CANDACE CAMP

THE *Bridal* QUEST

HQN™

ISBN-13: 978-0-373-77257-5
ISBN-10:   0-373-77257-2

THE BRIDAL QUEST

www.HQNBooks.com

Printed in U.S.A.

Praise for the novels of

CANDACE CAMP

"Camp delivers another beautifully written charmer, sure
to please fans of historicals, with enough modern appeal
to pull in some contemporary romance readers."
—*Publishers Weekly* on *The Marriage Wager*

"A clever mystery adds intrigue to this lively
and gently humorous tale, which simmers with
well-handled sexual tension."
—*Library Journal* on *A Dangerous Man*

"Camp has again produced a fast-paced plot brimming
with lively conflict among family, lovers and enemies."
—*Publishers Weekly* on *A Dangerous Man*

"The talented Camp has deftly mixed romance
and intrigue to create another highly enjoyable
Regency romance."
—*Booklist* on *An Independent Woman*

"Camp continues to prove herself capable of
twisting traditional plotlines into powerful stories
to touch readers' hearts."
—*Romantic Times BOOKreviews* on
An Independent Woman

"Romance, humor, adventure, Incan treasure,
dreams, murder, psychics—the latest addition to
Camp's Mad Moreland series has it all."
—*Booklist* on *An Unexpected Pleasure*

"Camp spins a tale that commands attention."
—*Romantic Times BOOKreviews* on
An Unexpected Pleasure

Also available from

CANDACE CAMP

**Watch for the next installment of
Candace Camp's Matchmakers series**

The Wedding Challenge

Coming in September

For my sisters:
Mary Elizabeth, Barbara and Sharon.
You're the best.

THE *Bridal*
QUEST

PROLOGUE

London, 1807

THE FRONT DOOR SLAMMED. Startled, Lady Irene Wyngate, in the library upstairs, turned, and the book she was holding tumbled to the floor.

It was well past midnight, and everyone in the house besides herself was tucked into their beds, sound asleep. Indeed, she had gone to bed an hour ago and had arisen only because sleep had eluded her, so she had decided to slip into the library and find a book to read. There should be no one about—especially no one slamming doors.

As she stood there, listening, the silence of the night was once again broken by a crash, this time followed by an oath. Irene relaxed, grimacing. Though the knowledge gave her no pleasure, at least she now realized who had made the noises downstairs. No doubt her father, Lord Wyngate, was home and stumbling about in his usual drunken state.

Quickly she bent and retrieved her dropped book from the floor; then, picking up her candlestick, she tiptoed out the door. Even though she was only sixteen years old, she was the only one of the household who would stand up to her father's bullying. Frequently she placed herself between him and her mother or brother, the people on whom he was most likely to take out his anger. However, Irene was not foolish;

like everyone else, she did her best to stay out of her father's way, especially when he came home roaring drunk.

Now she hurried silently along the hallway, hoping that she could make it to the sanctuary of her bedchamber before her father made his way up to the second floor. Downstairs, a voice was raised, angry and deep, and was followed by a response. Irene paused, her brows drawing together, wondering who was talking to her father. There was a loud smack, as of flesh hitting flesh, followed by another crash.

Irene darted to the railing at the top of the stairs and peered over it to the foyer below. Her view was partially obstructed by the lower tier of the sweeping staircase, but she could see her father sprawled on his back, the remnants of a shattered vase scattered around him on the Persian rug. The old-fashioned powdered wig that he insisted upon wearing, despite the fact that it was quite out of fashion, had been knocked askew and now tilted precariously to one side, rather like some small furry animal clinging to his bald head. A line of blood trickled down from his nose.

As Irene stared, astonished into momentary immobility, a man moved into her line of vision, striding rapidly over to Lord Wyngate. The stranger's back was turned toward her, so she could see only that he was tall and was dressed in the same sort of formal black suit that her father wore, though he eschewed the unfashionable wig and his black hair was hanging loose.

As Irene watched, the stranger reached down and grasped her father by his lapels, yanking him to his feet. Lord Wyngate put both his hands up to the other man's chest and shoved ineffectually.

"Damned puppy," Lord Wyngate growled, his voice slurred. "How dare you?"

"I dare a bloody lot more than that!" the other man snapped, drawing back his fist.

Irene did not wait to see the blow land, but whirled around and ran to her father's study. She raced across the room and jerked open one of the glass-fronted cabinets, then pulled out a case from one of the shelves, laid it on the desk and opened it.

Inside, on red velvet, rested a set of dueling pistols. Her father, she knew, kept them loaded, but she quickly checked, just to make sure, before she ran back out of the room, carrying one in each hand. The sounds of fighting and shouting grew louder as she neared the staircase. She could not see the men; they had moved. But it was clear from the sounds that the fight was still being waged in earnest.

Irene fairly flew down the first set of stairs to the landing. As she turned the corner, she could see them again, grappling at the bottom of the stairs. Just then, the younger man broke free and slammed his fist into Lord Wyngate's stomach. As her father doubled over, the other man brought his fist up sharply, landing a hit flush on the older man's chin. Wyngate staggered back and crashed onto the floor.

"Stop it!" Irene shouted. "Stop this at once!"

Neither man paid the slightest attention to her, didn't even turn to look at her. The stranger pursued her father, reaching out to grab him and pull him up again.

"Stop!" Irene shrieked once more. When she was again ignored, she raised one pistol and fired up into the air. She heard the ping as the ball hit the chandelier above, and a few prisms fell, crashing to the floor.

Both men froze. The stranger straightened and swiveled his head to look up, and her father, too, turned his wavering eyes upon her. Irene scarcely noticed her father's gaze. Her eyes were riveted to the other man.

He was tall, and his wide shoulders filled out the suit admirably. Clearly his tailor was not required to resort to padding to give the jacket the shape it needed. His hair was black as coal in the light from the wall sconces, and he wore it a trifle longer than was strictly fashionable. His face was all sharp angles and flat planes—handsome, yet hard and unreadable. The only signs of temper lay in the faint color along the line of his cheekbones and the unmistakable glitter of anger in his eyes.

She had seen other men more handsome than he; there was something a little raw and rough about him that was different from the more elegant gentleman she was accustomed to. Yet he affected her far more than any gentleman she had ever met. Looking at him, she felt a strange, visceral tug, a sort of twisting deep in her core, and she found it difficult to pull her eyes away from him.

"Irene?" Lord Wyngate croaked, and struggled to his feet.

"Yes, it is I," she replied in some irritation, not sure whether she was more annoyed with her father for bringing chaos into their house or with this unknown man for evoking such an odd and unsettling reaction inside her. "Who else would it be?"

"That's my girl," Wyngate slurred, wobbling where he stood. "Count on you."

Irene's mouth tightened. It galled her to be forced to help her father.

Ever since she could remember, her father had been the major source of misery and discomfort in the lives of everyone around him. The servants, her mother, her brother and she herself had always walked in fear of him. He had a wicked temper, an unquenchable thirst for alcohol and an affinity for trouble. When she was a child, she had known only that he made her mother cry and the servants tremble. She had learned to stay out of his way, especially when he was staggering with drink. In more recent years, she had come to have a better understanding of the many sins in which he indulged—of the gambling and whoring that went hand-in-glove with his imbibing, of his many excesses, both financial and of the flesh. Lord Wyngate was a libertine, but worse than that, he was an often cruel man, one who enjoyed the trepidation that others felt around him.

Irene had been taught, nevertheless, that she should love him, that he deserved her respect simply because he was her parent. It was not a lesson that she had ever truly embraced. She was not, she knew, a good-enough person to forgive him or to love him despite his faults, as her mother seemed able to. Nor was she so given to doing what was expected of one as her brother, Humphrey, so that she would offer him loyalty and respect simply because tradition required it.

Irene was of the opinion that if someone had attacked her father, he had probably deserved it. Still, he was her father, and she could not allow this stranger to kill him.

"Don't you think it is a trifle late to be brawling in the foyer?" she asked in the coolly commanding tone that she had learned was best in dealing with her father.

Lord Wyngate tugged down his jacket and brushed it off in the heavy-handed and supremely careful way often adopted by those in an inebriated state. He wiped his hand across his face, then looked down in apparent surprise at the blood on his palm.

"Damn—I think you broke my nose, you jumped-up cardsharp!" Lord Wyngate glowered at the other man.

His companion, however, did not so much as spare him a glance. His eyes remained on Irene.

She remembered suddenly how she must look. She had not bothered to throw a dressing gown on over her nightdress when she had decided to search for a book to read. Her feet were bare, and her thick blond hair, released from its pins for the night, tumbled in wildly curling abandon over her shoulders and down her back.

It occurred to her that the wall sconces from the floor above must be casting a light behind her, probably revealing the outline of her body, naked beneath the cotton nightgown. She blushed to the roots of her hair. *Why would he not look away?* Clearly the man was a mannerless ruffian.

She tilted up her chin and gazed back at him, refusing to let this boor see that she was embarrassed. Out of the corner of her eye, however, she saw her father sneak back step and wrap his hand around a small statue that sat on pedestal against the wall. He raised it, starting toward the other man.

"No!" Irene snapped, swinging the loaded pistol in her left hand toward her father. "Put that down this instant!"

Lord Wyngate cast her a sulky look but set the statue back on its base.

The other man glanced over at Lord Wyngate, his lip curling in contempt. He turned back and sketched a bow toward Irene.

"Thank you, my lady." His voice was deep and rough, his accent not that of a gentleman.

"I do not care to have any more blood on the Persian rug," Irene retorted tartly. "'Tis far too difficult to clean."

Her father leaned against the wall, still sulking, and refused to look at her. To her surprise, however, the other man let out a bark of laughter, and amusement lit his face, briefly warming and softening it. She was barely able to stop herself from smiling back at him.

"'Tis past my understanding that this old goat should have so fair a daughter," the man said.

Irene grimaced, annoyed at herself as much as him. The man had an enormous amount of gall to grin at her that way. And how could she be tempted to return the ruffian's smile?

"I think you should leave now," she told him. "Else I will be forced to call the servants and have you ejected."

He raised an eyebrow to convey how little her threat moved him, but said only, "Of course. I would not wish to disturb your peace."

He walked over to Lord Wyngate, who backed up a bit nervously. The man grasped Wyngate's shirt front in one hand, clenching his fist in it to hold the man still, and leaned in a little.

"If I ever hear of you bothering Dora again, I'll come back and break every bone in your body. Do you understand?"

Irene's father flushed with anger, but he nodded.

"And do not come back to my place again. Ever." The stranger gave her father a long look, then released him and strode toward the front door. Opening it, he turned back and looked up the stairs at Irene.

A faint sardonic smile touched his lips, and he said, "Good night, my lady. It was a pleasure to meet you."

Then, with a bow, he was gone.

Irene relaxed, realizing now that it was over, how tense she had been. Her legs felt weak under her, and she dropped her hand back down to her side.

"Who was that?" she asked.

"Nobody," her father replied, turning toward the stairs. His steps were weaving, and he had to grasp the railing to keep from stumbling. "Filthy lout…thinks he can talk that way to me…I ought to show him." He looked up at Irene, his expression sly and calculating. "Give me that pistol, girl."

"Oh, hush," she said, feeling suddenly weary, "Don't make me regret keeping him from killing you."

She turned and started back up the stairs. Just to be safe, she thought, she would take the pistols to her bedroom, where her father could not get at them.

"That's no way to speak to your father," Lord Wyngate bellowed after her. "You'll show me respect."

Irene whirled back around. "I will show you respect when you deserve some," she told him tightly.

"You're a poor excuse for a daughter," he returned, his eyes narrowing. "And no man'll marry you, with the airs you put on. What'll you do then, eh?"

"I'll rejoice," Irene replied flatly. "From all I can see, a life without a husband would be quite pleasant. I, sir, will never marry."

Pleased to see that her words had at least startled him into momentary silence, Irene turned and swept back up the stairs.

CHAPTER ONE

London, 1816

IRENE COVERED A SIGH as her sister-in-law continued her description—in detail—of the gown she had purchased yesterday. It was not that Irene disliked talk of fashion; indeed, she was fonder than she cared to admit of conversations regarding styles and colors and accessories. It was listening to *Maura* converse about clothes that bored Irene to the point of unconsciousness, for anything Maura discussed was ultimately more about Maura and her own taste or perspicacity or beauty than it was about the subject at hand.

Maura was, quite simply, the sun around which all interests and all people circled, at least in her own mind. She was unremittingly self-centered, which Irene would not have minded so much if she had not been thoroughly dull and prosaic, as well.

Irene glanced around the room at the faces of the other women. None of their three visitors, she saw, looked as indifferent or bored as she felt. She wondered if her own expression conveyed as little of her inner reaction. It was difficult to tell, no doubt because all the well-bred ladies had been brought up, as she had, to convey a polite interest in other people's conversations, no matter how tedious they were.

Irene's mother, Lady Claire, was one of the women now listening to Maura with a pleasant and interested look on her face. She would, of course, have considered it bad form to have allowed any other expression to mar her features, but Irene knew that more was involved; her mother was frightened to express a dislike for, or even a disinterest in, anything her daughter-in-law had to say. For the past year, ever since Humphrey had married Maura and brought her back here to live with them, Lady Claire had walked on eggshells, knowing that Maura was now the true power in the household, and could make her and her daughter's life a misery.

Of course, in Irene's opinion, having to bow to Maura's every whim already made life a misery, so it seemed foolish to work so hard to avoid the woman's ire. Nor did she think that her brother Humphrey was so weak-willed as to turn his mother and sister out of their home if Maura took it into her head to demand that. However, she knew that it was certainly within his power to do so, as well as in Maura's nature to selfishly demand such a thing. And it was, unfortunately, quite true that she and her mother had been left virtually penniless upon Lord Wyngate's death and were completely dependent upon her brother's generosity.

Lord Wyngate had died three years ago in a fall from his horse after a particularly heavy bout of drinking. Irene had been, frankly, somewhat surprised at the grief she had felt. After all the years of battling with the man and despising him, there had, it seemed, been a core of love inside her that even his wicked behavior had been unable to entirely squelch. However, there was no denying that his demise had also evoked a great sense of relief in all those connected to him.

There were no more bill collectors lurking outside their

door; that had stopped once Humphrey had sat down with their creditors and worked out a plan to pay his father's debts in full. Nor were shady characters popping up looking for Lord Wyngate anymore. They had no further need to fear that he would bring some scandal to the family name. And, most of all, his presence no longer hung over the house like some dark cloud, forcing everyone do whatever they could to avoid running into him or doing anything that might set off one of his fits of rage.

It was not until after Lord Wyngate was dead that, upon hearing one of the upstairs maids singing a cheerful song as she polished the furniture, Irene realized just how silent and cold the house had been. Suddenly, despite the black wreath on the front door and the black cloth draped above Lord Wyngate's portrait, the house was a lighter, brighter place.

Her younger brother, Humphrey, a rather serious, shy young man, had, of course, inherited the title and estate from their father. Aside from the entailed land and the house in London, Lord Wyngate had left little but debts for his heir; for his widow and daughter there had been nothing.

However, Humphrey was a loving son and brother, and he was happy to provide for Irene and Claire. Two years younger than Irene, he had always looked up to and relied upon her. In their childhood, it had been she who had shielded him from their father's curses and blows.

Humphrey had set about settling his father's debts and re-building the estate, leaving it to his sister to run the household, as she long had done for her mother. Life had moved along smoothly enough as they emerged from the period of mourning into a resumption of social activities. The debts had been largely repaid, and though there was a heavy mortgage on the entailed land that had passed to Humphrey, the money situation had loosened enough to allow for new dresses and the giving and attending of parties.

Irene knew that some found her life pitiable, as she was in her midtwenties and still unmarried, facing life as a spinster, but she did not care. The fact was that she was happy and useful, and she was not one of those women—those she privately characterized as foolish females—who found her life empty if it was not connected to a man's. Indeed, having witnessed the storms of marriage, she was certain that her life without a husband was far preferable to the one most married women endured.

Then Humphrey had taken a hunting trip to the North of England with a friend. His visit had been extended by first one week, then two, and at the end of the third week, he had returned home, flushed and happy with the news that he was engaged to be married.

Maura Ponsonby, the daughter of a local squire, had caught Humphrey's eye…and then his lonely heart. She was a jewel, he informed them, and he was the luckiest man alive. They would, he assured them, love Maura just as he did.

When they met Maura, it was easy enough to see why he had fallen in love with her. She was pretty, and she showered Humphrey with attention and affection. However, it did not take them long to see how she also controlled him with her pretty pouting and lively flirtation turning stony and un-yielding when she did not get her way.

All smiles and charmingly deferential to Lady Claire before she married Humphrey, she swept into the house after the wedding full of self-importance. As the new Lady Wyngate, she made it quite clear to both Claire and Irene that she was now in charge. Though Irene had intended to turn over the running of Wyngate Hall to Maura, the woman gave her no opportunity to do so, merely informed the house-keeper and butler that she would now be in charge of all de-cisions regarding the household.

Maura seized every opportunity to show that she was of primary rank in the house, inserting herself into any conver-sation, informing the butler whom they would or would not receive as callers and when they were at home to such visits, and boldly accepting or declining invitations for Irene and Claire, as well as for herself and her husband.

Lady Claire, as was her way, had submitted meekly to such behavior. Irene, of course, had refused to knuckle under, and the result had been a long series of skirmishes between the two women.

Now Maura, perhaps sensing Irene's disinterest, broke off in the middle of her description of the bows that adorned the hem of her dress and turned toward Irene, eyes wide, smiling in an arch way that made Irene itch to slap her. "But we are boring poor Irene with our talk of frills and furbelows, aren't we, dear?" She turned gaily toward the other women, saying, "Irene has little interest in fashion, I fear. Try as I might, I can hardly ever convince her to let me buy her a thing to wear."

Maura shook her head, a picture of loving despair over Irene's odd ways, setting her soft dark curls bobbing.

"You are so generous, my dear Lady Wyngate," mur-mured Mrs. Littlebridge.

"I am well content with my clothes," Irene responded coolly.

Lady Claire, as always, quickly stepped into the conver-sation to avoid the possibility of conflict. "Miss Cantwell, you must tell us about the wedding at Redfields. I am sure we are all eager to hear about it."

Irene's mother had chosen the topic well. The marriage of the Viscount Leighton to Constance Woodley a week before had been the highlight of the social year, and an invitation to witness the wedding at Leighton's family estate had been highly sought after. All those who had managed to attend were assured of being welcomed almost everywhere for their description of the wedding.

"Yes, indeed," Mrs. Littlebridge agreed. An inveterate social climber, she loved nothing more than gossip and storing up tales that she could repeat to make herself appear more important than she was. "Was the bride radiant?"

"She is pretty in her own way," Miss Cantwell admitted. "But no family to speak of. One cannot help but feel that the viscount has married down."

"Of course." Mrs. Littlebridge nodded sagely. "A bit of a country mouse, I hear."

"Exactly." Miss Cantwell gave the other woman a thin smile. "But then, Leighton always has been a bit…well, unconventional."

Irene, who felt sure that Miss Cantwell's opinion of the viscount's oddity sprang more from that very eligible bachelor's complete disinterest in her own person than from anything else, said, "I quite like Miss Woodley—or I should say now, Lady Leighton. I find her refreshingly unpretentious."

Maura let out a little brittle laugh. "You *would* find that admirable, of course, Irene. Not everyone admires a lack of refinement as you do, I fear."

"I believe Lady Leighton was a good friend of the viscount's sister, was she not?" Lady Claire said quickly.

"Oh, yes, Lady Haughston took her on as one of her

projects," Mrs. Littlebridge affirmed. "She introduced the girl to her brother, of course."

"And before that, she completely made the girl over." Mrs. Cantwell spoke up. "Constance Woodley was an utter dowd before Lady Haughston came along and turned her into a swan."

"She has a knack for it," Lady Claire commented. "There was that Bainborough girl last Season, and before that, Miss Everhart. Made excellent marriages, both of them."

"Indeed." Mrs. Cantwell nodded. "Lady Haughston has a golden touch. Everyone knows that if she takes a girl up, that girl is destined to make a good marriage."

"Why, Irene," Maura said playfully. "Perhaps we should ask Lady Haughston to help you find a husband."

"Thank you, Maura, but I am not looking for one," Irene replied tartly, looking the other woman in the eyes.

"Not looking for a husband?" Mrs. Littlebridge said lightly, and gave a laugh. "Really, Lady Irene, what young girl is not looking for a husband?"

"I, for one," Irene replied flatly.

Mrs. Littlebridge's eyebrows lifted a little in disbelief.

"Such words are fine for pride's sake," Maura commented, casting a knowing smile toward their trio of callers. "But you are among friends here, Irene. We all know that any woman's true aim in life is to marry. Otherwise, what is she to do? Live in another woman's house all her life?" She paused and turned her gaze to Irene. "Of course, Lord Wyngate and I would like nothing better than to have you as our companion for the rest of our lives. But I am thinking of you and your happiness. You really should talk to Lady Haughston about it. She is a friend of yours, is she not?"

Irene heard the bitterness that underlay her sister-in-law's sweet tone. It had always been a thorn in Maura's side that she had come from a provincial family of genteel breeding but unimportant name, that she had not spent her life, as Irene had, among the *ton,* known to and received by anyone of consequence.

"I know Lady Haughston, of course," Irene replied. "But we are no more than social acquaintances, really. I would not call Lady Haughston my friend."

"Ah, but then, there are so few who could be called your friend," Maura tossed back.

There was a moment of startled silence at that cutting remark, but then Maura adopted an expression of embarrassment and raised her hands to her cheeks. "Oh, my, how that must sound! Of course, I did not mean that you have no friends, dear sister. There are a number of them, of course. Are there not, Lady Claire?" She cast an appealing glance at Irene's mother.

"Yes, of course." Color stained Claire's cheeks. "There is Miss Livermore."

"Of course!" Maura exclaimed, her expression clearly stating her relief that Irene's mother had managed to come up with an example. "And then the vicar's wife back at the country house is so fond of you." She paused, then shrugged, as though abandoning the futile search for friends, and leaned forward, looking at Irene earnestly as she said, "You know that I want only what is best for you, don't you, dear? All any of us want is for you to be happy. Isn't that true, Lady Claire?"

"Yes, of course," Claire agreed, glancing unhappily at her daughter.

"But I *am* happy, Mother," Irene lied, then turned back to Maura, continuing in a flat tone, "How could I be anything but happy, after all, living here with you, *dear sister?*"

Maura ignored her words, going on in the same earnest, helpful way. "I want only to help you, Irene. To improve your life. I am sure you must know that. Unfortunately, not everyone knows you as I do. They see only your demeanor. Your sharp tongue, my dear, keeps people at bay. However much they might want to get to know you better, your, well, your acerbic wit, your bluntness, frightens people away. It is for that reason that you have so few bosom friends, so few suitors. Your manner is most unappealing to men."

She looked to her friends for confirmation. "A man does not want a wife who will correct him or who will ring a peal over his head if he does something amiss. Is that not true, ladies?"

Irene's eyes flashed, and she said tightly, "Your information, while no doubt *well intentioned,* is of little use to me. As I told you, I am not interested in acquiring a husband."

"Now, now, Lady Irene," Mrs. Cantwell began, with a condescending smile that grated on Irene's nerves.

Irene swung toward her, and the light in her eyes made the other woman swallow whatever she had been planning to say. "I do not wish to marry. I *refuse* to marry. I have no intention of giving any man control over me. I will not meekly become some man's chattel or let some man with less wit than I have tell me what to think or say or do."

She stopped, pressing her lips together, regretting that she had let Maura push her into revealing so much of herself.

Across from her, Maura let out a little laugh and cast a wry look at the other women, saying, "A woman does not have to be under a man's thumb, dear. She simply makes him think that he is in control. She just has to learn how to lead a man into doing exactly what she wishes. The trick, of course, is in making him believe that it was all *his* idea."

Their visitors joined Maura in her arch laughter, and Mrs. Littlebridge added, "Indeed, Lady Wyngate, that is the way of the world."

"I have no interest in such pretense and trickery," Irene retorted. "I would rather remain a spinster than have to cajole and lie to be able to do what I should have every right to do."

Maura clucked her tongue, looking sympathetic. "Irene, my dear, we are not saying you should *deceive* anyone. I am merely talking about making the most of your looks and covering up…certain aspects of your character. You dress much too plainly." She gestured with disdain toward Irene's body. "That gown you are wearing, for instance. Why must it be that drab shade of brown? And you have no need to wear such a high neckline. Why not show off your shoulders and arms a little? Even your evening gowns have such an air of severity—it is no wonder men rarely ask you to dance! Is it not enough that you are so tall? Must you stand so arrow straight and hide your shape?"

Irene could hear the real frustration creeping into Maura's saccharine tones, and she knew that however much her sister-in-law might enjoy pointing out Irene's defects under the guise of helpful advice, Maura was also honestly put out by Irene's lack of suitors. Maura would love to be rid of her altogether, and marriage was the only option open to her, short of murder—which not even Irene would accuse Maura of being capable of. No matter how much Humphrey was under his wife's thumb, even Maura must know he would not agree to turning his own sister out of the house, and in any case, the woman surely knew that such callous treatment of her husband's sister would earn her the disapproval of the *ton*. No, as long as Irene remained unmarried, Maura was saddled with her—a fact that doubtless irritated her almost as much as it did Irene.

"And your hair!" Maura went on relentlessly. "Heaven knows it is a trifle…unruly." She frowned at Irene's curling mass of dark golden hair, pulled back ruthlessly into a knot. "But the color is quite nice, really. And your lashes are long and luckily brown, not fair, so that you do not have that hairless look that one sees in some blondes."

"Why, thank you, Maura," Irene murmured drily. "Your compliments overwhelm me."

Maura shrugged. "I am simply saying that you could make yourself look much more attractive if you would just *try* a little. Why, one would think that you are trying to drive men away rather than attract them."

"Perhaps I am."

There was a moment of stunned silence; then Miss Cantwell let out a nervous titter. "Lady Irene! One might almost suppose you are serious."

Irene did not bother to respond to the woman's remark. Miss Cantwell would never understand, any more than any of the other women present, that Irene truly did not want to marry. Marriage was the goal of every woman's life, as far as they were concerned. The pursuit of a husband was the focal point of a woman's coming out—and of every Season thereafter, until she finally managed to snag one.

Marriage-minded mothers mapped out campaigns for their daughters like war-hardened generals. Skirmishes were played out on the fields of ballrooms, opera boxes and open-air carriage rides through Hyde Park, and the weapons of choice were frocks, curls, flirtatious glances over the top of one's fan and—most lethal of all—gossip. Victory lay in snapping up an eligible bachelor, and few considered the years that lay ahead after the all-important ring was placed upon their finger.

No doubt Miss Cantwell and her mother were in the midst of that vital fray now. They would assume that any protestations Irene made were simply sour grapes for having lost that battle herself, for being a twenty-five-year-old spinster with no prospects other than living with her family for the rest of her life.

Irene sighed. She did not envy Miss Cantwell the marriage she hoped for. But she did wish that she could muster more equanimity to face the future she would have because she would not marry.

Maura leaned forward and laid her hand on Irene's arm, smiling sweetly. "Now, dear, do not sigh. 'Tis not so bad. We shall find you a husband yet. Perhaps we *should* pay a visit to Lady Haughston."

Irene grimaced, irritated that she had given Maura any glimpse of her discontent by sighing. "Don't be absurd," she told her crisply. "I told you, I am not seeking a husband. And if I were, I would not ask some silly butterfly like Francesca Haughston to help me."

She stood up, too annoyed to worry about her bad manners. "Excuse me, ladies. I fear I have something of a headache."

Then she turned and strode out of the room without waiting for a reply.

A FEW BLOCKS AWAY, unaware that she was the topic of conversation among Lady Wyngate and her friends, Francesca Haughston sat in the sitting room that was her favorite spot in the house, a smaller and more intimate chamber than the formal drawing room, and decorated in a sunny yellow that seemed to catch every stray ray of sun that flowed in through the west-facing windows. It was a pleasant place, furnished with pieces that, if a trifle shabby, were comfortable and dear to her. It was the room she used most, particularly in the fall and winter, for it was warmer than the other rooms, and it was cheaper to keep a fire here than in the larger drawing room. Of course, the fire was not of importance now, as it was the middle of August, but it was still the room she chose whenever she was alone.

Since the Season was over and many of the *ton* had returned to their country seats, she had few visitors these days, only her closest friends. As a consequence, the formal withdrawing room was kept closed, and Francesca spent her time here.

She was seated at the small secretary beside the windows, her accounts ledger open before her. She had been poring over the figures, but the pencil now lay in the trough between the pages, and she was gazing out at the small side garden, where the roses were putting up a last colorful show before autumn arrived.

Her problem, as always, was money—rather, a lack of it. Her late husband had been a profligate spender and unwise investor, and when he had died a few years ago, he had left her with little but her fashionable clothes and her jewelry. His estate, of course, had been entailed, passing to his cousin so that she no longer had a home except in London, a house that Andrew himself had purchased and had been able to bequeath to her. She had closed off all of one wing in an effort to economize, and had, with regret, let many of the servants go, keeping only a skeleton staff. She had also greatly curtailed her spending.

Even so, Francesca barely managed to scrape by. The

easiest and most obvious way by which she could become wealthy—marrying again—she had rejected out of hand. She would have to be in much worse condition than she had yet fallen into to be willing to embark on that path once more.

There was a noise at the door, and she turned her head. Her personal maid, Maisie, stood there, looking uncertain. Francesca smiled and gestured to her to enter.

"My lady, I did not wish to disturb you, but the butcher's man is here again, and he has been most insistent. Cook says he refuses to sell her any more meat until she pays her account."

"Of course. Yes." Francesca opened the slender drawer of the writing table and took out a coin purse. She pulled a gold coin from it and held it out to the girl. "This should be enough to hold him off."

Maisie took the coin but continued to stand there, looking worried. "I could take something to sell for you, if you want. Maybe that bracelet."

Over the years since her husband's death, in order to survive, Francesca had sold off much of her jewelry and a number of other valuable items. It was Maisie who had taken such things to the jeweler's or the silversmith. Of all the people in the world, it was Maisie who knew her best and whom she trusted the most. Only a few years older than Francesca, Maisie had been her maid since she married Lord Haughston, and had been with her through every up and down. Maisie alone never suggested to Francesca that she ease her situation by accepting one of her many suitors.

For the past few years, Francesca had ingeniously supported herself by bringing out young girls and helping them find husbands on the marriage mart. Faced with the harsh reality that she was running out of items to sell or pawn and that there was little opportunity for a woman such as herself to earn her way other than to marry or to sell her virtue, she had sat down and assessed her skills. There was one thing at which she was an expert: attracting suitors.

She had, of course, some natural advantages in that area. Her figure was elegantly slender, her hair a guinea gold, and her large eyes were a vivid dark blue. But there had always been a great deal more to Francesca's success in the social world than her physical attributes. Just as her family's long and respected lineage could only place her in the upper reaches of society, not make her a leading light of the *ton,* so, too, could her looks account for only a portion of her appeal.

Francesca had style. She had personality. She knew how to smile to make the dimple flash in her cheek, how to look at a man over her fan in a way that made his pulse speed up, or to gaze up at him in a manner designed to make the hardest heart melt. Quick of wit, she could engage in conversation on almost any topic and bring a smile to almost any lips. She knew how to dress for every occasion, and, moreover, she had an unerring sense of color and cut that rarely steered her wrong. Social occasions were her natural milieu, and she not only gave memorable parties, but she could enliven even the dullest gathering.

All her life she had helped her friends with questions of style and taste, and when she had guided the daughter of one of her late husband's relatives through the treacherous social waters of a Season and been rewarded by a gift of a large silver epergne from the girl's grateful parents, she had seen a way to maintain her style of living without really appearing to engage in that object of horror to English aristocrats: gainful employment.

She had pawned the silver epergne she was given, and paid her servants and many of her household bills with it. Then she had proceeded to maneuver herself into the path of mothers with marriageable daughters, especially those whose daughters had not really "taken." A suggestion here, an offer there, and soon she had a steady stream of young girls whom she helped to turn out and find an eligible husband.

Her most recent project had been the result of a wager with the Duke of Rochford. The duke had promised her a bracelet if she won, against Francesca's promise to pay a visit with him to his rather terrifying great-aunt Odelia. It had been absurd, and she had entered into it only because Rochford had goaded her. However, to Francesca's surprise, the whole thing had resulted in Francesca's own brother falling in love with and marrying Miss Constance Woodley. It had scarcely been what Francesca had envisioned, but it had turned out in the end to be something much better.

The duke had given her the bracelet, as well—a circlet of perfect deep-blue sapphires linked together by sparkling diamonds. The bracelet lay upstairs in the bottom compartment of her jewelry box, next to a set of sapphire earrings, given to her long ago and never sold.

Francesca looked up at her maid, who was watching her shrewdly. Francesca shook her head. "No, I won't sell it just yet. One must keep something in reserve, after all."

Maisie said only, "Yes, my lady," in a noncommittal tone as she tucked the coin into her pocket and turned to leave the room. At the door, the girl paused and cast a last, considering look at her employer before she went out into the hall.

Francesca saw the glance. She knew the maid was curious, but Maisie was not one to pry, and, in any case, Francesca had no answer for her, really. The bracelet, and Rochford, were topics best left alone.

What she really needed to think about was what she was going to do to get by until the next Season began. It was unlikely that she would come upon a mother or father eager to marry a daughter off until next April, when the new social Season would start and there would be debuts at court and a large number of routs, balls and soirees at which parents could show off their nubile young daughters and see what prospective husbands awaited.

There *was* what was often termed the Little Season, which took place roughly from September to November, during which some of the sophisticates, bored by their sojourn in the country, returned to London to enjoy its entertainments. However, it was not the prime husband-hunting venue that the full Season was; there were far fewer young girls and, indeed, fewer people in general. Francesca knew that it would be unlikely that she could find a prospect to "help" during this time.

And while the payment she had given him would hold the butcher off for a few weeks, there were a number of other creditors who would soon be importuning her, and she hadn't enough to hold them all off. Perhaps she could come up with a stray silver tray or some such thing to sell; she would have to go up to the attic and dig through all the trunks. Even so, she did not think that one or two small silver pieces would get her through until April.

Of course, she could shut down the house and go to stay at Redfields, where she had grown up. She knew that her brother Dominic and his new wife would welcome her graciously, but she hated to impose upon the newly married pair. They were scarcely back from their honeymoon. It was bad enough that the couple had his parents living in the manor house just down the lane from them. It would be unfair to saddle them with his sister, too.

No, she would spend a month at Redfields at Christmas, no more. She could, she supposed, follow the example of her good friend Sir Lucien, who, on the frequent occasions when he found himself short of funds, always managed to wangle an invitation to this estate or that for a few weeks. Of course, a handsome, entertaining bachelor was a most sought-after guest to round out the numbers of a house party; it always seemed that there were extra women. Besides, she hated having to maneuver someone into inviting her for a visit.

Perhaps it would be better to visit one of her relatives. There was Aunt Lucinda, with her deadly dull daughter, Maribel. They would be happy to have her join them in their Sussex cottage, and after a time there, she could spend a few weeks with Cousin Adelaide, who lived in a large rambling manor house in Norfolk and always welcomed visitors to help her oversee her enormous brood of children.

On the other hand, Francesca decided, it would not hurt to sit down and write to a few friends and mention how deadly dull it was in town now that everyone had left….

She was distracted from her thoughts by the entrance of the parlor maid. "My lady, you have visitors." She cast an anxious look over her shoulder and turned back to Francesca, saying quickly, "I asked them to let me see if you were at home—"

"Nonsense!" came a booming woman's voice. "Lady Francesca is always home to me."

Francesca's eyes widened. The voice sounded familiar. She rose to her feet, pulled up by a vague but powerful sense of foreboding. That voice…

A tall, stout woman dressed all in purple swept into the room. The style of her clothes was at least ten years out of date. This oddity was no indication of a lack of funds, for it was quite clear that the velvet from which they were sewn was new and expensive, and the hand at work was that of a master. Rather, it was simply proof that Lady Odelia Pencully had ridden roughshod over the desires of some modiste, as she was wont to do over everyone who came into her path.

"Lady Odelia," Francesca said faintly, stepping forward on leaden feet. "I— What an unexpected pleasure."

The older woman let out an inelegant snort. "No need to lie, girl. I know you're scared of me." Her tone indicated no regret over this fact.

Francesca's gaze went past Lady Odelia to the man who had followed her down the hall. Tall, with an aristocratic bearing, he was as elegant as he was handsome, from the top of his raven-black hair to the tips of his polished black boots, made by Weston. Not a hair was out of place, and his countenance was politely expressionless, but Francesca could detect the glimmer of devilish amusement in his dark eyes.

"Lord Rochford," she acknowledged him, her voice cool, with just an overlay of irritation. "How kind of you to bring your aunt to visit me."

His mouth twitched a little at her words, but his expression remained imperturbable as he executed a politely perfect bow. "Lady Haughston. A pleasure to see you, as always."

Francesca nodded toward the maid. "Thank you, Emily. If you would bring us some tea…"

The girl left, looking relieved. Lady Odelia strode past Francesca toward the sofa.

As the duke moved forward, Francesca leaned in a little toward him, whispering, "How could you?"

Rochford's lips curled into a small smile, quickly gone, and he replied in a low voice, "I assure you, I had no choice."

"Don't blame Rochford," Lady Odelia boomed from her seat on the sofa. "I told him I would come to see you with or without him. I suspect he is here more to try to curtail me than anything else."

"Dear aunt," the duke responded. "I would never be so audacious as to curtail you in any way."

The old lady let out another snort. "You'll note I said 'try.'" She cast him a roguish glance.

"Of course." Rochford inclined his head respectfully toward her.

"Well, sit down, girl," Lady Odelia commanded Francesca, nodding toward a chair. "Don't keep the boy on his feet."

"Oh. Yes, of course." Francesca quickly dropped into the nearest chair.

The duke took a place beside his great-aunt on the sofa.

Francesca felt about sixteen again, as she always did in the intimidating Lady Pencully's presence. She had no doubt that Rochford's great-aunt had immediately seen her dress for what it was—over four years old and resewn into a more contemporary style—and at the same time had noted that the draperies were faded and that one leg of the table against the wall had a large nick in it.

Francesca forced herself to smile at Odelia. "I must admit, I am rather surprised to see you here. I had heard you no longer traveled into London."

"Don't, if I can help it. I'll be frank with you, girl. Never thought I'd come asking you for help. Flighty thing, I always thought you."

Francesca's smile grew even stiffer. "I see."

The duke stirred a little in his seat. "Aunt—"

"Oh, don't get your feathers ruffled," the old lady barked. She cast a glance at Rochford. "Don't mean I don't like her. Always had a soft spot for the girl. Not sure why."

Rochford pressed his lips tightly together to suppress a smile and carefully avoided looking at Francesca's expression.

"Francesca knows that," Lady Odelia went on, giving her a nod. "Thing is, I do need your help. I've come to beg a favor of you."

"Of course," Francesca murmured, her mind skittering anxiously over what no-doubt unpleasant task the woman could have in mind for her.

"The reason I am here…well, I'll just be plain about it. I am here to find a wife for my great-nephew."

CHAPTER TWO

THERE WAS A MOMENT of stunned silence in the room after the formidable old woman's announcement. Francesca gaped at the woman, and her eyes slid involuntarily toward Rochford.

"I…um…" she stammered, feeling a blush rising in her cheeks.

"No, not him!" Lady Odelia exclaimed, and let out a crow of laughter. "Been trying for the best part of fifteen years with this one. Even I have given up hope. No, the Lilles line will have to go down through that foolish Bertrand, if it is to continue at all." She heaved a sigh at this prospect.

"I'm sorry." Francesca's cheeks were thoroughly aflame now. "I didn't— I am not sure I understand."

"I'm talking about my sister's grandson."

"Oh! I see. I'm not—um, I don't believe I know your sister, my lady."

"Pansy," Lady Odelia said, and sighed. It was clear from her expression that Lady Odelia found her sister lacking. "There were four of us—besides the three children that died in childhood, of course. I was the eldest, and then there was my brother, who, of course, grew up to be the duke. He was Rochford's grandfather. After him was our sister Mary, and finally, the youngest, Pansy. Pansy married Lord Radbourne.

Gladius, his name was. Damned silly name. His mother chose it, and a more foolish woman never lived. But that's neither here nor there. The problem is Pansy's grandson, Gideon. Lord Cecil's son."

"Oh." Francesca recognized the name. "Lord Radbourne."

Lady Odelia nodded. "Aye, you understand me now, I warrant. You'll have heard the gossip."

"Well…" Francesca demurred.

"No point trying to deny it. It was all over the *ton* the last few months."

Francesca nodded. "Of course."

Lady Odelia was right. Francesca—along with all the *ton* and, indeed, much of the rest of London—had heard the gossip. Many years ago, when he was only a lad of four, Gideon Bankes, the heir to the Radbourne title and estate, had been kidnapped, along with his mother. Neither the boy nor his mother was ever seen again. Then, years after he had been long-presumed dead, Gideon Bankes had reappeared.

His reappearance, and his inheritance of the title and estate of the Earl of Radbourne, had been the talk of the town for several weeks. Everyone Francesca knew had had an opinion on the matter—what the suddenly reclaimed heir was like, where he had been all these years and whether he was, in actuality, an imposter. There had been more questions than there were facts, for few people had actually met the new earl, and very few of those had offered any gossip.

Francesca looked again at the duke. She had seen him here and there, at various parties, over the past few months, but never had he said a word about the recovery of the lost heir. Indeed, she had not even realized that Rochford was in any way connected to the Bankes family. This fact only served to confirm her opinion that the Duke of Rochford was the most tight-lipped gentleman she knew. It was, she thought with a little flash of irritation, quite typical of the man.

"I am sure that what you have heard is mostly wrong," Lady Odelia remarked. "I might as well tell you the whole of it."

"Oh, no, I am sure that is not necessary," Francesca began, torn between curiosity and the strong desire to get Lady Odelia out of her house.

"Nonsense. You need to hear the truth of it."

"You may as well let her tell it," Rochford advised Francesca. "You know it will be easier."

"Don't be impertinent, Sinclair," his great-aunt admonished him.

Francesca noted somewhat sourly that Rochford, of course, did not seem at all in awe of the intimidating woman.

"Now," Lady Odelia went on, "I am sure you don't remember it, as you were just a child then yourself, but my nephew Cecil's wife and son were abducted twenty-seven years ago. Frightful business. They received a letter demanding a ransom—a necklace of rubies and diamonds, dreadfully ugly thing, but worth a fortune, of course. It had been in the family for generations. Legend said it was given to them by a grateful Queen Elizabeth when she came to the throne. Cecil gave them what they asked for, but they did not give him back his wife and child. We all assumed both had been killed. Cecil was grief-stricken, but he held out hope that they would somehow, someday, return. Years went by before he remarried. Of course, when he did, he had to go through legal proceedings to have Selene—that was the first countess—declared dead. She had been missing for almost twenty years by then. But still, he did nothing about the boy.

I presume he could not bring himself to admit that his child was dead."

She shrugged and went on. "But then, a year ago, when Cecil himself died, something had to be done. If Gideon was still alive somewhere, then he would be the heir. However, Cecil's second wife, Teresa, had given him a son, so if Gideon was dead, then Timothy would be the heir. Before we started legal proceedings, I set Rochford to see if he could turn up anything about Gideon."

Francesca looked over at the duke. "Then…you are the one who found him?"

Rochford shrugged. "I can scarcely claim credit for it. All I did was hire a Runner to investigate the matter. He found Gideon in London. He was going by the name Gideon Cooper, and he had made something of a fortune for himself. Had no idea who he really was."

"He didn't remember anything?" Francesca asked in surprise.

"Apparently not—other than his given name, of course. He was only four when he was taken. He can remember nothing before the time when he was a street urchin in London."

"But someone must have taken him in, cared for him," Francesca protested. "Did they know nothing about how they came to have him? Where he came from?"

"Nothing," Lady Odelia declared with disgust. "He says he never had any parents, that he grew up with a bunch of disreputable children in the stews of the East End. Imagine, the son of an earl, a boy with Lilles and Bankes blood flowing through his veins, living hand to mouth in some hovel, consorting with God-knows-what sort of riffraff!" She shook her head, the purple plumes that curled over her unfashionably high hairstyle bobbing wildly with her movements.

"But how did you know that it was Gideon?" Francesca asked curiously. "If he could not even remember, and there is no one around who raised him…"

"Oh, it was he, all right," Lady Odelia's tone suggested that she was less than pleased about the fact. "He had the birthmark—a little raspberry-colored blotch beside his left shoulder blade. Gideon had exactly the same mark from the time he was born. Pansy and I both remembered it. Of course, it looks smaller on an adult, but there is no mistaking it. A bit like a lopsided diamond. And, of course, he has the look of the Bankses. The Lilles jaw and hair, as well."

"I see," Francesca said somewhat untruthfully. The truth was that while Lady Odelia's story was certainly interesting, she did not really understand why the woman had told it to her. She hesitated, then said, "I am sure you are quite happy to have him back after all this time." She looked from Lady Odelia to the duke, but there was nothing in his carefully schooled face that offered any enlightenment to her. She turned back to the older woman. "I'm not sure…that is…well, why do you need my help—or anyone else's, for that matter—to find a suitable wife for Lord Radbourne? You know everyone. Indeed, you know them better than I."

"It is not finding a *suitable* woman. It is finding someone who is *willing*," Lady Pencully replied.

Francesca stared. "But surely, with his title and property…"

"Lord Radbourne has not been out much in society. No doubt it has been remarked upon," Lady Odelia said, fixing Francesca with her penetrating gaze.

"Well, um…" Francesca tried to think of a suitable reply.

The truth was, gossip had been rampant regarding the newly found earl's absence from Society's rounds. Though he had turned up several months ago, he had not appeared at any parties this Season. Rumors had run the gamut from his suffering from some hideous deformity to his being a criminal to his being utterly mad.

"Don't knit your brow over how to tell me," Lady Odelia went on brusquely. "Believe me, I have heard all the stories. He isn't crook-backed or stunted or covered in boils. Nor is he stark-staring mad. But the truth is…well, he is…quite common."

Lady Odelia uttered the words in a hushed voice, as though admitting the darkest of secrets, and she squared her shoulders as she gazed at Francesca, waiting for her retort.

"Aunt Odelia, aren't you being a trifle hard on the man?" Rochford remonstrated. "I think Radbourne's done quite well for himself, particularly given the circumstances."

"Yes, if you are talking about making money," Lady Odelia sniffed. "He has done a good deal of that." Clearly her great-nephew's financial success had not met with her approval.

"Scarcely the mark of a gentleman," she went on flatly. "The truth is, his past is, well, unsavory. I am not aware of the particulars—and, frankly, I do not care to be." She turned her fierce gaze on Rochford again, then swung back to Francesca. "He lived among the worst sort of people, far from the influence of his family and peers. The result is that he is lacking in the qualities that make up a gentleman. His speech and manners are quite unrefined, and his education is woefully short."

"Gideon is very well-read, Aunt." Rochford came to the

man's defense again, but his great-aunt waved away his words.

"Pshaw!" she exclaimed contemptuously. "I am not talking about *books,* Sinclair. I am talking about his education in the things that count—he cannot dance, and he has no idea how to make polite conversation. The man can barely sit a horse." She paused to let that horror sink in. "He is much too familiar with the servants and the tenants, yet he scarcely says a word to his family or even the local gentry. Fortunately, we have managed to get him to stay at the Hall most of the time, but now he insists on returning to London."

"He does have business here," the duke pointed out mildly.

"And what if someone we know sees him conducting his…business?" Lady Odelia gave a theatrical shudder at the thought.

"Aunt Odelia, I think there is little for anyone to remark upon on seeing a man going into a bank or meeting with his clerks," Rochford protested, his voice edging into irritation. "Come now, you will make Lady Haughston think that he should be locked up in the attic."

"Would that I *could* lock him away," Lady Odelia retorted.

The duke's dark brows drew together, and he took a breath before answering her. It occurred to Francesca that she might soon have a battle between these two right here in her sitting room.

"But, Lady Odelia," she intervened hastily, "I am afraid I still do not quite see what I have to do with all this. How can I introduce him to anyone if he has no interest in Society?"

"She wants you to help her arrange the poor chap's life for him," Rochford responded in a biting tone.

Francesca's eyebrows sailed upward, and she said coolly, "I beg your pardon."

"Don't be difficult, Sinclair," Lady Odelia admonished. "There is no need to snap at Francesca just because you are annoyed with me."

Rochford's mouth tightened, and he flashed a hot glance at Francesca, but he bowed his head in polite acquiescence and said, "Of course. Forgive me, Lady Haughston. I meant you no disrespect."

"Do not worry," Francesca murmured in a silky tone. "I have learned not to put overmuch importance on what you say."

She was rewarded by a sardonic look from beneath his brows, but the duke said nothing more.

"It isn't that I dislike the boy," Lady Odelia went on, ignoring their exchange. "He is my great-nephew, after all, and I hope it never will be said that I denigrated any of my own blood—although God knows, Bertrand has tested my limits often enough. However, Gideon is a Lilles, at least in part, and it is scarcely his fault that he does not know how to act. So I put my mind to it and came up with a solution." She paused and looked at Francesca, then announced, "Gideon must marry. And you are just the woman we need."

"Oh." Was the woman suggesting that she herself marry the man, Francesca wondered with horror.

"We must attach him to a thoroughly respectable, quite proper woman. One of unquestionable breeding and taste. It is to be hoped that she will be able to influence him, direct him into better behavior. Smooth some of his rough edges and cover up his flaws. And if she cannot, well, at least she will insure that his children will be suitably well-bred."

Lady Odelia paused, then went on didactically. "A proper

marriage goes far in overcoming the taint of scandal. If a woman of impeccable lineage is willing to ally herself to him, then everyone else will prove more amenable to over-looking his various…problems."

"Well," Francesca began carefully, "As I said, I should think you would have no problem finding a suitable candidate. Surely there are a number of women of good name who would be quite happy to marry a man who has both Bankes and Lilles blood flowing through his veins, as well, no doubt, as that of several other prominent families."

"Of course there are," Lady Odelia said impatiently. "I've brought at least five girls to Radbourne Hall and made introductions. The problem is, in more than half those instances, they or their families cry off once they've met him. And the rest of them, Gideon has rejected. Imagine…girls I personally vetted, and he disapproves of them."

"Oh. I'm sorry," Francesca offered lamely.

"The Bennington girl does have a squint," Rochford pointed out. "Miss Farnley is a goose, and Lady Helen is dull as ditchwater."

"Well, what does that matter?" Lady Odelia queried. "He doesn't have to talk to them."

Rochford's mouth quirked up on one side, but he said only, "Yes. Well, I suspect he would have to at some point."

"I suppose I should have expected it of him," his great-aunt opined, ignoring his remark. "The Lord only knows what sort of woman he would prefer. That is another reason why it is so imperative that we find a proper wife for him, and soon. When I think of who he might bring home if left to his own devices…" She shook her head. "Of course, we cannot force him to marry anyone," she continued, looking quite annoyed at the thought. "So we decided to turn to you."

She looked at Francesca.

"Everyone says you have had such success in this area. Well, look at the way you matched up that Woodley girl with your brother—though I cannot think but that you could have found someone with a bit more funds to her name. Still, she seems a very pleasant girl."

"You want me to help find a wife for Lord Radbourne?" Francesca exclaimed, flooded with relief that Lady Odelia was not trying to persuade Francesca herself to marry the man.

"Of course, girl. What have we been talking about this past half hour?" Odelia retorted. "Really, Francesca, you must pay more attention."

"Yes, I'm sorry," Francesca replied quickly.

"Though I scarcely see how you can manage to marry him off, when all our best efforts have failed," Lady Odelia went on. "But Rochford assured me that you were best person for the task," the older woman added.

"Really?" Francesca glanced with some surprise at Lord Rochford.

"Yes," he answered, and he leaned forward, his face serious. "I hope that you will be able to find the right person for Gideon. The man has suffered quite enough already in his life. He deserves some happiness."

His black eyes were intent upon her face. Francesca had wondered how Lady Odelia had trapped Rochford into accompanying her on this errand, but she saw now that the duke was here out of a real concern for Lord Radbourne. Unlike his great-aunt, he seemed to hope that Francesca would come up with a wife for Gideon not to please the family, but to help the man.

"If you could come to Radbourne Hall and meet Gideon,

see what he is really like, I think that you could find the right woman for him," the duke went on.

"I see." Francesca felt strangely touched. Before this, she would have said that he thought her matchmaking efforts were at best harmless foolishness.

"That is precisely the thing," Lady Odelia agreed. "You must come to the Hall and meet him. Then you'll understand. And perhaps you might be able to polish him up a bit before he actually meets any of the girls you choose. Whatever else anyone might say about you, your manners are always impeccable."

"Why, thank you," Francesca responded drily. "But I am not sure whether I should do this. Whether I can…"

She looked at Lady Odelia, imposing in her outdated purple satin dress and towering hair. Francesca did not relish the idea of dealing with Lady Odelia on a daily basis. She had little doubt but that the woman would poke her nose into everything that Francesca did, questioning and quibbling at every turn. Moreover, Lord Radbourne did not sound like a very pleasant person to deal with, either. *And what if she would have to deal with the duke, as well?*

Francesca stole a glance at him. Things never went smoothly with Rochford.

Her instinct was to refuse to do what Lady Odelia asked. But on the other hand, Francesca could not help but think that it would be foolish to do so. After all, had she not just been wondering how she would survive until next spring? This seemed the answer to her problems. Lady Odelia, she knew, would reward her with a handsome gift if she managed to pull off the feat of marrying her great-nephew to an acceptable woman. And if she were living at the Hall, her own expenses would be decreased quite considerably.

Besides, there was the way the duke had asked for her help with finding Gideon a wife. How could she refuse?

"Very well," she said. "I will do what I can."

"Excellent!" Lady Odelia nodded her head sharply. "Rochford said we could count on you."

"He did?" Francesca glanced at the duke in surprise.

"Of course," he responded with that slow, sardonic smile that rarely failed to irritate her. "I knew you could not resist something so clearly doomed to failure."

"Now," Lady Odelia said, "we can get down to details. She must be a biddable girl, of course, who is aware of her responsibilities to her family. It will not do to find one who will get her back up at the slightest suggestion."

In other words, Francesca thought, someone whom Lady Odelia could bend to her will.

"She must be able to wield a beneficial influence over Gideon."

Meaning that she must be able to bend her husband to her will, Francesca interpreted.

"And well-educated, though not, of course, a bluestocking."

"Naturally," Francesca murmured.

Lady Odelia continued to list the many qualities she sought in a wife for her great-nephew, a large number of which were contradictory, and Francesca smiled and nodded politely, though her mind was busy elsewhere. She was more interested in reviewing the unmarried women of the *ton* in the hopes of finding a few who would be suitable—and willing—to attach themselves to the new Earl of Radbourne than she was in hearing Lady Odelia's opinions on the matter. Clearly Lady Odelia had been unable to come up with the right lady, so Francesca saw little point in being guided by her wishes.

Having finally ground to a halt regarding the qualities she felt necessary in the future Countess of Radbourne, Lady Odelia launched into a list of possible candidates. "You might start with Lord Hurley's daughter. Good name. And a steady sort. Not one to get up in the boughs over every little thing."

A pained look crossed the duke's face. "Aunt Odelia," he remonstrated, "the woman's horse mad."

Lady Odelia turned a blank look on him. "Of course. She's Hurley's offspring."

"But Gideon scarcely rides."

Lady Odelia rolled her eyes. "Well, he scarcely needs a wife who'll be forever in his pocket, does he? It isn't as if we are talking about a love match."

"Of course. What was I thinking?" the duke murmured.

Before Lady Odelia could continue her roster of available girls, the parlor maid once again appeared at the doorway, bobbing a curtsey.

"The Earl of Radbourne, my lady," she announced.

Even Lady Odelia fell silent at her words. As the three occupants of the room turned to stare, a man strode past the maid into the room.

"Gideon!" Lady Odelia exclaimed, looking astonished.

Francesca studied her visitor with interest. She did not know what she had expected the lost heir to look like, but this man was not it. She supposed that she had assumed he would be rather bumbling and ill at ease, an obvious fish out of water.

This man appeared about as ill at ease as a slab of marble. Though less tall than the lean and elegant duke, Lord Radbourne gave the impression of being a larger man. He was powerfully built, with a wide chest and muscular arms. His solid body was packed into a well-cut but plain black suit and mirror-polished boots, and he gave off an aura of wealth and strength.

Yet despite the expensive clothes and his air of confidence, there was some indefinable quality about him that hinted that he was not a gentleman. It was perhaps his thick black hair, worn a trifle longer than was fashionable and carelessly combed back. Or the hard set of his handsome face, tanner than that of most gentlemen. But no, Francesca thought, the difference lay in his eyes—cold and slightly wary, looking out on the world with the hard readiness that bespoke a life spent on the streets rather than in the lap of luxury.

When he opened his mouth, the impression that he did not belong among the aristocracy was confirmed. His grammar was correct, and only the merest tinge of an East End accent clung to his words, but there was some quality in his speech that would have hinted to any astute listener that he was not "to the manor born."

"Lady Odelia." Gideon nodded shortly to his great-aunt; then his gaze swept dispassionately across to the duke. "Rochford."

"Radbourne," Rochford replied, the ghost of a smile on his lips. "What an unexpected surprise."

"No doubt." Gideon's voice was dry. He turned next to Francesca, executing a brief but serviceable bow. "My lady."

Francesca rose, holding out her hand to him. "My lord. Please, join us."

He nodded to her and walked across the room to take a chair just past where Lady Odelia sat. "Well, Aunt," he began in a flat voice. "I presume you are once again engaged in arranging my life for me."

Lady Odelia's chin went up, and she looked back at Gideon somewhat defiantly. Francesca realized, with some amazement, that the intimidating Lady Pencully was actually a trifle afraid of this man.

"I hope to find an appropriate wife for you," Lady Odelia replied. "I trust you realize that your position requires it."

He gave her a long look from his bottle-green eyes, then said, "I am well aware of what my position requires."

Gideon turned once again to Francesca. His gaze was cool and assessing, and Francesca reflected that his face was as unreadable as Rochford's, but unlike the politely veiled expression the duke turned to the world, the Earl of Radbourne's face was like stone.

Now, she thought, he would tell her that he did not require her assistance in finding a wife.

"I know that my grandmother and great-aunt are seeking a bride in an attempt to tame me. To make me more presentable—I cannot imagine that I will ever be 'acceptable.'"

Odelia made a soft noise of protest, but when his gaze flickered her way, she fell silent.

Gideon turned back to Francesca. "I, of course, realize that it is a necessity that I marry. I am agreeable to it. Doubtless you will be as able to find a spouse for me as my grandmother and Lady Pencully have been. I do not think you could be less successful at it. I will rely on the duke's assurance that you know what you are doing."

"You told Gideon we were coming here?" Lady Odelia asked Rochford in some amazement.

"It seemed to me only fair, as it involves him," Rochford replied calmly.

"Pray proceed, Lady Haughston, in your search for a suitable bride for me," Lord Radbourne went on. "However, I feel I should point out that the woman in question will have to meet my approval, not Lady Pencully's." He paused, then added, "I prefer, you see, not to be saddled with a fool."

"Of course," Francesca replied. "I understand."

"Very good. Now, if you will excuse me, I must take my leave." He rose to his feet. "There are a number of matters regarding the business my family so disapproves of that require my notice."

"Of course, my lord. No doubt we will talk again."

He gave her a short nod, and bade goodbye to his cousin and great-aunt. He strode to the door, then turned and looked back at Francesca. "Lady Haughston…may I suggest one woman whom I would like to consider?"

Francesca caught Lady Odelia's expression of amazement out of the corner of her eye, but she kept her gaze on Gideon, saying only, "Of course, my lord. Whom would you suggest?"

"Lady Irene Wyngate," he replied.

CHAPTER THREE

IRENE WATCHED HER mother as she moved gracefully through the steps of a country dance with her cousin Harville. Sir Harville, whose party this was, was one of the few people with whom Lady Claire felt it was appropriate for a widow such as herself to dance. He was also one of the few people who could always bring a smile to her mother's face.

For those reasons, Irene always looked forward to Lady Spence's birthday ball. And since Sir Harville, instead of his penny-pinching wife, arranged the ball, the affair was also beautifully decorated and offered a midnight supper that would tempt even the faintest of appetites.

"Such a sweet little dance," Irene's sister-in-law said beside her, glancing about the ballroom with an expression that mingled approval with condescension. "Not nearly so grand a ballroom as we have at Wyngate House, but they have done it up very well."

Irene suppressed a sigh. Maura was the mistress of the insult wrapped in a compliment. However, Irene had promised her mother that she would not quarrel with Maura tonight, so she made no comment.

"Lady Claire is in good looks tonight," Maura went on. "Don't you agree, Humphrey dear?"

She turned a sugary smile on her husband, standing on

her other side. Humphrey smiled back, pleased at his wife's comment, "Yes, she does look lovely. So like you to point that out."

It never ceased to amaze Irene that her brother, so intelligent in so many other ways, never saw through Maura's pretense of sweetness to the sharp claws beneath.

"No matter what others may say, I think it is wonderful for her to dance."

Humphrey frowned a little. "Say? What does anyone say?"

"Nothing," Irene assured him firmly, shooting Maura a daggerlike look.

"Of course not," Maura agreed smoothly. "Why, there is nothing at all wrong with a woman of her age dancing with her cousin—even if it is such a *lively* dance. And while one would be quite correct in presuming that some women would do it to call attention to themselves, of course your mother would never do that."

"No, never." Humphrey blinked, looking at his wife with some concern. "Do people say that?"

"No," Irene interrupted flatly. "They do not. There is nothing wrong with Mother's dancing, even if it were not with her cousin, and no one *of any consequence* would say so." She shot a fierce look at Maura as she spoke the last few words.

"Indeed not," Maura agreed, assuming a prettily determined expression. "And so I shall tell anyone who has the audacity to say so."

"Yes, quite." Humphrey smiled down at his wife, though his eyes remained a little troubled. He turned to look at his mother again.

"And I beg you will not say anything to Mother about it,"

Irene went on, iron in her voice. "It would be most unkind to make her worry in any way over doing something that she enjoys so much."

"Oh, indeed." Maura nodded. "Though one cannot help but wonder whether Lady Claire, with her sensibilities, might not decide that she would prefer to stand up to one of the more sedate tunes."

"That is true," Humphrey agreed, casting a fond look at his wife. "You are always so solicitous of Mother."

"Humphrey!" Irene said sharply. "If you or Maura say anything to destroy Mother's happiness in taking an innocent dance with her cousin—"

"Irene!" Maura looked shocked. Tears welled up in her blue eyes. "I would never hurt Lady Claire. Why, she is as dear to me as my own mother."

"Irene, really," Humphrey said, exasperated. "How could you say something so cruel? You know how Maura feels about Mother."

"Yes," Irene replied drily. "I do."

"Sometimes your tongue is just too sharp. You know how sensitive Maura is."

"Now, Humphrey, darling," Maura said before Irene could speak, "I am sure that Irene did not mean to hurt me. She is so much stronger than other women. She does not understand how words can wound a softer nature."

Irene curled her fingers into a fist by her side, willing herself not to lash back at Maura with cutting words. That would be playing right into her hands. For all her silliness, Maura was amazingly clever at manipulating a situation to her advantage.

As Irene swallowed her words, Maura cast her a maliciously triumphant look, then turned her head away. "Oh, look, Irene, here is Lady Haughston coming toward us. Now might be your chance to talk to her, as we were discussing the other day."

"Talk about what?" Humphrey asked. "I didn't realize you and Francesca Haughston were friends."

"We are not," Irene began.

"Never mind, dearest," Maura put in, smiling at her husband. "It was just girl talk."

"Ah." He nodded, looking pleased at the thought of his wife and sister sharing girlish confidences. "Then I shall not press you."

He bowed to Francesca as she reached them. "Lady Haughston. How good to see you."

"Lord Wyngate. Lady Wyngate. Lady Irene." Francesca favored them all with a smile. "Such a lovely ball, is it not?"

They spent a few minutes on the usual niceties, discussing the lovely fall weather, the lack of entertainment in London now that the Season was over, and the health and happiness of Lady Haughston's brother and his new bride.

At a pause in the conversation, Francesca turned toward Irene and said, "I was about to take a stroll about the room. Perhaps you would care to join me?"

Surprised, Irene looked at her blankly for a moment, then said, "Why, yes, of course."

Francesca smiled and stepped away, and Irene followed her, casting a suspicious glance at Lady Maura as she did so. Had Maura arranged this meeting with Lady Haughston? The surprise on Maura's face appeared quite genuine, yet…

They strolled toward the opposite wall, where a bank of French doors had been opened to let in the evening air. As they walked, they exchanged the same sort of small nothings that they had been bandying about earlier, and Irene's curiosity grew with each step. It seemed too odd a coincidence that Francesca Haughston should make an obvious effort to meet her only two days after Maura had been urging Irene to talk to the woman.

Irene had assumed that Maura was simply using Lady Haughston as an excuse to needle her about her spinster state and her many deficiencies of charm and character. But perhaps Maura had been serious. Perhaps Maura was willing to go to any lengths to see Irene marry, given that it would mean that Irene—and perhaps her mother, as well—would leave Maura's house.

Color flooded Irene's throat as she thought about the embarrassing possibility that Maura had been talking to Francesca Haughston about Irene's failure to marry. She could well imagine how Maura would have smiled sweetly as she spoke of how sorry she felt for poor, unwanted Irene.

Irene set her jaw and cast a glance over at her companion. Would Francesca Haughston have any interest in doing Maura a favor? She could not imagine that the two of them were friends. Maura had only been around Lady Haughston a few times, and only in large social settings. And it seemed unlikely that Francesca would have sought out Maura's friendship. However much Irene regarded Francesca as frivolous, she knew that Francesca was not goose-ish. She was a sophisticated hostess, a light of the *ton*. Her favor was pursued by many, and she was knowledgeable about the world and about people. Francesca surely would not be fooled by Maura's manner, nor would she be impressed by the fact that Maura was married to Lord Wyngate.

No, Irene thought it unlikely that Francesca would have been particularly interested in doing Maura a favor. And even though she and Irene moved in the same circle, Francesca was seven or eight years older than Irene, and the two of them had never been what Irene would have termed friends, so Irene did not think that Francesca would have been moved by Maura's pleas into doing Irene a favor, either. Moreover, Irene could not forget that look of surprise on Maura's face when Francesca had taken Irene away from them. Surely Maura was not *that* good at dissembling.

But that left the question of why Francesca had sought her out. Irene was not naive enough to think that it was simply because she was interested in Irene's company.

"Lady Haughston…" Irene said abruptly, breaking into the amusing little *on dit* that Francesca was relating.

Francesca looked at her, somewhat surprised, and Irene realized that she had probably been rude again. It was a fault of which she was frequently accused.

"I beg your pardon," Irene said. "I should not have interrupted you. But you have known me long enough to know that I believe in straight dealing. I cannot help but wonder why you asked me to promenade with you about the room."

Francesca let out a little sigh. "I am aware of your preference for plain speaking. And while I am in general of the opinion that it is as easy to employ tact as to be blunt, I, too, find truth to be the best course. I asked you to accompany me because a longtime friend of my family asked me for a favor. I was asked to introduce you to someone who wishes to make your acquaintance."

"What?" It was Irene's turn to look astonished. "But who— Why—"

"I can only assume it is because he admires you," Francesca answered, and smiled in that small catlike way she had, a little secretive and yet at the same time alluring.

Her words so took Irene aback that for a moment her mind was blank. Finally she rallied enough to retort, "Really, Lady Haughston, I am not fresh from the country. Do you expect me to believe that?"

"I see no reason why you should not," Francesca responded, widening her eyes. "I do not know his reasons, of course. I did not think it my place to quiz him regarding his motives. However, I find that is commonly the reason why a gentleman wishes to meet a certain lady. Surely you do not count yourself so low that you think no man would find you worthy of his notice."

Irene regarded Francesca thoughtfully. Lady Haughston had rather neatly boxed her in. Finally she said, "'Tis not false modesty. It is more that I have found I have a certain reputation among the *ton* that makes gentlemen disinclined to pursue my acquaintance."

Francesca's eyes danced with amusement, and her smile broadened. "A reputation, Lady Irene? Indeed, I cannot imagine what you mean."

"I thought you believed truth was the best course," Irene shot back. "We both know that I am regarded as something of a shrew."

Francesca shrugged. "Ah, but while you are not fresh from the country, this gentleman is."

"What?" Irene, puzzled, started to say more, but Francesca's attention had focused on something over Irene's shoulder, and she smiled. Irene dropped the rest of her words as she turned to see what had claimed Francesca's attention.

It was a man. Tall and broad-shouldered, he strode toward them with purpose, and it seemed to Irene that those around him were dwarfed in comparison. It was not that he was so much larger than the other men, but there was a certain aura about him, a sense of toughness and strength, that set him apart.

His hair was jet-black, thick and a trifle long, giving him the faint look of a ruffian, despite the quality and cut of his clothes. His face was all angles and lines, with high, sharp cheekbones and a firm chin. The straight slashes of his eyebrows were as dark as his hair, and the eyes below them were an intense green.

She did not recognize him and yet there was something about him that tugged at her, some sense of familiarity that she could not place. Irene was aware of a peculiar sensation inside her, a dancing of nerves through her midsection that seemed both excitement and trepidation, mingled with another, unknown feeling that coiled down into her abdomen, hot and disturbing.

Who was this man?

"Ah, Lord Radbourne," Francesca said, holding out her hand in greeting.

"Lady Haughston." He bowed perfunctorily over her hand, and then his gaze slid past Francesca to Irene.

His eyes were not leering or bold, simply watchful, but there was a directness in them that was slightly unsettling. There was something different about him that intrigued her. She realized that she wanted to know more about him, that she wanted to talk to him, and the fact that she felt that way both surprised and annoyed her.

"Pray, allow me to introduce you to Lady Irene Wyngate," Francesca went on smoothly, turning from him to Irene. "Lady Irene, I would like you to meet Gideon, the Earl of Radbourne. Lord Radbourne is Lady Pencully's great-nephew."

It dawned on Irene then exactly who their visitor was. He

was the long-lost heir to the Bankes family fortune and name, around whom so much gossip had swirled over the last few months. Though she knew no one who could say they had actually met the man, she had heard a great deal about him. She had been told that he was a criminal, found in prison and hauled out of it by a powerful family member. Others had declared that he was mad, still others that he was simple-minded. A few had hinted at perversions the depths of which they could not even name in front of a lady. A number had held that he was deformed, hideous to look at.

Obviously the ones who had made the last assertion were wrong, Irene thought. She extended her hand, schooling her face into a polite expression that she hoped masked the leap of interest she had felt when she realized who he was. "How do you do, Lord Radbourne?"

"Lady Wyngate." He took her hand, giving her the same brief sketch of a bow that he had given Francesca.

Irene felt a little frisson of excitement run through her hand at the brief touch of Radbourne's fingers upon hers. It was absurd, of course, she told herself—the merest of touches, nothing more than a polite exchange that had happened on countless occasions. It meant nothing, indicated nothing… yet she could not deny that what she had felt was different from all the other times she had given her hand in greeting.

Irritation welled in her—with this man, with Francesca for manipulating her into meeting him, but most of all with herself for feeling this hitch of excitement and interest. It was most unlike her, and Irene found it decidedly annoying. She was, after all, a woman who always knew what she was about.

There was a moment of awkward silence as the earl looked at Irene and she returned his gaze coldly. She told herself that he was no doubt used to any unmarried woman he met fawning over him. Whatever the rumors about him, he was, after all, an earl and reputedly quite wealthy. She had no idea why he would want to meet her, but she was determined that he see that she had no interest in him.

Francesca cast a glance from Irene to the earl and back, then said, "A lovely ball, isn't it? I do hope that you are enjoying the party, Lord Radbourne."

The earl barely spared her a glance. Looking at Irene, he said, "May I have this dance, my lady?"

"I do not care to dance," Irene responded bluntly. From the corner of her eye, she could see Francesca's eyebrows vault upward at this bit of rudeness, but she ignored her.

Lord Radbourne, however, did not even flinch at her setdown. To Irene's astonishment, amusement flickered for an instant in his face, as he replied, "That is good, then, as I am not at all proficient at dancing. Why don't we simply take a stroll and talk?"

His effrontery left Irene speechless. But Francesca, a trace of laughter in her voice, spoke up beside her. "That sounds like an excellent idea. While you two are occupied, I shall pay my regards to our hostess."

With those words, Francesca turned and hurried away, leaving Irene alone with Lord Radbourne. There was little she could do except take the arm he extended, for she could see that they were the object of several interested gazes. If she gave him the direct cut now and stalked off, ignoring his arm, it would be gossiped about all over Mayfair tomorrow.

So she gave in with a regal nod, laying her hand on his arm. As they turned and began to stroll around the edge of the dancers, Irene nodded at one or two of the women watching them. She could feel Lord Radbourne's muscles like iron beneath the sleeve of his jacket, and it startled her to find that the fact stirred a warmth in her.

"Lady Haughston intimated that you wished to meet me," Irene began in her usual direct way. This approach, she had found long ago, was the easiest method of deflecting any man's interest in her. It was unladylike, with none of the flirtation and deception that marked the common course of interaction between men and women.

"That is true," he replied.

She shot him an annoyed look. "I cannot imagine why."

"Can you not?" He looked at her again with an expression of faint amusement, an expression that Irene realized she quite disliked.

"No, I cannot. I am twenty-five years of age and have been on the shelf for quite some time."

"You assume my interest in you is matrimonial?" he countered.

Irene felt a flush rise in her cheeks. "I just told you, I cannot imagine what your interest in me is. However, I have rarely found that men had any interest in spinsters."

"Perhaps I merely wished to renew our acquaintance."

"What?" Irene turned her head to look at him, startled. She had thought there was something familiar about him, and the feeling tugged at her again. "What do you mean?"

"We have met before. Do you not remember?"

Her interest was thoroughly caught now, and she studied his face, scarcely noticing as they stepped through one of the open doors onto the terrace.

"Let me refresh your memory," he said, leading her toward the hip-high stone wall that edged the terrace. "At the time, you tried to shoot me."

She dropped her hand from his arm and turned to face him. "What in the world are you—"

Suddenly the memory fell into place. It had been years—surely almost ten. She had heard a fracas downstairs in the entry and had gone to look into it. She had found this man punching her father, and she had stopped the fight by firing a shot from one of her father's dueling pistols into the air.

"You!" she exclaimed.

"Yes. Me." He looked back at her levelly.

"I did not try to shoot you," Irene told him caustically. "I fired over your head to get your attention. If I had tried to shoot you, you would be dead."

She expected him to turn on his heel and leave her at that remark, but to her surprise, he let out a short bark of laughter. His face shifted and changed, his eyes lightening with amusement, and he was suddenly so handsome that her breath caught in her throat. The heat that flooded her cheeks this time was not from embarrassment.

"Well, I am glad to see that you bear me no ill will," she said tartly, to cover her odd and unsettling reaction. She turned and strolled away from him along the stone wall.

A little to her surprise, he kept pace with her, saying, "It was natural, was it not, for a child to protect her father? I could scarcely blame you."

"Since you apparently knew my father, I imagine you know that he was little deserving of protection."

Radbourne shrugged. "What one deserves has little to do with the relationship between parent and child, I would think."

"My father would have told you that I was an unnatural child."

He looked at her. "You stopped me from hurting him any further, did you not?"

"Yes. I did." She did not look at him, instead turning her gaze out over the garden. She had no interest in discussing her father or her feelings toward him. "Still, I see little reason why you should wish to meet someone who held a gun on you."

"I was finished with Lord Wyngate, anyway. I had made my point to him." He paused, turning his own attention toward the garden. "But you seemed…interesting."

Irene turned to him. "I fired a shot at you and you found it interesting?"

The smile tugged at the corners of his mouth again. "It was over my head. Remember?"

She frowned. "I am not sure what you are getting at."

"You were correct in your first assumption, my lady. Matrimonial concerns are what brought me here."

"I beg your pardon?"

"My family is interested in marrying me off to a proper young lady. I am, you see, an embarrassment to them. The facts of my life are, apparently, somehow a scandal, a reflection upon them. And an earl who cannot ride, and whose vowels are not rounded and plummy enough, is a disgrace. As for my business interests…well, they cannot even be spoken of."

Despite his light tone, his words were biting and his eyes were hard. It seemed clear to Irene that the man had little liking for his newly discovered family—or perhaps it was simply disdain for the nobility in general. She could not help but feel a certain sympathy for him. After all, she had for several years been viewed by many of her peers and even some members of her family with disfavor, if not actual dislike, for her forthright manner and blunt speech.

Radbourne went on, "They have come up with a plan to cover my shortcomings by shackling me to a woman of good family. I think it is their hope that she will guide me into more appropriate behavior—or at least hide some of my inappropriateness."

"You are a grown man," Irene pointed out. "They cannot force you to marry."

He grimaced. "No. Only talk me to death on the matter."

Irene hid a smile. She knew the power of an incessant harangue all too well.

He shrugged. "But I know that I must marry and produce an heir. If I refuse now, I am only delaying the inevitable. I toyed with the idea of marrying an opera dancer or some such, just to put their noses out of joint. But it would be unfair of me to put someone else in that position. Nor would I want to doom my children to gossip and whispers. I will not make them pariahs among their peers. Therefore, I agree that I need to marry a suitable wife. You are, I understand, not yet married or betrothed, and according to my great-aunt, your family fits the requirements very well. Lady Haughston has apparently agreed to help Lady Pencully in this endeavor, so I suggested to her that you be considered as one of the possibilities."

Irene gaped at him, so astonished that she was momentarily robbed of the ability to speak. Finally she blurted out, "You are considering marrying me because I once threatened you with a pistol?"

"I thought that you might be less dull than the simpering misses they have presented to me," he replied, smiling a little.

She stared at him for a moment longer, then drew herself up to her full height, her eyes flashing. "Are you mad? Your words are insulting in so many ways that I scarce know where to start."

He stiffened a little, his face settling into hard lines. His voice was silkily dangerous as he said, "The idea of marrying me is an insult to you?"

"Do you expect me to feel flattered because you decided to 'consider' me as a 'possibility' in your parade of brides? Am I to be honored that you picked me out from the others, like a mare at a sale? Because you deemed me somewhat less boring and unworthy of you than the other unmarried women of the *ton?*"

His mouth tightened. "It is not the way you make it sound. I am not purchasing a wife. It would be a practical arrangement, something that would be advantageous for you, as well. I assumed that you had passed the age of holding girlish fantasies about love."

"Believe me, I was never so young as to hold that sort of fantasy," Irene shot back. Anger vibrated through her, making her oblivious to everything else.

She took a step forward, hands clenched into fists at her sides, and glared up into his face, finding his icy calm more infuriating than any raw display of temper. "Did you think that I was so desperate to marry, so unable to make my way through this world without the guidance of a man, that I would jump at such an opportunity?"

"I thought you would be mature and logical enough to see the advantages for both of us in such an arrangement," he retorted. "Obviously I was mistaken."

"Yes. Obviously. You may find me 'suitable,' but I can assure you that there is nothing about *you* that suits *me!*"

His eyes sparked at her words. It occurred to Irene that perhaps she had gone a step too far in her anger. But she refused to back down and appear intimidated before this fierce man looming over her. Instead she gazed straight back at him, setting her jaw defiantly.

His hand lashed out and wrapped around her wrist, holding her where she stood—though it was not necessary, for Irene would never have revealed weakness by stepping back from him. He looked into her face, his eyes as cold and hard as glass.

"Is there not?" he murmured in a tone all the more dangerous for its softness. "I think, my lady, that you might just find out differently."

With that he bent his head, his other hand coming up to cup the back of her neck, and fastened his lips to hers.

CHAPTER FOUR

IRENE WENT STILL, shocked into immobility. No man had ever had the audacity to kiss her before. His lips were warm against hers, firm yet soft, and they awakened in her a host of sensations that she had never experienced. She felt at once flushed and cold, and a tremor ran down through her body, bursting in a ball of heat in her abdomen.

His mouth pressed harder against hers, and her lips opened instinctively. His tongue slipped inside, startling her even more and starting up a new thrum of pleasure deep inside her. Radbourne wrapped his arms around her, pressing her more tightly against him, so that she felt the hard line of his body all down the length of her own. She was surrounded by his strength and warmth, her breasts crushed against the hard muscles of his chest. Later she would think to herself that she should have been frightened at how easily he held her still, but in this moment she felt no fear, only the eager rush of excitement, the breathless pleasure of her blood pounding through her veins, the sudden awakening of her entire body.

She felt the hot outrush of his breath against her cheek, heard the rough sound he made low in his throat, and she trembled in his arms, unprepared for the myriad of feelings that poured through her. Something seemed to open deep within her, aching and hot, spreading outward. She squeezed her legs tightly together, amazed at the yearning that was blossoming there.

His hands slid down her back and curved beneath her buttocks. His fingers dug in, lifting her up and into him, so that she felt the hard line of his desire pressing into her flesh, and his mouth shifted on hers, digging deeper, his tongue taking her.

Irene dug her fingers into his shoulders, holding on to him as desire swirled through her, urgent and compelling. Her tongue met his and twined around it, and she felt a shudder shake him. He wrapped his arms around her again, so tightly that it felt as if he wanted to melt into her. Irene wound her arms around his neck, lost in sensation, hungry in a way she had never imagined, eager for something she could not even name.

There was the sound of voices as someone stepped outside onto the terrace, the scrape of a foot upon the stone. As the noises penetrated Irene's consciousness, Radbourne dropped his arms abruptly and stepped back, sucking in a long breath. His eyes glittered, wide and dark in his face, and the skin seemed stretched across his cheekbones, stark and taut. They stared at one another. Irene's mind was blank, aware only of the feelings coursing through her body.

For a moment he looked as stunned as she, but then he blinked and half turned away, glancing toward the other end of the terrace, where a couple had emerged and were standing, talking together. The woman's laughter floated across the night air toward them, and the couple turned, strolling in the opposite direction.

As if the others' movement had broken her trance, Irene came crashing back to earth. Her body still hummed with the passion that had overtaken her, but her mind was alert again. She realized with horror that she had been wrapped in Radbourne's arms, kissing him passionately, and that anyone at any moment could have stepped out of the ballroom and seen them. Her reputation would have been ruined, of course, but that was not what most exercised her mind.

What truly horrified her was the fact that she had, for a few moments, completely lost herself in passion. She had not thought about that—not about her good name or what she was risking or, indeed, about anything at all. She had been held entirely in the grip of physical hunger, blind with need, driven solely by desire, like the basest animal.

Irene had always prided herself on her control, on her intellect and reasoning. She had told herself that she was nothing like her father, who had been ruled by primitive urges and basic emotions. She thought before she acted; she wanted a rational life, free from the turmoil of emotions.

Yet here she had been under the control not of her mind, but of her lowest instincts. She had thought of nothing, wanted nothing, but to satisfy her physical craving. Like her father, she had been filled with a primitive hunger, and she had let herself be ruled by it. When Lord Radbourne seized her in his grip and kissed her, she should have pulled away and slapped him. She should have given him the sort of brutal set-down his actions had deserved.

Instead, she had melted in his arms. Flooded with desire, she had kissed him back, had thrown her arms around his neck and clung to him. She had given herself up to him like the most feebleminded of maidens, letting him control her. Dominate her.

She was filled with anger and disgust for herself—equal to the anger and disgust she felt for the man who had brought her to this state. She glared at the earl, relieved at the surge of anger within her, as it pushed out the passion that had filled her earlier.

He gazed back at her, and she could see that he, too, had recovered from whatever desire had gripped him. Gone was the fierce gleam in his eyes. His face was devoid of expression, his lips thinned into a straight line.

"It seems I am not so unsuitable after all, am I?" he asked quietly. "At least in one way."

Rage shot through her, and without thinking, she lashed out, slapping him hard. His head turned aside from the force of her blow, but when he swiveled back to her, the mark of her fingers stood out, white against the tan of his skin, before turning red. He clenched his jaw, and for an instant his eyes sparked with fury, but he said nothing.

"I will not marry anyone," Irene choked out, close to tears. "But if I did, through some bizarre circumstance, marry, it would certainly never be *you!*"

She whirled and stalked back to the ballroom, not looking back.

FRANCESCA HAD FOUND a vantage point from which she could keep an eye on the dancers and also watch the two doors leading out onto the terrace. She was removed from most of the other guests and slightly shielded by a potted palm, and therefore she had been able to pass the last fifteen minutes or so without being pulled into conversation with anyone. She had found the spot shortly after Lord Radbourne strolled off with Irene Wyngate.

She had been rather surprised when the earl had managed to maneuver Irene into a stroll about the room, and unless she was very much mistaken, she thought that Radbourne had led Lady Irene out onto the terrace. The earl, she thought, must be a great deal more determined or clever than most men, for Irene rarely allowed a man to persuade her to do anything. Of course, few men were brave enough to try. Her sharp tongue and dislike of flirtation were well-known among the *ton*. It was something out of the way for a man to even try to woo her.

Of course, Francesca had to admit, the stern expression on the Earl of Radbourne's face scarcely made him look like a man who was wooing. Perhaps that was the reason Irene had gone along with him. Francesca wondered if it was possible that the earl might succeed where other men had failed.

Her curiosity had been aroused when Radbourne had suggested to her that she include Lady Irene on her list of possible matches. To begin with, she wondered how he even knew her. Until Gideon had been found by Rochford and returned to the bosom of his family, he had not moved in the same circles as Irene, and after he came home, it sounded as though he had more or less been secluded with the family at their country estate. Where and when had he seen Irene?

More than that, she wondered why he was interested in her. Irene was not unattractive. Indeed, in Francesca's opinion, Irene was one of the most intriguing-looking women in London. Her large eyes were a clear light brown, almost a golden color, and they were nicely accented by long lashes and nicely arched brows of a slightly darker shade than her hair. Her features were clean-cut, if a trifle strong, and her thickly curling dark blond hair gave her a leonine look that was slightly exotic. She was not the typical beauty, perhaps, but she was appealing—or would be if she did not make such an effort to dispel any interest in her looks.

She usually wore her hair pulled ruthlessly back and pinned into a severe knot, thereby negating the most beautiful aspect of her looks. Her clothes were likewise severe; though of good cut and material, they were plain to the point of dullness. She allowed nothing to soften her looks—or for that matter, her personality.

"Hiding?" A dry male voice said from behind Francesca, and she turned her head, startled.

She smiled. Sir Lucien Talbot stood there, his handsome face set in its usual wry lines, his eyebrows arched in amused question.

"Or are we spying?" he went on, moving up beside her and peering out across the ballroom. "May I join you?"

"Of course," Francesca replied, smiling back at him.

Sir Lucien was her oldest and dearest friend, and the only one who knew the dire state of her finances. As one whose pockets were frequently to let himself, he had long ago recognized that Francesca was living on the edge of financial disaster. He had even, especially in the early days right after her husband's death, taken a few of her items to pawn or sell for her, as a lady could scarcely be seen doing such a thing. Though Francesca had never told him that the projects she had taken on over the past few years were chosen for the monetary benefit she received in one form or another, she thought that Sir Lucien at least suspected she was not shepherding difficult girls through the marriage mart that was a London Season simply for the fun of it.

"I am waiting for Irene Wyngate to come back into the ballroom. She went out onto the terrace a few minutes ago with the Earl of Radbourne."

"Irene Wyngate?" Sir Lucien asked, his eyebrows vaulting

up again in a genuine expression of surprise. "You are putting her forward as a candidate for the position of countess?"

Francesca had told Lucien yesterday about Lady Odelia's scheme to marry off the newfound heir to the earldom, as well as of her own part in the matter. Sir Lucien, as one of the best-known arbiters of good taste and fashion, had on more than one occasion in the past been quite useful to Francesca in putting forward one of her "girls."

"Lord Radbourne specifically asked me to include her," Francesca told him now. "I agreed to introduce them tonight. As soon as I did, he whisked her off."

"Out to the terrace?" her friend asked, his voice assuming a lower, more suggestive tone. "Well, well…I never would have imagined it of the Iron Maiden."

"Pray, do not use that silly appellation. I cannot imagine why men have to come up with such odious nicknames."

"My dear girl, because it suits her, and you know it." He shrugged.

"Well, I hate to think what I am known as," Francesca went on.

"Why, my love, you are referred to only as 'The Venus,' what else?" he replied with a grin.

Francesca chuckled. "Flatterer."

He was silent for a moment, scanning the room with her. Then he said, "Why do you suppose he singled her out?"

"I don't know. I wonder how he even knew who she was. I suppose he must have seen her somewhere and been struck by her. She is quite attractive in her own way."

"She could be stunning if she made a bit of effort," Sir Lucien agreed. "I suppose he could have enough eye for beauty to see that." He paused, then went on drily, "Do you suppose his infatuation will outlast a stroll on the terrace with her?"

"I don't know. That is why I am looking for them. I do hope he does not cry off immediately. The more I thought about the matter, the more I realized that Lady Irene would be an excellent match for him."

"Indeed?"

Francesca nodded. "Obviously he is for some reason already interested in her. And she would suit Lady Odelia's requirements. Her lineage is excellent on both her mother's and her father's sides."

"Old Lord Wyngate was something of a rogue," Sir Lucien objected.

"Yes, but his scandalous behavior has never reflected badly on Lady Irene, or her mother and brother," Francesca pointed out. "And certainly she has the strength of will to make the man presentable, if any woman can."

"And the wit to hide the faults she cannot change," Sir Lucien added.

"Yes. And, most importantly, Irene can hold her own with Lady Odelia. She will not allow the old woman to ride roughshod over her."

"As we all know she will try to do."

"Naturally," Francesca agreed. "And I think, from what I have seen of him, it might require some strength of character to deal with the earl himself, as well."

"Really?" Sir Lucien turned toward her, intrigued. "I assumed he was, well…" He shrugged.

"Under Lady O's thumb?"

Sir Lucien nodded.

"I think not. When he came into the room, he seemed…a trifle rough around the edges, I suppose, but not intimidated in the slightest. In fact, when I looked at Lady Odelia, it occurred to me that perhaps *she* was a little wary of *him*."

"Well, well… That would be a first," Sir Lucien mused.

"I thought as much myself. He seemed to be going along with her plan but not obeying her, if you see what I mean. Oh, wait." Francesca straightened, reaching up to grasp Sir Lucien's sleeve. "There she is. Oh, dear. She does not look at all pleased."

Lucien looked in the direction of her gaze and saw Irene. She had just entered through the open doors onto the terrace, and she was now striding through the crowd of people, her back ramrod straight. She did not glance to either side as she walked. Her jaw was set, her face flushed, and there was a furious light in her eyes. He noticed that people stepped out of her way as she approached.

"I would not say it went well," he murmured to Francesca. She sighed. "No, I fear not."

Francesca glanced aside and saw that the Duke of Rochford was making his way toward her from the direction of the card room. "Now what?" she muttered.

Sir Lucien glanced over at her and then toward the duke. He chuckled. "It could be worse. It could be Lady Pencully."

Francesca rolled her eyes in her friend's direction. "Curse your tongue, Lucien. Now she is certain to appear."

Lucien smothered a laugh and said to the approaching duke, "Rochford. Dear fellow. Pleasure, as always, to see you."

"Sir Lucien. Lady Haughston." Rochford stopped beside Francesca, nodding to them both. "I must say, my lady, you do not look at all pleased."

Francesca gave the man a frosty look. "That depends on whether you brought Lady Pencully with you."

"No, I did not, I am pleased to say," Rochford replied. Then he smiled faintly and added, "However, I do believe that I saw her in the card room a moment ago."

"So that is why you left it," Francesca retorted sourly.

"But of course," Rochford admitted without a trace of guilt. "You may think yourself reluctant to see her, but you do not have the misfortune to be tied to her by blood. If you were, you would know just how craven you could be."

"What nonsense you talk," Francesca said reprovingly. "You have never been afraid of anything in your life."

He studied her for a moment, a quizzical look on his features, then said, "If only you knew, my lady."

Francesca made a face and turned away from his gaze. She was aware of a faint heat rising in her cheeks, and she was not even sure why. Rochford had the most damnable talent for unsettling her.

As her eyes swept across the room, she noticed the Earl of Radbourne entering the ballroom through the other set of doors. He looked, if anything, even more thunderous than Irene had. Francesca sighed inwardly. Obviously that opportunity had been lost for good. Perhaps she should not have introduced them so early. But he would have had to talk to Irene at some point, and it would simply all have unraveled then. Better, she supposed, to have gotten it over quickly instead of wasting her time on the match.

"Your Lord Radbourne seems a trifle fierce," she commented to Rochford.

"Hardly mine," Rochford protested mildly. "But I imagine he can be rather…hard. I suspect that is the only way he could survive the streets of London. He grew up in a very different world from the one in which we did, Lady Haughston."

"Indeed. But ours was dangerous, too, in another way."
Francesca glanced toward him, and Rochford turned to look
at her, his eyes sharp.

He made no answer, but Francesca looked quickly away
from him, suddenly aware of Sir Lucien's curious gaze.

The duke shifted, then said in a low voice, "Fair warning,
my friends. Lady Pencully is approaching." He bowed toward them. "I fear I must take my leave of you."

"Coward," Francesca whispered.

He merely smiled and strode away. Beside her, Sir Lucien
made a move, but Francesca turned and pinned him with a
look. With a sigh, he remained where he was and forced a
smile onto his face.

"Lady Pencully." He swept her an elegant bow. "What an
unaccustomed pleasure to see you."

"Don't try your folderol with me, Talbot," Lady Odelia
said bluntly, though Francesca saw that she could not keep
her face from softening a little. "Go sharpen your skills on
someone else, why don't you? I need to talk to Francesca."

"Of course, my lady." Sir Lucien cast an amused glance
at Francesca as he bowed to them both and strolled away.

"I've decided what to do," Lady Odelia went on without
preamble. "We shall have a party at Radbourne Park."

"I beg your pardon?"

"To search for a mate for the earl," the older woman said
with some asperity, as though Francesca were a bit dim.
"That is what we are about, remember?"

"Of course I remember. I just, um, wasn't sure why a
party—"

"It will be the best way to present him to the girls we pick.
I am convinced that we will never find him a spouse in
London. It is too elegant, too sophisticated. He is bound to

stand out here among men of Talbot's sort. Too smooth by half, that one, if you ask me, but he's the sort that women like, you know. Or Rochford. Though, of course, women would fawn on him if he were as rough as an old boot. Only stands to reason, being a duke and all. But that is neither here nor there."

She looked accusingly at Francesca, as if she had been responsible for her wandering off subject. "The point is, if we separate these women from civilization, they will no doubt find my great-nephew more acceptable."

"I think there are a number of women who would feel the earl's title and fortune make him acceptable enough anywhere," Francesca replied wryly.

"Yes, perhaps, but I am unwilling to take the chance. So I shall get Pansy to arrange a house party. We will work on a guest list. Go over the girls who will do. Then you will come up early to Radbourne Park, so you can work on Gideon himself. Smooth out some of his rough edges, if you can. You know what I mean. I am sure that he will receive suggestions better from you. He seems to resent the hints I give him."

"Surely not," Francesca murmured.

Lady Pencully gave her a narrow look. "Don't think I don't know when you are being facetious, girl. I am well aware that any man would much rather get instruction from a winning girl like you than from an old lady who doesn't couch the truth in sweet-sounding phrases." She gave a short nod, ending the matter. "When will you be at Radbourne Park?"

As always, Lady Odelia's commands rankled, but Francesca had to admit that the older woman's idea made sense. And a visit to Radbourne Park for a few weeks would also take care of her problem with maintaining her household for a while.

"I am not sure. A few days, surely, to pack and set things in order," Francesca told her.

"Well, don't dawdle, girl. We need to set this thing in motion."

"Of course, but—" Francesca broke off as she saw Lord Radbourne approaching. "Ah, Lord Radbourne. Good to see you again."

It was a lie, of course. She did not look forward to talking with him. He looked decidedly put out, and Francesca suspected that he was about to ring a peal over her head for whatever had transpired with Irene Wyngate.

He nodded shortly to Francesca and then to his great-aunt. "Lady Haughston. Lady Pencully."

"Gideon," Lady Odelia responded. "Saw you talking to Lady Irene a few minutes ago." She looked at him hopefully.

His lips tightened. "Lady Irene Wyngate is arrogant, stubborn and a snob. I am certain that she would not do for my wife."

Even Lady Odelia seemed unable to find a response to that.

Francesca jumped into the silence that followed his statement. "I see. Well, all the more reason to move forward with other plans. Your great-aunt and I were just discussing having a party at Radbourne Park. I hope you will find that agreeable. It seems a good way for you to meet several young women and get to know them, and for them to get to know you. A week or two allows one many more opportunities than attending rounds of balls and such here in the city."

He nodded. "No doubt. I will leave it in your capable hands. And my aunt's, of course."

"Very well." Francesca relaxed. At least he was not going to make a scene or, apparently, even blame her for whatever Irene had said to him.

"I will take my leave of you, then. I have business to attend to. If you will excuse me?"

"Of course." Francesca was quite content to see him go, though she could not help but wonder what sort of business he could have that required attending to at this time of night.

Lady Odelia paled a little and glanced around to see if anyone had overheard the earl's mention of business. He bowed toward them and turned to walk away.

He had taken only a few steps, however, when he abruptly stopped, pivoted on his heel and returned to them. "Lady Haughston," he said grimly. "When you make up the guest list…" He hesitated, then added shortly, "Invite Lady Irene."

CHAPTER FIVE

THE NEXT MORNING, Irene glanced across the table at her sister-in-law. Maura was unaccustomedly pale, and her lids were heavy and dark. If it were another person, Irene would have wondered if she had not imbibed too freely at the Spences' ball last night. Perhaps, she thought, Maura was not feeling well. She had been remarkably silent ever since she sat down at the breakfast table this morning, and she had merely picked listlessly at her food.

Irene glanced down at her own plate. She noticed that she, too, had not eaten much. However, she knew the reason for her own state. After her ill-fated stroll with Lord Radbourne, she had spent the remainder of the ball fuming. She had wanted to leave the party altogether, but Maura had refused to consider it, and Irene had finally slipped out of the ballroom and found a quiet nook along the gallery, where she had spent the rest of the evening.

Though she had been undisturbed, it had scarcely been a pleasant hour, for in her mind Irene had gone over and over Lord Radbourne's rude behavior and her own appalling lapse of good sense. Even when they finally left the ball and she was able to seek the sanctuary of her own room, she had not found any peace. She had gone to bed but had tossed and turned, her thoughts still occupied with the shocking kiss on the terrace.

It had been hours before she could go to sleep, and even after she finally slipped into slumber, she had been disturbed by hot, lascivious dreams, awakening with her heart pounding and her skin sheened with sweat.

As a result, she had come down to breakfast a trifle late, feeling as if she had not slept at all, and had pushed her food around on her plate, eating little of it.

Irene nibbled another bit of egg and glanced around the table at the others. She noticed that Humphrey and her mother were also sneaking small worried looks at Maura, and Irene wondered again what had gotten into Humphrey's wife.

Almost as if in answer to Irene's thought, Maura raised her head and looked at Irene, saying, "I don't know why you were so anxious to leave the party last night, Irene. It quite spoiled the evening."

Irene raised her brows. "I had a headache. But we did not leave, so I cannot see how your evening was affected."

"Irene…" her brother said quietly, a note of warning in his voice.

Irene glanced at him, a twinge of hurt going through her. Was her brother so in the thrall of his wife that he would discourage her from expressing her opinion?

"Well, Humphrey, it seems a reasonable question, does it not?" she asked levelly.

"It isn't that." He looked distressed, casting another glance at his wife. "Must we discuss this at the breakfast table?"

Lady Claire spoke up hastily, saying, "It was a lovely party, was it not? I enjoyed myself thoroughly. Didn't you, Humphrey?"

"Yes, Mother, of course I did." Humphrey smiled at the older woman fondly. "I was glad to see you so entertained."

"It was a very pleasant time," Maura agreed. "And I do not mean to criticize, Irene. I just wish that you would make a little more effort. It was so good of Lady Haughston to single you out, and then I saw you walking with that man. Who did you say he was, Mother?"

"Lord Radbourne," Lady Claire answered. "Yes, I was quite amazed when Maura pointed him out to me and said you had strolled about the room with him. I had not seen him before, but Mrs. Shrewsbury told me that he was the Bankes' heir who was kidnapped years ago. Such a sad tale…" She shook her head, tsk-tsking over the story.

"Yes, but the important thing is that he is said to be worth a fortune," Maura put in. "A highly eligible man. And you did not make the slightest push to interest him, I warrant. Instead, you came back wanting to leave straightaway."

"I am not interested in Lord Radbourne," Irene said flatly.

"Of course you are not!" Maura exclaimed. "You are never interested in any man! You are the most unnatural person…. I cannot understand you. Sometimes I think you simply want to thwart me." Maura glared at Irene, her mouth drawing into a childish pout.

Irene stared at her sister-in-law. Even for Maura, this behavior was a little unusual. "Maura, it has nothing to do with you," she began reasonably.

"Oh, do not speak to me that way," Maura snapped, picking up her napkin and tossing it down onto the table. "I am not a child. You talk to me as if I were a fool. Of course it has something to do with me! You refuse to marry, when any normal woman would be eager to do so. But you would rather remain here the rest of your life, even if it means being a spinster with no life of your own. You would much rather interfere with Humphrey's life—always telling him what to do and how to act—"

Irene gaped at the other woman, stunned by Maura's words.

"And you!" Maura went on, turning on her husband. Tears welled in her eyes. "You cannot seem to get through the day without asking your sister what you should do. 'What do you think about this, Irene?'" she mimicked, her voice dripping with bitterness. "'What should I tell Lord This or Sir That?' You never ask my opinion, yet I am your *wife!*"

Humphrey blinked in surprise, for a moment speechless. Then he leaned forward, reaching out a hand to Maura, saying, "My dear…how can you think that? Of course I am interested in your opinion."

"Hah!" Maura jumped to her feet, shaking off his hand. "You care nothing about me. Nothing at all!" With a sob, she turned and ran out of the room.

The other three people at the table stared after her.

"Humphrey! Irene!" Lady Claire said, her voice worried. "Why— What—"

"Perhaps I should leave, Humphrey," Irene began stiffly. She had always known that Maura did not like her any more than she liked Maura, but she had been unprepared for the level of dislike in her sister-in-law's voice.

"No, no," her brother said hastily, pushing back his chair and standing, looking from the door to Irene, then back to the door. "I suppose I should go after her. I don't know…she is so…volatile these days." He turned back to Irene, a frown forming on his forehead. "I apologize. I am sure Maura did not mean it. She is fond of you, of course, just as she is of Mother. It is just— Well, she did not want to tell anyone just yet, but I can see that I must tell you. Maura is in a delicate condition." His face pinkened slightly at his words, and he smiled in an almost abashed way.

Irene looked at him blankly, but Claire cried out in pleasure, "She is going to have a baby? Oh, Humphrey!" She clasped her hands together at her bosom, her face bright with excitement. "How wonderful! You must be so happy."

"A baby?" Irene looked at her mother, then back at her brother. She smiled and stood up, then circled the table and hugged him. "I am so happy for you."

"I knew you would be. I told Maura it was foolish to think you might not be," Humphrey said with naive candor. "She is not herself these days. You can understand why she said what she did. It is foolish, of course, but I know she did not mean to say anything unkind."

"Of course not," Irene lied.

"But, Irene…" He took her hand between his. "Will you try to avoid any unpleasantness for the next few weeks? I am sure she will grow less emotional. Right now it is laughter one minute and tears the next with her. It seems that the slightest thing upsets her."

"Of course. I promise I will mind my words," Irene agreed, though her heart sank at the prospect of walking on eggshells around Maura for the rest of the pregnancy. Unlike her brother, she suspected that Maura would play up her condition for all it was worth until the very end. Even longer, in fact. After Maura gave birth, she would doubtless demand even more consideration as the mother of Humphrey's child.

"Thank you." Humphrey beamed at her. "I knew I could count on you." He gave her hand a final pat and turned away. "Now I had better go up and talk to her. She will be feeling so distressed at the thought that she may have wounded you."

Irene watched her brother go without comment. She seriously doubted that Maura felt any remorse for what she had said, but she would not say so to him. She was well aware that Humphrey's love for his wife blinded him to all her faults.

She turned back to her mother, who was looking after Humphrey, her face soft with a tender happiness. Lady Claire shifted her gaze to Irene, and Irene watched the pleasure slowly fade from her face.

She felt a pinprick of guilt. If anyone had been distressed by her exchange of words with Maura, it had been her mother.

"Oh, dear," her mother said with a sigh. "I fear it will be a difficult few months. Maura will doubtless be…very sensitive."

"Doubtless," Irene agreed drily. "Do not worry. I promise that I will try my utmost to curb my tongue with Maura."

"I know you will, dear." Lady Claire mustered up a smile, but it quickly fell away. She glanced toward the open door guiltily and dropped her voice. "I fear it will be hard to do. I mean no disparagement upon your brother's wife, but…"

"I know you do not, Mother. No one could be sweeter tempered than you are. The truth is that Maura is difficult at the best of times."

"It is hard on a young couple, having a mother live with them. I do wish that your father had left us a larger portion. Would it not be darling to have our own little cottage?" She smiled to herself as she thought about it.

"Yes, it would." Irene's musings were less sweet than her mother's. "Father should have provided better for you."

"Well, what's done is done." Even now, Irene knew, Lady Claire was reluctant to speak ill of her husband. "We must simply work as hard as we can at making the house run smoothly. Maura will need help, surely, as she becomes more advanced in her condition. Of course, she may prefer having her own mother and sister, although the house will be a little crowded if they come."

Lady Claire paused, frowning a little as she thought. "Perhaps I should not have danced so much last night. I could see that Maura was not well pleased with my standing up so frequently with my cousin. It might not have been appropriate."

"You would never conduct yourself any way but appropriately," Irene assured her mother. "There was naught amiss with you dancing with your cousin and friends. You have lived among the *ton* all your life, and you know far better what is appropriate than some daughter of a Yorkshire country squire recently arrived in the city."

"Irene!" Her mother cast an anxious glance at the doorway, then turned back to her. "You must not say such things. You promised that you would make more of an effort to get along."

"I will," Irene said disgruntledly. "But that does not mean that I cannot have my own opinions. However, I promise that I will refrain from mentioning them in front of Maura. But only for your sake, Mother, not because I feel any regard for Maura's opinions or her sensibilities. As far as I'm concerned, Maura's skin is about as tender as an elephant's hide."

Her words surprised a gurgle of laughter from Lady Claire, who quickly covered her mouth with her hand to hide the sound as she shook her head reprovingly at her daughter. Then she took a sip of tea and set her cup down, saying brightly, "Well, now, after we finish breakfast, we must go through the yarns and pick out something for a baby blanket. Won't it be fun, making things for the baby?"

"Oh, yes."

Her mother chattered on, paying no attention to the dryness of Irene's tone.

"Booties and caps and little sweaters—oh, there is nothing sweeter than baby clothes."

Irene supposed it would be a pleasant task if she had more affection for the mother-to-be. However, it was important to keep her mother's mind on enjoyable topics and off the worry of displeasing her daughter-in-law, so Irene went along without protest, retiring to her mother's room to pull out yarns and knitting instructions, and listening to her mother chatter on about cradle caps, embroidered gowns and receiving blankets. It seemed that the arrival of a baby would require more articles of clothing than a bridal trousseau.

She tried to steel herself for the task of keeping Maura happy. It would be, she thought, an impossible goal, but still, for her mother's sake, Irene knew that she had to try. It galled her to think of catering to Maura's whims, of biting back her own opinions whenever they disagreed with her sister-in-law's, of putting on a pleasant smile whenever Maura chose to criticize her. However, if she did not do those things, she would, she knew, subject her mother to endless worry. Claire would take it upon herself to apologize and excuse and try to please Maura if Irene crossed the woman, and Irene could not bear to think of her mother debasing herself in that way to a woman who should be thanking her stars that she had Lady Claire for a mother-in-law.

More than ever, Irene wished that she could take her mother away from this house. But she was well aware that the few options for earning money that were open to a gentlewoman, such as hiring out as a governess or a companion, would not provide enough income even for them to let rooms. Part of the compensation in such jobs was the provision of a genteel place in which to live, but one could not bring along a dependent to live there, as well. And even if she could provide enough money by doing one of those things, or by taking in sewing or working in a shop somewhere, her mother would be aghast at the idea of leaving her son's house to move into some small place on their own. It would reflect badly on Humphrey for them to do so, Claire would explain, and she would never do that to her son.

Irene's thoughts were bleak as she contemplated how their lives would change with the coming of a new baby. Maura would be even more puffed up with her own importance at producing a child for Lord Wyngate, especially if it turned out to be a boy and heir. Irene could well imagine the sort of sweetly pitying remarks she would make to Irene regarding the fact that she would never know the satisfaction and joy of motherhood, the needling about Irene's wasted opportunities and lack of effort to acquire that most basic of necessities for a woman: a husband.

She was relieved that Maura stayed in her room all morning, not emerging until after luncheon. But the pleasant interlude could not last, and early in the afternoon Maura rejoined Irene and Lady Claire in the sitting room, where Claire had already begun work on knitting a blanket.

Maura was a trifle paler than usual, and she played the role of invalid to the hilt, sending servants to fetch her shawl, then her fan, then a stool upon which to set her feet, and letting Lady Claire tend to her, tucking the shawl in around her and jumping up to reposition the stool when it did not exactly suit Maura. However, Irene kept her tongue still, maintaining a pleasant smile on her face as she listened to Maura prattle on about the upcoming blessed event, interspersing her remarks with frequent sighs and complaints.

When one of the maids came into the room to announce a visitor, Irene was grateful for the diversion. It was with some amazement, however, that she heard the maid announce that Lady Haughston had come to call. She glanced toward her mother and saw an equally puzzled look on her face. Francesca Haughston had never been a frequent caller to their home, and since Maura had arrived, her calls had stopped entirely. Irene could scarcely blame her; she would have avoided Lady Maura's conversation herself, if only she could.

But it seemed strange that Francesca should suddenly have reappeared, especially after she had sought Irene out last night at the party. However, Maura clearly saw nothing strange about the other woman's arrival. She beamed at Lady Haughston and greeted her effusively, then proceeded to chatter away for the next few minutes without giving Francesca a chance to interject anything more than an occasional "Indeed?" or "Oh, really?"

It did not surprise Irene that Francesca soon began to stir a little restlessly in her seat, and she suspected that their visitor would cut the call short at the first chance she had. Sure enough, when Maura at last paused for a moment, Francesca quickly jumped into the brief silence to tell them that she was sorry she could not stay any longer.

"I was about to take a ride through the park," she explained. "And I just thought I would drop by to ask Lady Irene if she would care to join me."

Maura's face fell almost comically, and Irene hastened to

speak before Maura could come up with some reason why she could not spare Irene's company this afternoon.

"Why, yes, Lady Haughston, that sounds most pleasant."

Irene rang for a servant to fetch her a bonnet and pelisse, and whisked Francesca out of the room, warding off Maura's broad hints about a ride doubtless being just the thing she needed to cure her feeling out of sorts.

"Oh, no, dear sister," Irene told her with syrupy smile to match Maura's own. "I am not at all sure that that would be the best thing for you. You must be very careful now, mustn't you? You know how your back was aching just a few minutes ago. I fear a carriage ride would not be at all the thing for you." She gave her a significant look and appealed to Lady Claire. "Don't you agree, Mother?"

"Oh, yes. Lady Maura and I will be just fine here," Claire agreed, patting Maura's arm. "Won't we, dear?"

As they left the house, Francesca made no mention of Irene's clear desire to escape her sister-in-law but kept up a light conversation about the weather, her open-air brougham— "so unfashionable now, I suppose, for it must be all of ten years since Lord Haughston gave it to me, but it was his first gift to me, so I could not give it up, could I?"—and the ball at the Spences' home the evening before.

As soon as they were settled in the aforementioned brougham, the driver started forward, and they wheeled down the street and turned toward Hyde Park. For a moment they were silent, enjoying the soft golden sunshine and crisp air of the autumn day. Irene turned her head to study her companion.

Francesca, feeling Irene's gaze upon her, glanced at her, and the distinctive dimple creased her cheek as she smiled.

"I vow, I can almost hear the wheels in your head spinning," she said lightly. "Go ahead. Why start holding back now?"

A little breath of laughter escaped Irene. "You surprise me, Lady Haughston."

"Please, call me Francesca. We have known each other since your come-out. Do you not think it is time we call each other by our given names?"

"Why?" Irene retorted. "Are we about to become bosom friends?"

Her blunt words did not seem to bother Lady Haughston, whose smile merely widened. "Why, as to that, I know not. But I would not be surprised if we were to know each other better soon."

"And why is that? I do not mean to complain, for I am excessively grateful to you for inviting me for a ride this afternoon, but I confess that I am at something of a loss to explain your sudden interest in me."

"I could say that I found your candor refreshing yesterday evening—it is quite true, after all—and I thought I might liven up this afternoon with your company."

"What would you say if you were to tell me the actual reason I am in your carriage right now? Did Lady Wyngate approach you? Has she asked you to…help me find a husband?" Red spots of anger and embarrassment bloomed on Irene's cheeks.

Francesca turned to her, surprise marking her features. "Lady Wyngate? Your mother? Why would she— No, no, she has never said such a thing."

"Not my mother. Lady Maura, Humphrey's wife. Did she talk to you about me?"

"No. I assure you. I scarcely know Lady Wyngate. Why would you think she would say something like that to me?"

"Because she wishes me to be married and out of the house," Irene retorted with some bitterness. She cast an abashed glance at Francesca. "I am sorry. You must think me quite foolish. I know you are not friends with Maura. It is just that she was plaguing me the other day about my spinster state, urging me to talk to you. She said that any girl you took up ended by marrying well. She thinks you have the golden touch, I suppose. I was afraid…"

"I would not have discussed you with your sister-in-law," Francesca told her mildly.

Irene looked at her and saw the sincerity in Francesca's face. "I am sorry," she said quickly. "I should not have assumed you would go along with one of Maura's schemes. It was just so odd, right after Maura telling me that I should get your help."

Francesca nodded. "I understand."

Irene could see the sympathy in the other woman's face, and she realized that Francesca understood even more than Irene had expressed. "I am sure that it is difficult for you," the older woman said delicately. "Living with a new sister-in-law."

"I despise it," Irene replied candidly. "A good deal of it is my own fault, I know. I am accustomed to running the house, you see, to being my own mistress. It is hard to give that up, I suppose."

"I would not think that you and Lady Wyngate would ever have been likely to be bosom friends."

"It is a wonder that we have not yet gotten into a hair-pulling fight," Irene said with a wry smile, a little surprised to find herself talking to Francesca about her problems. Irene would never have thought that she would particularly like Francesca, but she was finding her very easy to talk to.

Francesca laughed. "Well, perhaps you *should* think of getting married, then. It would get you away from Maura. You would be the mistress of your own house."

"No, I would be the mistress of my husband's house, with nothing of my own and under a man's entire control. 'Tis far easier to put up with Lady Maura's barbs and petty attempts to run my life. At least at Humphrey's house I have a brother who defends me, at least sometimes, from his wife's edicts. And I am not legally under her thumb. With a husband, one is entirely at his mercy."

Francesca cast her a startled look, but said only, "There are those who are loved and cherished by their husbands."

"It is always a gamble, though, is it not?" Irene shot back.

Francesca shrugged. "Most women want to find husbands. They are quite happy with the married state."

"I must point out that you have not remarried, though it has been several years since your husband died," Irene told her shrewdly.

Francesca blinked in surprise, but recovered quickly. "Perhaps I felt I could not again find such love as I had with Andrew."

Irene grimaced. "Forgive me, but I was acquainted with Lord Haughston. He was one of my father's boon companions. I am well aware of how he spent his time, for I know how my father spent his."

Francesca replied levelly, "It would be false to say that you are wrong. However, my position as a widow is much less uncomfortable than yours as a dependent in-law. It is far easier for me to avoid marriage. Anyway, I am not a good example to use." She turned her head away, gazing out across the street, as she went on. "I married foolishly. I am sure you would not make the same sort of choice I did."

"I am sorry," Irene said, feeling a flash of regret for her blunt words. "I should not have spoken so about your husband. My tongue often gets the better of me. As you know, I have a reputation for it. I did not mean to hurt you."

"Nay, do not worry about it." Francesca smiled at her. "There is no harm in telling *me* the truth…although I would not advise you do so with others in the general course of things. Most people, I believe, would take your candor amiss."

Irene smiled back, and they drove on in silence for a moment. Then she said, "After you introduced me to Lord Radbourne last night, he informed me that he was searching for a wife and was willing to consider me as a candidate."

"I see." Francesca raised her eyebrows fractionally. "The earl is not, I think, known for his subtlety."

"Indeed. I informed him that I was not interested in marrying, and I would have thought that would be an end to it. But then you came to the house to invite me out for a ride, and here we are, once again talking about marriage. Am I to believe it is a coincidence?"

Francesca gazed back at her for a long moment, then gave a little shrug. "Lord Radbourne's great-aunt is Lady Odelia Pencully, and she asked for my help. You are right in saying that I seem to have acquired a certain reputation for—" she gestured vaguely, her expression amused "—for making matches. The earl's family is eager to find him a wife. You know, I am sure, of the tragedy of his past. They feel that the proper spouse would facilitate his taking his rightful place in the *ton*."

"And they thought that I would be the proper spouse?" Irene asked in disbelief. "What makes me a good candidate for that position? Do they think that because I am a spinster,

I must be desperate enough to wed any man, even one I hardly know?"

"There is no need to wed without coming to know him first," Francesca pointed out mildly.

At the spark that flared in Irene's golden eyes, Francesca held up her hands placatingly, her inviting laughter tumbling out. "No, no, do not fire up at me, pray. I was making a jest. No one is asking you to agree to marry the man. His family wanted me to think of eligible young women who might be willing to consider marriage, and Lord Radbourne asked to meet you, so I introduced you to him. His grandmother intends to hold a party at their country estate—or at least Lady Odelia intends that his grandmother will do so, which means that it will be done. I feel it is only fair of me to point out that if you were to go to the party, you would be able to become better acquainted with Lord Radbourne."

"I do not need to become better acquainted—with him or any man. My mind has long been set against marriage." Irene turned to Francesca, looking straight into her face. "You knew my father, did you not?"

Francesca glanced away. "Yes. I realize the sort of man he was."

"I am not sure you do," Irene went on. "I imagine that much of the *ton* knows that he was a libertine. A rake. He gambled and drank and indulged himself with countless barques of frailty. He made my mother's life a misery. But her misery was not solely because of his actions outside our home. When he was in the house, believe me, we all wished that he were out. He was loud, overbearing and bad-tempered, and when he had been drinking, which was much of the time, he was completely unreasonable and apt to use his fists to make his point. Everyone in the house, from my mother down to the servants, was afraid of him. I swore that I would never put myself in the position that my mother was in. I would never subject myself to the whims of any man."

"But you see, with this marriage, you would not be without power," Francesca pointed out. "His family is talking about an arranged marriage, a businesslike arrangement. You would have a great deal of bargaining power. No doubt you could get them to agree in writing to an assured allowance or some sort of guaranteed settlement."

"Even so, once we were married, I would be under his control. I would no longer have any rights. I would be subject to my husband's decisions."

Francesca did not reply, and Irene continued. "In any case, if I were to agree to such a marriage, it would certainly not be to the Earl of Radbourne." Color mounted in her cheeks again, and her eyes took on a golden glow. "He is insufferably rude and boorish. I have never met a man I would like less to marry. He is arrogant and bullheaded and—"

She stopped, visibly pulling herself back under control. She took a shaky breath. "In any case, I do not imagine that it matters now. I rebuffed him last night at the dance—rather decisively. I feel sure that Lord Radbourne would no longer be interested in me."

Francesca, who had been watching Irene with a great deal of interest, opened her mouth to speak, then stopped. She paused for a moment, looking thoughtful, then went on. "Well, as to that, I do not know. And, of course, if you are so set against it, I would not push you. I would not think of asking you to do anything you would not want to. I merely thought, when Lady Odelia told me, that it might be a proposition in which you would be interested. You always were,

I thought, that rare sort of woman who is more ruled by her head than by her heart."

Irene regarded Francesca narrowly for a moment. She was not sure whether Francesca was simply being truthful or attempting to maneuver her into changing her position. Francesca was correct that she was a woman who believed strongly in running her life with thoughts rather than emotions, and in that regard, she supposed it did seem a trifle peculiar that she would dismiss a practical marriage, one that others would consider a logical proposition. Could it be that she was allowing her fears to sway her from doing what was best for her and her mother?

But she quickly shook aside that thought. "I am ruled by my head. I know what can result from marriage, and so I refrain from allowing my hopes to sweep me into something foolish."

Francesca nodded. "Of course. Then let us say nothing more about it."

She then began to chat of other things, surprising Irene somewhat with her easy acquiescence in letting the topic drop. Irene joined in the conversation, thinking that it was very easy to like Francesca. She did not speak of anything serious or remarkable, perhaps, but she made conversation easy and somehow infused ordinary things with interest. Her laughter was quick and appealing, and it occurred to Irene that perhaps she had never given the other woman a chance, merely dismissed her as foolish and superficial. Though she did not touch on important issues, she was possessed of an agile wit, and there was a certain warmth about her that took away the sting from gossip.

They made their way slowly through the park, stopping frequently to talk to a rider on horseback or the occupant of another carriage. Clearly Francesca knew most of the *ton,* and everyone seemed eager to address her.

Lady Fenwit-Taylor, who was riding in a lumbering old black carriage with her timid daughter beside her, hailed Francesca, leaning out of her window to carry on a conversation in a booming voice. The woman was, it appeared, a fast friend of Francesca's mother, and it was clear that they would be stuck there for a goodly time.

Irene settled back in her seat, paying only cursory attention to the other women's conversation, and let her mind wander. It went, annoyingly, back to her encounter with Lord Radbourne the evening before, and she jerked her mind away from that subject. She would not, she told herself, allow that man to dominate her thoughts.

She heard the sound of another carriage behind them. Irene did not turn to glance back, but then a man's voice jolted her.

"Lady Irene! I have found you."

Hot, then cold, slashed through her. It seemed for a moment, absurdly, as if her very thoughts had conjured him up. She turned, her heart pounding.

"Lord Radbourne."

CHAPTER SIX

THE DARKLY HANDSOME MAN jumped down from his high-sprung yellow curricle and tossed the reins to his tiger before he strode toward Francesca's carriage.

Irene whirled toward Francesca, her mind filled with suspicion.

"Did you arrange this?" she hissed.

But Francesca was staring at Lord Radbourne in astonishment. "No!" She shook her head. "I swear I did not. I had no idea he would be here."

If Lady Haughston was not telling the truth, Irene thought, she was a consummate actress.

"Blast," Irene muttered under her breath. "My luck is always out."

"Lord Radbourne, I am surprised to see you here," Francesca said to him as he approached. "I would not have thought you were the sort to take an afternoon drive through the park."

"I am not," he replied shortly. "I was looking for you."

"Indeed?" Francesca's eyebrows rose a little at his words, her face assuming the sort of hauteur that was usually quite effective at dampening pretensions or reprimanding rudeness.

Her expression had no effect on the earl, however. He

merely stopped beside them and, casting a short nod toward the women in the other carriage, continued speaking to Irene and Francesca.

"I accompanied Lady Pencully to Lord Wyngate's house a few minutes ago," he told Irene, skipping any form of greeting or pleasantries. "Lady Pencully came to extend an invitation to you to attend a gathering at Radbourne Park. Unfortunately, you were not there."

"No, I was not," Irene replied. Though Lord Radbourne seemed to have no care for the curious onlookers in the carriage beside them, she had no desire to give them anything to gossip about.

"Lady Wyngate told us where you had gone," he went on.

"I see." She did see, indeed. No doubt Maura, scenting the possibility of marriage in the air, had been eager to send him after her. She cast a sidelong glance at the other carriage. "Perhaps I should return home to see Lady Pencully."

"She left," he told her. "She bade me deliver her invitation to you."

"Of course. Well…" Irene cast a look of appeal at Francesca.

Francesca, at least, quickly understood. She glanced at the other carriage, then at Radbourne, and said to Irene, "Why don't you and Lord Radbourne take a stroll while you discuss Lady Odelia's kind invitation? I believe I will be fulfilling my duties as chaperone if I watch you from here." She favored the women in the other carriage with a smile. "And I shall manage to keep myself well-occupied talking to Lady Fenwit-Taylor."

The lady in question looked decidedly let down at not being allowed to witness the rest of the conversation between Radbourne and Irene, but Radbourne, at least, seemed at last to realize that he was exposing their conversation to the ears of strangers, for he threw a quick look at the avidly waiting Lady Fenwit-Taylor, then nodded and reached up his hand to help Irene down from the carriage.

Irene put her hand in his, intensely aware of the size and strength of his hand as it closed around her fingers. The same bizarre shimmer of excitement that had seized her last night again ran through her at his touch. Though he offered her his arm as they turned to walk away, she did not take it, clasping her hands together in front of her instead.

She made her way from the wide path used by carriages and horses across the grass and onto a footpath, careful to remain respectably in sight of Francesca's brougham.

Lord Radbourne said without preamble, "I hope that you will be able to attend the party at the Park. Your friend Lady Haughston will be there, as well as a number of other people."

"A number of other young women of marriageable age?" Irene asked shrewdly. "Are you gathering all your marital prospects in one place so that you can easily compare and judge them?"

He frowned. "No, it is not like that."

Irene arched one brow. "Indeed? What is it like, then?"

"It is just…well, it seemed an easy course to meet several people." His mouth tightened at her expression. "Yes, all right, several young women. But it is not that I am comparing or judging. It is simply a convenient way to get to know someone."

"Several someones."

"Yes. Several," he agreed impatiently.

"Thank you, Lord Radbourne. Please convey my regrets to Lady Pencully. However, I am afraid that I must decline her invitation. I have no interest in joining the competition to win your hand."

Color rose in his cheeks, and he said shortly, "It is not a competition!"

"I don't know what else you would call it," Irene replied coolly. "There will be one prospective bridegroom, you, and 'several' prospective brides from whom you will select one. Therefore, all of the women will be competing to win your favor, will they not?"

"Bloody hell! You have the most irritating ability to twist any conversation into knots." He gave her a fulminating glance.

"If you find it so difficult to talk to me, I can only wonder that you would wish me to attend this party," Irene retorted.

"I wonder at it myself."

"There, you see? Doubtless you will be much more comfortable without me there."

"I am sure I will be," he agreed in a grumbling tone, and they walked on in silence for another minute.

Irene stopped and turned to look back at Francesca's carriage. "I had best turn around. We will be out of Lady Haughston's sight in a few more steps."

"Of course." His cool tone matched hers, and he started back toward the carriage. After a moment, he said, "I wonder what it is that you are so frightened of."

"I beg your pardon?" Irene turned to look at him, indignation rising in her. "I am not afraid. I cannot imagine why you should say that."

"Are you not?" He looked down at her quizzically. "What else would you call it, when you are so reluctant to even pay a visit to Radbourne Park? I am not asking you to marry me. Nor even to consider it."

"I have no interest in marrying you, so it seems quite pointless to me to attend. Let some other young woman who is more eager to marry an earl take my spot."

"Of course you don't want to marry me. Any more than I desire to marry you. We hardly know each other. But that is the purpose of this visit—to get to know one another. To obtain some better idea whether we might suit each other."

"I know you well enough already," Irene shot back, coming to a halt and turning to him.

He stopped also and faced her. "Do you? And how can that be, when we have spent no more than fifteen minutes in one another's company?"

"You showed me your nature last night," she told him, the cool calm she had tried to maintain faltering as her anger rose. "That was quite enough for me."

A light flared in his eyes, and he leaned down a little, bringing his face closer to hers. "It appeared to me that you responded to my nature eagerly enough."

The low timbre of his voice thrilled along her nerves, and Irene felt the memory of her desire the night before flutter deep in her loins once again. She stiffened in chagrin.

"It is clear that whatever your title, you are no gentleman," she snapped.

"Why? Because I bring up the bothersome matter of the truth?" he retorted. "You are right, my lady, I am no gentleman. I believe in speaking honestly. I had thought that you were of a like mind. Obviously I was mistaken."

Her cheeks were fiery, her eyes snapped, and all traces of the remote icy lady of a few minutes earlier were gone. Irene did not see, as he could, the splendid beauty she showed now, aglow with emotion. It was the wild and primitive glory of face and form that he had seen in her years earlier, and he could not help but respond inside, even as he tightened his jaw and turned away from her.

"How dare you—" she began, then stopped in astonishment as he ignored her, simply turning and walking away.

Her hands clenched in the material of her skirt as she struggled to contain her temper. She wanted, quite frankly, to shriek at him like a shrew, but that would be resorting to behavior as rude and classless as his, and she forced herself not to give in to the impulse. Instead, she swallowed hard, pushing down the heated words that surged in her throat, and stalked after him.

He glanced at her out of the corner of his eye but did not turn his head. For her part, Irene did not even deign to look at him. She caught up with him in a few quick strides and kept pace with him.

They soon reached Lady Haughston's brougham, and Irene climbed up into it, ignoring the hand that Lord Radbourne held out to help her. Francesca's gaze slid over his out-thrust hand and up to his face, stonily lacking in expression, his eyes cold and hard as glass. She said nothing, merely shifted her attention to Irene's equally frozen face, noting the color that stained her cheekbones and the fierce gold that shone in her eyes.

"Well," Francesca said, with a bright smile. "You are back just in time. I find that I am growing a trifle weary and should like to return home. Lord Radbourne, so pleasant to see you again."

"Lady Haughston." His tone was short, and he barely glanced at her before he turned to Irene. "Lady Irene. I trust you will think over your decision and join us at the Park."

Without waiting for a reply from her, he nodded to them,

then strode away, not even looking toward the occupants of the other carriage.

It took all Francesca's considerable social skill to separate them from Lady Fenwit-Taylor before Irene lost the pretense of calm that she was clinging to, but she managed to bid the other woman a polite farewell and get her driver to pull away from the carriage with seconds to spare.

"Oh!" Irene exclaimed, bringing a clenched fist down hard on her knee. "That dreadful, *dreadful* man!"

"I take it that your conversation with Lord Radbourne did not go well," Francesca observed wryly.

"He is the most bullheaded, irritating, smug, unlikable man I have ever met! I cannot imagine his family finding any woman who would be willing to marry him. She would be letting herself in for a lifetime of—"

Francesca waited as Irene paused, groping for words. After a moment, she prompted, "Of what?"

"I cannot even imagine what it would be like," Irene said grumpily. "My wits cannot stretch that far. He would be the most awful husband, demanding and infuriating and—" Once again she broke off, releasing her breath in a low noise of frustration.

"Goodness," Francesca said mildly. "He must have said something terrible during your conversation. What was it?"

"Well…" Irene started, then paused, and finally went on. "Well, it was not so much what he said as the way he said it. He has no manners whatsoever. And he accused me—me!—of disliking his honesty. He likes to hide his rudeness under the cover of 'truth' and seems to think that I should not take offense at what he says. Do you know that he accused me of being afraid to accept Lady Pencully's invitation? Afraid!"

Francesca, taking in the dangerous sparkle in Irene's gold eyes, replied candidly, "I cannot picture you afraid."

"Of course not! I have never— Well, of course, I have been afraid in my life. Who has not? But I have never let anyone see it! I have never refrained from embarking on a course because I was frightened of what might happen."

"I am sure not," Francesca agreed. "But of course Lord Radbourne does not know you well enough to know your true nature."

"Exactly. Yet he speaks as if he knows what I think. What I feel. It is absurd."

"Well, he is not accustomed to polite conversation. No doubt it is the result of his unfortunate upbringing."

Irene let out an inelegant snort at Francesca's offering. "I have met stableboys with better manners than he. It is his personality. He could have been reared as a prince, and he would still behave like a boor."

"Even so, I do not doubt that he will have little trouble finding a woman who is willing to put up with his manners," Francesca said. "Not someone like you, of course. But someone else who hasn't the courage to keep him from riding roughshod over her as you would. Or the wit to teach him how to act appropriately."

"No doubt," Irene replied shortly.

"She will see only the advantages of the situation, the opportunity, and none of the dangers and drawbacks." Francesca looked at Irene as she went on. "And of course, some women cannot resist the lure of a handsome man. His features are rather arresting."

"I suppose." Irene shrugged, adding, "If you like that sort of look. Personally, I find him too rugged. He is so large. And there is such a hard appearance to him. His cheekbones are so sharp, and his jaw is too square for true handsomeness. Do you not agree?"

Francesca nodded. "Yes, of course. Nor am I fond of brown eyes."

"No, his eyes are green," Irene corrected. "I find his coloring odd, for his hair and brows are black, and his skin is dark, so one would expect his eyes to be dark, as well. But his eyes are quite green. Not attractive at all."

"You are quite correct."

"And he wears his hair too long."

"Most unfashionable."

"The sort of hair you would expect a ruffian to have, not a gentleman." Irene paused thoughtfully. "And he has a scar at the corner of his eyebrow. It quite detracts from his looks."

"Really? I am surprised I did not notice."

Irene nodded and pointed to her right eyebrow. "It is here, just before the end of the brow."

"And he does not smile," Francesca pointed out.

Irene looked away. "Well, I did see him smile once, and it was—" For just an instant her face softened. "It made him look quite different." She shook her head. "But of course, one could not spend one's life waiting for a smile every now and then."

"No," Francesca agreed. "I suppose not, even if it was a very special smile."

"Yes."

"And good looks are not that important, really," Francesca continued, watching her. "It is superficial, after all, to choose a husband because he makes one's pulse flutter."

"Very true." Irene released a little sigh and turned to look out at the buildings they were passing.

After a moment of silence, Irene said, "The worst thing

about his invitation is that he and his aunt went to our house to invite me. Now Maura knows that I have been invited to Radbourne Park. She will be impossible if I do not go. She is desperate for me to marry and leave the house, and if I refuse to make a push to catch the earl, she will be furious. She will badger me night and day to change my mind. Worse, she will run Humphrey and Mother mad, trying to enlist their support."

Francesca studied Irene. "Perhaps you should go to the party." Hastily, seeing Irene's scowl, she went on, "Do not fire up at me. Hear me out. Consider the advantages. You could get away from your sister-in-law for a week or more. And you could even take your mother with you, for I imagine that she would not mind a respite from the woman herself. It would appear to Lady Wyngate that you are following her wishes, so she would not harangue you. Just think of it, a blessed week of freedom, of being able to do as you like, no arguments—"

"If I am around Lord Radbourne, then I am sure there will be arguments," Irene stuck in drily.

"No arguments with Lady Wyngate," Francesca corrected with a smile. "And you do not have to become engaged to the man just because you pay a visit to the family seat. You simply return and say that you did not suit."

"I would still have to be around him," Irene pointed out. "I am not altogether certain that I could be with him for so long without getting into a raging argument with him. That would scarcely brighten up the house party. Besides, I would feel awkward attending under false pretenses. If I do not mean to even consider him as a husband, I feel that I would be deceiving Lady Pencully and Lady Radbourne. It would be wrong to accept their hospitality in those circumstances."

"Nonsense. However much his family may wish to marry him off, they can scarcely hope that each and every woman whom they invite would accept his proposal. They simply hope that he will be more appealing to a prospective bride if she is able to spend more time with him."

"I cannot imagine why they should think that would help," Irene said sarcastically. "I would think that the less time a woman spent with Lord Radbourne, the more likely she would be to agree to marry him. A few minutes in his company are enough to scare away even the most marriage-hungry female."

"Well, perhaps if one spends long enough with him, one is able to get past the initial roughness. Or perhaps one might grow accustomed to his manner."

Irene shrugged. "I suppose. But I am certain that will not happen to me. I cannot pretend that I am willing to consider him as a spouse."

Francesca released a little sigh. "I am sorry. I would have enjoyed your company. Now I shall probably be surrounded by nothing but giggling young girls…and Lady Odelia."

She pulled a face, and Irene had to chuckle.

"I am sorry, Francesca. Indeed, if it were nothing more than a week in your company, I think I would enjoy it. But it would be unfair to the Bankes—and even to Lord Radbourne."

"What if—" Francesca straightened in her seat and reached out a hand, putting it on Irene's arm. Her face became more animated as she leaned a little closer, saying, "What if you did not go under false pretenses? What if you stated clearly up front that you had no intention of marrying him?"

"I don't understand. What would be the point of inviting me then?"

"To help me," Francesca replied, a triumphant expression on her face. "I would explain to them that you were adamant about not marrying Lord Radbourne—though I would, perhaps, couch it in a more general way than your intense dislike of the man. But you see, Lady Pencully wishes me to arrive a week earlier than the other guests and see what I can do about making Lord Radbourne more acceptable to a lady."

"How do you intend to accomplish that?" Irene asked.

"Of course I cannot change his character. But I think there are things that we could do to make him more appealing to a less discerning lady than yourself."

"Less critical, I believe you mean," Irene countered, smiling to take away any sting from her words.

"Lady Odelia says his dancing is poor. We can practice with him on that, and it would be much easier with two of us. We can school him in etiquette and making social chatter and such."

"Well, he certainly is in need of schooling in that regard," Irene said. "Although there are those who would tell you that I am scarcely a good example of those qualities."

Francesca shrugged. "Ah, but I am, and I shall use you for making blunt appraisals of his abilities and progress. He will have to be told what he is doing wrong, and I may rely on you for that, may I not?"

She cast a roguish little smile at Irene, who gave her a grin in return. "Yes, you may. I would be most willing to inform Lord Radbourne of his missteps."

"There. You see how well we would work together? I think you really could be of value in improving his lordship. I realize that you would have to spend a fair amount of time in his company, but surely it would not be so bad as long as he was aware that you had no intention of marrying him. I shall make it clear to him, and to Lady Odelia, that he is not to importune you to change your mind."

Irene hesitated. The idea appealed to her. Perhaps it was the thought of getting to point out to the irritating earl his innumerable faults. Or perhaps it was simply the idea of getting away from her sister-in-law—and all the baby plans—for two weeks. Or of spending time with Francesca, whom she was unexpectedly growing to like. Irene was not sure why, but she could feel her spirits rise at the prospect of going to Radbourne Park.

"I'm not sure," she said slowly. "It sounds reasonable enough, but I am not certain that Lord Radbourne is the sort of man who would necessarily accept my refusal."

Francesca shrugged. "Oh, he might hold to the idea that he could persuade you to change your mind, but I do not think that he would use any force. I do not think he is a bad sort of man, only…inelegant."

"No! Oh, no," Irene agreed quickly. "He is not wicked. Merely stubborn, I think. And confident in himself. Those are not bad qualities."

"And you, I am sure, would be quite able to resist his attempts at persuasion," Francesca went on.

"Of course." Irene grinned again at the other woman. "I would venture to hold my stubbornness up against any-one's."

"I have no doubt of that," Francesca replied. "And, you know, once the other young women are there, you would not have to be around him a great deal. He will doubtless spend most of his time talking to them, and they will all be eager to capture his interest."

"I suppose." Irene's smile slipped a little.

"I do wish you would come as my assistant. You would get to be away from your sister-in-law, and if you would like, you could bring your mother with you, as well."

"Mother would enjoy it, I am sure," Irene said, looking thoughtful.

"Of course. Both Lady Pencully and Lady Radbourne will be there, and though they are older than she is, I think that she would enjoy their company. Lady Odelia can be quite entertaining. And it would be a great help to me."

"Really?" Irene turned a penetrating look on Francesca.

"Oh, yes," Francesca answered honestly. "I think that your presence would greatly enhance the possibility of Radbourne getting a wife. I have not dealt with him, really. Certainly not in the way he deals with prospective brides. You have. You know all the things he does that irritate and offend. You can direct us in exactly where he needs to improve. Moreover, your presence will take a great deal of the burden from me. You can introduce him to the other girls when they arrive, and assist me in setting up situations where he can talk to them. It is always much easier if one has more than one chaperone, after all."

"Yes, of course it would be. Though I refuse to try to influence any young woman to accept his suit. I cannot in good conscience recommend him to anyone, particularly a young and vulnerable girl."

"Oh, no, I would not suggest such a thing!" Francesca answered, looking horrified. "The last thing that he needs for a wife is a weak girl. She must be strong, and well able to deal with him and his family. In any case, it would be quite wrong to try to persuade someone against her will. But allowing him the opportunity to endear himself to a woman is quite another thing."

"I see little likelihood of that," Irene said in a skeptical tone.

"Perhaps not. But I think it is worth a try. I cannot help but feel a trifle sorry for the man, given the horrible things that have happened to him over the years. Torn from his family, forced into a life of poverty and neglect. It is a wonder he even survived, much less that he was restored to his title and inheritance. And of course, that inheritance cannot make up for the fact that he grew up not knowing his mother and father. So much of his life has been stolen from him."

Irene felt a tug of sympathy in her heart. "You are right. It must have been very hard. No doubt it is wrong of me to be so critical of his manners and address. I should look beyond them. They are, after all, the result of things beyond his control." Her gaze turned thoughtfully inward.

"True." Francesca looked over at her companion. "So tell me, will you come with me to Radbourne Park? It would be such a favor to me."

Irene turned to her and smiled. "Yes. I think that I will. I should like to help you, as long as it is made clear to Lord Radbourne that I am not one of the girls competing for the honor of becoming his wife."

"Of course," Francesca agreed quickly. "I shall make it perfectly clear to him and to Lady Odelia."

Irene's smile widened. "Very well, then. It is settled."

The carriage had reached Irene's house and stopped. Swiftly they agreed to meet again to make arrangements for the actual journey after Francesca had discussed the whole affair again with Lady Pencully. Then Irene climbed lightly down from the carriage and, with a little wave of her hand to Francesca, went up the front steps of her house and in the door.

Francesca watched her as she walked away, her brain

busy with plans. She had told Irene the truth: she would make it quite clear to those involved that Irene had no intention of agreeing to marry Lord Radbourne.

Of course, that would not be the end of the matter. His lordship was not one who readily accepted defeat. And given Irene's detailed description of the man she professed to dislike, Francesca was inclined to think Irene was not really aware of the workings of her own heart.

Francesca did not mean to apply pressure to Irene to marry the man. But that did not mean she could not present the younger woman with ample opportunity to change her mind.

She gestured to her driver to take her home. It was time to get to work.

CHAPTER SEVEN

THE HEAVY OLD CARRIAGE rolled along the road, carrying the three women into the village of Wooton Beck. It was a quiet little town, with a village green, an unremarkable stone church, and rows of shops and cottages that marched up the rising slope. It was significant, however, to the occupants of the carriage, because only a mile or so past Wooton Beck lay the sprawling home of the Bankes family.

Lady Odelia had provided Francesca, Irene and Lady Claire with her own carriage for the journey. Although old-fashioned, it was well-sprung and luxurious. No effort had been spared to provide for their comfort. There was a basket of food and drink if they became hungry or thirsty. And there were lap robes to lay across their knees if it became too cool.

Irene glanced across at her mother, who was napping, her head nestled into the corner of the carriage, and wondered whether she ought to wake her. Lady Claire, she knew, would want to have enough time to put herself to rights before she met Lord Radbourne and his family. Still, she hated to interrupt her slumber. Between the excitement of the coming visit and the added work of getting ready for it, Irene's mother had been missing sleep the last ten days.

In Irene's opinion, there had been little need for the multitude of preparations that Lady Claire and the others had so enthusiastically embraced. First, there had been the apparent necessity for new clothes. Irene had argued against it, pointing out that she had ample garments, but her mother and, somewhat to her surprise, her sister-in-law had agreed that she could not face the house party without at least two or three new frocks.

"You must have a good evening gown—one that hasn't been seen time after time this past Season," Lady Maura had insisted, her interest diverted for the moment from her plans for her upcoming baby. "And a few new day dresses, as well. Do you not think so, Lady Claire? We cannot have Irene looking dowdy at Radbourne Park."

Irene had been so shocked by such a generous gesture from her brother's wife that she had agreed to the trip to the dressmaker's shop, and Humphrey had been so pleased at the sight of his little family basking in such seeming harmony that he had opened up his purse, giving Lady Maura free rein for their purchases.

Of course, Irene had quickly realized that Lady Maura's eagerness to get rid of her troublesome sister-in-law through marriage lay behind her sudden burst of goodwill, but it had nevertheless been pleasant indeed to go on an outing with Maura in which there was almost no verbal sparring between the two of them. Francesca, when told of the trip to the mantua makers, had decided to come along, and her presence had, of course, enlivened the excursion. Somehow, amidst all the laughter and chatter and unaccustomed bonhomie, Irene had found herself purchasing far more than she usually did and, moreover, purchasing dresses that were softer and more attractive than those she normally wore.

Francesca had insisted that only the gold satin ball gown

would do, and indeed, Irene had been so swayed by the soft golden glow of the material that she had at last agreed, though she insisted that there be only one row of festooned flounces, not three, around the bottom of the skirt and that the low neckline be raised an inch. Then there had to be soft dancing slippers to match and a gold-tissue wrap to drape around her bare arms, not to mention ribbons and flowers for her hair.

After that, it had been a quick slide into agreeing to the gray bombazine carriage dress trimmed with black gauze, a hunter-green evening dress, and two new day dresses of jaconet muslin, as well as the accessories that the other women agreed were absolutely necessary to complement the clothes.

Sated and tired, they had then retired for the day, but Maura, dazzled by this newfound friendship with one of the leading lights of the *ton,* jumped at Lady Haughston's offer to come by the following day and help them go through Irene's closet to select the rest of her clothes for the trip. Irene, tired as she was and rather embarrassed by her strong affection for the gold ball gown, put up only a faint protest.

The next day, Francesca had descended on the house, accompanied by Maisie, whom she proclaimed was a wizard with a needle, and all the women repaired to Irene's room, where her entire wardrobe was sifted through and talked over. No one could deny that Francesca's eye for fashion was impeccable, and her maid's prowess with a needle and thread was equally impressive. Almost before Irene knew it, with an added ruffle here or a ribbon there, a lowered neckline, lengthened or shortened sleeves, a bit of lace or a row of satin knots, her dresses were transformed into something altogether more flattering and fashionable.

She protested a little at their ruthless handling of her clothing, but the results were so attractive that she could not bring herself to make them return the dresses to their former state. What did it matter, she asked herself, if she did not dress as severely as she usually did? After all, she had made it plain to Lord Radbourne that she was not interested in being his wife, and in any case, he clearly was a man who sought a wife only for the most practical of reasons, not for her appearance. It would not matter if she looked her best; she did not need to deter his suit.

Moreover, in general there was no longer any actual need to look quite so…plain, she thought later that evening as she studied her reflection in the mirror. She had established herself as a spinster; she was past the age when most men would even look her way if they were considering a wife. So there was really no need to downplay her looks. She could, for instance, loosen the plain knot in which she normally wore her hair. It would not hurt to try the French style of a cascade of curls that Maisie had suggested, or to put an ornament in her hair.

And even though she was wont to consider the time and effort that females spent on clothes as a foolish waste, she had to admit that the last few days had been the most pleasant she had ever spent around her sister-in-law; she had, in fact, quite enjoyed the laughter and gossip and camaraderie that the women had shared as they worked on her clothes. The pleasant atmosphere was, she knew, largely the result of Lady Haughston's efforts.

Things had not continued so pleasantly, of course. Maura could not spend ten days in an uncritical mood, nor could Irene refrain from resenting the other woman's advice and, worse, her rule-making. But the prospect of escaping

Maura's presence in a few days made it much more bearable, as did the arrival of her new clothes. She could not resist trying them all on and preening, just a little, before the mirror. Nor could she resist the little spurt of pleasure she felt at thinking about the surprise with which the other young ladies would regard her when they saw her in the unaccustomed finery.

After all, while Irene was perfectly happy with being a spinster, she could not help but feel a bit of resentment at the way other young women consigned her to the social rubbish pile because of it.

Excitement had built in her over the last week and a half while she worked on her clothes, making sure they were clean and pressed, with every loose button resewn and any torn bow or ripped-out hem mended. Just packing them required a great deal of time and effort.

Although she expected to be at Radbourne Park for no more than two weeks, such a visit required a large wardrobe. She must take slippers for dancing, and an extra pair in case the first was damaged in some way. There must be riding boots in case there was an opportunity to ride, as well as sturdy walking boots in the more likely event that she decided to take a tramp through the countryside. And, of course, there must be less elegant slippers to wear during the days, at least two or three to go with her different frocks. All the shoes must be cleaned and inspected and wrapped carefully in cloth, then packed away. And that took care of only the footwear.

A large number of dresses must be packed, for she could not be seen wearing the same few garments every day. She must also take a riding habit, a carriage dress for traveling, a walking dress or two made of heavier material for the long walks she was looking forward to taking in the country, several day dresses, evening dresses for the formal suppers, and of course, two of her very best ball gowns for whatever elegant parties the Bankes might have during the two-week visit.

Then there were nightgowns, petticoats, chemises, and stockings of differing quality and weight, as well as a practical flannel petticoat in case it turned chilly and the Radbourne house was drafty. On top of that there were outer garments. It was, after all, almost September, and the weather was likely to get cooler while she was at Radbourne Park. She must have her best long velvet cloak to wear if she had to venture outside in one of her evening or ball gowns, as well as a couple of pelisses for daytime wear.

Last, but certainly not least, a number of accessories must be taken: gloves, both long and short, everyday and elegant, including leather riding gloves; ribbons and other hair ornaments; her small amount of jewelry; fans; and, of course, a number of hats. And Maura, much to Irene's astonishment, had lent Irene her own small sable muff to keep her hands warm.

"It's not yet cold enough for it, of course," she had told Irene. "But you might get a bit of cold weather by the end of your stay. And nothing makes a woman look so elegant and fragile as carrying a fur muff for her hands. You do have quite passable hands. You should play up that feature."

"Thank you," Irene had stammered in surprise. "I shall take very good care of it."

"See that you do," Maura had retorted, her brows drawing together, and Irene had hastily tucked the fur away in her trunk before her sister-in-law could change her mind.

There had been so much to do that Irene had managed to

keep her excitement tamped down, but finally the day before, as she watched all their trunks being loaded onto the wagon in which Lady Haughston's maid and coachman would follow them, Irene had at last allowed the suppressed excitement to blossom within her.

She was leaving London and the stifling constraints of the *ton* for the freedom of the country. She and her mother would be free for weeks from the carping and antagonism of Lady Maura. There would be no talk of Maura's "delicate condition" or the months of sacrifice that lay before her, or the faintness, nausea and a dozen other ills that afflicted a woman during this time. And her mother would blossom once outside of Maura's clutches. That fact alone was enough to make Irene very glad that she had agreed to accompany Francesca to Radbourne Park.

Irene thought of Lord Radbourne; he would probably be there to greet them when they arrived. She wondered if he would be frosty in tone toward her and stubbornly sure that he would be able to change her mind. He would not woo her, of course; Irene doubted that the man was capable of something as socially skilled as *wooing*. But she suspected that he would in some way or another attempt to convince her that she should marry him. After all, he still needed a wife, and she did not think he was a man who gave up easily.

Of course there would be other young ladies there, and there was always the possibility that he would turn to one of them. Irene unconsciously narrowed her lips at the thought. It would be a reasonable thing to do, of course—no doubt one of the other young women would be far more likely to accept his suit, willing to give up her freedom for the opportunity of being a countess—and, Irene reminded herself, she certainly hoped that the earl would set his sights on someone else. But she was honest enough to admit that it would be somewhat lowering to have it proved to her so clearly that she was not special in Lord Radbourne's eyes, and that any other woman would serve his purpose just as well.

She told herself that it was absurd to experience even a twinge of discomfort over the matter. Certainly she did not want the earl to continue his pursuit of her, and her visit would be far more pleasant if he did not. And she was not the sort to be dog-in-the-mangerish about things. Her pride might feel a twinge of hurt, but that would be quickly over. It would be a vast relief, really, to have him cease importuning her.

Along with her heavy old-fashioned carriage, Lady Odelia had sent her conservative old coachman, as well, so their trip was slow. However, Irene did not mind. Francesca was a lively companion, and her mother, once away from her critical daughter-in-law, had talked and laughed happily until she fell asleep, so the time had passed pleasantly. And when they fell silent, Irene always had her thoughts to occupy her. She enjoyed looking at the countryside, for she had never traveled this way. Nor was she accustomed to staying in inns, as most of her journeys, such as from their rural home to London, had taken no more than one day. It was a wonderful new experience, she thought, and she intended to squeeze every last drop of enjoyment from it.

Now, as they grew close to their destination, anticipation rose in her. She pushed aside the window curtain from time to time, hoping to catch a glimpse of Radbourne Park, but she saw nothing except a tall hedge beside the narrow lane along which they rode. The carriage turned from the road onto another lane, smaller and less well traveled, and Irene pushed the curtain back again and peered out, thinking that they must have turned onto the drive to the house.

They passed a small cottage, but after that they entered into a stretch of woods and were surrounded on both sides by tall trees, whose branches arched over the carriage. They rattled along, crossing a stone bridge over a stream, and then, a moment later, the carriage emerged from the trees.

Irene unashamedly stuck her head out of the window to get her first look at the house. Before them was a vast expanse of green lawn, sloping gently upward, intersected by the drive that curved in front of the house. The house lay at the highest point, alone in its splendor, with no trees or shrubbery in front or to the sides to soften its lines.

Irene sucked in her breath. "Oh, my."

It was not the largest house she had ever seen, but it was, in its way, perhaps the most imposing. The central square of the mansion, built as a magnificent gatehouse, was a full four stories tall, anchored on the ends by twin circular towers that rose another two stories into the air. The rest of the house spread out on either side of the towers in dormered wings of a more normal three-story height. The entire thing was built of red brick, its shading varying slightly from section to section, with a few darker bricks mixed in. The ornamentation atop the towers was of terra-cotta, a molded brickwork resembling stone, as were the window frames. The pale autumnal sun, low in the afternoon sky, glittered off the mullioned windows and cast shadows beside the towers, adding to the majestic appearance of the house.

Both Irene's mother, who had awoken on her own, and Francesca leaned over to join her at the carriage windows, and Lady Claire uttered a soft echo of Irene's words.

"Well," Francesca commented drily. "Obviously the Bankes family thinks well of themselves."

"It's… Well, I'm not sure what the word for it is," Irene

said, still gazing at the house. "It is not what I would call beautiful, but it is certainly grand. It has an appeal."

"It looks to me the sort of place that probably has a skeleton or two moldering in the cellars. Or mayhap a mad uncle locked up in the attic," Francesca told her.

Irene chuckled. "No, it looks to me more like—oh, something that one of those Elizabethan corsairs might have built for himself. Doesn't it have the look of an adventurer? Brash and bold?"

"Mmm, I suppose." Francesca cast a teasing glance at her. "Irene, you have deceived me. I believe that there is something of a romantic in you."

Irene blushed a little as she sat back in her seat. "Nonsense. Simply because one can see the appeal in something does not mean that one necessarily succumbs to it."

Francesca said nothing for a moment, merely smiled a little to herself, then changed the subject. "I feel sure that Lady Odelia will be there to greet us. Do you know Lady Pencully, Lady Wyngate?" she asked, looking toward Irene's mother.

"I have met her. I would not say I knew her, really," Claire replied carefully.

"I think to meet Lady Odelia is to know her," Francesca replied with a quick grin. "She is not a woman of subtlety."

Claire smiled back and admitted, "No. I believe that Lady Pencully is quite…true to herself. Which is an excellent quality."

"No doubt," Francesca agreed wryly.

"I have never met Lady Pencully," Irene said, and looked toward her mother. "Have I? She sounds the sort whom one would remember."

"Oh, yes," Lady Claire agreed. "I do not think that you

have met her. She does not get about much anymore. At least, she rarely comes to London."

"A fact for which we should all be grateful," Francesca told Irene. "I feel sure that she will not frighten you, Irene, but I was always terrified of her. Whenever she would come to Dancy Park to visit, I did my best to get out of calling on her. She never misses anything—whether it's a torn ruffle, a curl out of place or an unflattering style."

"You sound as if you know Lady Pencully well," Irene commented. "Is she a relation?"

Francesca's eyes widened, and she exclaimed, "Goodness, no! My family's home is near Dancy Park, one of the Duke of Rochford's estates. It is a pleasant place, and Lady Pencully, who is the duke's great-aunt, often came to visit him when he was in residence there."

"Do you know the others at Radbourne Park?" Lady Claire asked.

"No. Indeed, I have never been here before," Francesca explained. "I have never met Lady Pencully's sister. She is the present earl's grandmother, as I understand it. I am rather curious to meet her. I cannot help but wonder if she is like Lady Odelia. It is difficult to imagine two such in one family."

"Who else is in residence at the Park?" Irene asked.

"I would think that the late earl's second wife must live there, as well. He remarried late in life, I understand, but I have never met the countess. They did not visit London, I suppose because of the earl's advancing years and ill health. I do not even recall her name. They had a son, as well, only a boy still. I remember there was much talk about his losing his inheritance when Radbourne was restored to his family. I know little about them, though. And I am not sure if there are any other family members present. Lady Odelia has a way of skipping over 'minor details.'"

"Well, we will find out soon enough," Irene commented, looking out the window again.

They had almost reached the front steps of the house. The door had been opened, and a dignified-looking man dressed all in severe black made his way down the steps, followed by two liveried footmen. It was, Irene assumed, the butler.

He waited until the carriage pulled to a complete stop, then opened the door and bowed to the ladies inside. "Please allow me to welcome you to Radbourne Park, my ladies. I hope your journey was not too taxing."

"No, indeed. We made it in excellent spirits," Francesca assured him, taking his hand to step down from the carriage.

Irene and her mother followed Francesca. All three of them paused for a moment, looking up at the towering house. The butler allowed a brief smile of pride.

"The gatehouse was built by the first Earl of Radbourne," he told them. "Of course, there was an older home, a rather good specimen of the early Norman keep, but it has been unoccupied since the reign of King Henry VIII, when the first earl constructed his masterpiece. It was intended, you see, to rival Hampton Court itself, but sadly, Lord Radbourne died before anything more than this gatehouse was constructed. The second earl did not share his father's architectural vision and simply added the other wings to the gatehouse."

"Is there anything in the towers?" Irene asked, looking up to the tops of the round corner structures.

"Only winding stairs, my lady, and of course a magnificent view of the countryside from the top, if one is willing to make the climb."

"I should like to see it," Irene said.

"You will have to find a companion younger than I, then," her mother said. "I believe that I will be quite content to view the bottom floors."

"There is much to see everywhere in the house, my lady," the butler assured her. "My name is Horroughs. Please let me know if you need anything. Now, if you will allow me to show you into the house, the dowager countess and Lady Pencully are awaiting you."

While the footmen unloaded the carriage, the three women followed the straight-backed butler into the house and through the large formal entry hall to a large, well-appointed drawing room. Three women sat in the room, and they turned as the party of travelers entered.

Irene saw at a glance that Lord Radbourne was not there. Not that it mattered. It was actually a relief not to have to greet the man. Although, of course, it was rather rude of him not to be there to greet them. She wondered where he was and if he had meant to deliver a set-down to her by not being there when they arrived. Not, of course, that it mattered, she repeated to herself.

"There you are!" boomed one of the occupants of the room, an older woman with iron-gray hair under a lace-trimmed black cap. She was wearing a dark purple silk dress with old-fashioned wide skirts and a stiff bodice. She was a woman of large proportions that matched her voice, and she pushed herself up off the sofa on which she sat and came forward with all the power and majesty of a grand ship in full sail. She was, Irene assumed, Lady Odelia Pencully.

The woman who had been sitting beside Lady Odelia on the sofa was of a similar age, but the opposite of Lady Odelia in looks and style. Her hair under her lacy black cap was snow-white and softly curled, and the black dress she wore was of a modern style, slim-lined and high-waisted, and trimmed with black lace. She was thin almost to the point of frailness, and shorter than Lady Odelia, as well, though it was hard to tell her actual height, as she held herself in a hesitant, drooping manner. Everything about the woman seemed wispy and insubstantial, from the soft white curls escaping their pins beneath her cap to the folds of silk and lace that draped her body. A black fringed shawl was pulled around her shoulders, though one end slipped loose and trailed along behind her as she stood up, hesitated, then took a few steps forward, smiling tentatively.

"Hallo, Francesca," Lady Odelia greeted Irene's companion. "You look none the worse for your journey." She half turned back to the fragile-looking woman behind her and said, "You see, Pansy, I told you they were not likely to come to harm. Not everyone is such a bad traveler as you are."

"No, of course not, Odelia," the other woman responded with a smile and a shy bob of her head. Her voice was as slight as the rest of her, and though her smile was friendly and her eyes kind, there was a certain vagueness to her expression, as well, as though she were not quite connected to the others in the room.

Francesca introduced Irene and her mother to Lady Pencully, who in turn swept her hand toward her sister, the dowager Countess of Radbourne.

Lady Radbourne took Irene's hand in hers. Her hands were light, like bones covered with skin, the knuckles knobby, and they were chilly despite the warmth of the room. "I am so pleased to meet you," she said, smiling into Irene's eyes. "We will be good friends, I am sure."

"Thank you, Lady Radbourne. It is very kind of you to

say so." She was not certain why Lord Radbourne's mother seemed so eager to be her friend. She presumed it was simply the woman's way and hoped that she had not been misled by her sister into thinking that Irene was there to accept her grandson's proposal.

She shot a glance at Francesca, who gave a small shrug, but at that moment Irene's attention was drawn to the third woman in the room, who had stood up and was walking toward them.

The woman was blond and pretty, with pale skin and large, round light blue eyes. Her figure was voluptuous, and though her white and black dress of half-mourning was high-necked and her breasts covered, their fullness was unmistakable, accented by the high waist, sashed just beneath them.

"How do you do?" she said, her eyes sweeping coolly across Francesca, then Irene and Lady Claire. "I am the Countess of Radbourne."

"My son Cecil's widow," Pansy explained, sadness in her eyes. "He has been gone from us for a year now."

"Welcome to Radbourne Park," the younger Lady Radbourne went on coolly, ignoring Pansy and her words.

Irene studied the woman, intrigued. The widow of the late earl was quite a bit younger than Irene would have imagined. She was older than Irene and Francesca, she thought, but not by too many years. The countess did not seem especially friendly. Her words were polite, but her attitude was distant and formal, and there was a certain glint in her eyes that she could not conceal. Irene had the definite impression that she was not eager to meet the three of them. In fact, if Irene had to guess, she would venture that the countess would have preferred that they were not there at all.

What Irene was not certain of was whether the woman's dislike was aimed specifically at her and Francesca, or if she would dislike any woman who she thought wanted to become the new Countess of Radbourne. But then, given the way she had ignored her harmless-seeming mother-in-law, Irene supposed it could be that the woman was simply unpleasant.

"No doubt you would like a bit of refreshment after your trip," Lady Odelia said. "I'll ring for tea."

Then she marched over to the bell pull, not seeing, as Irene did, the hard glance that the younger countess shot at her back.

"Perhaps our guests would rather be shown to their rooms," the younger Lady Radbourne said. "I am sure it has been a tiring trip."

Odelia turned, a frown on her face. "They will want to say hello to Gideon."

The countess sniffed. "As if he would have the good manners to greet his guests."

Lady Odelia drew herself up, somehow attaining an even more formidable stature. "I beg your pardon, Teresa," she said in a voice as firm as iron. "I am sure that my greatnephew has been unavoidably detained—in all likelihood by some estate matter, for I can see that the Park has been allowed to fall into a shocking state of disrepair the past few years."

Lady Teresa shot a brief venomous glance at the older woman, but she clearly did not have the courage to stand up to Lady Odelia, for she said only, her voice taking on a bit of a whine, "My husband was not feeling well the last few months of his life. And I…well, I did the best I could, but I do not have a head for business, as some do."

This last comment, Irene suspected, was another swipe at the new earl, who had amassed a fortune of his own even before he was restored to his family. Irene knew that his business acumen was considered another of the many blots on his reputation. A gentleman, after all, was above the mundane matters of money, and a lady even more so. But frankly, as far as Irene was concerned, ignorance and incompetence on any matter were little cause for pride, and it was even more foolish when such ignorance caused one to lack for money. She had lived for too long with too little money, thanks to her father's extravagances, to find genteel poverty satisfying. And the fact that, despite his circumstances, Gideon Bankes had managed to not only survive but to thrive, seemed more admirable than despicable.

Clearly the widowed countess did not share Irene's opinion, however. Indeed, Irene was coming to realize that Lady Teresa held a rather healthy dislike of the new earl. It was somewhat understandable, of course, for if Gideon had not been found, Teresa's own young son would have inherited the title. Irene supposed that any mother would dislike the loss for her son—though she also suspected that, given this woman's proud manner, Lady Teresa equally disliked the loss of her own importance as mother of an earl still in his minority. And since Lord Radbourne intended to marry quickly, the woman's place would soon be completely usurped.

Although Irene could understand the lady's dislike of the new earl, she could not like her for it. Irene suspected that she would not be spending much time with Lady Teresa during her visit here and was glad of it. And, given the cold look in Lady Teresa's eyes when she spoke to her, Irene guessed that Lady Teresa had equally little interest in becoming friends.

It came as no surprise that Lady Odelia had her way, and the new arrivals sat down to tea with the other women. They discussed their journey with Lady Odelia in rather tedious detail, but finally the tea was consumed and the little cakes eaten, and Lady Odelia allowed the new arrivals to be shown to their rooms, even though Lord Radbourne had not yet made an appearance.

Irene's room was commodious and well situated, with a set of windows on either side of the bed looking out over the side gardens. She peered out of one window, her eyes going beyond the garden, largely denuded now that the weather was growing colder, to the stand of tall trees beyond. She could see, as well, a slice of the rear gardens, and past them a meadow. Far in the distance, a stream they had crossed earlier that afternoon curled like a bright ribbon through the rolling land. The place would provide a number of pleasant afternoon walks, she thought, something she sorely missed in London.

The wagon with the bulk of their luggage had not yet arrived, so her choice of garments was limited to those she had carried in the smaller bags that had been placed on top of the carriage. She thought that the deep blue evening gown that lay in one of those bags would do quite well.

One of the upstairs maids popped into the room, offering to return later to help Irene with unpacking and getting ready for supper. But Irene was not tired from the journey. Rather, she was still filled with a sense of anticipation. So, forgoing a nap to recover from the trip, she was soon bathed and dressed. Sending the maid on her way, she brushed out her own hair and began to pull it into a circumspect knot at the crown of her head.

However, she had barely begun when Maisie, Francesca's maid, came bustling in. "No, my lady, no!"

Maisie looked horrified as she hurried to take the brush from Irene's hands. "You must let me do your hair. You promised you would let me try a style I had in mind."

"But you must help Lady Haughston," Irene protested.

"Oh, no, not yet. Her ladyship never starts dressing for supper this early," Maisie told her, expertly pulling and twisting and pinning Irene's hair as she talked. "I will do your hair first, and then there will be plenty of time for Lady Haughston's toilette."

"Yes, but—"

"Oh, never say you aren't going to let me. I would so like to work with your curls. Her ladyship's hair is beautiful, of course, but entirely different from yours. You have so much of it—and those curls!"

"Those curls are a nuisance," Irene told her, but the girl just smiled and shook her head, promising Irene that she "would see."

And Irene *did* see a few minutes later when Maisie had finished and stepped back, highlighting the finished product with a flourish of her hand.

"Oh, my," Irene said, gazing at her image in the mirror.

The hairstyle Maisie had created was a far cry from the simple tight knot in which she usually wore her hair. Her hair was full and soft around her face, drawn up and back, then falling in a profusion of curls. Though tightly anchored with hairpins, it seemed loose and soft, as though it might fall free at any moment.

It looked, Irene thought, beautiful, and she smiled at Maisie in the mirror, nodding.

The maid left to tend to Francesca, and Irene sat for a

moment longer, looking at herself in the mirror. She supposed she should not indulge in such vanity, but she could not help but smile at her image. She looked prettier than usual, softer and more approachable. She tried to recapture the stern expression she usually wore, but somehow her face would not pull into the severe lines.

She stood up and strolled over to the window, but it had grown dark outside, and there was nothing to see. She turned back to the room, feeling restless and wondering how she would occupy herself for the next hour until it was time for everyone to convene for supper.

It occurred to her that she could slip downstairs and look for the library, and find a book to read, but the thought of something as sedentary as reading did not appeal to her at the moment. She wanted to walk, but of course she could not go out for a walk at this hour and in this dress. Finally she remembered that she had glimpsed a long gallery leading off from the entry hall this afternoon when they had arrived, and she thought that strolling along it, looking at the artwork, might be just the thing to occupy her time.

Irene picked up her black shawl to drape around her arms, bared by the short puffed sleeves of her gown, and left her room. She walked quietly, not really wishing any company, and went softly and quickly down the stairs. She had just started across the wide entryway to the gallery beyond when she heard a man's voice.

"Lady Irene. Not running away already, are you?"

Her stomach tightened, and she turned, knowing that voice even before she saw him. "Lord Radbourne."

CHAPTER EIGHT

GIDEON, TOO, WAS ALREADY dressed for dining. With his shaggy dark hair and hard angular face, he looked a trifle out of place in the formal black jacket and breeches and starched white shirt, a large pigeon's-blood ruby nestling in the snowy white folds of his cravat.

He strode toward her, and she watched him, trying to place what it was that made him look different from all the other men she knew. Perhaps it was the sun-darkened skin that gave him a slightly piratical look…or the shaggy cut of his thick black hair, which marked him as one who cared little about his appearance. But she thought it was mostly the eyes—as green as new leaves, but hard and watchful, as though he was always on alert, ready for an attack even here in the middle of this huge house.

"You are early for supper," he commented as he drew near to her. His comment was mundane, but his eyes swept down her in a way that heated her blood.

"As are you," she replied coolly, looking him in the eye. She felt, as she had before when she had been around him, the same curious blend of nerves and heat that she had never experienced around anyone else. It was a feeling she was determined not to let him see.

"Why don't we take a stroll through the gallery while we

wait?" he suggested, gesturing toward the long hall in front of them, lined with windows along one wall and with paintings along the other.

She nodded and turned toward the gallery, not taking the arm he proffered. Sconces burned along the wall all the way down the corridor, reflecting their flickering light in the mullioned windows across from them. The ceiling of the gallery was high and braced with beams of dark wood, giving it a dark and dramatic effect. Portraits of men and women whom she assumed must be Bankes ancestors decorated the wall, along with paintings of rural scenes and animals. There were statues and vases, some on pedestals and others freestanding, and here and there beneath the windows were benches upon which one could sit, presumably to admire the art across the way.

Most of the paintings were rather pedestrian, Irene thought, but she studied them as if they were masterpieces, for doing so kept her face turned from Lord Radbourne. She was discovering that looking at him caused too much tumult inside her.

After they had passed a number of ancestors in progressively dated styles of dress, they came to a large painting of a horse. Irene stopped, blurting out, "This is the best painting here!"

A grin spread slowly across her companion's face. "Yes, isn't it? Far better than the one of his owner." He gestured toward the man in the portrait that hung beside the one of the horse, then on past him to a picture of a pinch-faced woman. "Or the man's wife. But then, from what I have heard, the third Earl of Radbourne was much fonder of his horse than he was of his countess."

Irene could not help but smile, though she quickly suppressed it. "I suspect there are a number of people who could say that."

"You haven't a very good view of marriage, Lady Irene."

She did not reply, merely cocked an eyebrow at him and continued her progress down the hall.

"Or should I say that it is men of whom you take such a poor view, not marriage?"

Irene shrugged. "I am sure that I have no control over what you say."

They continued in silence for a few more minutes, then Lord Radbourne began again. "You are displeased with me yet again, I take it."

She cast him a brief glance. "Why would I be displeased with you? I have not even seen you until just now."

He gave a slight nod. "I see. You are miffed, I take it, that I was not there to greet you when you arrived. My great-aunt has already rung a peal over my head about it."

"Were you not?" Irene asked, instilling her voice with disinterest. "I am afraid I did not notice."

"Did you not?" he murmured, his mouth once more curving up into a smile.

It was a very good smile, Irene noticed; she had forgotten how it lit up his eyes. He should use it more often, she thought, for it made it difficult for one to remain annoyed with him.

"It *was* rather rude of you—to ignore your guests."

"Exactly the sort of behavior that you are here to polish out of me," he told her.

"Lord Radbourne, I fear that there is not enough polish in the world to make you anything but rude."

He did not appear to be offended by her remark, for the smile lingered on his lips. "Indeed. You know, Lady Irene, there are those who might say that you are somewhat less than courteous yourself."

She drew breath to argue, but stopped, then gave a little laugh and said, "Well, perhaps you have the truth of it there." She paused for a moment and looked back at Radbourne. "Perhaps we should start over. After all, you and I will be working toward the same goal, will we not? Getting you married to some appropriate young lady?"

He shrugged. "I think that is more my relatives' goal than mine."

Irene looked at him in faint surprise. "Then I was mistaken and you are not interested yourself in the matter? You do not wish to marry?"

"I know I must at some point, and I suppose now is as good a time as any. But I am not driven to become a husband and father, no."

They continued their stroll along the hall, though Irene found herself studying her companion as much as she did the artwork.

"I had thought you more eager than that in your pursuit of a bride," she said after a moment.

He lifted one shoulder in a ghost of a shrug and said, "I am not certain that eagerness enters into it. I am willing to marry—and I am willing to marry a woman from their class. But it is less than inviting to think of saddling myself with a wife who will spend the rest of my life looking down on me, or who will be forever schooling me on my accent, my dress, my commonness."

Gideon glanced at her out of the corner of his eye and asked, "Would *you* wish to be shackled to such a partner?"

"No, indeed. That is why I refuse to marry."

"But you would not be considered unworthy by an aristocrat."

"Lord Radbourne, you do not understand. Wives are regarded as inferiors by all men." She tilted her head to look up at him.

He came to a stop, looking at her in some astonishment. "That is what you believe?"

She raised her brows. "What else should I believe? Oh, I am not talking about the meaningless little courtesies such as standing until a woman is seated or walking closer to the street to protect her. I am talking about all the essential matters of married life. A husband makes decisions for his wife. He gives her an allowance to spend on her fripperies. He tells her what to do. Is that the behavior of a man toward his equals?"

He frowned. "Well, no, but—"

Irene gazed at him challengingly. "But what?"

One corner of his mouth quirked up in a half smile, and he said, "But I cannot imagine the husband who would dare to tell you what to do or make decisions for you."

"I intend to make sure of that. I only wonder that a man such as you would be willing to take on the sort of wife you just described."

"I have little doubt that I will be able to take care of myself in such an arrangement. And if I am lucky, perhaps I will find a woman more…interesting than those that have been presented to me before. Because in the end, marriage is something that will make me more acceptable in the eyes of my family." His mouth twisted as he said the words, and for an instant a certain bleakness touched his eyes before it was swallowed up in their cold depths.

"You sound bitter toward your family," Irene commented.

"What else should I feel?" he challenged. "They claim that blood is so important to them. But I see no indication of it. They have no joy in recovering a member of their family, blood of their blood. What is important to them is that I am the heir. The succession is what drives them. As to feelings for me, they have none. Their only worry is that my deficient upbringing will embarrass them, so they want me to marry in order to reduce their embarrassment."

Irene had to drop her eyes before his steady gaze. It was rather hard to argue against his assumptions.

"I grew up in the East End," he went on in a voice almost devoid of emotion. "I believed myself an orphan. I had no memory of this place or my parents, except perhaps for one vague feeling of a woman holding me. I remember nothing of how she looked, only of softness and a smell of lilacs. My earliest real memory is of hunger. I was always hungry. I belonged to a man who ran the lot of us as pickpockets and thieves. I was useful for wriggling into tight spaces and then opening a window or door for my accomplices. I was skillful at picking pockets and I was fast. So I had value to him. If I had not, he would have thrown me out into the cold. But as it was, he gave me food to eat—though it never seemed to be enough—and he gave me a place to stay. I had no schooling—I taught myself numbers and reading."

Irene's heart was touched with pity. "I am sorry."

He cast a sideways glance at her and said roughly, "I don't ask for your pity. I am merely telling you that that was my life. That was my world. And then, one day, Rochford walked into my life and informed me that I was Lord Radbourne and my family wanted me back. What am I supposed to feel for them? They are strangers to me. Strangers whose only interest in me is how to keep me from ruining the family name. They are noblemen, the kind of arrogant, useless, unfeeling people whom I have always despised. Members of the *ton*."

Irene felt the pain that lay beneath his words, and surprising herself a little, she took a step toward him, laying her hand on his arm. "But you are a member of that same class of people yourself," she reminded him softly.

He looked at her. "Not in my heart."

His hand came up to cover hers where it lay on his arm, and something shimmered between them—fragile, warm and light as gossamer—connecting them. It was a strange feeling, one she had never experienced, different from the desire that had melted her when they were together before, yet somehow joined to it.

She turned her face upward, looking into Gideon's eyes, and he bent his head closer to her, his eyes growing suddenly intent. His gaze drifted down her face, coming to rest on her lips. Irene could not speak, could not even move, caught for the moment in the web of something she did not recognize.

As she looked at him, her heart stirring in her chest, heat rising in her loins, Irene heard a woman's voice. It was too far away to be distinguishable, but it reminded her that they were standing in one of the main hallways of the house, where anyone might happen upon them at any time. She knew how they must look to anyone else, standing this way, their heads close together, her hand on his arm, with no one else around. It was a scene that would convey intimacy to any viewer—exactly the sort of assumption that she would not wish anyone to make. Worse, she suspected that if they stayed there any longer, the scene they presented would become decidedly more shocking.

She stepped back hastily, blushing. What was it about this

man that made her respond in such an abnormal way? It had never before been a problem for her to keep her distance from a man.

She turned slightly away from him, and more to cover her own awkwardness than anything else, she said to him, "Even though you have learned to dislike the nobility, still, they are your family."

He, too, stepped back, and whatever warmth had been in his eyes for an instant was now completely gone. "A family who never tried to bring a child of their blood home?" he countered. "My mother, I suppose, cannot be blamed, as she was presumably killed at the time I was taken. But what of the others? What about my father?"

"But surely you cannot blame him for not rescuing you," Irene protested. "Your family did not know where you were or what was happening to you. You had been kidnapped. They had no idea who had taken you, or where you were. They believed you must be dead."

He gave her a long, level look. "Even if a father believed one dead, don't you think that he would still search for his child?"

"But he did search, did he not?" Irene asked.

Gideon shrugged. "So I am told."

"Why do you doubt it? Do you count your father wicked simply because he belonged to a class of people whom you dislike?"

"When Rochford set out to find me, it was only a matter of months before he was able to track me down." Gideon paused, giving her time to let that thought sink in. "And, remember, that was more than twenty-five years after the kidnapping. If it was possible then, when the trail was so cold, why was it not possible to find me right after the kidnapping took place?"

Irene simply stared at him, struck dumb by his statement.

Gideon offered her his arm, and she took it, her brain humming busily as they strolled back down the gallery to the antechamber where everyone was gathering for supper.

When they reached the small drawing room, they found Lady Odelia and her sister Pansy seated against the far wall, engaging in a conversation in which Odelia's side could be heard all over the room and well out into the hall, and Pansy's contributions were impossible to make out. It made for a disjointed conversation that was difficult to follow but impossible to ignore, meaning that everyone else in the room could do little but stand about and awkwardly attempt to make chitchat of their own.

They were not a large number for the evening meal. Besides her mother and the members of the family whom Irene had already met, there was also a vicar, identifiable by his clerical collar, a plump, motherly sort of woman whom Irene took to be his wife, and an older man, tall and dark-haired, who stood alone by the window.

Lady Odelia paused in her conversation long enough to introduce Irene to the new guests. Irene had been correct in her identification of the vicar and his wife, who were named Longley. The other gentleman, she learned, was Pansy's younger son, Lord Jasper.

Gideon's uncle, Irene thought, assessing him as he bowed over her hand. She could see the family resemblance. Jasper had the same thick black hair, though touched with silver at the temples, and the lines of his face were similar. He was leaner and less muscular than Gideon, and there was about him an air of refinement that was missing in Gideon, an indefinable something that stamped him as a product of Eton and Oxford, a member of the elite.

His manner was somewhat aloof, and though he went through the usual polite chitchat with Irene—was her room comfortable? Had she enjoyed the trip up from London? Had she ever visited this area before?—it seemed clear to Irene that he had no interest in her answers. He looked at Gideon a time or two, but said little to him. She wondered how she felt about Gideon and his return to the family. Until Gideon reappeared, this man would have been next in line after the countess's son, and in the usual way of things, as the boy's nearest male relative, would probably have been the guardian of his assets until he came of age. Gideon's arrival would have relegated Jasper to a much less important role. While Jasper showed none of the animosity toward Gideon that she had noticed in Teresa, Irene could not help but think that Gideon must, just as he had said, have received a cool reception indeed when he returned home.

It was really no wonder that he felt spurned by his family. His uncle seemed at best awkward around him; his father's widow obviously disliked him; and clearly they all viewed him as something of an embarrassment that could somehow be covered up by marriage.

Though she did not want to, Irene could not help but feel for the man. Even though she had her share of problems with Maura, and before that had frequently clashed with her father, at least she had always been sure of her mother's and brother's love. What must it be like not to have known your parents? To be unceremoniously deposited in the midst of an unloving family?

Her thoughts were interrupted by Francesca's arrival. Lady Haughston was, unsurprisingly, the last to join the group, and soon after she entered the room, they went in to supper.

The atmosphere at the meal was rather stiff, and words did not flow freely. Lady Odelia, usually the sort to dominate the conversation, seemed more interested in eating than in talking. Pansy seemed unable to say anything without looking to Odelia or Teresa first, and neither Lord Radbourne nor his uncle contributed much to the conversation. Even Francesca's ample social skills were not enough to keep the talk flowing smoothly around the table, though she, aided by Lady Claire, strove valiantly to maintain polite small talk.

Finally Francesca seemed to give up, and the table lapsed into a heavy silence, broken only by the sound of the cutlery against the china plates and an occasional tinkle of crystal. The longer the silence lasted, the more uncomfortable it became, and Irene glanced across the table at Francesca in appeal.

But before Francesca could come up with something to say, Teresa spoke. "It is so kind of you, Lady Haughston," she said, with an insincere smile, "to come help us with Lord Radbourne."

Teresa cast a glance up the table at Gideon, whose face gave no indication that he had heard her. He did not even acknowledge her look, but continued to eat in a stolid fashion. Irene's nerves began to prickle and her stomach tightened, reminding her of mealtimes spent in her father's presence. There had often come a moment when suddenly she would realize that her father had passed some point in the course of his drinking, and that danger was once again hovering over the table. She would always grow taut with dread, knowing that at any moment he might do or say something that would lead to an inevitable scene.

"I am, of course, quite happy to help Lady Odelia," Francesca responded coolly.

"I fear it will be a test of your skills," Teresa went on, with a little titter. "Lord Radbourne has been away from society for a very long time."

Irene's fingers curled tightly around the handle of her knife, and she said, "Yes, what happened to Lord Radbourne was indeed a terrible thing. However, I am certain that his family was overjoyed to find that he was alive and well, were you not?"

Teresa turned her gaze to Irene. "Why, yes, of course. It is simply astonishing that he could have survived in that sort of place all those years. One would think that it would have been almost impossible for one of our sort to have lived in such conditions."

"I would think that being cold and hungry would be difficult for a child from any class," Irene responded.

"I suppose." Teresa looked doubtful.

"I can assure you, Lady Teresa, that it was equally difficult for my companions and for me," Gideon said, clearly surprising everyone by speaking up.

"Of course it was. What nonsense are you talking, Teresa?" Lady Odelia put in decisively.

Teresa shot the older woman a venomous glance, but said mildly, "I meant only that it would seem to me that such an existence would be very difficult for one of higher sensibilities."

"Ah, but then, my sensibilities are distressingly plebian, are they not, my lady?" Gideon responded, giving her title a sardonic stress.

Teresa again affected a little laugh as she cast a look around the table, inviting them to share in her amusement.

"I fear Lord Radbourne does not like to be reminded of his shortcomings. Do you remember the first night you were here, my lord?" She looked at him, challenge in her gaze. "La, that look upon your face when you saw the array of knives and forks and spoons beside your plate! I knew at once that we would have to do something to bring you up to snuff. I believe that is when Lady Pansy wrote to you, Lady Odelia."

Irene set down her utensils on her plate with a clatter, resentment burning in her on Gideon's behalf. She could not bring herself to look at him.

Across the table from her, Francesca said mildly, "I often feel that way myself. One wonders why it's really necessary to have a different utensil for every course. Could not one use the same fork for fish and meat?"

"Oh, Lady Haughston, you are jesting," Teresa said gaily. "I have been told that you are very light in spirit." She leaned toward Francesca and went on in a confidential tone. "However, I fear that you will find that explaining place settings will be only the beginning." She nodded wisely. "There simply are things that are ingrained in people, things that cannot be learned, which are the hallmark of good breeding."

"Indeed?" Francesca replied in so chilly a tone it would have warned someone less oblivious than Lady Teresa.

"Oh, yes. When one is lacking in refinement…" Teresa threw a little look at Lord Radbourne, just in case there might be someone at the table who missed her meaning. "Well, it shows, and it is very difficult to change that. How can one learn good breeding?"

She sat back in her chair, looking self-satisfied. For a moment the table was silent. Francesca glanced at Irene, looking decidedly and uncharacteristically uncomfortable.

Irene smiled, her eyes glinting with a dangerous light, and turned toward Teresa. "Lady Teresa," she began in a deceptively friendly tone, "I am surprised that I have never met you before. A woman of such obvious taste and refinement as yourself must surely have come to London. Why have I not seen you at any parties there?"

The face Teresa turned to Irene was cold. "I am afraid that Cecil—my husband, Lord Radbourne—did not care to visit the city. He was a man who liked his own home and hearth. And of course, I felt it my duty to stay with him."

"But before you married him, surely you made your come-out in London. When was that?"

A flush started in the other woman's pale cheeks. "I did not visit London then, either. My father was a not a social man, and he disapproved of the 'fripperies and foibles of the London life,' as he liked to say. And then, of course, I married Lord Radbourne when I was quite young."

"Of course. How sad that both your husband and your father kept you from the sophisticated life to which you are so obviously suited." Irene smiled at her. "It explains, of course, why we never met. But I am sure that I must have heard of your family. What was your father's title? I suppose he is an earl, like Lord Radbourne."

Teresa's cheeks flamed with color as she shook her head. "No. He is not an earl."

"He is of higher station, then?" Irene asked, looking impressed.

Across the table, Francesca raised her hand to cover her mouth, her eyes bright with laughter. She shook her head at Irene, but Irene ignored her, saying to Teresa, "Your father is a marquess? Or perhaps a duke, like Lord Radbourne's cousin, Rochford?"

"Goodness me, no." Teresa let out a nervous titter and glanced around the table with a trapped expression.

"Oh. A baron, then?" Irene pursued relentlessly.

"My father is Mr. Charles Effington, the son of Sir Hadley Effington," Teresa told her stiffly.

"I see," Irene responded, locking gazes with the other woman.

"One does not need a high title to be well-bred," Teresa said in a faintly defiant tone.

"No doubt you are right," Irene relented. "You are saying that it is not a man's family that makes a gentleman, but his manners—education and courtesy, a refinement of taste."

"Yes, exactly." Teresa seized on this explanation with an air of relief.

"So, then, a well-mannered, well-spoken, well-educated merchant is no doubt the equal—or even the better—of a nobleman."

"What?" Teresa stared at her. "No, of course not. I—I didn't say that."

"But if it is not one's bloodline that provides good breeding but a courteous air or the manner of one's speech—"

"I didn't say that!" Teresa cried. "No, you are twisting my words." Thoroughly flustered, she looked around the table as if for help.

"Irene, stop baiting the girl," Lady Odelia interrupted, sounding amused. "It is hardly fair to engage in a battle of wits with an opponent so ill-equipped as Teresa."

Francesca let out a short bark of laughter, quickly smothered and turned into a cough. Teresa shot Lady Odelia a murderous look but said nothing.

"Please forgive me, Lady Odelia," Irene replied, ignoring

the glare that Teresa had now turned on her, and returned her attention to her plate.

After the meal, when the gentlemen had retired to the smoking room for port and cigars and the women were making their way to the music room, Francesca slipped her arm through Irene's as they walked down the hall.

Leaning her head close, Francesca murmured, "It was quite admirable of you to defend Lord Radbourne as you did. However, I think you have made a bitter enemy of Lady Teresa."

She nodded toward the woman in question, who was walking alone ahead of all the other women. Irene knew that Francesca was right. Even Teresa's stiff back radiated displeasure.

Irene shrugged. "I have earned far worse anger than hers, I'll warrant." She smiled a little. "And I have survived. I have little doubt I will survive Lady Radbourne's wrath."

"I would put my money on you," Francesca agreed. "But I would not discount the countess. She dislikes you, and you stand in her way."

Irene glanced at Francesca in puzzlement. "Stand in her way? How can I do that?"

"Maisie filled me in on the gossip in the servants' hall. Apparently Lady Radbourne is counting on Gideon's not marrying. As long as he does not marry, her son Timothy is his heir. Once Gideon marries, Timothy's status is much less certain. Gideon will likely have a son—indeed, he could have several. So she would like to see the earl remain unwed."

"It seems a faint hope to me," Irene opined.

Francesca shrugged. "I imagine she hopes that if she plays up Gideon's impossibility as a husband, she will frighten off prospective wives."

"I should think the man's personality would do that well enough by itself," Irene commented.

Francesca looked over at her. "If you feel that way about Lord Radbourne, why did you come to his defense?"

It was something Irene had wondered about herself. She gave Francesca the only response that she had been able to come up with. "I liked Lady Radbourne's needling him even less."

Francesca just nodded, making no comment.

"I have always disliked unfairness in any form," Irene went on. She did not add that she herself had been somewhat surprised by the fierce blaze of anger that had shot up in her at the other woman's remarks.

"No doubt," Francesca murmured.

"I realize that it was quite unnecessary, of course. After all, Lord Radbourne is clearly a man who can take care of himself and needs no defense from me."

"Mmm. Well, I suppose that necessity had little to do with it," Francesca replied.

"What do you mean?" Irene cast a suspicious glance at her companion.

"Why, what *would* I mean?" Francesca asked, turning to look at Irene with an innocent expression.

"I did not do it because of any sort of *feeling* for the man," Irene pointed out.

"Oh, no. Of course not," Francesca said agreeably.

Irene drew breath to comment on Francesca's answer, which she felt was meant to imply the exact opposite of what she said, but at that point it struck her that to protest the other woman's words would only serve to make her look foolish. So, not without some degree of frustration, she swallowed her response.

But she could not so easily cut off her own speculations about her actions. Why had she been so quick to defend Lord Radbourne? One would think that she would have sided with a woman who disliked the man, for she herself had decided that he was a thorough boor. Certainly his childhood must have been filled with a great deal of pain and sorrow, and the man doubtless carried scars from those years. It made her shudder to think of any child being subjected to the sort of life he had led. But those facts did not change his personality. They did not make him better or kinder or less obnoxious.

True, Teresa had been rude and insensitive in her remarks, but Francesca had responded to the woman as most ladies would, with a chilly disdain. Why had Irene felt compelled to charge into battle with her?

It was her nature, she told herself. She simply could not sit idly by while Lady Teresa made such hurtful, arrogant remarks. She would have done the same if the remarks had been directed at anyone else. She was, she hoped, not so unfair as to allow comments that hurt someone to pass just because she disliked the man.

And yet…somehow she could not dismiss what had happened and what she had said quite that easily. Her thoughts kept circling back to the matter all through the next tedious hour in the music room, as Lady Odelia told the vicar's wife a seemingly interminable story about a woman whom she and her sister had known forty years earlier. Odelia paused now and then to urge Francesca to play a tune upon the piano, but then she returned to her tale, raising her voice to be heard above Francesca's soft playing.

Francesca obediently remained seated at the piano, running quietly through her repertoire of music, though she rolled her eyes comically at Irene from time to time. Teresa sat in a chair at some remove from Irene and occupied herself by staring daggers at Irene, and Lady Claire took up her place beside Irene on the narrow sofa, fretting quietly about Irene's having methodically sliced Lady Teresa's pretensions into ribbons at the supper table.

The men did not join them after the postprandial cigars and port. Irene could scarcely blame them. Doubtless they had experienced such excruciating evenings before.

When enough time had passed to satisfy the requirements of civility, Irene spoke up, pleading tiredness from the journey as an excuse to retire early. Francesca, she noticed, was quick to agree that she was ready for bed. Lady Odelia waved them off with a few caustic comments about the lack of hardiness in young women today, and Irene and Francesca wasted no time in escaping the room.

They spent a much more enjoyable hour in Francesca's room, talking, but when they heard sounds of the group breaking up downstairs, Irene slipped down the hall to her own room. She went to stand by the window again and looked out into the dark garden below. It was difficult to see anything, for there was only a quarter moon, barely illuminating the shapes of trees and shrubs. But Irene gazed out anyway, thinking about the evening more than looking at the view.

Then, at the edge of her vision, a light appeared, catching her attention, and she leaned closer to the glass, intrigued. The light was from a lantern, she realized, bobbing with the steps of a man. She cupped her hands around her eyes to cut out the glare of the light inside her room and narrowed her eyes. Who was walking about the garden at this time of night?

The man bent to open the latch of a gate, raising the lantern to see, and the light fell on his face. It was Gideon.

Irene straightened, her curiosity engaged. She watched as Lord Radbourne walked through the garden until he disappeared from her sight in the trees at the far end. Then, beyond the stand of trees, she caught sight of the bobbing light again. A moment later it was gone.

What, she wondered, was Lord Radbourne doing tramping about the grounds so late? It certainly did not seem as if he were out on a casual stroll or smoking a late-night cigar before he turned in. His stride had been purposeful, and he had taken a lantern to light the way. Nor had he stayed in the garden. The last time she had seen the light, it had surely been some distance away.

She supposed he could have been headed toward the tavern in the village; it seemed a likely enough place for a man to go, especially after a difficult evening with his relatives. And while it might be too common a place for many gentlemen to relax, it could very well suit someone who felt uncomfortable in his gentleman's role.

However, the village and the tavern were in the opposite direction from that which Gideon had taken, and, moreover, it seemed a rather long way to walk. Surely he would have taken a horse. But he had not been headed toward the stables, either.

What was he about, and where was he going? What lay in that direction besides fields and woods and the occasional cottage? Was he meeting someone? She could think of little reason to meet someone at this time of night. It seemed rather late for any sort of activity…unless, of course, he was meeting a woman. Could it be that he was heading for a romantic rendezvous?

Nonsense, she chided herself. No doubt there were a number of other logical reasons why a man might be setting out into the countryside—alone—at nearly midnight. The fact that she could not think of any of them did not mean they did not exist.

Besides, even if he *was* sneaking off for a tryst, it was no concern of hers. Irene could not imagine why she was even wasting her time thinking about it. And there was certainly no reason for that suspicion to cause such a painful little twist in her heart.

CHAPTER NINE

THE NEXT DAY Francesca and Irene began their campaign to improve Gideon's marriage prospects. There was, Lady Odelia had assured them, no time to waste. The prospective brides had been invited and were expected to arrive in a little over a week.

Irene and Francesca met in the dining room after breakfast was over. Gideon, however, was late by almost thirty minutes. Perhaps, Irene thought with some annoyance, the man had overslept this morning after his midnight tryst. The more she had thought about it, the more likely it seemed that Lord Radbourne had been sneaking away to meet a woman. He was clearly a sensual man; she had felt the power of his kiss, after all. And there would be a number of willing women around, she felt sure, given his looks, wealth and position.

It was only to be expected, she decided, and though of course it did not matter in any way to her, she could not help but feel irritated at this further example of typical male behavior. Gideon was about to court a wife, yet at the same time he was carrying on an affair with a mistress. Or perhaps not an affair with a mistress, just indulging in an even more meaningless encounter with some woman. Irene knew, of course, that she was jumping to conclusions, but that fact did not prevent her from feeling annoyed.

She wondered who the woman was—the wife or daughter of one of the tenants? It would have to be someone who lived close by. Perhaps there was a willing widow in the vicinity, happy to ease her loneliness with the handsome lord…or could it be one of the housemaids? Irene cast her mind over the ones she had met, wondering which of them might be pretty enough to catch Gideon's eye.

She considered how she might find out where Gideon had gone and whether he had met someone, and then in the next moment realized how foolish her thoughts were. What did it matter if he was meeting a woman? It was no concern of hers. She would do much better to control her imagination and her curiosity, and concentrate on the task at hand: getting Gideon married. Let his future wife worry about the rest of it.

Gideon arrived finally, looking rushed and irritated. Irene made a point of glancing at the clock on the mantel. He followed her gaze, and his lips twitched with obvious annoyance.

"Yes, I am late, Lady Irene," he said grouchily. "I am afraid I allowed some trifling little business matters to interfere with my main duty in life—learning to pretend to be a gentleman."

"You are forgiven," Francesca returned placidly. "However, you have no need to pretend. You already *are* a gentleman by virtue of your birth."

"Yes, you simply need to learn to act like one," Irene added caustically.

"And I am to learn manners from you?" Radbourne asked, raising one straight black brow.

"Oh, Irene *knows* her manners," Francesca replied before Irene could speak, casting a droll glance in her direction.

"She simply does not always choose to *apply* them." She paused, then added, "As, no doubt, you will choose, also."

Gideon allowed a smile to creep in. "Lady Haughston, I would say that you have put us both in our place."

Francesca nodded, giving her little smile, as of a secret shared, to remove any ill will from the situation. Irene, for the first time in her life, felt a curious envy of Francesca's winning manner. She looked at Lord Radbourne, who had come into the room with such irritation and resistance and yet who now seemed relaxed, almost malleable. He was smiling at Francesca, and Irene felt an unaccustomed twist of resentment inside her, a feeling so uncommon that it jolted her. Surely she did not— No, this could not be *jealousy.*

She turned quickly away, taking refuge in the task before them. "If you would be so good as to take a seat here, Lord Radbourne?"

He moved over to where she stood beside the table and looked down. There, spread out before his chair, was an elaborate setting of glasses and eating utensils, grouped around a folded white damask linen napkin in the center.

"Ah, I see," he said, with a derisive twist of his mouth. "The infamous cutlery."

"'Tis easy enough to learn," Irene began.

"Oh, my lady, I'm not so sure about that," he commented, dropping into the chair in front of the table. "Some of us are intolerably slow learners."

"I am sure that you are not," she retorted flatly. "And your first lesson is this— You must not sit down at the table whilst ladies remain standing. A gentleman waits to sit until the ladies have been seated."

"In fact, let us start before that," Francesca told him.

"When you go in to supper, you must offer your arm to a lady."

"Any lady?"

"Oh, no. There is an order, of course. Yesterday evening was an informal setting, merely family and a few close friends. But at a more formal dinner, you would, as host, offer your arm to the highest-ranking female, which would in the case of last night's group be your grandmother. Both she and Lady Teresa are dowager countesses, of course, but by virtue of your grandmother's age, she would be higher. And, after all, Lady Pansy is the daughter of a duke." She shot a mischievous look at Irene as she went on. "Which, as we all know, outranks the daughter of the second son of a baronet."

Irene colored a little at Francesca's reference to the evening before and stole a glance at Gideon. A smile twitched at his lips, and he looked at her, sketching a bow in her direction. She felt her blush deepen, but she could not keep from smiling back at him, and she was warmed by his look.

"Do not mention it to Lady Odelia, of course," Francesca went on with a glint of amusement in her eyes, "but even though she, too, is the daughter of a duke, her married title is only baroness. So she is behind the others in precedence."

"Strangely, her precedence would actually be higher if she had married below the rank of baron," Irene put in. "For then she would retain the rank she is owed as daughter of a duke, which is right after the wife of the eldest son of the duke, but before the wives of the younger sons of the duke."

Gideon looked at her, his brows drawing together. "Are you seriously suggesting that I remember such a thing?"

"It is not important at the moment," Francesca added

quickly. "And, of course, in the future it will be something that you can rely on your wife to remember."

"Ah, yes," he replied drily. "One of the many benefits of marrying an aristocrat."

"Right now, let us proceed to the meal. You escort the lady in. Irene, you be the lady." Francesca waved Gideon toward Irene. When the two of them stood stock still, gazing at her, Francesca nodded impatiently. "Go ahead, you must practice. Offer her your arm."

Gideon turned and walked to Irene, holding out his arm, bent at the elbow.

"Very good. Nice form," Francesca said encouragingly.

Irene put her hand on his arm, and the two of them walked over to the table.

"She will be seated in order of precedence, as well," Francesca went on. "But of course, at a formal dinner, there will be dinner cards, so there will be no confusion. Ordinarily she would sit here." Francesca pointed to the spot in question. "But as I have had the servants lay out the table settings here, for now just seat her next to you. Pull out her chair and then, as she sits, gently push it in a little."

Francesca gave him a nod of encouragement, and suppressing a sigh, Gideon pulled out the chair. Irene started to sit down, but Gideon slid the chair forward quickly, catching the backs of her knees, and she sat down with a graceless thump. Irene twisted to look up at him scathingly, and he returned her glare with a bland look.

"You might try it a little less energetically," Francesca offered.

"I am sorry, my lady," Gideon told Francesca.

"I believe I am the one to whom you should apologize," Irene reminded him, annoyed.

He smiled a little to himself as he sat down, saying, "Ah, but what would be the enjoyment in that?"

Irene arched one eyebrow, her eyes beginning to spark, and Francesca went on quickly. "Now, to the place setting… Irene, show him which utensils are which."

Irene cast a recalcitrant glance at Francesca, but said, "Oh, very well." She leaned closer to Gideon and reached in front of him to point out the different eating utensils. "They are in the order in which one uses them, the outermost being used first. You see? The spoon for soup is on the far right of where they will set the plate. Next comes the fish knife, matched by the fish fork on the left side, then the meat knife and fork, the pudding spoon and fork, and finally the savory knife and fork. The spoons for the ices and for the fruit at the end will be brought out with the plates."

As she talked, Irene was very aware of how close she was to him. She could smell the faint scent of his cologne, warmed by his body heat, and when she looked up from the place setting to see if he had followed her words, she found her face only inches from his. She moved involuntarily, startled, and had to put her hand briefly on his arm to steady herself. He gazed back at her, and she knew that he had been watching her face, not the utensils to which she had been pointing.

"Are you paying attention?" she asked sharply.

"Of course. But which was this one?" He indicated the small rounded knife on the little plate to the left of the place setting.

"That is the butter spreader." Irene straightened up, removing herself from such close proximity. "That is why it is put here across the bread plate."

"And which of these glasses is for the liqueur?"

"None of them. The servants will bring out the liqueur or port glasses at the appropriate time." Again she reached across him to touch the various glasses above the knives and spoons. "Sherry glass for the soup. White wine glass, with fish. Claret glass, with meat. And of course, water. But you do not really need to remember where they go. The glasses will be filled by the servants at the correct time."

"And which did you say was the savory fork?"

Irene reached across to tap the small fork that lay closest to where the silver savory dish would be placed by the servant. They continued in this manner for several more minutes, going over the uses and placement of the cutlery. It seemed as if every time he ran through a listing of them, Gideon forgot one or more, and Irene grew increasingly impatient.

With each mistake or slip of the tongue, his expression grew more stolid and his voice seemed to slip further back into his East End youth, *H*'s dropping and *A*'s drifting toward *I*'s. Even Francesca began to look nettled.

Francesca sighed and said wearily, "Now, once again, Lord Radbourne. Which is the fish knife?"

Gideon hesitated, looking down at the place setting in front of him. "Well…now, they're all startin' to look the same to me." His hand hovered over the plate for a moment. "I'd say it'd be…this one." His index finger fell decisively to the meat knife.

Irene let out a groan. "No, no, no. Really, my lord, we have gone over this twenty times, at least."

She reached over and took his hand, forcibly redirecting his finger to the smaller fish knife. "This is the knife for the fish. It goes with the fish fork over here on the left. They are both outside the meat fork and knife, as the turbot will come before the roast joint. I cannot conceive how you can still be confused over this."

She looked at him in some exasperation. His face was set in the same blank, stony expression he had worn for the last few minutes. But there was something lurking in his eyes that made her pause.

"It must be too 'ard for me, my lady," he started. There was a faint tremor in his voice, and he stopped, pressing his lips together tightly.

Irene's eyes narrowed, and she leaned a little closer, staring into his eyes. "You are trying to gammon me, aren't you!"

"I don't know what you mean," Gideon began, trying for a wide-eyed look, but his mouth began to twitch, and he brought his hand up, pressing his fist against his lips.

"Oh!" Irene jumped up, her hands doubling into fists. "You are doing it much too brown, my lord! You cannot be so abysmally stupid and manage to run a successful business!"

Gideon began to laugh, which only served to infuriate her even more. She turned away, and began to pace up and down the room, spewing forth a litany of complaints. "What is the matter with you? Why do I waste my time? You are the most ill-mannered, inconsiderate wretch!"

As Irene continued to pace and fume, Francesca stared at Gideon from across the table, her eyebrows shooting upward. "You mean this has all been a pretense?" Suddenly she began to chuckle, and soon she, too, was laughing.

"What is wrong with you?" Irene cried, whirling around to stare at Francesca now. "Have you gone mad? We have just wasted thirty minutes teaching this fool things he probably already knew!"

Gideon turned his head toward her, grinning. "It isn't that hard, my lady. I think you put too much faith in Teresa's words last night. I did not spend my life in a hole. I have been able for some time to afford a chef—far better than the one in this drafty pile, I might add—and my butler would not have dreamed of having anything less than the perfect setting at my table. Even if I had not known how to eat when I arrived here, it merely takes looking at what everyone else is doing to learn. 'Tis not Euclid, you know, or the writings of Plato."

Irene stared at him, hands on hips, perplexed. "Why?" she asked, throwing up her hands and walking back to the chair beside him. She sat down, shaking her head, and said again, "Why would you want us to think that you know nothing? Why would you try to act rougher than you are?"

"It pleases my family so," he replied. His eyes glinted, and he added beneath his breath, "And how else was I supposed to get you so close?"

Irene's eyes widened, a sudden warmth flooding her abdomen at his words. She glanced quickly at Francesca to see if she had heard his sotto voce statement. Francesca, still smiling from her spate of mirth and shaking her head in amused disbelief, did not seem to have noticed what Gideon said, and Irene relaxed a little and turned to look at him. He was watching her, his face relaxed from his laughter, but his eyes steady and watchful. Irene felt a blush rising in her cheeks, and she turned away, suddenly flustered and confused.

"Don't be absurd," she said, but her voice did not come out as sharply as she had intended.

"Very well, then," Francesca said, rising to her feet and settling her face back into a serious expression. "I apologize,

Lord Radbourne, for listening too much to what others have said that you need. Perhaps we should start over. Maybe you have no need to polish your manners, in which case, there is really little reason for Lady Irene and me to be here. So I will ask you—is there any area in which you feel you could…gain useful knowledge? Do something to make you fit in more easily with your new family and your peers? Or should Irene and I simply retire from our efforts?"

"No," he said without hesitation. "I am sure that you and Lady Irene can improve me. But I know as much as I care to about tableware. I have a valet who endeavors to keep me looking the part. And, as you said, I will have a wife to keep me informed as to the order of precedence on any occasion. I am aware that my speech is a trifle wrong, but I can tell you that I worked at some length to speak in the proper manner, and I am told that it is my nature, not my grammar, that is not quite up to snuff. So I have little hope—and admittedly, little interest—in learning how to speak like a swell." He paused, then added, "There *is* one area in which I would like to improve my skills. I am hopeless on the dance floor."

"Ah." Francesca looked pleased. "That, I am sure, is something that we can help you with." She looked over at Irene. "Don't you agree?"

"Yes, of course." Irene nodded.

They left the dining room and made their way to the music room. Irene had immediately seen the dangers inherent in teaching Gideon to dance. He would need to have a partner with whom to practice, and being his partner would require her to stand quite close to him the whole time, often with his hand on hers or even his arm around her. If being close to him at the table had stirred her in unaccustomed ways, she did not like to think of what she might feel while dancing with him.

"Why don't I play the piano?" she suggested as they entered the music room, heading for the piano where Francesca had played for Lady Odelia the evening before.

Francesca let out a little laugh. "Oh, no, my dear, you forget—I have heard you play. I think it will be better if I play the tune and you act as his lordship's partner."

Unfortunately, Irene knew that Francesca had the right of it. Irene was not musically gifted and had hated the tedium of daily practice, so she possessed only minimal skill at the piano. And both she and Francesca were well aware of that fact, as young unmarried ladies were often called upon to show off such talents at various social gatherings. If Irene insisted on playing, Francesca would know that there was something behind her stubbornness, and she had even less desire to set Francesca speculating on why she did not want to dance with Lord Radbourne than she did to dance with him.

"Of course." Irene gave in as gracefully as she could.

She glanced over at Gideon. He smiled at her in a way that told her that he understood why she had wanted to play the piano. Worse, he knew why she was reluctant to dance with him—not because she was repelled by him, but exactly the opposite. Quite despite her own wishes, she was attracted to him. She was afraid to be in his arms, to move to the music with him, because she was afraid of her own response.

"Shall we start with the waltz?" Francesca asked, going on without waiting for an answer. "I know it is not always done outside of London, but I think this will be a sophisticated enough gathering that it will be no problem. And it is the simplest to learn, I think. Irene, you explain the steps to Lord Radbourne while I find some music."

Irene turned to Gideon as Francesca started searching through the pile of sheet music on top of the piano. He held up his hand.

"I know the steps. I have been taught them. I am simply not expert at it. I think what I need is practice."

"Of course," Irene replied, goaded by the smugness in his smile into a determination to remain utterly cool and unaffected throughout the dancing lesson. "Shall we try a few steps without the music first?"

"If you wish." He held out his hand for hers, then drew her closer, putting his other hand at her waist.

His palm was heavy and warm upon her side, his grip firm, and she was very aware of just how large his hand was. It made her feel a little breathless to stand this close to him, to look up into his face from only a few inches away. He was, she thought, a rather overpowering man, and she had to remind herself that she, on the other hand, was a woman who was not easily dominated.

"The first thing to remember is that you must not grip a lady too tightly," she told him in an even tone. "Your hand should rest lightly at her waist."

He lifted his hand just a little, and she reached down and moved his thumb a bit so that it was in exactly the correct position.

"Now you must guide me in the direction we are going, but lightly. You must not be ham-handed about it, as if you are pulling and pushing a sack about. Merely a light pressure of your fingers. And you do not grip my other hand tightly, but cup it. Yes, just so. Now, let us start."

She began to count out the waltz, and they moved, their steps rather stiff and awkward.

Irene looked up at him and asked, somewhat suspiciously, "You are not pretending to be less able to dance than you really are, are you?"

He laughed. "No. I fear that this is, in fact, the way I dance."

"All you need is practice," Irene told him encouragingly.

"My dear lady, you have not taken refuge in the polite lie before. Please do not start now."

She had to chuckle. "All right. Then let me say truthfully that you are not the worst with whom I have taken a turn around the floor. Not the best, either, it is true. But I do believe that practice will bring improvement."

He bowed his head briefly in acknowledgment. "Thank you. Then we shall practice."

So they did, sweeping around the floor to Francesca's playing. Their task was made more difficult by the necessity of dodging the other pieces of furniture in the music room, which was not set up for dancing. But after knocking over a stool and backing into a chair, they paused to rearrange the chairs a little, forming a vaguely circular path around most of the impediments. They danced along it for a time or two, and Gideon began to relax and move less stiffly, without such concentration on his steps.

As his confidence increased, he looked more at her face and less at his feet. Indeed, he looked at her at such length that Irene felt a flush beginning to creep up into her cheeks.

"Have I grown a third eye, sir?" she asked somewhat sharply. "You have been staring at me far longer than is polite."

"I am sorry. No doubt it is more of my poor upbringing,"

he responded without the slightest trace of regret in his voice. "It is probably also impolite of me to point out that there is something different about you."

She cocked an eyebrow at him. "Different? Different from what?"

"From the way you looked when I first met you. Your hair, I think. It is not the same."

"A woman often chooses different hairstyles, my lord," she retorted.

"I like the one you chose last night and today," he told her. His voice deepened a little huskily as he went on. "It is softer, a little less…tightly bound. It makes a man think…"

Heat spread in her at his words. She knew she should not ask, should not permit him to go on in this way. It was not at all the thing. It was dangerous.

Yet she heard herself saying, "Think of what, my lord?"

"Of taking it down," he answered, and the huskiness of his voice sent a thrill through her. "Of seeing all that glory unbound and spilling over your shoulders."

This time it was Irene who stumbled a little, and his hand tightened on her waist, keeping her steady. She looked away. "This is not the sort of conversation we should be having. Your speech is far too warm, sir. Far too familiar."

"It is not polite?" he asked sardonically.

"It is not proper," she corrected. "A gentleman does not speak to a young unmarried lady in this manner." She raised her eyes to his face a little defiantly, thinking that she must not let him see how his words had affected her.

"Ah, but we both know that I am not a gentleman." His eyes were on her, and she could not mistake the heat in them any more than she could mistake the meaning of his words.

His low voice was like a caress across her skin, making her tremble.

"You must not say such things to the girls you will be courting," she said firmly, struggling to ignore the response she felt inside her.

"I am not saying this to any of them," he pointed out, adding, "I don't have any interest in any of them."

"You have not met them yet."

"I do not have to meet them to know that they will be by and large giggling and foolish, or proud and disdainful. And that none of them will have anything to say that is not what they have been trained to say since they were born. And not one of them will be as interesting to me as you are."

Irene drew a sharp breath. "I told you that I was not interested in marriage, Lord Radbourne."

"Do you not think, since you are engaged in correcting my every word and move, that you could at least call me by my name?"

"That is your name," Irene protested.

"No. It is not. The Earl of Radbourne is not me. It is some entity that has nothing to do with who I am at all." His voice turned hard as he spoke, his face drawing into its usual severe lines and angles. "I have been Gideon all my life."

It was not proper, she knew, to call him by his given name; they had known each other only a few days, after all. To call him Gideon would indicate an intimacy between them that was not right. And yet, after a long moment, she said, "All right. Gideon."

His face relaxed, and his hand tightened slightly around hers. Irene glanced away. She felt as if she were sliding down a rather slippery slope. How had this situation gotten away from her? She had started out correcting Gideon, quite rightly, for speaking to her in a most improper way, and somehow she had wound up agreeing to call him by his first name, something she did not do even with men she had known her entire life.

She was simply not accustomed to this—the man, the situation, the feelings that boiled within her, seeming to bubble up to the surface at inopportune moments. Irene knew that she had a certain reputation for prickliness; there were those who proclaimed that it was more her disagreeable nature than her lack of dowry that had kept her from receiving an offer when she was younger. However, she did not mind that people thought her difficult and sharp-tongued. She would rather be that than a spineless chit who giggled and simpered and looked up with awe at a man, no matter how idiotic the fellow might be.

Lady Irene Wyngate, she thought, was the sort who knew her own mind. She was not easily swayed, and she rarely felt mystified or confused—in particular, she was not confused about herself. Yet ever since she had met the Earl of Radbourne, she had surprised herself. She had felt things she had never felt before, had acted in ways that she would never have thought she could, and she had been pushed this way and that by a tumult of sensations and emotions. She felt, quite frankly, a loss of control that she had never experienced before, and the feeling left her a little shaken.

When the waltz ended and they stepped apart, Irene moved a few steps away from him. She turned toward Francesca, who was paging through her music, looking for another waltz to play while the dancers took a short rest.

Irene took a breath and said, "Lady Francesca, I think that I would like to—to stop now, if we may."

"Of course." Francesca looked over at her in surprise. "I

am sorry. Are you tired? I was not thinking. I should not have kept on playing."

Gideon frowned, starting toward Irene. "Yes, we should take a few minutes. Perhaps we should have some tea."

"No, I'm not—" Irene started to dispute the idea that the dancing had wearied her, but she stopped, seeing the easy opportunity. "That is, yes, perhaps you are right. But I don't need any tea. I think that I should go upstairs to my room. I—I have a bit of a headache, I believe."

She could not quite meet Gideon's eyes, and she turned quickly back to Francesca. "If you do not mind, perhaps we might continue this tomorrow?"

"Of course." Francesca smiled and waved a hand. "I feel sure that Lord Radbourne will be more than pleased to escape our clutches for an afternoon. I shall just go along and discuss the plans for the party with Lady Odelia."

"Thank you." Irene gave her a small smile and, without another look at Gideon, fled the room.

Once she was safely in her own room, she flung herself into the chair by the window and spent the next few minutes castigating herself for being such a coward. Whatever was she doing, hiding up here? It was yet more evidence of how unlike herself she had been behaving.

She was not the sort of woman to engage in the socially acceptable deception of a headache that she had just used in the music room. She did not flee from men because she could not handle them. Far less did she flee because she could not trust herself!

Irene drummed her fingers upon the arm of the chair. She did not understand why this one man affected her in this way. But she could not allow it to continue. She must return to her old self.

She should go for a long walk, she decided—the sort of ramble she was wont to take when they were at home in the country. A little fresh air and healthy exercise would restore her, make her see things more clearly.

Determined, she stood up and pulled on the sturdy boots she had brought for walking and a chip straw hat with a wide brim to shade her face. She ought, she knew, to change into an older dress to avoid getting dirt on the hem of the new one she had on, but she could not undo all the buttons of this dress by herself, and she did not want to ring for the maid to help her. She would just as soon not advertise that she was going out for a walk after she had just pleaded weariness and a headache.

She slipped down the backstairs and out the rear door into the garden. She did not linger along the tended walkways there, however, taking instead the shortest way through toward the meadow beyond.

It was not long before she came upon one of the small pathways that wound their way through so much of the English countryside. She was not sure which way it ran, but she turned in the direction that seemed least likely to bring her back in sight of the house and struck off.

The path led along a small ridge and offered a fair prospect of the countryside. Below her she could see the meadow stretching off to farms and, in the distance, the Cotswold hills. To her right were trees and then another slight slope, on the top of which stood an old square gray stone tower and partial walls of the same stone.

It must be the ruins of the old Norman tower that the butler had told them about when they first arrived. Irene thought it might be worth some exploration later. She stopped for a moment and shaded her eyes to look at it.

Suddenly she heard the jingle of a bridle on the pathway behind her and the sound of a horse's hooves. She turned to look and saw a man riding toward her on a large bay gelding. Her stomach dropped.

Lord Radbourne was the man on the horse's back. And she was well and truly caught in her little white lie.

CHAPTER TEN

IRENE THOUGHT FOR a single harried instant of turning and running, but she firmly clamped down on that impulse. Had she not just resolved to be strong, to return to her accustomed ways? She would meet this problem as she always had: straight on.

She stiffened her spine and watched Gideon approach. She recalled that Lady Odelia had told Francesca that Gideon was a poor rider, but Irene could not help but think that he showed quite well on horseback. He might not have the excellent form of many of her male acquaintances, who had ridden from childhood, but that fact did not detract from the picture of power he presented, with his wide shoulders squared and his large, leather-gloved hands holding the reins, his muscular thighs clamped against the horse's sides.

Irene swallowed and straightened even more.

"Why, Lady Irene," Gideon said as he drew near, laughter lurking in his voice, as he swept off his hat to her. "What a surprise to find you here."

"Indeed. I am equally surprised to meet you," she retorted. "Did you follow me?"

"No, I thought you ensconced in your bedchamber with a headache, if you will remember," he responded and swung down from his horse. He took the reins in his hand and led the horse closer to her. "I decided to take a look at one or two of my farms, as the rest of my day was suddenly free."

Feeling that some explanation was in order, Irene told him, "I thought perhaps a turn in the fresh air would relieve my headache."

"Ah, I see." He nodded. "Then I shall just walk with you…unless, of course, you prefer not to have company."

The roguish gleam in his eyes was too much of a challenge for Irene to resist. "Of course not," she replied. "Indeed, my lord, I believe that there are a few things that we need to discuss."

"Really? Points about my manners? Or my dancing skills? And I thought we had agreed that you would call me Gideon."

"Gideon," she said, deciding that she would give in on that small point. "Though, of course, it would not be proper to address you so when we are in company."

"Oh, no, indeed. Then I must definitely be Radbourne to you."

"I know this all seems a joke to you," Irene told him stiffly. "But these are the rules by which we live, and it does a lady little good to be seen breaking them. I am considered odd enough as it is. I do not wish to add any questions about my honor to the gossip."

He frowned. "Indeed, I cannot imagine that anyone would dare question your honor."

"I hope to give them no cause to do so," she countered.

He bowed his head in acceptance, and they continued to walk. After a moment, he said, "Now, what was it that you wished to take me to task for?"

"It is not that I wish to take you task. It is more…that I wish to clarify my position here. I agreed to come to your home to help Francesca, and that is all. I had hoped she made that clear to you and your great-aunt."

"She did."

"I tried to make it equally clear to you that I have no intention of marrying you."

"You did."

She shot him a sideways glance. "And yet, this morning, you made remarks to me—"

"Remarks?"

"Compliments, I suppose you might say."

His eyebrows vaulted up in an expression of innocent surprise. "Am I not allowed to compliment you?"

"It was your manner, sir. It was not the compliment of a… a gentleman to a woman he does not know. Or of a brother to a sister."

"No. They were not the compliments of a brother. But then, I am not your brother."

"You are being obtuse. Purposely so, I warrant. Your remarks were… You were flirting."

"Am I not allowed to flirt with you, either?"

"No," she answered crossly. "Oh, do not put that astonished look upon your face again! You know exactly what I am talking about. You spoke to me in a…well, in a seductive manner."

A faint smile touched his lips. "I am glad to see that my intention was clear."

"But I told you—"

"I know what you told me, Irene."

"Then why do you continue to pursue the matter?" she asked with some heat, not even noticing that he had used her first name, though she had not invited him to. "I repeat, there is no hope of my marrying you, so I see no sense in your making advances toward me. Do you hope to change my mind? You will not, I assure you."

"No, I can see that your mind is set in stone," he retorted.

Irene's brows drew together in a frown. "Now you are insulting me."

"You did not wish me to compliment you, if you remember."

She heaved an exasperated sigh and turned her face away. They walked on in charged silence.

After a moment, Gideon said mildly, "In any case, I did not ask you to marry me. Surely you noticed."

"No, but you were making advances toward me. You have admitted that."

"Well, you said only that you would not marry me. You did not forbid…other matters."

Irene came to an abrupt halt and swung on him, her face lighting with outrage. "What! Are you saying— Do you dare to think that I— That I—" She sputtered to a halt, unable to bring herself to say the words.

His smile was slow and knowing, an acknowledgment of the suggestive implication of his earlier words. Irene knew that she should have felt insulted by it, even repulsed, but instead she found that the curve of his lips, the light in his leaf-green eyes, set up an ache deep in the pit of her abdomen. She released a shaky breath, knowing she should step back from him, should tear her gaze from his, but she could not. She did not want to, and that was the most shattering realization of all.

"Even a woman so disinclined to marry…does not necessarily seek to bar herself from all relationships," he said carefully.

"You think that I would dishonor myself? Bring shame

to my name?" she asked, appalled at how shaky her voice came out. Would he realize that it matched the trembling inside her? Could he know, just by looking into her eyes, that he had awakened in her the lust that she denied?

"Never dishonor. I do not think you capable of dishonoring yourself." He took a half step closer to her, dropping the reins and bringing his hands up to curve around her upper arms. "What would you have us do? Deny what lies between us? Forget the fact that when I touch you, your skin turns hot beneath my hands? That when I kissed you, you kissed me back?"

Irene closed her eyes, unable to look into his face any longer for fear she would wantonly throw herself into his arms. She wanted, quite badly, to feel his lips against hers once more. She could remember their taste, their texture, and her own lips tingled at the memory.

"No," she whispered almost fearfully. "It is not true. There is nothing between us."

"I thought you were not a woman who lied," he shot back, and his hands tightened on her arms, pulling her closer.

Then his lips were on hers, hungry and seeking, and all rational thought left her. Irene went up on her toes, her mouth pressing into his with an equal hunger, and her arms went around his neck, holding on to him as heat rushed down through her in a storm, sweeping aside all else.

In this moment there was nothing but the feel of his hard body pressed against her all the way up and down her length, nothing but the harsh thrum of lust in her loins, the pounding of hot blood in her veins. Their kiss was long and deep, as though they could summon up each other's souls. Irene trembled in his arms, bizarrely weak, almost faint, and yet she had no desire to end the kiss. She wanted him, his taste and heat, the hardness of his masculine body. She yearned to drink him in, take him inside her, and was stunned at the very fact that such a feeling lived in her.

His hands slid up her back, moving to caress her sides, then sweeping down to curve over her buttocks. His fingers dug into the soft flesh, cupping her and lifting her up onto the hard, pulsing evidence of his desire. Irene had never felt a man in this way, indeed, had not even imagined the feeling, but she knew at once what it was, and a pulse began to throb between her legs.

She dug her fingers into his hair, aware of a wild desire to rub her body against his, to unbutton his clothes and let her fingers caress his bare skin.

"Oh, God!" Irene broke away, half turning from him, bringing her shaking hands to her face. "No! What am I doing?"

Gideon let out a groan of frustration, and his arms went around her from behind, pulling her back against him. His loins cupped her buttocks, hard and insistent against her. She could feel the rapid rise and fall of his chest, and hear the harsh rasp of his breath as he bent to nuzzle into her hair.

"You feel it," he murmured huskily. "Do not deny that you burn with the same desire I do."

"I cannot. I will not."

"You are so stern. So harsh," he went on, his lips teasing softly now at her neck. "Do you not care at all how you tempt me?"

"I do not try to tempt you."

"I know you do not." He let out a noise that was half laugh, half groan. "That is the devil of it. You have no need to try. You have only to look at me with those golden eyes. I have only to see a lock of your hair pull loose from its restraint and I can think of nothing else but watching it all come free, of pulling out the pins and sinking my hands into those curls…gold as honey…soft as satin."

"Gideon, stop!" Irene pulled away and faced him, clenching her fists at her sides to still the telltale trembling of her fingers. "I will not allow you to seduce me. Can you honestly think that I would set myself up as your mistress?"

"No," he replied, scowling blackly at her. "I want you as my wife, as you well know."

"Gideon, I told you I would not. Why will you not believe me?"

"What would you have me do?" he countered. "You have told me what you will not do. But you cannot make me cease trying. Did you really think that I would meekly accept your refusal? That I would not do my best to change your mind? To persuade you in whatever way I could?"

They stared at each other for a long moment; then Irene sighed, relaxing her taut stance. "No. I suppose I did not expect you to give in. Not really."

"Would it be so terrible?" he asked in a low voice, taking a step closer to her.

Irene backed up at his advance and found herself bumping against the side of his horse. The placid mount did not move away from her but stayed where he was, stretching his neck to crop at a tasty-looking tuft of grass.

Gideon moved closer, his eyes holding hers as he brushed his knuckles down her cheek. Slowly, as he continued gazing into her eyes, his hand moved lower, skimming over her jaw and down the column of her throat, then spreading wide over her chest. Irene could not pull her eyes from his, could not even make herself step away as his fingers moved boldly downward, molding her dress to her breasts, her stomach, the side of her hip.

"Would you find it such a chore to be my wife?" he asked, his dark eyes burning into hers. "To be in my bed…to feel my touch…"

"No," she answered honestly, though her voice shook from the fire that rippled through her in the wake of his hands. "It would not be terrible…for a few weeks, a month, until you were no longer filled with this lust for me."

She forced herself to jerk away from his hand. "But then, when your thirst was slaked, I would still be under your control."

"I think you underestimate how long I would desire you," he said mildly. "But let us say you are right. When the fire between us died, you would still be my wife. You would have my name, my respect, my fortune, still."

"I would have nothing but what you chose to give me," she shot back. "Once your fire has cooled, once you have gotten what you hoped to achieve, think you that you would find my blunt speech acceptable? No, then, I believe, you would find that I am impertinent and far too independent, that I speak my mind with no regard for what you think or prefer. You would realize that I am argumentative and opinionated."

His brows arched upward in amusement. "Do you think that I have not already realized those things?"

"Do not jest with me!" Irene exclaimed. "You may find such concerns silly and unimportant, but I assure you, I do not! If you were the one who would be under another's thumb, with nothing of your own, not even the right to your own body…dependent on someone else's whims, forced to live by another's rules, then you would not wish to enter into that state, either."

"Irene—" Looking somewhat alarmed, he held out a hand toward her. "Do you think me such a tyrant?"

"I don't know! I don't know you!" Her eyes were wide in her pale face, her cheeks splotched with a blaze of color. "But I know how easy honeyed words come to a man's lips when he hopes to gain something, and how quick he is to forget them later. I know that if I trust and I am wrong, then I will have bartered my life away. You could beat me and no one would interfere. The children I carried in my own body, born in blood and pain, would be yours, and I would have no rights over them. You could take them from me if you pleased. You could lock me away. The very clothes on my back would belong to you. Whatever money I had to spend would be only what you gave me. You—"

"My God," Gideon interrupted. "I am not such a monster! No, you do not know me—any more than I know you—but have I given you any reason to suppose that I would act in such a way?"

"No," she replied, and struggled to pull together the remnants of her composure. "And you doubtless find me foolish to think of such possibilities. Others have told me so, you need not reiterate it."

He paused for a moment, studying her, then asked quietly, "Is it because of your father that you have such a fear of marriage?"

Irene bridled at his words, retorting automatically, "Fear? I do not fear marriage. I look at it sensibly, that is all." But then she let out a sigh, her stiffened back relaxing a little, and she said quietly, "You knew him. You know what he was like. Obviously he must have wronged you in some way, since I found you trying to beat him into unconsciousness."

He looked at her a little quizzically. "I find it reassuring that you assumed that I went after your father because he wronged me first."

"Do not be overly proud of the matter. It was more the result of my knowledge of my father than my knowledge of you," Irene told him drily.

"I prefer to take it as a compliment, if you don't mind. Such things are hard to come by from your lips."

"You may take it any way you please," she replied, and began to stride once more down the path.

Gideon fell in beside her again, leading his mount. After a moment, he said, "I did know your father. I knew him in my world. He attacked a woman who worked for me. He had a habit of assuming that any woman who made her living dealing faro in a gambling den was available to him in other ways." His mouth tightened. "When she refused him, he hit her."

"And that is why you came to our house?"

He nodded. "Yes. But I must be fair and admit that the actions of a man in my part of London are not necessarily his actions among his own kind. In his family."

"I cannot answer for how he was among his peers, but I know how he treated those he considered his inferiors, and I can tell you that his wife and children were among that group. My mother is a woman of great patience and sweetness, but he constantly found fault with her. I do not know what she was like before she came under his power, but I know that around him, she was fearful and timid, uncertain about everything she said or did. None of us ever knew what might set him off. He would go for days, weeks, and do no more than roar about this or that 'mistake' one of us made. Then he would suddenly lash out and hit my mother for the least thing."

"I am sorry."

"It is over now. As you might imagine, I did not mourn his death overmuch."

His jaw tightened as he went on. "Did he hit you?"

"Once or twice he knocked me aside. I am not sure he intended to hurt me, as he was often clumsy with drink. He was, I think, in some way a little proud of me. I did not cower from him. He could not reduce me to tears or shakes, as he could Mother or Humphrey."

Gideon smiled faintly. "I am sure you were a little lioness."

She shrugged. "I saw early on that it only made him worse if one showed fear. It is much the same principle with animals, I think. But I did not need to feel his hand to know what the results of his anger were. I saw what he did to my mother often enough. I knew he was worse with her because she was his wife. She told me once what a fine gentleman he had been when he wooed her, how he had extolled her charms, her virtues. It was only after they were married that he found her foolish."

Irene glanced over at Gideon. She was a little surprised at herself for telling him about her father. Such stories were not something she normally shared with anyone. She was not sure why it was easier to tell him—perhaps because he had known her father's wickedness personally, or because the life he had lived had been far rougher than that of anyone else she knew, or simply because she sensed that any secrets would safely remain with him. Still, she could not help but wonder if he would look at her a little differently now. Men did not like a woman with too much knowledge of the darker side of the world.

Gideon stopped, reaching out to take her arm and turn her to face him. "Not all men are like your father, you know. Many men treasure their wives. They treat them with great care, even tenderness."

"I am no precious jewel," Irene replied bluntly, "to be coddled and wrapped in fine silk. No man would think it, and even if he were *foolish* enough to believe it, I can assure you that I would soon set him straight about the matter. I am, I suspect, more of a thorn in one's side."

She started to pull away, but he held her firm, saying flatly, "Do not mistake me for your father. Or for other men."

Irene raised her eyes, glinting golden in the afternoon sun, and stared at him. "I do not. But if I am wrong, I would not know until it was too late. I assure you, sir, I will not change my mind. I cannot marry you."

SHE PARTED FROM Gideon not long afterward. He went on to visit his holdings, and she walked back to the house, a little surprised by the vague feeling of sadness that hung over her. She felt sure that she must have gotten through to him this time; he would cease his pursuit of her and turn his interest to the women who would attend the party next week. She ought to be relieved, she told herself, not despondent.

Yet, despite her best efforts, she could not seem to dispel the downcast mood. She spent much of the afternoon in her room, staring moodily out the window. Somehow, she thought, she must have let herself slip into some silly girlish dream of love. Why else had she allowed Francesca and the others to talk her into buying those attractive new gowns?

Why else had she agreed to travel to Radbourne Park? Why else had she allowed Maisie to change her hairstyle?

Well, that had changed. She had set things straight with Gideon this afternoon. And tonight she would do her hair as she had done it for years, and she would wear one of her older dresses down to dinner. She had done the right thing, and she would soon be back in her usual spirits.

She did as she had planned, choosing a brown bombazine that had been enlivened only a little with lace at the neck and cuffs, and turning away Maisie's offer to put her hair up in the style she had worn last night.

Nor did she go down to supper early tonight, waiting instead until she heard Francesca leave her room, then joining her. In this way, she managed to avoid having to come face-to-face with Gideon before they all went in to supper. There, she knew, she would be distant enough from him that she would not have to talk to him.

Supper moved along at a glacial pace, seeming even slower due to the lack of conversation—except for that of Lady Odelia, of course, who could apparently always be counted upon to find something to talk about if she so desired.

Late in the course of the meal, however, Gideon spoke up, surprising everyone, as he had not joined the conversation before that point. "Grandmother, I should tell you that I have invited another guest to the party next week."

Irene saw little to shock anyone in such a pronouncement, but his words seemed to stun both Lady Radbournes, as well as Lady Pencully. The three of them turned to look at him, eyes wide and mouths ajar.

"I beg your pardon?" Lady Odelia said at last.

"I have invited one of my friends to join us next week.

Piers Aldenham. The party is rather overweighted with ladies. It seemed a good idea to add another man to the group. After all, there will be dancing." When none of the women said anything, simply continuing to stare at him in amazement and, Irene thought, horror, Gideon continued blandly. "I have already informed the butler and house-keeper, of course, so you needn't worry about that. But I thought I should let you know, as well, as you might need to make adjustments to your plans."

After a long moment Lady Odelia said, " A friend of yours? What do you mean? Someone you knew—before?"

"Precisely. Mr. Aldenham and I have been friends for, oh, ten or so years, I should say. I will be pleased to introduce him to you."

Teresa and Pansy both turned to Lady Odelia, who looked back at them, eyebrows raised, then returned her gaze to Lord Radbourne.

"You cannot be serious," she told him flatly.

"Indeed, I am."

"That is absurd! You cannot introduce one of…of…those people you used to know to the people we have invited."

"I cannot?" Gideon's voice was mild, but Irene detected an iron tone that seemed to escape his great-aunt completely.

Irene glanced across the table at Francesca, who was watching the exchange with interest, then returned her gaze to Lady Odelia.

"No, of course not," Lady Odelia boomed, looking as if she thought she were on firmer ground now. "You should have consulted me before you asked him. I would have told you that it would not do. It is very good of you, I am sure, to remember those people, but you cannot expect them to mingle with our sort."

"Indeed. So they will shun him, you think?" He continued meditatively. "It is a good thing then, I suppose, that Piers is not easily cast down."

"No, Gideon. You misunderstand me. You cannot invite him. You must send another note, telling him not to come. Perhaps next time you are in London you may visit with him."

"No, Aunt." Gideon's voice was level, but his eyes were cold as stone. "I fear it is you who misunderstand. I have invited him. He is coming here."

Lady Odelia gaped at him. Finally she snapped her mouth shut with a clack, then said, "No. I forbid it."

"You forbid it?" Gideon repeated, but his silky tone did not deceive Irene.

Lady Odelia regarded her great-nephew sternly. The woman was, Irene thought, in for something of a surprise.

"My lady." Gideon leaned forward slightly, and his words, cool and careful, dropped like hard stones from his mouth. "I fear that I have given you the wrong impression. I have gone along with your plans for my future because they coincided with my own intentions. Unfortunately, my acquiescence seems to have given you the impression that I have turned over the running of my life and this household to you. Allow me to remind you that Radbourne Park belongs to me, and that you and everyone else in this room are staying here on my sufferance. I will invite who I want to this house whenever I choose to do so. And while I will show you the respect your age and familial ties deserve, I am not now and never will be subject to your command. Piers will arrive here next week, and I expect him to be treated with courtesy. I hope I have made myself clear."

Lady Odelia, for once in her life, had no answer. She simply stared at Gideon, gaping.

He waited for a moment, then inclined his head briefly. "Ladies. As I am the only man present tonight, I believe I will take my port in my study. Excuse me."

He rose and strode from the room.

The stunned silence continued after his departure. Finally Francesca took a sip of her wine, then said, "Well, one can certainly see the Lilles blood in him."

Irene let out a chuckle, quickly covering her mouth with her napkin.

"What are we to do?" Teresa wailed, looking wildly around the table.

"It doesn't seem to me that you have much choice," Irene commented.

"You!" Teresa whirled on her. "Oh, yes, it's well enough for you. You won't be the one who is humiliated."

"Oh, dear," Pansy said anxiously, her eyes tearing up. "I'm afraid he's terribly angry with us now. Odelia…" She turned imploringly toward her older sister.

"Well." Lady Odelia looked shaken. "Well. He is an ungrateful pup, is he not? I have half a mind to wash my hands of him and go back to Pencully Hall."

"No! Odelia!" Pansy cried out, and now the tears spilled over, running down her cheeks. "Please, don't leave us with him."

Lady Odelia's face softened, and she reached out to pat her sister's hand. "There, there, now, Pansy, you know I shall not desert you. If I decide to go, you may come with me."

"Lady Radbourne," Irene said to Pansy, "I should not worry, if I were you. I do not believe that Lord Radbourne would harm you in any way. He does not strike me as a man who is spiteful."

"Of course he will not hurt you, Pansy," Lady Odelia told her sister. "Though I fear he is becoming recalcitrant." Her brow knitted in thought. "Why is he digging in his heels now?"

"Perhaps, my lady, he has simply become tired of being told what to do," Irene suggested. "No man of my acquaintance would meekly accept being told that he could not invite whom he wanted to his own party."

"There was something about him of our father, wasn't there, Pansy?" Lady Odelia said reflectively.

Pansy's only reply was a small moan of distress.

"Well," Lady Odelia went on. "Clearly the Ferrington chit will not do. No spine at all—she would never be able to direct him. Pity… Ah, well, good thing we have you, Irene."

"Excuse me?" Irene replied, facing Lady Odelia. "My lady, I meant what I said. I have no intention of marrying Lord Radbourne."

"Yes, well." Lady Odelia shrugged dismissively. "Easy enough to say, my girl. But we have all seen the way you jump to his defense."

"I was only being fair," Irene replied with some heat. "It does not mean I—I—have feelings for the man."

"Hmm. I suppose." Lady Odelia gave her a patronizing smile. "Still, I hope that you wake up to the truth…before Gideon gives up and chooses one of those other girls."

CHAPTER ELEVEN

IRENE WAS WISE ENOUGH to know that Lady Odelia was baiting her. She hoped, no doubt, to make Irene jealous with the mention of the other women and the suggestion that Lord Radbourne might choose one of them instead.

Irene, however, had no intention of being manipulated by Lady Odelia or anyone else. She reminded herself that it made no difference to her whether Gideon chose another woman for his wife, though she was honest enough to admit that she had felt a twinge of what she supposed might be jealousy at the thought of him marrying another. After all, over the course of the time she had been here, she had begun to like Gideon, and she could not help but think that if she were of a mind to marry, he might well be the man she would choose. And it was a rather heady sensation to be pursued by so eligible and attractive a man as Lord Radbourne.

But she was not going to marry, and she was not so weak as to allow her mind to be swayed by feelings of lust or pride. She sincerely hoped that she was not so ignoble as to wish for him not find happiness with some other woman if she herself would not marry him. So she was determined to ignore the little barbs that afflicted her now and then when she looked at Gideon and thought of him wooing another.

She stayed steadfast in her decision to quell the vanity that had inspired her to wear prettier dresses and arrange her hair in a soft, inviting style. There was no point in attracting Gideon's attention; indeed, it worked against her wishes. Moreover, she felt that returning to her old style sent an overt message to him and the matchmakers that she had no intention of trying to catch his favor.

They continued with the dancing lessons, as well as the rather stilted conversations between the three of them that were meant to improve the earl's social skills, but Irene made sure to maintain a correct distance between herself and Gideon, as well as a rather formal tone. She noticed a certain puzzlement in Francesca's eyes and an irritating amusement in his, but she strove not to let his attitude bother her. No doubt he wanted to goad her into one of their arguments. However, she was as aware as he that their arguments always resulted in an upheaval of emotions and produced a sort of intimacy that her pleasant-but-distant attitude discouraged.

Over the course of the next few days they developed a loose schedule of working in the mornings, then stopping their lessons just before luncheon. In the afternoons Gideon disappeared into his office or on business about the estate, and Francesca and Irene were left on their own to do as they wished—at least sometimes. Francesca spent much of her time helping with the plans for the upcoming week, and as a consequence, Irene often found herself involved in the preparations, as well.

Since interminable conversations regarding seating arrangements, floral decorations, menus and music bored her almost past bearing—and conversations about the merits of the various possible brides for Gideon were irritating in the extreme—Irene often avoided the drawing room after lunch, secreting herself in the library with a book or occupying herself in her room with the needlepoint she had been half-heartedly working on for the past month, or writing a letter to a friend or her brother.

She would have preferred to take a long walk, but after her experience the first day she was at Radbourne Park, she had been reluctant to run the risk of running into Gideon. However, she grew more and more restless, so on her fourth afternoon of inactivity, she decided that a walk through the gardens would be safe enough. After all, if Gideon was locked up in his study or out looking at his lands, he would not be idling about in the gardens. And in just a few more days the other guests would begin arriving, which Irene feared meant that she would rarely have much chance to be by herself.

She pulled her bonnet off the shelf and slipped out the back entrance onto the terrace, then down the steps into the upper garden, where she wandered onto the path, tying the strings of her hat as she went. With no destination in mind, she randomly took whatever paths forked off, looking at the autumn flowers. She stepped through a lattice archway, covered in ivy, and on the other side, as she turned to go through a gap in a hedge, she stopped.

There, in front of her, a small boy was crouched, intently studying the progress of a snail across the path. He whirled at the sound of her approach, looking alarmed. But when he saw her, he relaxed and stood up.

"Sorry," Irene said, smiling reassuringly. "I did not mean to frighten you."

"I thought you were Miss Tyning," he told her confidentially. He was a pleasant-looking, sturdy lad of five, with a thatch of sandy hair and a sprinkling of freckles across his snub nose. His eyes were the same light blue as Teresa's, confirming Irene's guess that this must be Timothy, Teresa's son, who had been rather inexplicably invisible since her arrival.

"She is my governess," he went on to explain. "And she will be ever so annoyed when she wakes up and sees that I've gone. But it was much too pretty a day to stay inside."

"Much too pretty," Irene agreed solemnly.

He regarded her for a moment. "You are the lady come to marry Gideon, aren't you?"

Irene lifted her eyebrows. "I am Lady Irene Wyngate. I am here to help his lordship, but no, I have no plans to marry him."

"That is what Mama says. She said it would never happen. But Lady Pencully said it would. And people always do what Lady Pencully wants."

"Indeed?" Irene smiled faintly. "I imagine they do, most of the time. But I think, this once, she will not get her way."

"Really? I hope not. I don't want Gideon to marry. Mama says that if he does, that will be the end of me."

"The end of you?" Irene repeated, shocked. "Whatever do you mean?"

Again he shrugged. "I don't know." He paused, then confided, "I think she does not like Gideon." He heaved a little sigh. "She does not like for me to be with him. But I like Gideon." His face lit up as he went on. "He is my brother, you know. I didn't have a brother until he came."

"It's very nice to have a brother," Irene commented. "I have one, too."

"Really? Is he as big as Gideon?"

"No, I do not think so. Your brother is rather large."

"I know. He says that I will be large one day, too. I hope so. I would like that."

"I imagine he is right. Your uncle Jasper is tall, as well."

Timothy nodded enthusiastically. "Yes, he is. Uncle Jasper is nice. But not as nice as Gideon. He doesn't say much to me. Mama doesn't like Uncle Jasper, either. But I don't think he's bad. Do you?"

"I don't know him well enough to say. Nothing about him struck me as bad, though. He is a little quiet and stiff."

"Gideon is much better," Timothy circled back to what was apparently one of his favorite subjects. "He likes to see the things I collect. Rocks and bugs and such. Sometimes in the afternoon he comes through the garden. That's why I come down here when Miss Tyning falls asleep."

"I see." Irene cast a look around, her heart suddenly picking up its beat. *Drat the man! Must he be everywhere?* "Do you think that he will be here today?"

"I don't know. Maybe."

"Perhaps I should go back into the house then—so that you and your brother can have your talk."

"He won't mind that you're here," Timothy assured her. "He likes people."

"Really?" This was a side of Gideon Irene had never noticed.

Timothy nodded. "He always talks to the gardeners and the grooms. Sometimes, when I sneak down to the kitchen for a snack, he's down there, talking and laughing with the cooks and the footmen and all. Except Horroughs." The boy pulled his face into a fair approximation of the butler's taut face. "I don't think Horroughs likes him."

"I'm not sure Horroughs likes anyone," Irene commented.

Timothy giggled and began to jump, chanting, "Horroughs doesn't like anyone. Horroughs doesn't like anyone."

Irene watched the boy's antics, smiling. It was hard to

imagine this cheerful, lively child being Teresa's son. Irene hoped that he would manage to remain relatively unspoiled by his mother's influence. At least he seemed to have disregarded her when it came to Gideon.

Because of the noise Timothy was making, she did not hear the crunch of boots along the path until they sounded right behind her. She whipped around to see Gideon stepping through the ivy-clad trellis that she had passed under a few moments earlier. He stopped when he saw her.

"Ah. Lady Irene. I wondered who Timothy was talking to."

"Lord Radbourne." She had delayed too long, she thought. She should have left as soon as Timothy had raised the possibility of Gideon appearing.

It occurred to her that he might think she had come this way in an effort to meet him. There were women, she knew, who spent a great deal of time making careful, precise plans to run into a man "accidentally." The practice was particularly in use at house parties.

"I was just out for a stroll when I ran into Master Timothy," she explained, then instantly regretted that she sounded as if she were making excuses for herself.

"I told her you might come," Timothy said, jumping happily into the conversation. "And you did!"

"Yes, I did. I am doubly glad that I did so now, as I get to see both you and Lady Irene." Gideon's face softened as he looked down at the boy, and he smiled, his usual wariness falling away. "What have you got to show me today?"

Gideon squatted down beside the boy to be face-to-face with him. Timothy smiled and began to dig in his pockets, pulling forth a variety of treasure: rocks, marbles, a ha'penny, a bent and rusty nail and an old key.

"My, look at that," Gideon commented, inspecting the items gravely. He picked up the key. "This looks as though it has been around for a long time. Someone must have been unhappy, don't you think, years ago when they lost it?"

Timothy nodded and began to explain when and where he had found each of the things he had deemed worthy of being shown to Gideon. When he had finished this rambling discourse, he pulled Gideon over to show him the snail he had been watching earlier, only to find that the creature had finally made its way across the path and had disappeared beneath a bush.

Irene, watching the two of them, was amazed at both Gideon's patience with the boy and his obvious affection for him. She would have said there was no softness in him, especially after the blunt set-down he had given the other evening to Lady Odelia.

But there was no hint of the autocrat in the man who listened so carefully to the small boy. Nor would she have guessed that the man she saw now would be intent on marrying for such cool, unemotional, businesslike purposes.

Gideon turned and saw her watching them, and he smiled at her. Her heart did a little turn in her chest as the full force of his easy, unfettered, genuinely happy smile hit her. The cold, hard angles of his face changed into a handsomeness that was both warm and compelling, pulling her in, and she could not have kept from smiling back at him even if she had wanted to.

Gideon rose lithely to his feet. "Well, much as I enjoy talking with you, Timothy, and seeing your treasures, I suspect that the excellent Miss Tyning is no doubt searching madly for you. We should take you back to the house."

The boy gave in without much complaining, and they

turned to go back down the path. Gideon paused beside Irene. "Won't you walk with us, my lady?"

"Yes, do," Timothy added, reaching out to take Irene's hand. He looked back toward Gideon and added confidingly, "I like her. She didn't scold me for getting dirty." He pointed toward the smudges on his knees where he had knelt on the path.

"Lady Irene is a jewel among women," Gideon agreed, casting an amused glance at her.

"I don't think she likes Horroughs, either," Timothy went on.

At that statement, Gideon chuckled. "Then she is definitely worthy of our friendship."

Timothy smiled happily. "I knew you'd like her." He turned to look up at Irene. "Are you going to come live here, too?"

Irene ignored the sideways look Gideon sent her and told Timothy, "I am merely visiting. I shall be here only for a week or two."

"Oh." Timothy looked downcast.

They emerged into the upper garden. As soon as they did, they saw a thin, nervous-looking woman in a plain brown bombazine dress hurrying along the main path, glancing anxiously down each row of shrubs she passed.

When the woman saw them, she let out a cry and hurried in their direction. "Master Timothy! There you are!"

She came to a stop before them, managing to look both furious at Timothy's escape and cowed by the sight of the Earl of Radbourne.

"I beg your pardon, my lord. I am so sorry if the boy has troubled you. I promise you it will not happen again," she said in a rush, reaching out to grab Timothy's other hand.

Irene gave Timothy's hand a reassuring squeeze before she released it, but in fact, she could not see that he looked particularly frightened at the prospect of his governess's wrath.

"Miss Tyning!" A shrill voice issued from above them on the terrace.

They all looked up and saw Lady Teresa standing there, her pretty doll-like features twisted into an expression of venom. She lifted her skirts and hurried down the steps toward them.

"Have you lost track of him again, Miss Tyning?" she exclaimed as she drew near, her voice high and shrewish. "I cannot conceive how a grown woman can be so easily outwitted by a five-year-old boy!"

"I am sorry, my lady," Miss Tyning said softly, curtseying before Teresa, her eyes turned down to the ground. "I— I thought he was playing in his room, and I—"

"He was merely in the garden," Irene put in, feeling sorry for the woman in the face of Teresa's anger. "He came to no harm."

Teresa turned her glare on Irene. "And you, an unmarried woman, know so much about children," she said with withering disdain.

Irene was not so easily intimidated as the governess, however, and she gazed back at Teresa with cool assurance. "I did not mean to discount the great worry that a concerned mother such as yourself must feel. Indeed, I am quite surprised that I have not seen Timothy before, for I am sure you must spend a great deal of time with him."

Teresa bridled at the ironic undertone of Irene's words, but Irene went on before she could speak. "However, though I may not know much about children, I have a great deal of faith in the fact that there is little harm that could come to Lord Radbourne's brother on the grounds of Radbourne Park. Timothy may have been out of sight of the house, but he was definitely not out of hearing, and I dare swear there are gardeners working about the grounds who could help him. Why, in the short time he was out there, both Lord Radbourne and I chanced past where he was. So I think you may rest easy that he was in no danger."

Teresa's glare remained unchanged. Without looking at either her son or his governess, she snapped, "Miss Tyning, take Timothy inside *now*. I will be up to deal with both of you later."

"Yes, my lady." Again the governess bobbed her obeisance to Teresa, then headed for the terrace, dragging Timothy with her.

The boy turned to look back at Gideon and Irene, and gave them an insouciant wave. Irene hid a smile at the gesture, but Gideon did not bother to hide his response and waved back.

"Stay away from my son!" Teresa ordered, turning to Gideon.

"I beg your pardon?" Gideon turned his gaze on her, flat and black, unyielding.

"You heard me," Teresa went on. "There is no reason for you to be around him."

"He is my brother," Gideon reminded her.

"He is none of your concern!" Teresa shot back.

Gideon raised his eyebrows a little at the force of her reaction, but he said nothing.

Teresa, however, was not finished. "You encourage him to misbehave. He did not escape from Miss Tyning nearly as often before you came to the Park."

"He knows that I frequently take a walk about this time in the afternoon," Gideon admitted. "I think perhaps he hopes to run into me here. If we were to set up a schedule, a time every day when he and I would go for a stroll, then he might not be tempted to 'escape,' and you would not have to worry that he might be in danger. It would be good for him."

"I am the one who will say what is good for Timothy," Teresa told him.

It seemed to Irene that Teresa looked even angrier than before at what seemed to her a very reasonable and even generous offer on Gideon's part. There were not many men who would suggest taking on the company of a lively five-year-old boy even for a few minutes each day. Irene started to give Teresa her opinion, then realized that would probably only annoy the woman even more and certainly wouldn't help Gideon and Timothy's case.

Teresa went on, her voice rising into a screech. "Do you think I want my son to spend more time with you? Do you think I want him to speak like a shopkeeper or have the manners of a street urchin?"

Irene drew in a sharp breath at the insult and glanced quickly at Gideon. His face was stony. He looked at Teresa for a moment, his lips pressed tightly together.

Then he said, "I am afraid that you are quite overset, my lady. No doubt your worry for your son impels you to say things that you will later regret. I suggest we both forget this conversation." He bowed slightly toward her. "No doubt you wish to get back to the nursery to look after your son."

He turned to Irene, offering her his arm. "Lady Irene? Shall we continue our walk?"

"Yes, of course." She put her hand on his arm, and they stepped away from Teresa.

Gideon's arm was like iron beneath her hand, and Irene cast a quick glance upward at his face. His expression was still like granite.

"You must not pay any attention to what Lady Radbourne said," Irene told him. "She is a fool."

"There is no denying that," he agreed.

"I am sorry."

"For what? You did nothing."

"I know. But still, I am sorry that she was…unkind."

"I have dealt with far worse than Teresa, believe me." He shrugged. "Anyway, she is merely the only one rude enough— or stupid enough—to say to my face what all my relatives feel."

"No. I am sure they do not," Irene protested. "Anyway, you don't speak like a shopkeeper. And your manners— well, perhaps you are not so polished as some gentlemen, but I have met a good number of gentlemen who are quite ill-mannered, I assure you."

He smiled, his face relaxing, as he flashed a look at her. "Are you trying to make me feel better, my lady?"

She lifted her chin. "I am simply telling the truth."

"Well, the truth is that I *was* a street urchin," he said.

"Yes, but obviously you became something much more than that," she pointed out. "As I understand it, even before the Duke of Rochford tracked you down, you had done well for yourself."

He looked at her. "I made a good deal of money, that is true."

"Well, that is admirable in itself, is it not?" she persisted.

"That you got out of the situation you were in, that you got away from that man you told me about—"

"Jack Sparks."

"And you stopped being a thief." She paused, then added, with a touch of concern, "Didn't you?"

Gideon laughed. "Yes. You need not worry that the Runners are going to track me down and toss me into gaol. All my business concerns are now legitimate. They were not always so, but I managed to become legal a good many years ago. I had no desire to end my days hanging from a gibbet."

They continued in silence for a moment, then Irene asked, "How did you do it?"

"Get out of the business of thievery, you mean?" he asked, looked surprised. "Do you really want to know?"

"Why, yes, why wouldn't I? It must be a most unusual story, I should think."

"It is not one that my family has been interested in hearing. Their main concern is to keep me from talking about my past, not encourage it."

Irene shrugged. "Well, I am interested in it. It would seem to me that it must have taken wits and courage."

"I think it was more bloody self-interest than anything like wit or courage," he responded. "I started thinking, why am I doing all the work, then giving this fellow all my money? Why do I have to settle for crumbs from him? So I started hiding some of the money I took from people, not giving it all to Sparks. I managed to get a bit of thread and a needle, and sewed a secret pocket inside my pants, and I'd take a bit out of each purse and hide it there. I had to take a caning a few times because he thought I hadn't brought back enough cash, but I considered it worth it to keep something for myself. Later I got big enough that when he tried to beat me, I was able to stop him."

He paused, and for a moment Irene thought that he had decided not to tell her any more. But then he said, "And after a while I went into business on my own."

"As a thief?"

"I was not perhaps always entirely honest, but no, my skills were not best suited to thievery. I grew too large to do well climbing into windows or slipping unnoticed through a crowd. I was bigger than most, and stronger. I knew how to fight. So I hired myself out to protect people."

"Protect people? Who?"

"There are always men whose lives are lived on the edge, who have enemies and no recourse to the authorities. They need someone they can count on to keep others from stealing from them or hurting them, and if you can do that well, they are willing to pay you a good deal of money. That was when I was still a lad, before I learned things. Before I figured out easier and better ways to make money."

"How did you do that?"

"I made it a point to learn from the men I worked for. I saw how they made money, and how others made money from them. I saw how the chain ran, and how those at the top used their brains instead of their muscles. And how those who made the most money made it legally. More importantly, they didn't wind up in gaol or dangling at the end of the hangman's noose."

"So how did you make the move from illegal to legal business?"

He shrugged. "Gradually, I suppose. I had my store of money, and I saved most of whatever I was paid. I wasn't going to be like the other lads I knew, spending every ha'penny they earned on gin and women. I lived lean. The last man I worked for owned taverns and gambling dens, along with some less savory businesses. I spent a good deal of time at them, too, and at one of them I got to know a chap who worked there. In fact, I saved him from having his throat slit by a dissatisfied customer."

"Really?" Irene turned wide eyes on him. "That sounds like more than dissatisfaction."

"Well, he was a rum 'un. One of your 'gentlemen.'"

"He doesn't sound like any sort of gentleman I would claim," Irene retorted.

"He resented losing all his money to Piers."

"Piers? The man you invited to the party?"

"Yes. He was the one who had won the money. Ask him— he'll be happy to show you the scar. An inch long, right here." He pointed to one side of his neck. "The fellow had a sword tip hidden in his cane. He waited outside until Piers left the place, then twisted the cane, and this thing popped out of the end. Piers was quick enough to bring up his hand and knock the thing aside, but he slipped and went down on the wet cobblestones. It would probably have been the end of him, but I happened to walk out right then, and I saw what was happening. So I took the cane away from the customer and sent him on his way."

"You make it sound so easy."

"He had little experience fighting. I did. The sword-cane did not improve his odds much. After that, Piers and I became friends. And eventually we went into business together. With a loan from my employer and the money I'd saved up, I bought a little place and turned it into a gambling den. Piers ran the place. Another friend of mine worked there, as well. And it was a success."

"Was it then that you met my father?" Irene asked.

He nodded, casting a sideways glance at her. "Yes. Lord Wyngate was a frequent customer…at least at first."

"Until you tossed him out."

"Yes."

"It seems that throwing him out must have been something of a risk," Irene commented. "He and his cronies would have been valuable customers."

"It was more important to establish control of my business. I had no intention of allowing anyone to dictate how I ran it. Nor did I have any interest in letting noblemen, or anyone else, abuse my workers." He shrugged. "In any case, it did me no harm. I might have lost a few customers, but my policy attracted others who appreciated knowing that the house was free of the rowdiness and low behavior with which many of the gambling dens were riddled. And those customers, it turned out, were generally more plump in the pocket than Wyngate and Haughston and their group."

"Then you knew Lady Francesca's husband, as well?"

He nodded. "Enough to know that she is better off being a widow."

"I imagine you're right," Irene agreed.

They continued to walk. Irene was very aware of the quiet around them and of Gideon's presence beside her.

"Odd, isn't it?" Gideon mused. "She did not manage for herself what she is apparently well-known for doing for others."

"'Tis easier, I suppose, to see clearly when one is not personally involved," Irene surmised.

"Or perhaps she learned from her own mistake." Gideon glanced at her. "It seems that ladies often do not take their opportunity to ensure financial success for themselves when they marry."

"It is looks and honeyed words that all too often sway them. It was so with my mother. Perhaps it was so with Francesca, as well. Lord Haughston was a handsome man. Desire can blind one to one's own best interests."

She cast a sideways glance up at Gideon, thinking of the way her own desire kept leading her astray with him, beckoning her into making the mistake she had always sworn not to. He caught her look, and a smile touched his lips.

Then he stopped and turned to face her, taking her hands in his. "Desire," he told her softly, "does not have to be a mistake. One can make the wisest decision and still take the path that passion leads one to."

"I am not sure that one's vision can be clear in that regard," Irene retorted. "Emotions and uh…" She cleared her throat, turning her gaze away from his eyes, for she found it difficult to speak looking up into their dark depths. "Sensations can make it difficult to think. To see one's way."

Gideon raised her hand and gently pressed his lips against the back of it. "Irene…I think in this instance that your 'sensations' give you a very clear picture of what this marriage could be. You have only to let yourself believe it."

He turned her hand over and laid another breath of a kiss in her palm. She felt the trembling in her hand—and the way it spread insidiously throughout her body. She looked at his head, bent to press his mouth to her skin. She saw the thick darkness of his lashes against his cheeks, the sensual curve of his mouth. His hair brushed against her wrist.

Had she always thought him this handsome? she wondered. When she met him, had other men paled beside him, as the thought of them did now? She could not remember any other man whose gaze had enthralled her as his did, or whose smile she had awaited with such anticipation. When and how had her heart taken to tripping like a hammer whenever she saw him?

She thought of the way she had held herself aloof from him the past few days, hoping to avoid a repetition of the kisses they had shared the other afternoon. And yet, after those days, those hours and hours of avoidance, all it took was a look from him, a smile, a kiss upon her hand, and she felt once more as if her knees were turning to jelly, that simmering burn beginning to bubble again deep in her abdomen.

It was frightening to feel so little in control of herself, scary to know that someone could affect her so effortlessly, so quickly, slipping past her defenses with the ease of smoke. And yet…and yet…

Where, she wondered, was the harm in taking a husband who could make one feel this way? Was what she felt the foolishness of women like Francesca or her mother, who had married those they had come to regret wanting? Or was this merely one of the benefits of a wise marriage—an extra dollop of sweetness on a practical course of action?

Gideon raised his head and looked into her eyes. She wondered if he could see the thoughts that danced in her brain, confusing her. She rather thought he must guess how he disturbed her. She could see the trace of male satisfaction in his eyes even through the heat that flamed in them.

He drew closer, his body only inches from her now. He still held her hand, and now he brought it up to his face, cradling it against his cheek. She felt the flash of heat, the smoothness of his skin, the prickles of the dark stubble that was beginning to roughen his flesh. She thought about feeling his cheek against hers, of his mouth pressing against her lips.

She remembered the way his hands had stroked her body that afternoon after their first dance lesson. Her breasts tightened at the thought, her nipples budding with yearning.

"You think that you have fooled me the last few days?" he murmured, and there was a raw ache to his voice that stirred her. "That I cannot see past the plain clothes? That I do not remember how full and soft your hair is, or how it curls around your face? I have seen how you dressed, how you have stifled your curls into a governess's knot." He bent close to her, his breath brushing against her hair as he talked, and Irene could not suppress the shiver that snaked through her.

"But I know you, Irene," he went on, his voice low and gravelly. "I have kissed you, and I have held you in my arms. I know the passion that lies within you."

He hooked his forefinger beneath her chin and tilted her face, so that she looked up into his eyes. She drew a shaky breath, unable to speak or move. He was going to kiss her, she thought. He would bend down and take her in his arms, and his mouth would lay claim to hers once more. She trembled, scared and excited and utterly uncertain.

For a long moment Gideon simply looked at her. When at last he moved, it was not to seize her in a fierce kiss, but to lean down and merely brush her lips with his.

"Do not deny us what we could have," he whispered, pressing his mouth gently to hers again. She found herself leaning into him, prolonging the contact.

He raised his head. "Think well before you decide, my lady."

He brushed his thumb over her bottom lip, then turned and strode rapidly away, leaving Irene looking after him, every nerve in her body alive and tingling.

CHAPTER TWELVE

IRENE WAS NOT CERTAIN how long she stood that way, dazed and shaken by the feelings swirling within her. She turned and moved back down the path toward the house, her steps slow, her face pensive. Her brain buzzed with thoughts, the encounter with Teresa and Timothy tumbling about with musings upon marriage and her feelings for Gideon, until she felt as if her head might explode from all that caromed around inside it.

She wished that there was someone to whom she could talk, but she was afraid to enlist either her mother or Francesca to aid her. She was certain that Lady Claire would urge her to marry Lord Radbourne, and she suspected that Francesca would probably do the same, though her words of advice would doubtless be couched in subtler language.

Irene was not accustomed to being confused and uncertain, and she did not care for the feeling. But she could not seem to bring herself back to her usual decisive state. She washed and dressed for dinner, half listening to the maid's friendly chatter. It was not until she was dressed that she realized she had chosen one of her new, more flattering dresses and had directed her maid to arrange her tresses in a softer style.

She looked at herself in the mirror for a moment and

wondered if she should change back into something plainer. But to do so, she thought, seemed even more foolish, and finally she left the room and made her way down to the anteroom where they gathered for supper.

She was surprised to find that Francesca was there before her. Usually Francesca liked to be the last to sweep into a room, but this evening she was here as early as Lady Odelia and her sister, and she seemed wrapped in a brown study, sitting by the window several feet from where Odelia and Pansy were talking together on the red velvet couch.

Irene crossed the room and sat down on a chair near Francesca, who looked up at her and smiled.

"Ah, there you are. I was just contemplating where to seat Lady Salisbridge, who, I just learned, is feuding with Mrs. Ferrington, who had the audacity to wear a dress just like one Lady Salisbridge owns."

"Oh, dear," Irene replied. "It does sound a serious matter."

"Yes. And made more so by the fact that the dress was rather more becoming on Mrs. Ferrington than it is on her ladyship. I just learned this by letter, and I now sincerely regret inviting both the Ferrington girl and Lady Salisbridge's daughters."

Irene shook her head, smiling. "I am sure it will resolve itself one way or another."

"No doubt. However, I would prefer that it not do so in a public hair-pulling." Francesca smiled, her cheek dimpling.

"I am surprised to see you down so early," Irene commented.

"Well, that is entirely your fault. You see, I had to escape from the drawing room this afternoon, so I had nothing to do except go up to my room and dress for dinner."

"And how did I cause that?" Irene asked.

"Ah, well, the reason I had to escape is that Lady Radbourne the younger was telling me, in great detail, about how she rescued Timothy from your clutches this afternoon. It seems that you and Lord Radbourne are corrupting her son."

Irene grimaced. "She was excessively insulting to Gi— to Lord Radbourne. I suspect the only reason he tolerates her is because of her son. He is fond of Timothy—who is such a winning boy that I can scarcely believe he is related to Lady Teresa."

Francesca chuckled. "I have not seen the lad. But it certainly could not be bad if he were corrupted from Teresa's ways."

"I would think she would be glad that the man spends time with Timothy. With his father gone, I'm sure it is good for him to have a man whom he can admire. But Lady Teresa told Radbourne that she did not want her son taking on his— manners and speech."

"Lady Teresa is a fool," Francesca replied dispassionately. "And I dare swear that her son is the least of her concerns. I have never met a less maternal woman. Lady Odelia is certain that the only reason she had the boy was because she thought she would be the mother of the Earl of Radbourne when Lord Cecil died." She smiled a little wickedly. "I would have liked to see her face when Rochford announced that he had located the rightful heir."

"Francesca…" Irene began, reminded by Francesca's comment of her conversation with Gideon on her first evening at Radbourne Park.

The other woman turned to look at her, her interest raised by the suddenly serious tone in Irene's voice. "What?"

"I have been wondering. Doesn't it seem a trifle odd that the family was unable to locate the earl all those years that he was missing, but then the duke was able to find him within a matter of months?"

Francesca looked at her for a long moment. "What are you suggesting?"

"I'm not sure. But the first evening we were here, Radbourne pointed out how easily Rochford tracked him down and wondered how it could have been so hard for his father. It…well, I cannot help but wonder."

"You would understand if you knew Rochford," Francesca assured her. "That is simply the way he is. I have never known a more irritating man. He is always right." Her eyes glinted and her mouth narrowed as she contemplated the duke's annoying ways. "He will be the one person who thinks to take an umbrella on an outing. Worse, you will point out that the day is sunny and the umbrella quite unnecessary, and then, naturally, it will rain. Or you will have looked for a book or an earring or something everywhere for days, and he will sit down and reach in between the sofa cushions and say, 'Oh, look, here's a book someone mislaid.' He is exasperatingly competent."

"Oh."

"Also," Francesca went on, obviously warming to her subject, "he is so utterly single-minded and completely stubborn that he will continue to pursue a subject long after any more reasonable person would have given it up."

Irene blinked. "I see. Forgive me, I thought you and the duke were friends."

"Friends?" Francesca repeated, her voice laced with irony. "I doubt that 'friends' would be an adequate description of…whatever it is we are." She paused, thinking, then said, "I suppose you could call us acquaintances—of a rather long duration."

There was more to this story, Irene thought, but at the moment she was too intent on the subject on her mind to pursue this secondary trail. "Still, doesn't it seem a bit strange that Gideon was not discovered before now? Even if the duke is a persistent man, one would think that Radbourne's father would have pursued his disappearance as diligently as a—what, second cousin?"

Francesca frowned thoughtfully. "Yes, I suppose he would have. But it could be that when Radbourne was a child someone was hiding him, trying to keep anyone from locating him. But now that he is an adult, he is no longer hidden. Indeed, he is a successful businessman and therefore easy to find." She paused, then continued. "What does Radbourne think—that his father did not try to find him?"

Irene shrugged. "I am not sure. It seems unlikely. But I have thought about it a good deal since Radbourne mentioned it, and there were a number of oddities about the whole thing."

"Oddities?" Francesca frowned and leaned a little closer. "What oddities?"

"Well…for instance, why did the kidnappers take both the boy and his mother? A child would be easy to handle. Less noticeable. But a woman and a child—one has two people to try to control. A woman is more difficult to conceal or to carry. And a mother bent on saving her child is certain to struggle, wouldn't you think?"

"Yes. But perhaps they could not snatch the child except when he was with his mother. He was only a little boy, so he was probably always with his nurse or his mother. They could also have presumed that they would get a higher ransom for both of them."

"Did they demand ransom for both?" Irene asked.

"I have no idea. I never asked about it."

"And what happened to his mother? If the boy was turned loose by himself, I can understand that he would not know where to go or what to do. He might not remember his home or be able to tell anyone where he was from or who his father was. And if he did, people might just assume it was a jest. But his mother would have come back here."

"Maybe he was not turned loose. Maybe they kept him and raised him."

Irene thought about this idea for a moment. She supposed that it was possible that the Jack Sparks Gideon had lived with could have been the one who abducted him. Still, that left questions unanswered. "Then where was his mother?"

"They may have killed her," Francesca responded.

"And why did they not give him back when his father paid the ransom? Everyone assumed that they had killed the boy, and that was why they did not return him. But obviously they did not."

"Give who back? What are you girls talking about?" Lady Odelia's voice boomed from across the room.

Francesca cast her an apprehensive glance. "Oh. Um. Why, nothing."

"Nothing?" Lady Odelia arched one eyebrow. "How can you talk about nothing?"

"We were discussing Lord Radbourne's kidnapping," Irene explained calmly. "Lady Haughston did not wish to disturb you."

Gideon's grandmother gasped, but Lady Odelia merely grunted and said, "Obviously *you* have no such compunction."

"It is my belief that if one asks about another person's

conversation, then one must be prepared to hear about whatever that conversation was," Irene retorted imperturbably.

Humor glinted for an instant in the older woman's eyes. "I see. Pert young thing, aren't you?"

"Yes, indeed she is," Teresa put in. Irene had not noticed that Teresa had come into the room while she and Francesca were talking. Now Teresa walked over to sit down with the older women, at some remove from Francesca and Irene.

Teresa looked at Irene with disdain as she went on. "I find that Lady Irene also seems to be remarkably concerned with other people's affairs."

Lady Claire, who was just entering the room, colored a little and hastened to intervene. "I am sorry, Lady Odelia, I am afraid that Irene can be a mite too blunt at times."

"Nothing wrong with honesty, Claire," the older woman said. "Don't worry yourself into a taking. Always better to be blunt, I say, than to be one of those dreadful girls who cannot utter a plain statement. I find nothing wrong in a having a healthy curiosity." She cast a significant glance at Teresa before returning her gaze to Irene. "What were you saying about the kidnapping?"

"Everyone has heard about it, of course, but I have never really known the details. Perhaps it is simply that I do not know the full story, but it seems to me that there were some curious circumstances."

"Indeed?"

"For one thing, is it not peculiar that the Duke of Rochford, while obviously a very capable man, was able to locate the earl with so little effort, yet no one was able to find him before?"

Pansy's eyes widened, but Odelia simply nodded. "Ah, is Gideon wondering about that? I must say, it does seem that

Cecil should have learned more." She shrugged. "I was not here at the time, so I don't know exactly what was done to find Gideon and his mother. I could not come, despite Pansy's pleading with me to, as my youngest girl was having her lying-in right about then."

She glanced around. "Pansy is the only one who could tell you about that time. It was long before you were here, Teresa."

"Actually, Lady Odelia, I was here," Teresa replied unexpectedly. When everyone turned to look at her in surprise, she added, "Not here at Radbourne Park. But my family lives only a few miles away. I remember all the excitement. Naturally I was still rather young—I had not yet made my come-out. I was— Oh, I must have been about fifteen. The abduction was the talk of the countryside for months. But of course, I did not know all the details of it, only the bits and pieces of gossip that I overheard. No one would speak to a young girl about such matters."

"I expect that Cecil mishandled the search," Lady Odelia commented. "He always was one to let his anger blind him to good sense."

"Odelia!" her sister cried out indignantly. "How can you say such a thing? Cecil did everything he could. Why, he sent Owenby all over the countryside looking for some clue to where they had gone. How could anyone be expected to track down the ruffians, with no idea who they were or where they went?"

"How were Lord Radbourne and his mother taken?" Irene asked the old woman gently.

"How?" Pansy looked at her blankly. "What do you mean?"

"Were they stolen from the house? Were they out for a stroll?"

"Oh. I...um...I'm not entirely sure. It has been so long." Pansy looked down at her hands, knotted together in her lap. "It was such a dreadful time. Poor Cecil was so overset."

Lady Odelia let out an inelegant snort. "I imagine he was! No doubt he strode about all over the place, shouting and slamming things and getting nothing useful accomplished."

"Odelia!"

"I am sure he was most upset," Francesca told Pansy soothingly.

Irene added, "Then you do not remember if Lady Radbourne and her son were in the house or were taken outside?"

"Outside," Pansy said quickly, nodding her head. "Yes, it must have been outside. No one would have been able to just burst in here and grab them. They were in the garden—yes, that is it. They were in the garden."

"Did no one see them taken?" Irene continued.

"No. They were quite alone. The kidnappers got away clean as a whistle."

"How did you learn what had happened to them?"

"What? Why, Cecil told me."

"But how did he come to know? Did he receive a note?"

"Oh! Oh, yes, he told me that they had sent him a letter, demanding that he hand over the Bankes rubies for his son— and Selena, of course. Beautiful necklace, given to the family by Queen Elizabeth herself. Part of a treasure trove captured from the Spanish queen."

She stopped after that, and finally her sister said impatiently, "Well, go on, Pansy, what happened after that? What did he do with the necklace?"

"Oh, well, he gave it to his man, Owenby. You probably don't remember him. He was Cecil's valet, had been with him from the time Cecil was barely more than a lad. Owenby was someone whom Cecil could trust absolutely."

"So Cecil did not think that this chap took the necklace himself and merely pretended to give it to the kidnappers?" Lady Odelia asked.

"No! No, of course not." Pansy looked shocked. "Owenby would never have done anything to harm Cecil. Never. He—he took the necklace and gave it to them, but they did not return Gideon."

"Or Lady Radbourne," Irene added.

"Yes, of course."

"Do you mean that this valet met the kidnappers face-to-face?" Irene asked, her voice tinged with surprise. "Was he able to recognize them?"

"What? Oh, no, of course not. I believe he left the necklace…somewhere, and then they were going to let Gideon go, but they did not. Gideon was supposed to be, um, up by that large old oak. The one along the road into town. So Owenby left the necklace for them, then went to the tree, but Gideon was not there. Owenby waited and waited, of course, but the boy never appeared. When Owenby went back to where he had left the necklace, it had been retrieved."

"What did Lord Radbourne do then?" Francesca asked, her interest obviously aroused.

"Why, he sent Owenby to look for them, of course. He looked everywhere. Went to Liverpool and Southampton, all the ports."

"The ports?" Irene asked, surprised. "He thought the kidnappers had taken them out of the country?"

The elder Lady Radbourne stopped, blinking, and color seeped into her cheeks. "Oh, well, I—I'm not sure. I suppose they would not have, would they?" She glanced around, as though seeking answers from the room.

Her sister fixed her with a firm stare. "Pansy, stop being so featherbrained. Where did Cecil send Owenby to look for them?"

"Well, I know the fellow went to London to make inquiries, but no one had seen them," Pansy offered weakly.

"And that is all you can remember about the affair?" Lady Odelia asked.

"It was a long time ago!" Pansy flared up. "And we were all rather overset at the time. I— My memory is perhaps not the best."

"It sounds as though this man Owenby is the person to talk to," Irene remarked. "Is he still alive, Lady Radbourne?"

Pansy turned to Irene with a look almost of horror. "No! I mean, well, yes, he is alive, but he no longer works here. He, um, left our employ after Cecil died."

"Does he live in the village? Gideon—I mean, Lord Radbourne—could go talk to him."

Pansy blinked, then said weakly, "Oh, I am sure that is unnecessary. My grandson needn't speak to the man. It would—it would be too painful, surely."

"Nonsense," her sister told her stoutly. "Why should it be painful? I imagine the boy would like to learn all he can about what happened to him. Better to know, isn't it, than to wonder?"

"Better to know what?"

Everyone turned to look at the doorway, where Gideon

stood looking at them. He repeated, "Better to know what? Wonder about what? Is this boy you are discussing me, Aunt Odelia?"

"Yes, of course. Irene brought up the subject of what happened to you all those years ago."

"Did she now?" Gideon's gaze flickered to her.

"Yes," Irene replied, facing him calmly. "I am sorry if you find the matter disturbing. I had some questions...."

"As you know *I* do," he told her. "And I do not find the matter disturbing. How like you, of course, to charge the battlements." A smile flickered across his lips. He turned toward his grandmother. "I should have broached the subject earlier with you."

"Pansy was telling us that the man your father sent in search of you is still alive," Lady Odelia told him, taking charge. "He could tell you much more about it, I am sure."

"Your grandmother was just about to tell us where Owenby lives now," Irene added, bringing the conversation back to the question she had asked Pansy just before Gideon came into the room, a question that she noticed the woman had never answered. Gideon's grandmother, she thought, seemed peculiarly reluctant to talk about the whole incident.

Pansy shot her a look that, coming from some other woman, would have been venomous, but which from Pansy came across as more agonized than fierce. "Lady Irene...it really..." She swiveled her head toward Gideon but obviously found no comfort there. "I—I'm not sure where the valet went. But really, Gideon, there is little point in your seeing him." Her face turned entreating. "It would be better if you just let this whole matter...remain in the past."

Gideon looked at her for a long moment. "No, I don't think

so. I am sorry if this distresses you, Grandmother, but I would like to talk to this man. Owenby, you said his name was?"

"Please, Gideon…" Pansy's voice was soft, seemingly on the verge of tears. "What good will this accomplish? Owenby probably does not remember it well. It was so long ago."

"Oh, stop being such a ninny, Pansy," Lady Odelia told her sister bluntly. "As if he wouldn't remember charging all over the country, searching for a gang of kidnappers!"

"Odelia!" Pansy looked from her to Gideon. "Please, can we not talk about something more pleasant?"

Gideon's expression hardened. "Why are you so reluctant to discuss this? Do you not want me to learn the truth? Are you afraid that I will find out how very little my father cared? How little interest he showed in finding me?"

"No!" Pansy cried. "Cecil cared! He was devastated! You must not think that your father was indifferent. He was in such a state—I have never seen a man more overset than he was. She didn't deserve his sorrow!"

Gideon froze. The air was suddenly thick with silence.

"What?" Gideon asked at last. "What do you mean, 'she didn't deserve his sorrow'? Are you talking about my mother?"

"No! I didn't mean—" Pansy cast a panicky look around the room.

"Pansy!" Lady Odelia's voice was sharp and commanding. "Stop dithering. Tell me right now—what *did* you mean by that?"

Pansy looked as if she might faint, but finally she squared her shoulders. "Forgive me, Cecil," she murmured, throwing a glance upward, then added, in a stronger voice, "But I refuse to let you believe that your father was not concerned about you, Gideon. It was Selene who separated you from your father and your family."

"What?" She was greeted by a chorus of astonished voices.

Pansy raised her chin somewhat defiantly. "You were not kidnapped, Gideon. Your mother ran off with her lover and took you with her."

CHAPTER THIRTEEN

FOR A LONG MOMENT no one spoke, too shocked to utter anything. Irene cast an anxious glance at Gideon, who had gone pale and was staring at his grandmother.

It was Lady Odelia, not unexpectedly, who spoke first. "Are you mad? Pansy!"

"No. I am not mad," Pansy replied, though her voice had dropped to so low a whisper that it was difficult to make out what she said. "It's the truth."

"No! It cannot be!" Lady Teresa's voice rose in a wail. "She was kidnapped. Everyone knows that. She died years and years ago!"

"Are you saying that Cecil lied to everyone all those years ago?" Lady Odelia pressed her sister. "That you lied?"

Pansy nodded, and suddenly her eyes flooded with tears that began to spill down her face. "Yes. Yes. We lied. To everyone."

She pressed her hand against her mouth, as if in a futile attempt to stop her words.

"No, no," Lady Teresa moaned, shaking her head.

"But why?" Irene asked, unable to keep still. Her heart clenched in her chest as she thought of what Gideon must be feeling now. His whole world had been overturned only a few months ago when the duke had found him. Now it had been thrown into a tumult all over again. "Why did you pretend that they were kidnapped?"

"Because Cecil could not bear for anyone to know the truth!" Pansy cried. "The scandal…"

"He did it to cover up a scandal?" Irene asked, appalled.

"Not for himself!" Pansy cried. "For her! He did it for Selene. Even then he loved her. He—he was certain that she would see the folly of her ways and return to him in a few days. He did not want her to have to suffer the sort of gossip that would ensue if everyone knew what she had done."

"More likely his pride would not let him admit that his wife would leave him," Odelia snapped.

"Odelia! How can you say that?" her sister protested. "Cecil's heart was broken. You were always unfair to him."

"And you were always a weak reed," Odelia retorted. "How do you know that she ran away?"

"Why, Cecil told me, of course." Pansy looked at Odelia with amazement. "He would not have withheld such a thing from me. He came to me, waving the letter Selene had left for him. It was all blotched with tears—as if she were the one whose heart had been broken. She told him that she was sorry, but she loved someone else, and that she was leaving with him that night. She begged him to let her go, not to look for her. Cecil found it in his study the next morning."

"And he just let her go?" Gideon asked. His voice was quiet, his face like stone. "He let her take his son from him?"

"I told you, he was certain she would be back. He was positive that she would regret her actions and return, full of apologies, so he made up the story of the kidnapping, pretended that the letter he had found in her room was a notice from the kidnappers. He had Owenby take the necklace and ride off as if he were fulfilling their demands, but of course the man just brought back the necklace and Cecil hid it away, then pretended that it was gone."

Pansy sighed, then went on, her voice quavering a little. "After a time, when he realized that Selene was not going to return or even contact him again, Cecil fell into a dark despair. He stayed in his room. He lost interest in everything. Why, the estate manager had to come to *me* to ask about problems that arose, because Gideon would not see him."

Pansy's face reflected the seeming horror of that memory.

"But eventually he must have come to his senses," Lady Odelia told her sister. "I know Cecil did not spend the remainder of his life locked away in his room, grieving."

"No, of course he did not," Pansy agreed. "Finally he returned to himself. He began to take an interest in things again, bit by bit. He did send Owenby out to try to find her and Gideon, but by then the trail had grown terribly cold. He could find no trace of Selene or their son. Cecil was sure that she and her lover must have had a plan laid out before they left. He thought they must have driven straight to a port and sailed out of the country almost immediately. Owenby went to London, even to Liverpool, but he could find no record of their having been there or having boarded a ship, though no doubt they would have been smart enough to use false names. And they could have sailed from anywhere. Cecil sent a man to Europe to look for them, but he had no success, either. In all likelihood they sailed to one of the Colonies. Any place where they would have been impossible to find."

"But what about his son?" Lady Odelia burst out.

Irene's eyes flashed to Gideon's face. The old woman's question was the same one that burned on her tongue, but she would not let herself speak it, knowing the agony that

Gideon must be suffering. He had learned that he had not been torn from his home and family and thrown into a life of hardship and poverty by villains, but by his own mother. And his father had not even tried to get him back, at least at first.

Obviously Lady Odelia had no such compunctions, however, as she said, "Gideon was his heir. I cannot believe that Cecil would not have gone after him and brought him back."

"I urged him to look for the boy," Pansy insisted. "I reminded him that he must have an heir. It did not matter if she was gone, but the succession was at stake." She shook her head. "He did not seem to care. He said it did not matter, that his brother was there to inherit after him. He refused to pursue a woman who did not want him. Who had gone to such great lengths to escape him."

She looked around at the others' shocked expressions, then added guiltily, "He did not know that Gideon was on his own in London. It never occurred to us that Selene would abandon the boy. How were we to know? We thought that Gideon was all right, that he was with his mother."

Lady Odelia shook her head, looking dazed. "I cannot believe it. Even of Cecil. How could you have let him? How could you have been so bacon-brained?"

"I didn't know!" Pansy wailed, bursting into full-blown tears. "I—I meant no harm!"

Gideon turned on his heel and strode out of the room.

"Oh, hush, Pansy!" Lady Odelia exclaimed in irritation, turning to her sister and mechanically patting her shoulder.

Only a foot away from her, Lady Teresa looked about to succumb to a similar bout of tears. Irene, ignoring them both, jumped to her feet and hurried out of the room.

"Gideon!"

He was already halfway down the hall, but he stopped and turned back to look at her. She hurried toward him.

"Wait! I will go with you," she said.

He shook his head. His face was dark with emotion, his eyes fierce. "No. I am not fit company right now."

He swung around and continued down the hall, not waiting for her. She ignored his words, trotting after him.

"I am sure you are not," she told him, catching up to him as he opened the door onto the terrace. "But neither are you fit to be alone."

Ungraciously he shrugged and strode off across the terrace. She walked with him, hurrying to keep up with his long strides. Wisely she did not try to talk to him, merely walked with him down through the garden.

Finally, as if he could hold it in no longer, he burst out, "Clearly he cared nothing for me! He let me go without even trying to get me back." Gideon cast a burning look at Irene. "How can that be? A father who has no interest in his son? Even my grandmother seemed to care nothing about me except for the fact that I was his heir!"

"Perhaps your father believed that you were best off with your mother. You were quite young, only four. And he did not know that you were on the streets of London, after all."

Gideon gave her a speaking look, and Irene did not try to continue her argument. Clearly it was weak, and, in truth, she could not even believe it herself.

After a few more minutes, Gideon came to a halt. They had reached a wide-spreading oak that stood at the far end of the garden, a large and solitary outpost of the woods that started not far past it. An iron bench stood beneath its shady branches, and during the day one could sit upon it and contemplate the countryside spread out before one.

Gideon clamped his hands around the back of the bench and looked out, as if he could see the vista before him. He shook his head and began to speak again, not looking at Irene but staring straight in front of him.

"My father's indifference to me does not really matter, I suppose. I have long suspected that he did not care enough to look for me. But to find out that my mother—" He bit off the words.

Irene reached out silently and laid her hand upon one of his. "I am so sorry."

"I always assumed that my mother was dead. Otherwise, I thought, she would not have let me go. Even as a child, I recall being certain that she must be dead or I would have been with her. After Rochford found me and I learned about the 'kidnapping,' I was more certain than ever that she was dead. I knew, deep down, that she, at least, had loved me. Now…to find out that she abandoned me, that she fled with a lover and left her child to whatever fate awaited him on the streets of London…! What sort of woman could do that? What kind of a woman was she?"

"You do not know any of that is true!" Irene protested. "Perhaps your mother *did* die. You cannot remember what happened—you were too young. Just because the two of you were not abducted, it doesn't mean that she abandoned you. After all, why would she have taken you with her at all if she did not want you? It would have been far easier to have left you behind. It is quicker to travel without a child. Easier to pass unnoticed. And she must have realized that a man would be more likely to chase his wife down if she had taken his son and heir with her when she left him." She shook her head. "No, I cannot help but think that she took you only because she could not bear to leave you behind.

She must have loved you very much. Whatever she might have felt about her husband or her marriage or this supposed lover, she must have loved you."

"Then how did I end up alone in London?"

"I don't know. I don't suppose we shall ever know," Irene replied honestly. "Any number of things could have happened. She might have fallen ill and died there, so the man she was traveling with left you. Or perhaps he abandoned her along with you, and then she grew ill and died, or was somehow taken from you."

"Or her lover could have grown tired of hauling a brat around with them and demanded that she leave the boy behind. She betrayed her husband. She besmirched her own name. Why would she balk at abandoning an inconvenient child?"

Irene's heart was heavy with pity for Gideon. She could not imagine how it must feel to have learned that his mother had abandoned him. Despite her troubles with her father through the years, she had at least always been certain of her mother's love. What, she wondered, must it be like to have had none of that sure, abiding love? Gideon had been on his own for as long as he could remember, with no one to depend upon or trust absolutely.

"I am so sorry," she murmured, aware of how weak her words must sound. She could think of no way to convey the depth of her sympathy, and of course, she could not fully understand how he felt.

Gideon shrugged, his face set and unemotional. "This news changes nothing in my life. After all, I have no real memory of my mother. It is not as if someone I knew betrayed me."

"Yes, but what you believed is as important as what you

actually remembered. You were certain that your mother did not abandon you or else you would have been bound to feel betrayed by her."

"What I believed did not change the facts. I was alone then, just as I am alone now."

"No, you are not alone!" Irene cried, taking a step closer to him, reaching out to touch his arm. She drew a breath, ready to point out that she was with him, but she realized at the last moment that she was committing herself to a closeness that was not true. She might be literally with him right now, but that situation would not last long. She would not remain with him as a wife or even as a friend when these two weeks were gone.

Her hand fell from his arm, and she looked away from him. "That is…I mean, you are about to get married. You will have the companionship and support of your wife, so you will no longer be alone."

He let out a short, unamused laugh. "A wife who is willing to marry such a disreputable sort as I in order to gain wealth and a title? Somehow I cannot feel that ours will be a close union."

"It does not have to be that way," she protested.

Gideon cocked an eyebrow in a look of disbelief. "You cannot really believe that. It scarcely jibes with your refusal to marry. How can I expect support and companionship, even affection from a woman whom I will, in your opinion, tyrannize and abuse?"

"I do not think that you will tyrannize or abuse your wife," she replied candidly.

"You certainly made a very good pretense of believing just that."

"No, I am simply not willing to subject myself to the life

I would have if I am wrong. But I am not like most women. Few women expect or even think of the worst that a marriage can provide. Many woman are in love with their husbands. There are those who maintain that marriage is a partnership, a true union of two people. At the very least, it will provide you with a wife and children—you will have the family you never had as a child."

"I am not looking to create a family for myself," Gideon replied curtly. "I told you that when I first met you. I am simply doing what is reasonable for a man in my position. What is expected of me. I have no intention of marrying for love."

"You offer a woman a cold sort of life," she told him, bristling.

"I offer a woman wealth, a title and an easy life. The only drawback in the arrangement for her is me, and I will make sure that she has to put up with my presence as little as possible." His face was hard and set, his eyes as cold as stone. He looked, Irene thought, like a stranger. "I can assure a woman that she will not be harmed by me nor smothered."

"No, only ignored," Irene retorted.

"Why do you care what my intentions are toward my wife?" Gideon snapped, anger flaring in his eyes. "You have made it very clear that you have no interest in that position. I would have thought that such an arrangement would have suited you admirably—being left to your own devices, with none of the inconveniences of a husband. But you have assured me over and over again that you have no intention of marrying me. So I fail to see why you should care what sort of marriage I have."

"I do *not* care!" Irene shot back, glaring at him.

For a long moment they faced each other stiffly, eyes

bright with anger. He half turned away, then sighed and swung back.

"I apologize. I fear that I am very poor company tonight. It is no doubt best if I take my leave of you now."

He pivoted and walked away toward the house.

Irene watched him go. Finally, with a sigh, she followed him back down the path. She was annoyed not only with Gideon but with herself. She did not know why she had said the things she had. He had been right on all counts. She was not interested in marrying him; she had more than once assured him that she would not. It was, therefore, no concern of hers what sort of marriage he made for himself. She might wish that he could find happiness in his marriage, but it would mean nothing to her life.

Looking back on it, she could see the absurdity of their conversation. She had been presenting him with exactly the sort of arguments that her mother and others had pressed on her for years. How many times had she heard that marriage was a true union of souls? How often had people assured her that her husband would provide her with happiness and love for the remainder of her life? She had always scoffed at such statements. Yet today she had been spouting the very same sort of pap to him.

Could it be, she wondered, that deep down inside she really believed those romantic notions about love and marriage? She did not. She *could* not. Yes, this afternoon, she had been in something of a turmoil after her talk with Gideon in the garden. He had perhaps shaken her resolve, made her wonder for a while if she was somehow making a mistake in rejecting him.

But that was just momentary nonsense, she reminded herself. She knew what marriage was really like. No, she did

not believe those things she had said to him. She had simply
been trying to comfort him in a time of distress, trying to
make him feel better. So she had told him the first thing that
had come into her head; she had told him what she wished
were true.

Irene came to a halt, struck by that thought. She would
not have suspected that such a longing lived in her, but now
she could see that it did. She had been too practical, too realistic, to believe in some rosy vision of love and partnership. But deep down inside her, hadn't she wished that such
a thing could actually exist? Was there a hunger in her for
that sort of love—a hunger that Gideon had awakened?

She sank onto a stone bench that lay beside the garden
path, her legs suddenly shaky beneath her. She felt as if she
no longer knew herself. She had always been so sure. So
right. She had, she knew, even felt a trifle smug that she was
not as weak as other women.

But what if it was not that she was strong in her convic-
tions but merely that she had never met a man who could
make her feel the way Gideon did? So giddy and excited and
fluttering with life?

Irene put her hand against her stomach, almost as if she
could hold in the turmoil that bubbled inside her. She liked
the way she felt when Gideon kissed her; it was wonderful in
a way she had never known, never even dreamed of. But it
was scary, as well. Where would that desire lead? Surely she
could not go against everything she had believed for all these
years just because she suddenly had this hunger inside her.

Even if she had had a secret wish that love could bloom
in a marriage, what did that matter? She knew that it was
nothing but a wish, a hope. It was not real. If she had needed
any reminder of that, she had just received it from Gideon

himself, who held out an offer of marriage so cool and indifferent that it could freeze even the most hopeful heart.

No, even if her feelings might have changed, the truth of the matter remained the same. Marriage was a trap for a woman, and wavering in that belief would lead to a lifetime of regret.

She realized that she had been behaving as foolishly as any of the women whom she had criticized in the past. But at least she knew better and could stop behaving in this foolish manner. However much she might feel sympathy for the man, however much she might enjoy talking with him, she was no longer going to indulge in any dangerously lax behavior. There would be no more long walks with him in the garden or flirtations with him as they danced.

She was here to help Gideon find a suitable wife. The women in question would be arriving the day after tomorrow. And she was going to concern herself only with making sure that one of them became the next Countess of Radbourne.

Irene nodded sharply, as though she had made a point to someone who opposed her, and stood up. There was an odd little ache deep in her chest that she was determined to ignore. It would go away soon, after all, and she would concentrate on doing what she had come here to do. Back straight, shoulders squared, she strode back to the house.

CHAPTER FOURTEEN

THE HOUSE WAS IN a turmoil the next day. Gideon left for the estate manager's office immediately after breakfast and was gone the remainder of the day. His absence excused Francesca and Irene from their usual dancing lessons, which meant that they were free to turn their attention to the upcoming party.

It was a good thing, Irene decided, for no one else in the house seemed able to do so. Gideon's grandmother took to her bed with a fit of the vapors. Her maid refused to let anyone in, but of course Lady Odelia eventually bullied the poor woman into submission and went in to talk to Pansy. However, since it was Lady Odelia's harsh assessment of the way Pansy and her son had dealt with what happened twenty-seven years earlier that had originally sent the delicate woman into hysterics, Lady Odelia's presence did little to improve the situation.

The younger Lady Radbourne was also suffering from a fit of nerves brought about by the news. She kept bursting into tears and moaning that she should never have married Cecil. Even the redoubtable Lady Odelia was clearly shaken by the situation.

It took all of Lady Claire's considerable skills at soothing fears and placating ruffled tempers to keep the three of them somewhat calm. Therefore, all the last-minute details of the large house party fell to Francesca and Irene. There were vases to fill and place cards to write out in elegant copperplate cursive, plans to be finalized for the ball, questions from harried servants to be answered, menus to be approved and changed, and of course, the swarm of problems that always seemed to arise at the final moment.

It was not until late in the afternoon that Irene managed to pry Francesca away from the housekeeper's clutches and lead her out for a restorative stroll about the gardens.

"Thank goodness you lured me away from the house," Francesca said with a sigh, linking her arm through Irene's and turning her face up, as though to drink in the warm sun. "Such a to-do. Of course, it couldn't have come at a worse time, with all the guests arriving tomorrow. And it is all the worse because I am not familiar with the house and servants. Horroughs, I think, absolutely delights in coming up with reasons why one thing or another cannot be done."

"You handled him far better than I would have, I can assure you," Irene told her.

Francesca smiled. "I have had practice. Our butler at the Haughston country house was much the same way. I was so very glad that he went with the entailed estate to Lord Haughston's heir."

Irene chuckled. "You make it sound as if he was tied to the land."

"He was the sort who practically was," Francesca retorted. "He was always saying, 'But that is not the way we do things at the Hall, my lady.' One would think that he had been there since the first Lord Haughston laid the first stone of it." She rolled her eyes. "I want to thank you for doing so much to help."

"I fear copying out names on place cards and arranging flowers is little enough," Irene replied with a smile. "And I have had plenty of time for it, since Gideon seems to have called quits to his lessons."

"I am sure he was overset by the news." Francesca shook her head. "It must have been a dreadful shock to him. Did you talk to him?"

"I talked to him, but it did little good. It was a shock, but he was very stony about it all."

"After being with Teresa these past two hours, I think stony would be a welcome relief. I never dreamed that she could turn out to be such a watering pot."

Irene rolled her eyes. "She was not even involved in the matter."

"Yes, but she is worried that this revelation has thrown her own marriage into question."

Irene shrugged. "I imagine she is right to be. If the first Lady Radbourne was not kidnapped but ran off with a lover, the possibilities are good that she is still alive. And if she is alive, then Lord Radbourne was not really free to marry Teresa."

"Exactly. And if so, poor Timothy is illegitimate and would not be Gideon's heir. It would be quite a comedown for Lady Teresa."

"Of course," Irene reasoned, "Lord Cecil did have Gideon's mother declared dead. He went through the legal process. And she had been gone all those years."

"Certainly he could have obtained a divorce, I would think, due to her desertion," Francesca agreed. "But what Lady Odelia said—which, of course, quite set Teresa off again—is that if Lord Cecil knew that Selene was probably still alive, then he may have committed fraud by petitioning the court to declare her dead. He would have had to swear that he thought her dead, wouldn't you think?"

"I suppose." Irene shook her head. "It certainly is a tangle. I even feel faintly sorry for Lady Teresa."

"I feel sorry for poor Pansy. Lady Odelia rang such a peal over her head!"

Irene grimaced. "I can understand Lady Odelia's irritation. Gideon's father and grandmother seem to me to have handled the whole thing most incompetently."

Francesca nodded. "Apparently, from what Lady Odelia says, Lord Cecil was the sort of man who always acted first and thought later. And Pansy is the most indecisive and weak-willed of people."

"Understandable, I suppose, having grown up under Lady Odelia's thumb," Irene put in.

"Yes, who can blame the poor woman? All the Lilles I have ever known are strong and commanding. They nearly always get their way, and when they clash, it can be horrid." Francesca gave an elaborate shudder. "I imagine that poor Lady Pansy got utterly ground into dust by the rest of them."

They had circled the central portion of the gardens and turned back to the house as they talked. Francesca sighed and looked up at the terrace before them.

"I suppose we should return," she said without any enthusiasm.

Irene nodded. "Yes. I have several more cards to write out before it is time for supper."

Francesca looked at her, then said, "What about you, Irene? Are you...all right?"

"Yes, of course." Irene smiled firmly at her. "The news was startling, but after all, it did not really concern me."

"It concerns Lord Radbourne, so..."

Irene shrugged. "Yes, but that affects me only in a peripheral way. Actually, his leaving the house today was a blessing. It gave us more time to deal with the other problems."

Francesca's brows drew together as she studied Irene, and Irene thought she would have pursued the matter, but at that moment they walked through the back door into the hallway and were stopped by the sound of raised voices.

A man's low rumble sounded from behind the closed door of the nearby small drawing room, rising to a loud, "Impossible!"

His words were followed by the sound of a woman's tearful rejoinder, though her more softly spoken words were difficult to understand.

Francesca and Irene glanced at each other uncertainly. It was an awkward situation, and neither was sure whether it would be better to retreat back onto the terrace and wait for an end to the argument or to slip down the hallway as quietly as possible in the hopes that they could get past before the door was opened. For a moment they hung there indecisively as the indistinguishable clash of voices went on.

"No!" the man's voice rang out. There was more rumbling, then, "—don't believe it!"

Irene glanced at her friend and nodded toward the other end of the hall. Francesca nodded, and they hurried forward as silently as they could. They had almost reached the foyer when the door to the drawing room crashed open.

Irene jumped at the noise, whirling around instinctively. A man strode out of the drawing room, glowering. Irene recognized him as Gideon's uncle, Jasper.

Behind him, through the open door, a woman's voice cried, "How do you know? You weren't even here! You had hared off to join the army."

Jasper swung back to the room, biting out, "No, I wasn't here, and I will always regret it! I would have found them and brought them back!"

He turned back to walk away, and for the first time looked up the hall to where Irene and Francesca stood, frozen in embarrassment. He pulled up short.

He let out a soft exclamation under his breath, and for a moment he stood, struggling to gain control of his anger. Finally he let out a sigh and bowed his head toward them. "Ladies. Please forgive me."

Pansy came to the doorway, wringing a handkerchief between her hands. Her eyes were red from crying, tears streaked her face, and she looked even more fragile than normal, as if a good gust of wind would topple her. "Oh!" she gasped when she saw the other women. "Oh, dear."

She brought her handkerchief up to dab at her eyes. "Jasper…"

"Yes, Mother. I know. Ladies, I apologize for creating a scene."

He half turned back toward Pansy, not quite looking at her as he went on. "Mother, I hope you will forgive me. The news was…a shock." His lips tightened, and then, as though he could not restrain himself, he added, "But you were wrong."

He looked back to Irene and Francesca, saying, "I never knew a better woman or mother than Cecil's wife. I am certain she did not run away. And she would never have abandoned her child."

With those words, he turned and strode past them out the front door.

His mother tottered into the hall, still dabbing at her tears.

"Jasper…" When he did not respond, she looked at Francesca and Irene.

"He doesn't understand," she told them mournfully. "He just doesn't realize what a scandal it would have been."

THE GUESTS BEGAN TO ARRIVE the next day, and nearly all of Irene's time was taken up with helping Francesca deal with them, as Gideon's grandmother insisted on keeping to her room despite Lady Odelia's best efforts to make her come down to greet their guests. Lady Teresa did come down to the drawing room, but it was soon apparent that, despite her earlier haughty manner, she was ill-prepared for a party such as this. She knew none of the arrivals, and she seemed somewhat overwhelmed at greeting a large number of blue-blooded guests. She was silent beyond a few commonplaces about the weather, and if asked a question, she quickly referred it to Francesca or Irene.

The first guest to arrive had actually been Gideon's friend, Piers Aldenham. As fair as Gideon was dark, he was slender and elegantly dressed, and when Horroughs, a look of disapproval writ plain upon his narrow features, ushered Piers into the drawing room, Aldenham swept a very creditable bow to the ladies of the house.

"It is an honor to meet you," he said with a winning smile. "As well as a pleasure. I must take my friend Gideon to task. He did not prepare me for the beauty of the ladies I would meet here. I am overwhelmed."

"Nor did he inform us of how smoothly you could talk," Irene replied with a smile, liking his merry grin and his complete lack of self-consciousness. Here was obviously a man who felt at home wherever he was.

"No doubt I wax more eloquent around fair ladies," he told her.

"Piers!" Gideon strode into the drawing room, smiling broadly. "Never tell me you got up early enough to make it here by this hour."

"Gideon!" Piers turned and clapped his friend on the shoulders, shaking the hand Gideon offered him. "I can assure you that I did not. I got in too late yesterday evening to call on you. I went straight to the inn and fell into bed."

"I shall send one of the grooms down to the inn to get your bags."

Piers shook his head, grinning. "Nonsense. I'm quite content there. 'Tis a very good room."

"Don't be absurd. Of course you will stay here."

Piers' gaze flickered toward the women in the room. "You may have been raised without a mother and sisters, my friend, but I was not. I can tell you that a last-minute guest throws all their plans into a terrible state, and they will hate both of us for it."

Irene saw the crease between Gideon's brows. She felt sure that he suspected, as she did, that his friend was staying at the inn in order to lessen Gideon's conflict with his relatives. It made her respect the man. However, she was also certain that Gideon would not be well-pleased with Piers doing so. Besides, at the present time, given what he had learned, Gideon was in need of every friend he had.

"Oh, no, Mr. Aldenham, you wrong us," Irene put in lightly. "We are more capable than that. We already have a room made up for you." That much was true. She herself had made sure that the room was ready for Aldenham's arrival.

Piers smiled at her, surprised. "You are kind and efficient, as well as beautiful, my lady. Still, I think it would be unpardonably rude of me."

"It is not rude of you at all," she rejoined. "The late notification of your arrival must be laid at Lord Radbourne's door, so if there is any rudeness, it is entirely his, and I can assure you that we are all quite accustomed to Lord Radbourne's rudeness."

Piers let out a bark of laughter. "All right, then. You have convinced me, my lady. Send for my bags, Gid."

"Of course." Gideon glanced at Irene, and for an instant the harsh look his face had worn the past day was gone, replaced by a flash of warm gratitude. Then his expression returned to its cool indifference, and he turned away. "Come, Piers, I will show you about the place. If you will excuse us, ladies?"

Piers favored them all with another grin and a bow, and the two men left the room.

"Well!" Lady Odelia said. "A well set-up young man, I must say."

"He is not quite what I had expected," Francesca admitted. "His speech and dress would certainly pass for those of a gentleman."

"I suspect that Lord Radbourne misled us a bit about what to expect from Mr. Aldenham," Irene said drily. "No doubt he enjoyed watching everyone squirm over the possibilities of embarrassment."

"Well, everyone will wonder who the man is," Francesca said. "But at least they will not declare themselves insulted and leave in a huff."

Irene grinned. "You may wish that he did drive off some of them before it's all over."

The next guest to be admitted to the drawing room was

Miss Rowena Surton, a pretty doll-like blonde with blue eyes and a strawberries-and-cream complexion. She arrived a couple of hours later and was accompanied by her brother, Percy, who had the same coloring as his sister and a pleasant, if rather vacuous, expression, and their mother, a plump, easygoing woman who, Irene thought, was probably the image of what Rowena herself would look like in twenty-five years.

Gideon, unsurprisingly, did not appear in the drawing room again, and Irene felt sure that it would be supper before any of the young women they had invited actually got to speak with him. She did not, however, offer any explanations or excuses for his absence. After all, the girls would have to deal with the man's nature sooner or later; they might as well find out about his manners up front.

In the middle of the afternoon Mrs. Ferrington and her daughter Norah showed up, and, most unfortunately, Lady Salisbridge and her two daughters swept in almost on their heels. As soon as she spotted the attractive dark-haired Mrs. Ferrington ensconced on the sofa in the drawing room chatting in a lively manner with Lady Odelia, Lady Salisbridge drew herself up to her full height and threw a furious look at Francesca.

"Lady Salisbridge. And Flora and Marian." Francesca hastened over to them, smiling and holding out both her hands. "How wonderful to see you again. I am sure you wish to go up to your rooms and freshen up a bit before you meet everyone. I am afraid Lady Radbourne is indisposed this afternoon, in any case. I am sure she will be here to greet you this evening, however. Irene? Why don't you show Lady Salisbridge and the girls to their rooms? You know Lady Irene Wyngate, do you not?"

Irene smiled and whisked the three women out of the room before Lady Salisbridge could comment on the presence of her rival at Radbourne Park. Diplomacy was not Irene's strong suit, but she managed to avoid any complaints from Lady Salisbridge by keeping up a steady stream of comments about the weather and questions about their journey as she led the three women up the stairs. Francesca had strategically placed them in rooms near the front of the house, at the greatest possible distance from the room given to Mrs. Ferrington and her daughter at the back, just as they would be seated as far apart as could be arranged every night at dinner.

As the Countess of Salisbridge was known to be a proud woman—though also always notoriously close to Dun Territory—Francesca had been careful to put her and her daughters in large and pleasant rooms close to the family. Mrs. Ferrington, on the other hand, was a realistic sort who knew that her husband's wealth was greater than his standing among the *ton,* and whose confidence was firmly embedded in her own status for the past twenty-odd years as a reigning beauty. She would be unlikely to quibble at where she and her daughter were placed.

Irene cast quick sideways glances at Lady Salisbridge's two daughters as she led them up the stairs. They were similar in looks, with medium brown hair and hazel eyes, and the same long, aquiline nose as their mother. They had, too, that woman's habit of looking at one down the length of that nose, giving them an air of disdain for the rest of the world.

She left the three women exploring their rooms and ordering about the abigail who had accompanied them, as well as the housemaid who had been sent to help with the unpacking. She returned to the drawing room, where she found that Mrs. Ferrington and Norah had also decided to seek the comfort of their room.

She had little chance to rest, however, for she was immediately embroiled in a crisis with the cook and after that had to soothe the ruffled feathers of the housekeeper, whom the Salisbridges' haughty abigail had offended with her demands.

It was not long afterward that Lord Hurley and his daughter came in, windblown and in high spirits, having chosen to ride instead of being cooped up in the carriage. The pair were as alike as a father and daughter could be, with the same hearty, pleasant manner, sandy hair and square, freckled faces. They told a long and detailed story of their ride, including, Irene thought, every fence, hedge, stream and other hazard their horses had jumped along the way, one of them taking up wherever the other dropped off. Listening to them, Irene suspected that Lady Hurley had probably been just as happy that the two of them had not ridden with her in the carriage.

Lady Hurley, arriving an hour later and in a more decorous state, was a small, languid woman who, after greeting Lady Odelia and the others, opted to retire to her chamber for a restorative nap.

The last guests were the Duke of Rochford and his sister, Calandra, a pretty young girl whose black hair and dark eyes were very like her brother's, but whose lively personality was most unlike the duke's imperturbable elegance.

By the time they arrived, even as spacious a house as Radbourne Park was stuffed to the bursting point, despite the Salisbridge girls and several mothers and daughters sharing their rooms. It was fortunate, Irene thought, that the duke, though leaving his sister at Radbourne Park, was himself going to stay with a friend who lived not far away and would simply ride over each day to partake in the festivities. Even Lady Odelia could not persuade the duke that familial duty required him to reside with his family at Radbourne Park.

Lady Calandra, standing beside Irene, cast a laughing glance at her and raised her fan to murmur, "What Aunt Odelia does not realize is that her presence is one of the reasons Rochford would rather be elsewhere."

Irene smothered her grin. "Still, it does seem too bad that he must ride over here each day."

"Nonsense," Callie, as she was called by her brother and Francesca, replied. "He will enjoy things far more as they stand. He will get to talk to Mr. Strethwick about all those boring subjects that he enjoys, like plants and rocks and things with long Latin names. Besides, Mr. Strethwick, being a scholar and very little aware of the world, shows Rochford no deference except for his brain, which Rochford quite enjoys. He gets so tired of everyone fawning over him because he is a duke. Not, of course," she added, "that he doesn't like being a duke, because he can be quite toplofty, too, if someone offends him, and he never gets anything but the very best. But really, I think he is often rather lonely, too."

Irene glanced at her in some surprise, for she had never met anyone who appeared more self-contained and aloof than the duke.

"Oh, dear." Calandra looked a little conscience-stricken. "There, I have said too much, as I so often do. My brother would not like for anyone to think that he felt—well, anything, really." Her irrepressible grin popped back onto her face.

"I will not give you away, I assure you," Irene told her.

"Nor will I think any the less of him to find that he does not go through life feeling nothing."

Irene found that she rather liked the pert girl, who displayed none of the haughtiness that might be expected of one in her position. Was she, too, here to enter into the bridal race? The thought left Irene with a strangely cold feeling in the pit of her stomach.

But she pushed the thought aside and took Calandra up to her bedchamber, regaling her with the entertainments that Francesca had planned for the next few days. Afterward Irene returned to her own room, for there was little enough time left in which to get ready for supper.

The dress she had chosen earlier was laid out on the bed, but when she looked at it and thought of going down to supper in this plain frock, while all about her the women would be dressed in their prettiest finery, she realized that she could not bear to do so. She might be here only as an assistant matchmaker, but she was suddenly determined that she would look her best while doing her job.

She rang for the maid and went to the wardrobe to pull out one of her new dresses, a silk evening gown of a dark green that would not flatter most complexions but that looked wonderful against her coloring. Once her maid, with a smile of approval at Irene's rejection of the plainer gowns she had been wearing recently, went off to get rid of any wrinkles in the chosen dress, Irene went down the hall to Francesca's room to ask Maisie for help with her hair.

She went downstairs an hour later, secure in the knowledge that she would look as attractive as any woman there. She walked into the anteroom where everyone had gathered and cast a glance around. She immediately spotted Gideon, who was standing near the windows talking to Miss

Surton—though, to be truthful, it looked as though it was Piers who was doing most of the talking, to which the pretty blonde was responding with much giggling and flirtatious wafting of her fan, while Gideon stood by looking grim.

Gideon turned to look at her, and for an instant Irene thought that he would leave his group and come over to her, but then he pulled his gaze away and turned back to Piers and Rowena.

Francesca joined Irene and turned to survey the room before them. "Well," she said, "what do you think of our candidates?"

Irene took a moment, looking about the room before she began. "I think that the Salisbridges are too proud."

"Oh, I assure you that either of them would accept him," Francesca replied.

"That is not what I meant," Irene replied. "I fear that Gideon will reject them. Miss Surton is far too giggly. As for Miss Hurley…" She cast a speaking look at the young woman in question, who was at the moment engaged with her father and Rowena Surton's brother in a discussion of broodmares.

"I know." Francesca shook her head despairingly. "I tried to dissuade Lady Odelia from including her. I fear that it will take an avid rider to the hounds to favor Miss Hurley—or to find favor with her. But Lady Hurley is Lady Odelia's godchild, and she was most determined to push her at Lord Radbourne. But what about Miss Ferrington? What do you think of her?"

Irene studied Miss Ferrington. "She is not such a beauty as her mother."

Francesca let out a chuckle. "Is there none among my girls that you like? I thought Miss Ferrington a very good possibility. She is not a beauty, perhaps, but she is quite above average, don't you think? And pleasant, as well."

"Yes, she is. But do you not think that she is, well, a trifle bland?" Irene pointed out.

Francesca smothered a smile and went on. " Miss Surton is quite pretty, even if she is a bit silly. And Salisbridge's daughters are not unattractive. Flora has more looks than Marian, of course, but Marian is quite acceptable, I would think. After all, Lord Radbourne is not looking for love in the arrangement."

"No, that is true," Irene agreed tartly. "And certainly he would not find it with either of those two."

"Irene, you are most disapproving of them all," Francesca said with an innocent air. "One might almost think that you are jealous."

Irene turned to look at her friend, her eyebrows shooting upward. "Jealous? I? I cannot imagine where you would get such a notion."

"Then it is not true? You have not formed a…*tendre,* shall we say?…for Lord Radbourne?"

"No. I have not formed a *tendre* or anything else for Lord Radbourne," Irene shot back. "You are very much mistaken."

"I suppose I must be. It just seemed to me that over the last few days Lord Radbourne has shown a preference for your company."

"Given the fact that the rest of the company is his family, whom he does not like, I do not think that indicates any great liking for me."

"And what of you?" Francesca asked. "How do you feel about him?"

Irene opened her mouth to make a hasty retort that she did not care for him at all, but then she glanced at Francesca and finally, somewhat reluctantly, said, "I do not know. But it does not matter, in any case, for we are not going to marry. You know well my thoughts on matrimony, and Lord Radbourne is interested in the sort of marriage that I could not accept. So it really makes no difference how I feel."

"Doesn't it?" Francesca asked softly.

"No," Irene told her firmly. "It does not. I am here to help find Lord Radbourne a wife—some other wife. I believe that he has finally accepted that I am not the proper candidate for that position."

"I see." Francesca nodded, looking at Irene shrewdly. "Well, I will be glad for your help. Everyone liked the idea of a ride about the estate tomorrow, but all the mothers are inclined to stay at home. So I will have four men and six young women to oversee, and I feel quite certain that Lord Hurley will be of no use whatsoever in that regard. I would enormously appreciate your help to chaperone them."

"Yes, of course," Irene agreed. "I intended to do so."

She watched as Gideon's group was joined by his greataunt, who brought with her Lady Salisbridge and her daughters. Gideon turned his attention to them, making a perfectly acceptable bow. The conversation looked as if it was slow-going, but he remained, and if his expression was not enthralled, at least he did not appear as if he might bolt at any moment, even after Piers slipped away from the group.

Gideon was, Irene thought, making an effort. He was trying to get to know Francesca's candidates, the first step in choosing his wife. She was aware of a little prick of pain in her chest at the thought.

Was Francesca right? Was she jealous of these women and the attention Gideon was paying them? She told herself that was ridiculous. She had not dismissed any of the women as unacceptable for Gideon for any reason other than the ones she had given Francesca. She simply did not think that he would want any of them. None of them were right for him. None of them were good enough.

With, of course, one notable exception.

"Lady Calandra," Irene said to Francesca, almost forcing the words out.

"What?"

"I was just saying that I find the duke's sister quite attractive and very pleasant, not at all bland or boring. She is a woman I am sure will meet with Lord Radbourne's approval."

"Oh, Callie." Francesca waved a hand in dismissal. "She is not someone I selected for Lord Radbourne. There isn't the slightest reason for her not to marry exactly as she pleases. She has an extremely nice portion, and she is the daughter of a duke. Nor would Rochford ever urge her to marry unless she truly wanted to. She is the apple of his eye, no matter now stern he likes to pretend he is with her."

Irene tried to ignore the fact that her chest suddenly felt much lighter. "Then you do not think she would choose Lord Radbourne?"

"I would not believe so," Francesca replied, then added, "I suppose it is possible, but, well, I would think he is a trifle *dour* for her. And in any case, they are related, are they not? Not first cousins, of course—is it second or third? But I do not think she would even regard him as a potential match. I invited her and Rochford merely because they are relatives, and I thought having them here might make it seem more normal. Less like a…well, what it is."

"Oh. Well." Irene struggled a little to keep her lips from twitching up into a smile. "Pity."

"Yes, isn't it?" Francesca added drily. She leaned in a little closer and murmured, "My dear Irene, I think that you must be rather better at lying to yourself than you are at lying to others."

Then, with a smile, she walked away.

CHAPTER FIFTEEN

IRENE TOLD HERSELF that Francesca was wrong. She was not lying to herself about her feelings for Gideon. She was quite aware of how dangerously close she was to tumbling into love with him. But she also knew that she could not allow that to happen. She would not let her heart sweep her into making foolish decisions, as had happened with so many other women.

So she kept her distance from him, settling into the role of chaperone and helping Francesca with whatever task needed doing. She spent the first day touring the estate with the other young people, but she did not ride beside Gideon or talk to him. She watched as he rode alongside first one young woman, then another, talking to each one, even, she thought, flirting a little with Norah Ferrington. In the drawing room after supper that evening, she watched him exchange pleasantries with the girls and listen politely as they played the piano or sang, even standing beside Marian Salisbridge to turn the music for her. And the following day, through a session of lawn tennis in the warm August afternoon and then tea afterward, she watched him devote his attention to each one of the women in turn.

It surprised her somewhat that he was actually making an effort to mingle with the marriage candidates whom Francesca and his great-aunt had selected for him. He had apparently accepted her own refusal to marry him and was intent on pursuing someone more willing. He did not seek Irene out for conversation or even ask her for a dance when the girls cajoled Pansy and Odelia into letting them roll back the carpet in the center of the music room and engage in an impromptu party. Piers asked to stand up with her, as did Gideon's uncle Jasper and Mr. Surton and even Lord Hurley, but Gideon did not approach her.

It was a slight that, she realized, was noticed by others, for as she stood, watching the couples go through an energetic country dance, Lady Teresa came up beside her and said, "Fickle creatures, men."

Irene looked at her coldly. "I am sure I don't know what you mean."

"Do you not?" Teresa smiled and shrugged. "If you wish to pretend you had no hopes of landing him, well, who am I to deny it?" She paused, then went on. "It is just as well that you did not set your cap for him. Whoever he marries will not have his heart. He has a low-born mistress in London, and she is the one he loves."

"What?" Startled, Irene turned to look at Teresa in amazement. She realized then that she had shown too much of her feelings to this woman, and she shrugged, striving for an expression of indifference. "Many men have mistresses, especially before they marry."

"Well, he intends to keep her. Her name is Dora. I heard him arguing with Lady Odelia about her. Radbourne said that he would never give up Dora."

Irene felt for a moment as if she could not breathe, and the intensity of the pain that stabbed through her chest shocked her. *Dora*. It had been years, but she remembered that name clearly. It had been the one Gideon had spoken that very first time she saw him, the name of the woman whom he had warned her father to stay away from. The woman he had been so determined to protect that he had attacked a peer of the realm.

And now, so many years later, she was still his mistress. Clearly this Dora held his heart, and so no wife would ever be able to.

"Indeed?" she said at last, striving to keep her voice cool. "It would seem that he has the same problem as his father—marrying one woman while still bound to another."

Teresa's eyes flared with fury at Irene's words, and she turned and stalked away, leaving Irene feeling a trifle guilty over what she had said. She should not have been so cruel, she thought, even if Teresa had hurt her. But she had been unprepared for the pain it caused to hear that Gideon loved another woman, and she had lashed out without stopping to consider her words or the injury they would inflict.

Was what Teresa had said true? she wondered. Or had the other woman made it up only to hurt Irene, and to drive a wedge between her and Gideon? Francesca had been sure that Teresa wanted to keep Gideon from marrying Irene in the hopes that Teresa's son would remain the heir to Gideon's title. But Teresa must have seen that Gideon was no longer pursuing Irene, that he was, instead, dancing attendance on other women. There seemed, therefore, little reason for her to have made up such a story.

Of course, Teresa could have acted simply out of spite, letting her venom spew out over the nearest target. But why, even out of spite, would she have made up such a story? The words she said she had heard Gideon say to his great-aunt had a ring of truth to them. And surely Teresa could not have settled on the name by coincidence or accident. Dora was indeed the name that Gideon had flung at her father years ago, warning him never to try to touch her again. Gideon had told her that he attacked her father because he was protecting one of his faro dealers, but had not the very heat of his fury indicated some deeper feeling than that?

It would explain, as well, his lack of interest in finding a wife whom he could love. If the love of his life was a woman whom he could not marry, given his suddenly acquired position in life, he could very well plan to marry for duty and keep a mistress in the city for love.

Irene swallowed, feeling a little queasy. Had he kissed her as he had, all the time knowing that he was in love with another woman? She had known that he did not love her, that all that lay between them was desire, but…she hated the thought that his desire could have had so little in it of caring, that in his embrace there had been nothing but carnal lust.

Irene glanced around. All eyes were on the center of the floor, where Gideon and the others were dancing. No one was looking at her, and no one would notice if she left, least of all Gideon.

She turned and slipped out of the room. Outside in the hallway, she hesitated. She had thought to go up to her bedchamber, but she was too restless, she realized. Instead, she turned and hurried down the corridor and out the rear door onto the terrace. She stood for a moment, drawing a calming breath.

Finally she started down the steps to the garden. It was a trifle cool, but the evening air felt good against her overheated cheeks, and she did not want to go back for a wrap. In any case, she would not stay long, as the partial moon did not provide enough light for her to venture farther back into the gardens, where trees and hedges created deeply dark spaces. She strolled along the central path to where it split around the fountain and stood for a moment, gazing down at the cheerily splashing water.

"Irene."

She whirled around, her heart suddenly hammering in her chest. Gideon stood a few feet behind her. The noise of the fountain must have covered his steps. She straightened, lifting her chin a little. She must not let him think that she was mooning over him.

"Are you all right?" he asked. "I saw you leave the room."

"I stepped out for a breath of air," she told him nonchalantly. "It had grown rather warm in the music room."

Her statement would have sounded better, she knew, if she had not involuntarily shivered right afterward as the night breeze touched the bare skin of her arms.

"But now you are cold." He shrugged out of his jacket and came forward, laying it about her shoulders.

The jacket was still warm from his body, and his scent lingered on it. Irene clutched the edges together, feeling suddenly as if she might burst into tears. Whatever was the matter with her? *He had rudely ignored her all evening, and now a tender gesture from him was enough to make her cry?* She was not, she reminded herself sternly, one of those females.

It did not matter that she wanted to lean against him, to rest her head against his hard chest. It did not matter that his nearness was intoxicating to her, that the heat emanating from his body drew her, that the unique scent of him set up a fluttering deep in her loins. She would not be weak.

Irene swallowed and said, "You seemed to be enjoying the dance."

He made a face and said, "I would rather—"

He broke off as a voice from the terrace called, "Gideon!"

They turned and looked up to see Gideon's uncle approaching rapidly.

"Oh, excuse me, Lady Irene," Jasper said. "I did not see you standing there."

"It is perfectly all right. I left the music room and Gi— Lord Radbourne came after me to make sure that I was not ill."

"Are you all right?" Jasper asked, trotting down the steps to join them.

"Perfectly." Irene forced a smile onto her face, hoping that it looked more natural than it felt. "I just came out for a stroll, and then I found it a trifle too cool."

"I wanted to talk to you, Gideon. I had not been able to catch you alone this evening," Jasper told his nephew.

"Pray excuse me," Irene said quickly. "I will leave you gentlemen so that you may talk."

"No, please, my lady, I did not mean to be rude," Jasper said quickly, looking embarrassed. "You are welcome to stay. Indeed, I already spoke to you on this subject the other day."

"Oh." Irene knew that he was referring to the afternoon two days before, when she and Francesca had inadvertently overheard Jasper's argument with his mother. "About Lady Selene?"

"Yes."

Beside her, Gideon stiffened, and Irene suspected that he was searching for a way out of the conversation.

"Please stay," Jasper said, addressing both of them. "It is important. I want both of you to hear. I fear you have been misled about your mother, Gideon."

"Yes, I know. My father pretended that she had been kidnapped."

"No. Not that. About her running away. She would never have done that. I swear to you. As soon as my mother told me, I knew there was something terribly wrong. Selene would never have run away."

"What are you saying? What do you mean?" Gideon looked at him. "What else could have happened?"

"I don't know," his uncle admitted, looking uncomfortable. "But I know she would not have run away with a lover. I will not have you believe that of your mother. She was a-a wonderful woman, good and kind."

"Uncle…" Gideon's face softened a little, and he reached out to touch the older man's arm in a gesture of comfort. "I know that you regarded my mother highly. I am sure that when you knew her, she was as you said. But you were not here at the time. You don't know what she might have been doing or—or how she might have changed."

"I know!" Jasper jerked away. "Do not patronize me or try to calm me down. Blast it! This is important. I am not some doddering old fool. You were the most important thing in the world to her. She would never have taken you from here, and she would never have abandoned you. Never."

"Perhaps she did not," Irene offered. "We have no idea what happened after she left Radbourne Park. She could have been abandoned by her lover or she could have died, leaving her son alone in London, with no one knowing who he was."

"She did not have a lover," Jasper grated out. "And she would not have removed Gideon from Cecil and his inheritance. She would not even have left Gideon here and run away by herself."

"You cannot be certain—" Gideon began.

"I can! And I am!" His uncle cut him off, his face harsh and lined in pain. "I know—because I asked her to leave with *me,* and she would not!"

His words were followed by a stunned silence.

"Oh, my," Irene murmured at last and sat down abruptly on the low stone wall around the fountain.

"You…" Gideon stared at his uncle.

"I loved her," Jasper said simply, and sank down onto the wall beside Irene, resting his elbows on his knees and supporting his head with his hands. "God help me, I loved her. I betrayed my brother. My honor."

"Bloody hell," Gideon said in a low voice and turned to look out over the garden.

"I was mad for her," Jasper went on in a dull voice. "I begged her to leave Cecil, to run away with me. Time and again I begged her. I said we would go to America or the Colonies. I didn't care about giving up my family, my name. Nothing mattered to me except her. She was the most beautiful creature, the most charming and gentlest… But you do not want to hear the lovesick maunderings of an old man."

He stood up and turned toward Gideon. "I know that she would not have left, because she refused to leave earlier with me. She told me that she could not do that to you. You belonged here, at Radbourne Park. You would be the earl someday, and she would not take that away from you. Nor would she leave without you. So she would remain with Cecil, without love, without hope, because of you. And that is how I know that she would not have run away with her lover, if such a man even existed, and taken you with her. And never, no matter what, would she have abandoned you."

"Is that why you joined the Army?" Irene asked.

Jasper nodded. "Yes. I was in despair. I could not stay here, loving her as I did, and see her daily as his wife. Cecil was not worth a single one of her tears. I hated him because she belonged to him, and because he did not even realize what a treasure he had. I began to realize that if I remained at Radbourne Park, I might someday kill him just to free her from him. So I bought a commission and requested an Indian regiment. I wanted to be as far away as I could be, so that I could not break my vow and return, even for leave." He sighed and rubbed his hands tiredly over his face. "If only I had not been so weak, so impulsive. If only I had stayed here, it would not have happened."

"You must not blame yourself," Irene told him sympathetically. "You could not have known that anything would happen."

"I left because I was too weak," he replied, his voice like iron, and his eyes were filled with a regret that she knew would never leave him. "I could not bear it. And God only knows what happened to her."

"What *did* happen?" Gideon asked, his voice hard and clipped.

"I don't know." Jasper looked at him. "But I am sure that Selene did not walk away of her own accord."

IRENE WENT DOWN to breakfast the next morning looking composed, if somewhat pale, with nothing to give away the fact that she had spent a restless night. The evening before, after she and Gideon had walked with Jasper back into the house, she had gone upstairs to her room, leaving the two men to talk together.

She did not know what had transpired between them, but she had been unable to fall asleep for a long time, her head full of jumbled thoughts and tangled emotions. She kept thinking of Gideon's mother, alone and in love with a man far away. What had she done? What had happened to her? Irene's mind was filled with frightening possibilities. When she finally slept, she had dreamed, jerking awake time after time, sweating, her heart pounding.

This morning she had come awake from the last jarring dream to find that the early morning sun was slanting through the cracks at the edges of the drapes. She would not, she knew, be able to fall back asleep again, and after the night she had spent, she thought that she would rather not. So she rang for her maid and dressed, then walked down to the dining room. At least, she thought, it would probably be empty this early.

It was, save for one person. Gideon raised his head at the sound of her entrance.

"Irene." He stood up quickly.

"Lord Radbourne." She hesitated, then went to the chair he pulled out for her and sat down, determined to act naturally. "Very little company this morning, I see."

"Yes, it is rather early, and I think everyone was tired from the dancing last night."

A footman came forward to offer her dishes from the sideboard, and for the next few minutes Irene was able to occupy herself with filling her plate and eating. Gideon was already through with his meal, and the servant took away his plate, but Gideon himself remained, sipping a cup of tea.

Irene felt his eyes upon her, but she kept her attention on her food. She felt distinctly uncomfortable. The strain that had grown between them the last few days was exacerbated by the too-private knowledge his uncle had shared with them the night before. At last the silence grew too awkward, and she set down her fork and looked across the table at him.

"What do you plan to do?" she asked him.

"About what?"

She made a face. "About what your uncle told you last night. Do you not…wonder what happened?"

"My uncle and I talked at length last night," he admitted. "I had already ascertained from the housekeeper that my father's valet still lives here in the village. I had thought I would talk to him, but then…" He shrugged. "I told myself that there was little use in it. And I delayed it. Now, however—well, I have to find out what I can. My uncle told me that the woman who was my mother's personal maid also lives there. I am going to see both of them, and I thought…I would appreciate it if you would go with me."

"Of course," Irene replied without hesitation. "But would you not rather take your friend? Mr. Aldenham?"

"No. I have told Piers nothing of this. He is my friend, but this…" He shrugged. "It is not the sort of thing we talk about."

"When would you like to leave?" she asked.

He smiled faintly. "If you are through with your breakfast, we can go immediately. I will have the carriage brought around."

She did not pause to think the matter over, nor wait to see whether Francesca might have some task that needed doing. She only nodded and went up to her room for her gloves and bonnet, and to throw on a light pelisse to cover her arms and shoulders. When she returned downstairs, she found the carriage waiting in the drive in front of the house and Gideon standing beside it, ready to hand her inside.

Once she was enclosed with him in the carriage, she again

felt awkward. She could think of nothing to say that sounded natural, and her brain seemed to hum primarily with thoughts of how close he was to her, how little effort it would take to reach out and touch his arm…and yet he seemed more remote than ever before.

Finally, stiffly, she said, "You have been quite diligent in getting to know the various young ladies."

"Yes." He glanced at her, his face unreadable, then turned to gaze out the window. "I have talked with each of them. And danced with them."

"I saw." She swallowed the sudden lump that developed in her throat.

"I hope you found my steps acceptable."

"Yes, of course." She was pleased to find that her voice came out light and unconcerned. "You did quite well."

She looked out the other window, and after that silence settled between them. It was a relief when, some minutes later, they reached the outskirts of the village. They turned from the main road and took a twisting lane that led them finally to a comfortable little half-timbered cottage.

A maid in a neat gray dress and white cap answered the door and bobbed a curtsey, then ushered them into the small front parlor.

She left the room, and a moment later they heard her calling out the back window, "Mr. Owenby, sir, you've visitors."

Before long an old man entered the parlor, his gaze going first to Gideon, then to Irene. He was a compact man, not tall, but sturdily built, with close-cropped iron-gray hair. He wore a gray jacket over dark breeches and a plain collarless shirt, and it was clear that he had been out in the yard working. A sheen of perspiration still dotted his forehead.

He bowed his head toward Gideon. "My lord."

"You are Mr. Owenby?" Gideon asked.

"Just Owenby, sir. That is what his lordship always called me."

"My father?"

"Yes."

Gideon introduced Irene, and the other man gestured toward the chairs grouped before the small fireplace. "Please, sit down, my lord. My lady. May I bring you a cup of tea? Water?"

"No, thank you. We came here to ask you a few questions about the night my mother and I…left Radbourne Park."

"Of course, sir. When you were kidnapped."

"Is that what happened?"

"Of course, my lord." He flicked a glance at Irene. "Lord Radbourne got a note asking for that necklace, and he gave it to me in a little velvet pouch and told me where to take it. So I did. I left it beneath a pew in the church, and then I went down the road to a certain oak tree and I waited. Only nobody ever came to give you to me."

"Owenby, stop," Gideon said shortly. "There is no need to pretend. My grandmother has already told us that the kidnapping was a hoax, something my father made up to cover up what really happened."

"Did she now? What did she say happened?"

"I'd rather hear it from you," Gideon told him flatly.

The man shrugged. "Lord Radbourne went to Lady Radbourne's chamber, but she was not there. He thought she was downstairs, but he did not find her there, either. He wasn't worried at first. He looked around the house a bit, then in the garden, thinking she had gone for a walk. He asked the servants, but none of them had seen her. Then the governess came down, screeching like a madwoman, saying as how you were gone. Everybody started searching like mad then. And finally, in his study, his lordship found the note she had left for him."

"Did you see this note?" Gideon asked.

"Me, sir? No. He wasn't likely to show a private letter to me. But he told me that she had run away. She'd taken you and gone off with a man." His lips curled contemptuously. "No surprise to me."

"Why not?" Irene asked, rather taken aback by the man's tone.

The man barely spared her a glance. "I could see what kind of woman she was—begging your pardon, sir. Anybody could see, except his lordship."

Irene could not help but be struck by the difference between this man's opinion of Gideon's mother and the one expressed by his uncle. It was unusual for a devoted servant to speak ill of his master's wife—and even more so for him to express such an opinion in front of that woman's son. Clearly Owenby's bitterness toward the countess ran deep.

"And what did my father do after he read the letter?" Gideon asked.

"Sent me after them, that's what," the older man answered simply. "He wasn't one to let her go without a fight, least not at first. He didn't tell anyone else what had happened. I took a horse and rode to the village. His lordship took the road the other way." He shrugged. "We couldn't find anyone who'd seen a woman and child, with or without a man."

"Did she take a horse from the stables? How did she leave?"

"I don't know the answer to that. His lordship questioned the head groom, but he said no horses had been taken. I figured she must have taken the boy and run down to the road to meet her lover. That he was waiting for her with a carriage or horses."

"How long did Lord Cecil search for her?"

The man shrugged. "He didn't search, not after that first morning. He thought she'd see the error of her ways and come back. But he had to tell the servants and the neighbors something, so he came up with that tale of the two of you being kidnapped. He figured nobody would question her being gone a few days and then coming back if she had been taken. Only she didn't. He didn't hear from her. A week or so later, he sent me to try to track them down. But it was useless. The trail was cold. I couldn't find anyone who'd seen them, and I had to be careful not to let the truth get out. I checked some ports. I asked at the docks. Nobody remembered seeing a woman and child or a family, at least not a particular one."

"Then what did you do?"

"I came back. What else could I do? They had done a good job of covering their tracks. We had no way of knowing where they went. I think Lord Radbourne hired another man later to look for you and the lady on the Continent, but he never found aught." His mouth tightened. "His lordship was never the same after that."

"You remained in my father's employ?"

"Of course." The valet nodded. "Until the day he died. I gave him his medicine and brought his food to him, what little he could get down. He was a good man, Lord Cecil, and a good master."

"Less good as a father, it seems to me," Irene offered.

The valet shot her a scornful look. "Begging your pardon, miss, but you didn't know the man. Or the woman. She broke him, she did. He deserved better than that—" he bit off the clearly derogatory remark he had been about to make, casting a quick glance at Gideon, and said instead "—that woman."

"I would think a man would make more of an effort to find his own son," Irene countered.

"He thought the boy was better off with his mother," Owenby shot back. "He didn't know she had let him go in the city to fend for himself."

"How do you know she did?" Gideon asked.

"What? What do you mean?"

"How do you know that she let me go in London?"

"I don't. I just assumed…I mean, that's where they found you, didn't they? That's what the rumor is, that the duke found you in some gaming hell in London and knew it was you."

Gideon arched his brows. "A little more colorful, perhaps, than the literal truth, but yes, London is where I lived."

"And can you remember nothing else?" Owenby asked. "Nothing about your mother or how you came to London?"

"No. Nothing. I would like very much to find out what happened."

"I wish I could help you, my lord," Owenby said. "But I've told you all I know."

"My father never heard anything from her? No letters? No rumors? No one ever claimed to have seen her?"

"Not that I know of."

That was all they were able to get out of him, though Gideon asked him a few more questions. His reply was always the same: He had told them everything he knew. Gideon's mother had run away with her lover, taking her son with them.

It was clear that he was through. Finally Gideon nodded and bade the man a polite goodbye. Then he and Irene left the cottage.

"Well," Irene commented as they settled into the carriage and drove away from the valet's cottage, "he is certainly consistent in his answers."

"And not inclined to elaborate on them, either," Gideon added. "I cannot help but wonder if he knows more than he is saying."

CHAPTER SIXTEEN

IRENE GLANCED AT GIDEON, surprised. "That sounds ominous."

He shrugged. "I don't know. I am not sure there is anything have-cavey there, but…some things were odd. He was quite frank in his poor opinion of my mother, for one thing."

"Yes, I noticed. He certainly saw her in a different light than Lord Jasper."

"Which, I wonder, is the true picture?" Gideon mused. "The devoted mother and sweet and charming woman of my uncle's view? Or the callous, deceptive strumpet who Owenby saw?"

Impulsively, Irene reached out to lay her hand upon his arm, sympathy swelling in her chest. "I imagine that the truth lies somewhere between those two. But I think Lord Jasper's opinion of her must be more accurate. Owenby's perception is no doubt colored by his love for and loyalty to your father."

Gideon smiled down at her, his hand coming up to cover hers. "Thank you for your kindness, but I am not hurt by what he said. Whatever my mother was, the truth is that I have no memory of her. And while, God knows, I would prefer to believe that she was not a cold, wicked woman, it would not make any difference in my life if that is true. But I cannot help but be struck by the peculiarity of the man's response. It is true that Owenby was a most devoted servant—he was with Lord Cecil from the time he went off to Eton, so I understand. And in my father's will, he left Owenby a nice retainer for his years of service. Still, in general, I find that servants are reluctant to speak ill of *anyone* to those of higher station. And people of all sorts are reluctant to speak ill of one's mother."

"Yes. He was…well…ruder than I would have expected."

"And another thing—he did not seem to have any particular fondness for me." He looked over at her. "Did you notice?"

"He was not effusive," Irene agreed. "Still, he did not seem a demonstrative sort. And he probably would not have been around you that much as a child. Children generally are relegated to the nursery."

Gideon nodded. "True."

Irene said carefully, "I am sure that had you grown up there, he would have known you better and had fonder remembrances of you."

Gideon glanced at her, and a smile quirked up one corner of his mouth. "Irene, are you trying to soothe my wounded feelings?"

She cocked an eyebrow and replied somewhat testily, "Well, you seemed perturbed about the fact that he did not greet you with enthusiasm."

"Thank you for your concern." He bowed his head toward her, grinning in a way that warmed her. The awkwardness between them was gone for the moment, and she felt a closeness to Gideon that had been missing since their conversation after his grandmother's revelation.

"However," he went on, "I was not hurt by his manner any more than by his words. I merely found it rather odd.

Wouldn't you think, as devoted to my father as he was, that there would have been some expression of relief or pleasure that his father's son had been found safe all these years later? I thought an old family retainer would have been more…" He trailed off, shrugging.

"'Oh, Master Gideon, thank heaven you've been brought back to us after all these years'?" Irene suggested lightly.

He smiled back at her. "Exactly. Something along those lines. Perhaps you did not notice it, but every time he looked at me, his eyes were cold. Even disdainful." He paused. "Do you think me fanciful?"

"No. I can think of few people I would call less fanciful than you," she answered honestly. "I did not notice any particular coldness toward you, but then, I was not on the receiving end of his gaze. If that is the opinion you formed, I would think you had good reason for it." She hesitated, then went on. "What, then, do you suspect? That Owenby might have…killed her?"

His expression turned rueful. "It sounds a bit far-fetched."

"Well…Owenby did seem to dislike her a good deal. Perhaps he discovered her affair with your uncle, and he wanted to rid your father of her. He could have forged the letter. Or perhaps your father knew what he did and helped him conceal the crime. Maybe Lord Cecil did not want to lose the man, no matter what he had done."

If their reception at Owenby's cottage had been cool, it was more than made up for by the rush of pleasure that appeared on the face of his mother's maid when they arrived at her cottage and she saw Gideon.

"My lord! Oh, my!" She reached out to touch his arm, then remembered herself, blushed, and curtsied instead.

"Lord Radbourne, it's so wonderful to see you! Please, come in, come in."

The maid, whose name was Nancy Bonham, whisked them into the single large room of her tiny row cottage, quickly picking up a basket of sewing and stowing it behind a sofa and in the same motion directing Gideon toward the comfortable-looking chair beside the fireplace.

"Please, sit down. Could I get you a cup of tea? I'm so happy, so happy, you came," she chattered, beaming and wiping a tear from the corner of her eye. "You must excuse me. I'm not usually so easily overcome, but to see my lady's boy…" She stopped, choking up.

"No, don't apologize," Gideon told her, smiling back at her. "I should have come to see you earlier. I am afraid I did not realize—I have no memory of my life here before."

"You do not remember your mother?" Nancy exclaimed in a shocked tone. "Oh, my, how terrible for you. She was such a sweet, kind woman. A fine lady, so good to me. And she loved you so very much. You were the light of her life, you know. There are some ladies as don't pay much mind to their children, leaving them to the nurse or governess, but not her ladyship. Whenever you were sick, she was right there at your bedside. And she would tuck you into bed each night and read you a little story. You loved that, you did."

"Tell me about my mother," Gideon said.

The woman needed no urging. She launched into a long paean to the Lady Selene's temperament, looks and character. "Her eyes were much like yours, you know. That same clear green. People always said you favored Lord Radbourne, but I thought you had more the look of Lady Selene. Her hair was dark, too, and she was tall. So refined she was, a true lady in every sense of the word. His lordship was lucky to have married her, I'll tell you that, though he never would have admitted it. The Bankeses were always a proud lot. And, of course, his mother was a Lilles, and we all know how they are. But your mother was a Walbridge, and her line went back as far in Norfolk as ever the Bankeses were here."

She went on at some length about Lady Selene's family and her own family's long tradition of serving them, from there launching into a description of her ladyship's many kindnesses, not only to Nancy herself, but to the poor of the village.

Finally, when she paused, Gideon said quickly, "Nancy, can you tell me about that day she left. What happened?"

"Oh, that horrid, horrid day!" She teared up again, bringing her handkerchief back out of her pocket and dabbing at her eyes. "I never dreamed…I saw she wasn't in her bed, of course, as soon as I went into her room. The bed was turned down, just as I'd left it the evening before. She hadn't slept in it at all. I didn't know what to do. I—" Nancy looked down at her hands "—I didn't want to tell Lord Radbourne. I didn't want to…get her in trouble with him. He—" She glanced up at Gideon a little uncertainly.

"Go ahead," he said calmly. "It does not matter what you say about him or my mother. They are… I have no attachment to them. I did not know either of them, so I do not feel as one would normally feel about a parent. You will neither please nor offend me with what you say. I simply want to know the truth."

"Your father was a man with a quick temper. He was not always kind. And she— She was not happy." Again she looked away.

Irene leaned toward the woman. "You said you did not want her to get in trouble with him. Why did you think that she would? Why would he have been angry? Why wouldn't he simply have been worried because she had gone missing?"

The older woman shifted uncomfortably in her seat, and this time her eyes went to Irene. "She was a good woman. You have to understand that."

Irene nodded. "I am sure that she was. Was— Had there been other mornings when she was not there?"

"No," Nancy replied slowly, shaking her head. "But sometimes, well, there was a time or two when, earlier in the night, she was not in her bed. She was always there the next morning, though."

Irene kept her gaze on the woman so reluctantly answering her question. She knew that the maid would be more willing to communicate what she knew about Lady Selene to another woman, and she wanted her to forget as much as possible that Lady Selene's son was sitting right there.

"Was she meeting a lover?"

Nancy's chewed at her lip nervously, and her hands twisted in her lap. "Yes. I mean— I think she was. I fell asleep sitting in her room one time, waiting for her so I could help her undress. I woke up when she came in. It must have been four o'clock in the morning. Why would she have been up that late? And there was something about her face— so flushed and happy. And there were other times when— she would just seem so much happier for a bit. She would come in from the garden, her arms full of flowers, and she would be humming and smiling. There were periods when she was happier for weeks at a time. And then she would be sad—I would catch her sitting, looking out a window, and there would be tears in her eyes."

"Do you know who the man was?"

Nancy shook her head. "No. She never talked to me about him. She wouldn't have wanted to burden me with it, for fear his lordship might question me. But she needn't have worried." The woman set her jaw defiantly. "I would never have told him anything."

"Of course you wouldn't," Irene agreed. "So that morning, you thought that perhaps she had just been out late with someone."

Nancy nodded. "I couldn't think of any other reason for her not to have gone to bed—though I thought she had stopped seeing him. It had been a long time since she had…acted so happy."

This time Irene could not help breaking contact with the woman to glance at Gideon. It seemed likely that the signs Nancy had seen had been when Lady Selene was having an affair with Jasper.

"So I was a little surprised and worried," Nancy went on. "But I didn't dare tell his lordship." She let out a little moan of regret. "Oh, I wish I'd gone straight to him! Maybe if I had he could have tracked those terrible men down." She turned toward Gideon. "He could have found you and your lady mother safe and sound."

"You must not blame yourself," Irene soothed her. "It was not your fault. You did the only thing you could do. And even if you had gone straight to him, obviously she had been gone for some time, since the bed had not been slept in. They would have been far away by then."

"That's right," Gideon agreed, his voice kind. "You could have done nothing else."

"Thank you, my lord," Nancy sniffed, giving him a grateful smile. She cleared her throat and wiped at her eyes again, then went on with her story. "But then the governess came running down, babbling about the young master. She said he was gone when she got up, and she'd looked all over for him. And then Lord Radbourne came to me, and I had to tell him that my lady was gone, too. I thought he would be furious with me for not telling him sooner, but he wasn't. He didn't even ask why I hadn't said anything earlier. He was— he was scared."

She said the words with a touch of amazement in her voice. "I'd never seen him look like that before. Usually he was a hard, cold man, but he looked scared that day. I could see his hands trembling. And then I realized that he must have loved her, even with the way he was. He told me that her ladyship and Master Gideon had been taken, stolen away and held for ransom." She sighed. "He sent that Owenby fellow out to give them the ransom, but then they didn't give you back. And I knew she must be dead."

"Did you ever think that perhaps she had not been taken?" Irene asked. "That she might have run away?"

Lady Selene's former maid looked at her a trifle guiltily. "I—I did, my lady. Right at first I did. It seemed odd, you know, that kidnappers could have come into the house and taken her and the boy without waking anyone up. I thought maybe she had deceived the earl, though it seemed too cruel a trick for her to play. But she had been so unhappy, and I thought it must have been because she had broken it off with the man, whoever he was, and I thought maybe she could not bear it anymore and decided to just run away and go to him. She would have taken you with her, sir, if she had left, for I know she could not have borne to leave you behind. So I— Well, I didn't tell his lordship, but I went to her room and checked her clothes, just to see if there were any missing."

"And were there?" Irene prompted when the woman fell silent.

"No. The only missing dress was the one she had been wearing the night before. But there was a nightgown gone, the one I'd laid out on her bed, and I couldn't find her dressing gown. And it seemed to me that one or two of her petticoats were not there. I couldn't be sure. She had a number of them, and there were some in the laundry to be washed."

"It doesn't seem like much to take with her if she had run away."

"No, ma'am. But that would have been like her. She wouldn't have wanted to take anything from him. She wouldn't have thought it was right."

"None of her jewelry was gone? Her hairbrush? Perfume?"

Nancy shook her head. "That was why I thought she must have been abducted after all. She wouldn't have wanted anything of his, but she would have needed her brush and mirror, wouldn't she? And what use would her perfume be to him? So I knew it must have been true—that they came in and took her and the boy. They must have just grabbed up the nightgown and dressing gown because they would have been lying right there, wouldn't they?" She frowned, started to speak, then stopped.

"What?" Irene asked quickly. "Was there something else?"

"Only…her little clock was missing."

"Her clock?"

Nancy nodded. "It's odd, isn't it? Doesn't seem like something someone would take if they were abducting someone, does it?"

"No, not really," Irene agreed.

"But neither does it seem the sort of thing someone would take if she were running away," Gideon added.

"That's true, sir, except it was something special to her. It was her mother's, a French ormolu clock. Pretty, it was, and not too big. You could hold it in your hand. She kept it on her dresser. It made me wonder, because it was something she might have wanted to take—it was hers, after all, not his, and she treasured it because it was her mother's. Her mother died when she was but a girl, you see," she added in explanation. "So I thought it might show she did run away, but…"

Her voice hitched, and she paused to regain control, then went on. "But I think maybe it was just that I wanted so much to think that she wasn't dead. That somebody hadn't taken you and her, and then killed you both." She shook her head. "Hope's a powerful thing, can make you think things that aren't true. More likely one those ruffians just figured that clock was small and easy to snatch, and would bring a few pounds."

Nancy lapsed into silence then.

"Are you sure that the times when she was late to bed had been some months prior to when she was abducted?" Irene asked.

The woman nodded. "Oh, yes, my lady. She had been sad for some time."

After that Nancy had little else to say, beyond a few more reiterations of how glad she was that Gideon had come home and how happy his mother would have been that he had survived. Gideon and Irene soon took their leave of her and returned to their carriage.

For the first part of the ride back to the Park, Gideon was silent, and Irene remained so, as well, suspecting that he needed some time in silence to come to terms with what Nancy had told them.

Finally, when they were well away from the village, he broke the silence, saying, "She was right about hope. You want to believe so much that eventually you do. I don't suppose we will ever know the truth of what happened."

"No, probably not," Irene agreed. There was a sadness in his eyes that made her want to lean across and take his hand, but she refrained.

"The thing is—if my uncle is correct and my mother did not run off with a lover, it raises a difficult question."

Irene looked over at him. "What actually did happen to Lady Selene?"

He nodded. "Yes. Was she killed? Did someone steal her from her bedroom?"

"But we know that your father made up the story about her being abducted. So that is not a possibility. He told his valet—if we are to believe him—that Lady Selene left him a letter telling him that she was taking you and running away."

"A letter that only he read," Gideon put in. "He told my grandmother about it, too, but I did not get the impression that she actually read it, only saw him waving it about. Convenient."

"Are you saying…do you think that your father…murdered her?" Irene's voice grew hushed as she said the words, as though saying them aloud would give reality to the events.

He shook his head. "I don't know. I—the maid seemed frightened of him. Even his mother agreed that he was quick-tempered. It is not something I like to consider, the possibility that I was sired by a murderer. But what other options are there, if she did not run away? Are we to believe that someone else crept into the house, stole her from it and killed her? After forcing her to write a note to my father, of course, making it look as though she had left voluntarily?"

Irene sighed. "It seems unlikely." She paused thoughtfully, then went on. "On the other hand, if your father killed her, what happened to you? How did you end up in London by yourself? It makes no sense. You were his only child, his heir. He would not have taken you to London and abandoned you there."

He shrugged. "That is odd. Nothing seems to concern the aristocracy more than the succession of their title. The same is true if Owenby killed her. He would not have taken me away to London. But who else could it have been? Who would want my mother dead and me gone?"

"Well, the likeliest candidate would have been your uncle," Irene pointed out. "He is the only one who would have benefited by your no longer being here. He was, after all, your father's heir after you. And if your father was grief-stricken enough, perhaps Jasper could have thought that Lord Cecil would not marry again."

"Yes, except for a couple of minor points—the first being that Uncle Jasper loved my mother."

"According to him," Irene countered.

Gideon raised his eyebrows at her. "My, you are a suspicious one. All right, we have only his word for that. But the second objection is that he was in India at the time it all took place. And my grandmother confirms that."

"He could have hired someone," Irene argued. "He might have sent a man to get rid of both of you, but the fellow wasn't able to bring himself to kill a child, so he simply abandoned you somewhere."

Gideon gave her a long look. "You have a frighteningly vivid imagination."

She grimaced at him. "Or—and this one sounds like an excellent candidate to me—Lady Teresa. Did you know that she and her family actually lived in this area?"

"No." He looked surprised. "But wouldn't she have been a child then?"

"She isn't that young. I think she said she was fifteen at the time." At his look, she went on. "Well, yes, it is a trifle young, but she could have had her sights set on being the Countess of Radbourne and eliminated the obstacles in her way—you and your mother."

"If I were murdered now, I think she would be an excellent candidate for the crime. But it's a bit far-fetched that at fifteen she even hatched such a plot, let alone carried it out. And how would she have gotten me to London?"

"All right. It was not a very viable idea," she conceded.

"And don't forget the letter. Whoever killed her would have had to get my mother to write that letter beforehand."

He was silent for a moment, then said, "Or maybe it simply was just as my father and Owenby said. My mother fled with a lover and took me with her. Perhaps Uncle Jasper simply cannot bear to believe that the woman he loved would have left with another man. She was unfaithful to my father with his brother. Why would she be so unlikely to be unfaithful again with someone else? And who is to say she did not want to be with the other man more than she had wanted to be with my uncle?"

"Or she reached a point where she could not bear to be with Lord Cecil any longer," Irene added. "There is another possibility that I have thought of. She was very sad, her maid said. It might be possible that she would have…"

Gideon's eyes narrowed. "Taken her own life?"

Irene nodded.

"Then why all the secrecy? Why make up such a tale?"

"There is a great deal of stigma attached to suicide," Irene pointed out. "The church…"

"You think the local church would not have bent to my family's influence? For that matter, that the coroner would not have conveniently found her death an accident?"

"There is still the scandal."

"Yes. But I cannot imagine it would outweigh what they would have had to do. What about her corpse?" he pointed out bluntly. "If she did not leave of her own free will, if she was murdered or took her own life, then they would have had to do something with her body. Hidden her somewhere."

The thought made Irene feel a trifle queasy. "Yes. It seems unlikely that they would have done so because of a suicide."

"And what else is there? That she went mad and was locked for years in the attic?"

"I know. It is all rather…unrealistic," she agreed.

"I think perhaps my uncle's belief is based more on what he wants to believe than what was true," Gideon said.

"But both Nancy and your uncle agree that you were the center of Lady Selene's life," Irene pointed out. "Whatever happened to her, I do not think she would have abandoned you. At least you have that."

"True—if you accept Nancy's and Uncle Jasper's accounts of what Lady Selene was like. What about Owenby's? According to him, it was my father who was good and she was wicked. I suppose it does not matter, really, either way. Clearly my parentage was deficient. An unfaithful wife for a mother, one who conceivably would have taken her child away from his home, his heritage. And a father who did not care enough to try to get his own child back."

"Or maybe it is simply that both your parents were human. A little wrong, a little weak. Perhaps your mother was guilty only of loving someone to the detriment of everything else."

"The sort of love that poets praise, no doubt." His mouth twisted cynically. "That, at least, is one failing I shall not have to worry about."

"I suppose not," she agreed, aware of the drag of regret in her chest. "Neither one of us shall."

The carriage turned into the lane leading to Radbourne Park, and a few moments later they were rattling across the small bridge. Gideon cast a look toward the house looming in the distance, and his expression turned reluctant. Suddenly he reached up and rapped upon the roof of the carriage. The vehicle rolled to a stop.

"Come," he said to Irene impulsively, and opened the door to climb down. He turned back, holding up his hand to help her out. "Please? There is something I would like to show you."

She raised her eyebrows in surprise, but she took his hand and climbed down. He struck off on a course parallel to the edge of the woods, and intrigued, she followed him.

CHAPTER SEVENTEEN

THEY WALKED for perhaps twenty minutes, staying close to the woods, then cutting through the swath of trees that curved back toward the house. Irene saw that they were close to the ruins of the Norman keep that had once kept watch over the Bankes land, long before the earldom had been bestowed on them.

She had seen the place on her first walk here and had wanted to explore it, but she had not yet done so. The riding party a few days earlier had gone past the ruins, and Lady Calandra, unsurprisingly, had thought it would be fun to explore. They had not stopped, however, for Miss Surton had declared with a shiver that it was eerie, and Gideon had prosaically commented that the place was too unstable to poke about in.

"The ruins?" Irene said now, casting a quizzical glance at Gideon. "Is that what you wanted me to see?"

"In a way. Something inside the tower."

"I thought it was too unstable, that it was dangerous to go inside," she reminded him.

A quick grin flashed across his face. "For Miss Surton, it is, certainly."

Irene let out a gurgle of laughter. It pleased her more than she cared to admit to hear Gideon's dismissal of Rowena Surton.

He led her into the tower. It was dim inside, but as they climbed the stairs, chinks and even holes in the stonework let in more and more sunlight. They emerged onto the top floor, and he opened the sturdy wooden door, revealing a room beyond. Irene drew in her breath in surprise.

Unlike the rest of the tower, dust and ruin had been banished here. A large piece of canvas slanted from the remains of the fallen roof down across to the waist-high southern wall of the tower, closing out the elements. A rug was spread across the portion of the room farthest from the half-ruined wall, and upon it were a pile of large comfortable pillows and a low table, as well as a small bookcase. A kerosene lamp sat on the table, and two candles stood on the bookcase. Close to the canvas-covered wall, by itself, with only a stool nearby, was a telescope.

"Gideon!" Irene looked around her, amazed. "I had no idea!"

"No one does." He walked over to the wall and unwound a rope from a bracket, then pulled on it on it, and the canvas rolled up, opening the room to the outside.

"It's beautiful," Irene breathed, looking at the suddenly revealed view of the countryside. She raised her head, looking up at the late afternoon sky.

"So this is where you come at night!" she exclaimed.

"What?" It was his turn to look surprised.

"I've seen you once or twice, late in the evening, walking out through the gardens, and I've wondered where you went." She paused, then added candidly, "I thought perhaps you were having an assignation."

"Indeed?" He arched his brows. "How…interesting to hear your opinion of me. And who did you think I was coming to meet? One of my tenants' wives? A maid?"

"I had no idea. But I could not imagine why else you would be slipping out this way, on foot, at that time of night. I had no idea you were an astronomer."

"I scarcely qualify for that title," he replied easily, strolling over to the telescope and running a hand along it. "Actually, I had no interest in it—indeed, had never thought of it—until I came here. But this telescope was in the house— a hobby of my grandfather's, apparently—and I decided to try it out. I found the skies fascinating, and then, when I was roaming about, learning the grounds, I came upon the tower and saw how, with a little rebuilding, it could be used for an observatory." He looked out across the landscape. "I find it soothing. An escape." In an undertone, he added, "I have used it a great deal the last few days."

Irene glanced at him sharply, then looked away. "You… have not enjoyed the party?" she asked in a determinedly casual tone, keeping her eyes on the landscape beyond.

He made a low, inarticulate noise. "Bloody hell, Irene! Of course I have not enjoyed it. Who could enjoy listening to conversation so treacly it makes one's teeth ache? Everything is so 'sweet,' so 'cunning,' so 'pretty' and 'pleasant.' If I ask for an opinion, all I receive is a laugh or a wave of the fan, or perhaps, 'Oh, my lord, I do not know. What do *you* think?' What sort of an answer is that? I *know* what *I* think."

She could not help but laugh, and he swung on her with a dark look.

"Oh, yes, well you may laugh. You are not the one having to endure it. Don't think I have not seen you sneak away every chance you get."

She should not have been so pleased, she knew, to learn that he was not enjoying the dogged pursuit of the young women at the party—or that he had noticed when she left the room.

"There is little for me to enjoy," she replied, and though she knew she should not, she added, "You did not even ask me to dance."

He glanced at her, something sparking in his eyes. "Ah, that rankled, did it?"

"Is that why you did not ask?" she countered, his remark sparking the dry tinder of her hurt and anger. "To rankle me? Were you punishing me?"

"I did not ask you," he said, each word short and sharp, "because you do not care to be my wife. You have made that plain. Therefore I must turn my mind to those who are willing."

Irene burned to make a sharp retort, but she could think of nothing that was not foolish. He was right. She was not in the running, and it would be a waste of his time to dance or talk with her when he could be measuring the others' assets as a bride.

"Of course. I forget that friendship and emotions have no place in your scheme of things."

She shot him a flashing glance, head high and chin up in a defiant pose.

Gideon took a step toward her, his eyes suddenly burning hot, and for an instant the air between them was charged, heavy and humming with anger and heat.

She thought that he was going to pull her to him and kiss her as he had before, and her loins blossomed with warmth, her nipples tightened. Her body felt as if it were opening to him, and she knew that if he kissed her, she would go up in flames like straw at the touch of a match.

She wanted nothing more than that. And nothing scared her more.

She turned abruptly, striding away from him to the center of the room. Almost before she knew what she was going to say, the words came tumbling out of her mouth. "Tell me about Dora."

There was an instant of stunned silence following her request, and she swung around to look at him.

"What?" he asked. "Why do you ask about Dora?"

"That was the name you said, the woman whom you were protecting from my father's advances," Irene went on. "That night, when I found you downstairs…"

"Yes. She is the faro dealer I told you about."

"Is that all she is to you? An employee?"

"No," he replied, his eyes searching her face. "Why are you asking me this? Who told you about Dora?"

"Teresa. I remembered the name when she said it. I remembered how you told my father never to touch her again."

"And do you have a difficulty with Dora?" he asked, his voice tight, his eyes guarded.

"I?" Irene responded with a sinking heart. His attitude was certainly not that of a man speaking about an employee. "No. How should I have a difficulty with Dora? I have never met the woman."

"Then what is your interest?"

"Curiosity, I suppose," she answered in a voice she hoped was as cool as his. "I wonder if you will tell your wife about her."

"I will," he responded, his eyes still fastened on hers. "She is a part of my life. My wife will have to realize that."

"So part of the price she must pay to become countess is to endure your mistress?"

He looked at her for a long moment. "Is that what Teresa told you? That Dora is my mistress?"

"Yes. She said that she had heard you arguing about her with your grandmother. She said you told Lady Radbourne that you would never give her up."

Gideon released a sigh. "Dora is not my mistress."

Irene tried not to sag with relief.

"I have known Dora for years, since I was a child. We grew up together. She was another of the children Jack collected about him. She was a little younger than I, smaller, weaker. We were friends. I protected her. We shared our food, our blankets. She is…for all my life, she has been the closest thing that I have had to a family. She is like my sister. But I have never—just the thought of *that,* with her, is inconceivable."

He looked, Irene realized in amazement, almost embarrassed.

"Indeed, she is engaged to Piers," he went on. "But one thing Teresa said is true. I will not give her up. Ever. Any more than I would give up Piers." His gaze was defiant.

"Of course not." Irene's smile was dazzling. "No one should ask you to."

He let out a noncommittal grunt. "You should speak to Lady Odelia and my grandmother."

"I suspect, deep down, even Lady Odelia admires your loyalty."

"And do you think any of those young ladies will?"

Irene hesitated. Quite frankly, she doubted it. What was disturbing, she realized, was that the idea of his prospective brides falling short pleased her.

"If she is the proper wife for you, she will," she answered finally, somewhat primly.

He looked at her for a long moment, and suddenly nervous, Irene turned away. "We should leave soon, or we will be late for supper."

"Yes. Of course."

He rolled the canvas back, securing it in place, and they left the tower.

THE LARGEST EVENT of the weeklong house party was the ball scheduled for the following evening. There was only another day planned for the guests after that, and then the visitors would pack up and leave. The ball would be an opportunity for everyone to dress up in their finery and look their very best, and Irene felt sure that most of the girls planned to put their utmost effort into the evening.

She had spent almost a week watching the five young women flirt and chatter with Gideon—with the exception of Amanda Hurley, who seemed to be forming an attachment for Rowena Surton's equally horse-mad brother Percy— and planning entertainments to give them the opportunity to carry on their flirtations. Irene was, quite frankly, thoroughly tired of the whole lot of them, and she would be glad to see them gone in another two days.

As for the ball…well, she had quite selfishly decided that she would do no more planning or assisting or maneuvering to aid any of them. She intended, instead, to set herself to the task of enjoying the evening. Her time here was coming to an end, too, and soon enough she and her mother would be back with her brother and Maura, a thought that was enough to quite depress her spirits. So, she decided, she would dress up in the lovely ball gown she had bought for the occasion, and she would dance and talk and laugh. And if Gideon again chose to ignore her…well, that would be his loss.

The next evening—when she was dressed for the ball in the gold satin gown, her hair swept up into a soft arrangement of curls, tiny golden sparkling ornaments glittering here and there among her darker gold curls, and the gossamer-thin wrap of gold tissue draped across her bare arms—she knew her decision had been the right one. The soft shining material turned her eyes a pale, compelling gold and warmed her skin. She might be returning soon to a lifetime of spinsterhood, but tonight she was lovely and glowing. The very air shimmered with promise.

She went down to the ball with Francesca, who assured her as they descended the stairs that she would be the most beautiful woman in the house tonight. Irene smiled; the words were pleasant to hear. But the feeling was nothing compared to the warmth that filled her when she stepped into the ballroom and Gideon turned and saw her. His eyes widened, and the fire that sprang to life in them was swift and fierce.

He continued to gaze at her for a long moment, his eyes boring into hers, and it was not until one of the people with whom he was standing reached out to touch his arm that he finally turned back to his conversation.

"Well," Francesca said beside her, "I believe that Lord Radbourne's response was precisely what you intended."

Irene turned to look at her. "I did not intend anything."

Francesca let out a light laugh. "Irene, please, do not try to gammon me, I beg you."

Irene narrowed her eyes. "I don't know what you are talking about."

"The way you look, of course. The hair, the dress—you have taken particular care with yourself tonight, and the result is obvious. You look like a goddess. A golden goddess, at that. Who else would anyone think all this effort was for?" She cocked a knowing brow.

Irene flushed. "If you are talking about Lord Radbourne, I can assure you that I do not care a whit what he thinks."

"No, I am sure not." Francesca smiled in her catlike way. "Nor was that a look of triumph I saw in your eyes when he turned and stared at you as if he could eat you up."

Irene's cheeks turned even hotter. "Francesca! No!"

"Yes."

Irene wanted to protest, but she knew it would be foolish to do so. She had wanted to bring that look into Gideon's eyes. The question, of course, was why? And why did she feel such a rush of excitement and satisfaction at her success?

Did she want so much to outshine the other young women here? She did not really dislike any of them, and it seemed a very petty thing to do. After all, they were interested in becoming the next Countess of Radbourne, and she did not even want the prize.

But even as she had the thought, she knew she was not being entirely honest. It was true that she did not seek to be the Countess of Radbourne, but she had wanted the prize: the look in Gideon's eyes.

She did not want to marry. But she wanted Gideon.

"I am a terrible person," she confessed in a low voice to Francesca.

Francesca shrugged. "Not terrible. Only human. What female does not want a man's admiration…? Especially the admiration of the man she loves?"

"Francesca! You are quite wrong. I do not love Gideon. I did, I admit, feel a certain low satisfaction in—in making him notice me. And I have been foolishly bothered by the fact that he has been dancing attendance on all the other young women here. But that is utter nonsense, I know. I intended for him to pay attention to them. That is why we worked with him so much."

"No. I worked with him to force you to be around him long enough to realize how you felt. The other women are here only in case you never come to your senses, or he gets so annoyed with you that he chooses someone else."

Irene stared at her. "What?"

"Irene. Really." Francesca linked her arm with Irene's. "My dear girl, I saw how it was with you two as soon as I watched you together in the park that day. It was utterly clear to anyone—or at least to anyone as accustomed as I am to watching people tumble into love—that the two of you were, well, in a word, *destined*."

"Destined?" Irene repeated blankly. "You mean, destined for each other? Are you mad? We argued the whole time we talked in the park."

"Yes, you did. But it was the way you argued. You were both clearly upset because you challenged each other's preconceptions. You each had very orderly arrangements, and the other one did not fit into them at all. Naturally you were upset. But the…attraction was unmistakable. I knew it was just a matter of time until you figured it out. You are a clever girl."

Irene gaped at her. "All of this…" She waved her hand vaguely around the room. "All of this was just a…a ruse?"

"Oh, no. It wasn't a ruse at all. I did need your help. Your assistance was absolutely essential." Francesca smiled at her, amusement brimming in her eyes.

Irene was torn between anger and laughter, but Francesca's smile was too infectious, and after a moment she lost the battle and chuckled. "You are outrageous," she told her friend, shaking her head. "Well, I hope you will not be too disappointed when your plans do not work out as you had hoped. I have no intention of marrying Lord Radbourne."

"Indeed, that is too bad," Francesca said without any visible sign of distress. "I fear he will be exceedingly unhappy. But…" She shrugged. "When your heart is not engaged, it simply is not. Poor man. You still find him disagreeable, then? Maddening, I think you called him. Selfish, annoying…"

"No! I mean, yes, he is all those things," Irene agreed. "However, I do not dislike him. No, indeed. I have come to quite appreciate the man. He is strong and capable, and once you come to know him, you realize that he possesses a sharp wit. He is an excellent man. Everyone—his relatives most of all—have grossly misjudged him."

"Have they?" Francesca murmured.

"Oh, yes." Irene nodded. "It is a wonder, really, that he puts up with them. A lesser man would have tossed them out on their ears by now."

"If you hold such admiration for him, I am at a loss to understand why you would not marry him," Francesca told her.

"You know why I have no plans to marry."

"Yes, but when one meets a man who stirs one so, then such plans usually fail, and the reasons you used to cling to no longer apply."

Irene shook her head. "I am not, I hope, so inconsistent. And he—he does not want a true marriage. To love him would be a futile exercise. He does not want love. Marriage is a business arrangement for him. A practicality."

"Indeed." Francesca frowned. "Is it truly so? The look he sent you did not seem so cold."

"Oh, he is not cold," Irene responded, and again her cheeks turned pink. "He is, in fact, quite bold in that way. But that is not love."

"Ah. Well, many women I know would feel that they could turn such 'boldness' into a deeper feeling. They might believe that with a little effort, such a man could come to love a woman who loved him."

"Perhaps. But…it does not matter. Marriage is not something I long for. And 'tis better, surely, to avoid the pain that could come with such hopes. To love a man who does not return your love must be painful indeed."

"Yes, I suppose it must be." For an instant, sorrow shadowed Francesca's lovely face, but then she shrugged it off. "Well, you are a very strong woman, Irene. I admire you. Few women would be able to turn away as you can. To face not seeing Gideon again. To return to the life you have lived until now. Many would be unable to bear the thought of the loneliness. The pain."

Irene's smile wavered. "I will manage, I am sure."

"Of course you will."

Determinedly, Irene sought to change the subject. She glanced around, saying, "There are a number of new people here tonight."

"Yes," Francesca agreed. "A few local people whom Lady Odelia considers good enough for a large gathering—the squire and his family, the vicar and his wife. And Lady Odelia's invitation is command enough to bring several others here just for the night. They have been tucked into the undamaged rooms in the old wing."

"Not the best of accommodations."

"No, but 'quite well enough for them,' as Lady Odelia would say." Francesca shrugged a shoulder. She stiffened suddenly and stared across the ballroom, muttering a soft, "What is *she* doing here?"

"What? Who?" Intrigued, Irene followed Francesca's gaze. She saw a woman with dramatically good looks standing across the ballroom, chatting with Lady Odelia and her sister.

The woman was older than Francesca by a few years, but she was still lovely, even though she must now be on the far side of thirty-five. She was tall and voluptuously built, with auburn hair and large pale blue eyes.

"Lady Swithington?" Irene asked, a little surprised. The woman, until recently married to her second elderly lord, was no longer a mainstay of London society. She had been living with Lord Swithington on his Welsh properties for some years, until his recent death, only rarely returning to London for a Season.

"Yes. Lady Daphne." Francesca looked at her for another moment, then turned back to Irene, offering her a tight smile. "I would have thought that, so soon after Lord Swithington's death, she would not..." Francesca stopped and offered up a brittle smile. "But of course, I should have known Daphne's mourning would pass swiftly. And she has always been connected to the Lilles. I believe Lady Odelia dotes on her."

"I cannot imagine Lady Odelia doting on anyone," Irene retorted honestly, but she did not pursue the matter. She watched as Francesca glanced around the room, stopping when her gaze fell on the Duke of Rochford, who stood chatting with his sister Callie.

"Well, it is of no matter anyway," Francesca went on brightly. "If you will excuse me, I must check in with all our girls."

"Of course." Irene's curiosity was aroused, but she was too polite to press Francesca on the matter.

The older woman started to walk away, then turned to give Irene a shrewd look. "He may profess no interest in love, my dear, but I think it is safe to say that Lord Radbourne has a decided interest in *you*."

With a nod, she was gone.

Irene was not alone long. Soon Piers strolled up to ask her for a dance, then stayed to chat with her and survey the scene. And long before the night was over, she had danced with almost every man in the room, including the somewhat intimidating Duke of Rochford. Only one man did not talk to her or ask her onto the floor—the one man she wanted to do so.

Gideon watched her. She knew that, for she had glanced up a time or two and found his eyes on her. They had swirled around the ballroom to the lilting strains of a waltz, each with another partner, but she had been aware the whole time of where he was, and she knew that he was just as aware of her. Yet still, he did not ask her to dance.

It grew close to midnight, when the music would stop and everyone would go down to the lavish supper laid out in the assembly room. Irene was beginning to despair that Gideon would ever appear when suddenly she looked up and saw him walking straight toward her. He did not look to either side or pause to talk to anyone, but kept his eyes on her, his intent clear.

Her hand clenched around her fan, and her stomach began to jangle with nerves. Her eyes met his and held. She felt as if her heart might jump right out of her chest.

"Irene." He stopped in front of her.

She nodded to him, striving for at least a modicum of cool aplomb. "My lord."

Gideon sent a single hard look at Mr. Surton, who had been standing talking to Irene, and the man was quick to take the hint. "Excuse me. I, ah, I must go speak to…"

His voice trailed off as he executed a bow in her direction and left.

"I believe this is my dance," Gideon said to her.

"Indeed?" She arched an eyebrow, nettled by his tone. "I do not remember your asking me."

"I am asking you now."

She was somewhat inclined to argue, but then she looked into his eyes and the words died in her throat. Desire stirred and coiled deep within her belly, awakened by the heat in his gaze. She simply nodded and took his arm.

They strolled out to the dance floor. His arm was like iron beneath her palm, and Irene knew that her hand was trembling just a bit. She wondered if he could feel it, and if he understood the jittering tumble of emotions that was dancing through her.

She turned to face him, and he took his hand in hers, his other hand going to her waist. They stood poised for a long moment, as the first haunting strains of the violins began, and then the whole orchestra came in with the surging, unmistakable rhythm of the waltz, and they began to dance.

Gideon did not speak, nor did Irene try to find anything to say. There was too much pleasure, too much emotion, in this moment. It was enough to feel his arm around her, his hand upon hers. It was enough to look up into his face and see the hunger that was written there.

She needed no words to know what he felt; the same

needs roiled in her. And when, as the song ended, he whisked her out onto the terrace, she went easily.

There were other couples there, enjoying the cool evening air, and Irene nodded and smiled to them, wafting her fan as the other ladies did, in the pretext of cooling her face. They drifted farther down the terrace, until finally, with a glance back at the others, Gideon slipped around the corner of the house, pulling her with him.

His hands clasped her arms, turning her to face him, and he gazed down into her face. "God, but you are beautiful. You bewitched me tonight."

"I did?" Irene could not suppress a slow, satisfied smile. "I would not have known it. You did not speak to me all evening."

"I tried my best not to," he retorted. "I have tried my best all week. Blast it, Irene!" Temper flared in his eyes. "I thought—I hoped that you would care, that you would notice, at least, if I stayed away from you. I danced attendance on those ninnies, praying all the while that you would see, you would realize. But clearly jealousy does not exist in you, at least not for me. I told myself that if you so disliked the idea of wedding me, then I must find another." He glared at her in frustration. "But I could not! I know I will not ever!"

Gideon pulled her to him, and his mouth came down to cover hers. His lips were hot and eager, his kiss searing, and the hunger in it shook Irene down to her toes. She let out a soft noise, and her hands went to his waist, sliding beneath his jacket. He jerked a little in surprise, and she started to remove her hands, but he clasped them in his own, holding them to him.

"No," he murmured. "Don't leave. You have no idea how much I have longed to feel your hands upon me." He nuzzled his face into her hair, moving to lay a soft kiss upon her ear, then turning his attention to her neck. "You've no idea how hard it is to stand there listening to one of them giggle and chatter, and all the time, all I can think of is the line of your throat when you lift her head and laugh, or the soft curve of your breast, or the way the material of your dress drapes around your legs."

She shivered, as much from his heated words as from the silken touch of his lips. "Gideon…"

He pressed his lips into the soft hollow of her throat, then worked his way back up her neck. Her head fell back, offering up the soft, vulnerable expanse of her throat. She felt heavy and languid, her blood pooling hotly in the depths of her loins.

"How can I choose one of those silly, insipid girls—" he rasped "—when you are here? Do you honestly think I could settle for their giggles and niceties, when all I long to hear is one trenchant remark from you? I burn for you. Every night I lie in bed thinking of you, with desire dancing over my skin like fire until I think I shall go mad. And not once— not once—do Miss Surton's blue eyes come into my head. Not once do my hands itch to slide over Lady Flora's curves. All I can think of are golden eyes, like molten metal. All I want beneath my fingertips are your breasts…your hips…."

His hands slid over her, punctuating his words, curving around her breasts and sliding down over her hips.

"All I want is you," he finished, his lips hovering at the corner of her mouth. Then his lips were on hers, hard and hungry, opening her mouth to his seeking tongue.

Irene shook under the force of the passion sweeping through her, and she dug her hands into his shirt, clinging to him. Her breasts felt swollen and aching, the nipples tightening in need, and she pressed herself up into his body, yearning to feel his hardness against her. Desire blossomed between her legs, hot and damp.

His hands clamped over her buttocks, grinding her against him, and he pulled his mouth away to string hot kisses down her throat and onto the soft curves of her breasts.

"Marry me," he murmured urgently against her soft skin. "Take me from this misery and be my wife." He raised his head and looked down into her eyes. His face was soft and slack with hunger, his eyes ablaze with desire. "I want you in my bed. I want you beside me every day. I want your face to be the last thing I see at night and the first thing I see in the morning."

"Gideon…" Irene breathed, swamped with emotion.

"I haven't a poet's way with words," he went on. "I am a blunt, hard man, I know. I cannot offer you words of love. I think that love is…not in me any longer, if it ever was. But I know this—I want you as my wife. I want to share my life with you. I want to know you in every way a man can possibly know a woman. And I can promise that I will protect you and care for you. I will not harm you. I swear it. Marry me, Irene."

She stared up at him, her mind a jumble of thoughts and emotions. His words had melted her; she burned with desire, and yet felt strangely weak and tender. He did not love her; he had made a point of saying so. How could she hope to live a happy life without her husband's love? Yet how could she choose anything but a life with him?

"Gideon, I—I don't know what to say."

"Bloody hell!" he cried in a low voice. "Can you not, just for once in your life, say yes?"

"I must think," she told him shakily. She had always prided

herself on thinking, on not being ruled by her emotions. How could she throw all caution to the winds?

"Don't think!" he shot back. "Damn it, Irene…"

They stared at each other for a long moment. She felt frozen, unable to move or speak.

With a low oath, he broke the embrace, took a step away, then swung back. "I cannot go back in there. I am going to the tower."

He did not finish, just broke off and strode away across the terrace and down the steps into the garden.

CHAPTER EIGHTEEN

IRENE HURRIED AFTER Gideon to the top of the steps, watching him as he disappeared into the dark of the garden. She stood there, her hands clenched into tight fists, struggling to hold back her tears. She felt bereft, as if something had been torn from her. And she knew in that moment that what had been taken from her was her heart.

She loved Gideon. No words, no logic, no amount of thinking could change that. She was not sure when she had fallen in love with him, when the immediate, intense desire she had felt from the moment she met him had turned into something deeper. But somehow, somewhere along the way, she had given her heart to him.

She loved him, and she knew that the last thing she wanted was to turn away from him. She had thought the worst that would happen when she refused him was that she would have to return to live with her brother and sister-in-law. But now she realized that her life would be far worse than that—she would have to live without Gideon for the remainder of her years. Just the thought of it sent pain slicing through her.

She brought her hands up to her flushed cheeks. She knew deep down that she could trust Gideon. He would not harm her, would not control her, would do none of the things that had always made the thought of marriage so frightening. Such fears were, in the end, not what had held her back. What was truly frightening was the realization that she could give her love to him and not receive his love in return.

And that, she thought, was what held her poised over the precipice now.

If she went to him, if she married him, she would be giving herself entirely to him, offering up her love, her very self. Yet Gideon had just told her that he did not love her—indeed, did not think himself capable of love. Could she allow herself to step into such emotional danger? To love even though she might never receive his love in return?

But even as she wondered whether she could, she realized that not to give him her love would lead to a worse fate, much worse. To hold back from marrying him now would be sheer cowardice. The only true course that her love could take was to commit herself to him. If she did not follow that path, she was denying her love, denying her very self. She would be giving herself over to a life of lonely bitterness, and all because she was afraid to take the ultimate step.

Irene let out a low cry and ran down the steps. Lifting her skirt to her ankles to keep from tripping over it, she hurried through the garden, following the path Gideon had taken. The light of the moon was all she had to see by, and when she came to the darker reaches of the garden, where trees and shrubs grew up to hedge her in and block the light, she had to slow to a walk.

She arrived at the edge of the gardens finally and emerged onto the narrow path leading to the ruins. To her right lay the woods, dark and impenetrable. At another time she might have been frightened of passing this way by herself at night, but tonight she thought of nothing but Gideon.

There, ahead of her, stood the ruins of the tower, and her pace quickened until she was almost running. "Gideon!"

She called his name again as she hurried up to the base of the tower. She stopped at the ruined doorway, one hand upon the stone to steady herself, and drew in her breath. Suddenly she felt a little shy, and when she said his name this time, it came out more tentatively. "Gideon?"

There was the screech of wood on stone, and light spilled into the stairway above her head. "Irene?"

"Yes." Her heart was pounding so hard that she thought he must hear it even from the floor above her. "I am here."

"Irene!" Feet pounded down the stone steps, and he came to a stop on the landing, looking down at her. His eyes were dark in the dim light; his skin seemed stretched tautly over his facial bones.

"My answer is yes," she said, unable to hide the little catch in her voice.

He took the stairs two at a time and wrapped his arms around her, lifting her up and burying his face in her hair. "Irene, Irene…I've been half mad. I thought I'd been an utter fool, leaving like that, making you choose."

He kissed her ear, her hair, her face, as his words spilled out. "I was about to go back and tell you that I was an idiot, that I would wait for as long as it took you to decide."

Irene let out a delighted chuckle. "But you needn't, for I am here now, and I have decided. I want you. I want to marry you."

"Then we are of one mind." He swept her in his arms and started up the steps. "That is no doubt a first for us—and it may be the last time, as well."

"You think that we shall argue?" Irene asked him, opening

her eyes wide in mock dismay. "But, my lord, we shall be as one."

"If you ever stopped arguing with me, I am sure I would not know what to do. In fact, I think I would be certain that something was very, very wrong."

Gideon carried her into the room he had made in the tower and set her down, kicking the door closed behind them. He stood looking down at her for a long moment, then set her on the floor and cupped her face in his hands.

"Lady Radbourne. My wife," he said experimentally.

"I am not your wife yet," she reminded him.

He took one of her hands and raised it to his mouth, kissing her knuckles. "We are promised now. Bound. I will tell my grandmother tomorrow, and then I shall go back with you to London to formally ask your brother for your hand. But I have received the only answer I need tonight."

He opened her hand, turning it up and laying another kiss in her palm. "I have only one requirement," he said, then kissed her hand again.

"And what is that?"

"That we be married soon," he replied, a wicked grin curving his lips.

He traced the line of her jaw, watching the progress of his finger as it curved down over her chin and onto the tender flesh of her throat, gliding lower and lower until it skimmed the soft fleshy tops of her breasts and slid down into the dark crevice between them.

Irene's breath caught in her throat, and her heart began to hammer like a mad thing. "Have you no patience, sir?"

She cast a long golden look up at him from beneath her lashes, full of invitation, and was rewarded by the faint trembling of his fingertip against her skin.

"I have no patience at all where you are concerned," he answered, and his smile was a little vulpine. Yet Irene found it did not frighten her at all; it only stirred her blood more.

He lightly traced the neckline of her ball gown across the tops of her breasts with the fingertips of one hand, then spread his hand out flat across her chest before sliding it up to curl around her neck.

"I want you now," he said thickly. "And always."

He bent his head to brush his mouth across hers lightly, returning again and then a third time, tracing the seam of her lips with his tongue. Irene drew in a little breath of surprise at the intimate touch, and she felt him smile against her lips as his mouth settled onto hers.

He kissed her for a long, leisurely time, exploring and teasing sensation after sensation from her. She felt as if all her muscles and bones were melting, and she leaned into him, her hands going up to his chest to support her.

Gideon spanned her waist with his hands, holding her upright as his mouth continued to plunder hers. When at last he raised his head, she sagged weakly against him, her cheek upon his chest. He bent and kissed the top of her head, murmuring her name.

"You are so beautiful," he told her. "You looked like a goddess tonight. Rich and golden. All I could think about was putting my hands on you."

He matched his actions to his words, sliding one hand down her back and lingering over her hips. With the same slow care that his lips had used on hers, he caressed her, moving his hands slowly, intimately, over her. He turned her so that she leaned back against him, and she went easily, willingly, luxuriating in his touch. Looping one arm around her waist, he held her against him, while his other hand smoothed over her breasts and down onto her stomach.

Gently he aroused her through the material of her clothes, his fingertips teasing over the sensitive tips of her breasts and curving beneath them to cup their weight, then sliding down over the flat plane of her stomach and abdomen to delve into the notch between her legs.

Irene let out a startled noise then, stiffening a little at the unexpected touch, but his fingers moved slowly, gently, igniting the myriad of sensitive nerves that gathered there, and before long it was a soft moan of pleasure that escaped her lips. Moisture flooded between her legs, and she was aware of a deeper, hungrier yearning.

She moved against him, rubbing herself against his body behind her, and she was pleased to hear his low groan. The sound of his desire further stirred her, and she realized that she wanted very much to arouse him as he had aroused her.

Irene turned into him, setting her hands to roam across his body. "Show me how to please you. Let me give you pleasure."

"Everything you do gives me pleasure," he assured her, stiffening and suppressing another groan as her fingertips slid across the front of his breeches.

"I like it when you do this," she said, running her hands around behind him and gliding over his buttocks. "Do you like it?" she asked, sinking her fingertips into his flesh.

His response was a choked noise and the sudden jerk of his body against hers, and it was answer enough for her. She smiled, caressing him again. Then she took a step back and reached up to pull the pins from her hair.

"You told me once that you wanted to see my hair come down," she said softly.

His eyes glittered in response. "I do."

He watched her, his chest rising and falling rapidly as her fingers worked through her hair, loosening curl after curl. The long tresses tumbled down over her hands and arms, caressing her skin. He watched her until at last he could stand still no longer, and then he reached out, sinking his hands into her springing curls.

He kissed her again, but with increasing urgency now, as if he could not get enough of the taste of her mouth. He pulled away at last to unfasten her gown with hands that trembled. With equally clumsy fingers, she worked at his buttons until she opened his shirt wide enough that she could slide her hands beneath it. Slowly she roamed the bare ridges and curves of his chest.

Gideon went still, his hands going to her shoulders to steady himself as she caressed his bare skin. His teeth sank into his lower lip, holding back the moans that threatened to break from him as her inexperienced fingers aroused him almost past bearing. She explored his ribs and chest, fingers curling around his flat masculine nipples and gliding downward over the softer flesh of his stomach until she came up against the barrier of his waistband.

"Sweet Lord, you are killing me," he murmured.

Irene raised her head, concerned. "Should I stop? Did I hurt you?"

He shook his head, seizing her hand and bringing it up to his lips. "Only a pleasure so sweet 'tis near pain." He shrugged out of his shirt and tossed it aside. "But let me please you now."

Gideon hooked his hands into the shoulders of her gown, now unfastened to below her waist, and peeled it down, revealing her soft white curves encased in only a chemise and petticoats. After untying the strings of the petticoats, he let them fall in a puddle at her feet. Watching her, watching his hands on her, he undid the ribbons of her chemise and opened it, freeing her breasts from all constraint. He slid the cloth off her shoulders, his eyes intent on the soft cotton as it dragged over her rosy, peaked nipples.

Irene's breath hitched. She had never dreamed that it would stir her so to have Gideon's eyes on her naked body, to see the desire that darkened his gaze and softened his mouth.

He reached out and slowly, delicately drew his fingertips over her breasts, circling the centers, which hardened even more at his touch. She trembled, unprepared for the intense pleasure that speared down through her, spreading in a hot pool deep in her loins. She had never known, never guessed, that a man's touch could make her feel this way—so unsettled, so eager, so tingling with pleasure.

Gideon cupped her breasts in his hands, his thumbs circling around her nipples. Then he bent his head and drew one nipple into his mouth, stroking it with his tongue as his thumbs had done a moment before. Irene's knees buckled at the new sensation, and she was grateful for the strong arm he looped around her waist, holding her up. His mouth tugged at her breast, hot and wet, while his tongue teased the tight bud. It seemed to Irene that some invisible cord of pleasure ran straight down through her, connecting her tender nipple to the core of her being, and with every pull of his mouth, every caress of his tongue, the cord pulsed, flooding her loins with heat and need.

She dug her fingers into his thick hair, holding on as the sensations swirled and built within her. Even the feel of his hair between her fingers excited her, she realized. She could not hold back a moan as his mouth left her nipple. She waited, panting a little, as his mouth trailed across her breasts. She felt supremely alive and sensitive to every slight sensation; even the touch of the evening air upon her dampened nipple made the hunger in her swell. And then his mouth fastened on her other breast, slowly, leisurely, bringing it to life.

Irene choked back a little sobbing breath, and her hands slid down the firm column of Gideon's neck to his shoulders. She stroked the bony ridge of his collarbone and curved her palms over his shoulders, then let them drift down over the smooth skin of his arms, underlaid with muscle, and found herself fascinated and aroused by the combination of textures.

He lifted her, carrying her over to the pillows that lay tumbled across the floor near the wall. After setting her down, he went to the last garment that covered her, untying the ribbons at the waist of her pantaloons. The waistband sagged, and he slipped his hands beneath it, slowly shoving the material down as his hands slid down over the sides of her hips. The undergarment fell to her feet, leaving her naked to his gaze except for the thin stockings on her legs, more provocative than concealing, and her flimsy dancing slippers.

He looked at her, his eyes heavy-lidded with desire, his face flushed. A lady, she supposed, should have been repulsed by the lust stamped upon his features, but she found that the way he looked at her only made her want him more.

Gideon curved his hands over her backside, then around, and after going down on one knee, he rolled her stockings down, one by one, taking the garters with them, then lifted each foot and took off her dancing slipper and pulled the stocking free. She reached a hand to his shoulder for balance. His flesh was searing.

He pressed a soft kiss against the inside of her thigh just above her knee, and repeated the action with the other leg. Then he reached up and pulled her down onto the pillows beside him. Irene lay back, watching Gideon as he stood and divested himself of the rest of his garments, carelessly kicking off the formal shoes, and peeling down the breeches and stockings.

He looked, she thought, magnificent naked—powerful and muscled—and even though it was a little frightening to see for the first time the hard evidence of his desire, it was also compelling. She could not imagine taking him into her, and yet at the same time heat expanded between her legs, making her want to open to him.

He lay down beside her, propped up on one elbow. He looked down at her, slowly moving his hand over her body, caressing and teasing, arousing ever more delightful sensations in her. Irene's skin felt deliciously alive, sensitive to the slightest touch, and she was aware of a very wanton desire to spread her legs for him, a desire she suppressed until he slid his hand down the center of her body, over her stomach and between her thighs.

She drew a shaky breath and closed her eyes, feeling sure that this should be embarrassing, not wonderful, but unable to feel anything but eager pleasure. Delicately, his fingers explored this innermost secret part of her, separating and stroking the tender folds, slick with moisture. Irene could not hold back a moan, and she arched up against his questing fingers, seeking release.

"Gideon…" His name was a shaky whisper.

He bent and brushed his lips over her mouth, murmuring, "Not just yet. Let me make it easier for you."

"I want you," she said more clearly, opening her eyes and gazing up into his.

He tightened as if she had touched him and drew a slow breath. "I know. I know. And you have no idea what that does to me." He nuzzled against her neck, his breath sending shivers through her. "But first…this will help."

He kissed her breasts, playing with her nipples with his tongue and lips, fanning the flames of her desire. And as he did so, he slipped a finger inside her, stroking her, and then another, stretching and filling her, opening her.

Irene moved her legs restlessly, digging her heels into the pillows beneath her and moving against his hand. He let out a little laughing groan, and then, at last, he moved between her legs. His hands beneath her hips, he lifted her and slowly, carefully, sank into her.

Irene gasped, pain flashing through her briefly and she tightened. Gideon paused, waiting, and gradually she relaxed. Gently, inexorably, he slid into her, filling her. Irene wrapped her legs around him, moving a little to take him in more fully. He began to move within her, slowly pulling back and thrusting in, and with each movement something tightened within her, coiling harder and tighter.

She sobbed, moving with him, yearning for something that she could not even name. And then she felt it explode within her, a pleasure so deep and intense that she was rocked by it. She shuddered, clinging to him, as Gideon thrust hard and deep inside her, crying out as his own release took him. Waves of pleasure washed through her, rippling outward to every part of her body. He collapsed against her, and Irene wrapped her arms around him, stunned by what she had felt.

Whatever happened, she thought hazily, whether Gideon ever came to love her or not, she knew that she had found her home.

CHAPTER NINETEEN

THE NEXT MORNING, when Irene went downstairs to breakfast, she wondered a little nervously how she would act when she saw Gideon.

The night before, after their lovemaking, he had walked with her back to the house, his arm around her. They had said little, peaceful and content in the moment, stopping now and then to kiss or just to stand with their arms around each other. They had waited until after everyone else had gone to bed to return, and she had slipped in the back door and crept up to her room, while he had waited for several minutes before he came in more boldly. Tired and happy, she had gone immediately to bed and, hugging her happy knowledge to herself, had drifted off to sleep.

This morning, however, she could see all the problems that might present themselves. For one thing, it seemed likely that someone—or more than a few someones—would have noticed that both she and Gideon had been absent for the last part of the evening. What if someone mentioned it? What would she say? She could not allow herself to blush and stammer, for then it would be immediately apparent that she was guilty of some indiscretion.

But more than that, she feared that when she first looked at him, it would be clear to everyone what she felt for him…

what they had done. And deep down somewhere there lay a little niggling fear that when he saw her, he would regret everything, that in the time since she had last seen him, he would have come to wonder why he had ever thought he wanted to marry her.

But when she walked into the dining room and saw him sitting at the table, all her doubts and worries disappeared instantly. He glanced up from his plate, and though he did not smile, there was a swift, intense look in his eyes that welcomed her more than any words could have.

"Lady Irene," he said, rising and stepping over to pull out her chair. "I trust you slept well last night, after all the exertion…of the dance."

He looked down into her eyes, his own vivid green eyes brimming with intimate laughter.

"Thank you, Lord Radbourne. I spent a very pleasant night," she replied, casting back her own flirtatious glance as she took her seat. "It must be the air here."

"I always find country air most salubrious," Lady Salisbridge offered. "Though my two girls," she added with an indulgent smile, "are rather slugabeds this morning, I am afraid. But then, they do so love to dance."

"It was a wonderful ball," Mrs. Surton said. "Such talented musicians, such lovely flowers. I must applaud your talents, Lady Radbourne, to offer so excellent an entertainment in the country."

Everyone else joined in to compliment both the countesses, who received the praise with gracious smiles. Irene cast an amused glance up the table at Francesca, who gave her a slow wink in return.

Irene's gaze went next to Lady Odelia, who gave her such a regal nod and smile that Irene suspected Gideon had already told his great-aunt about their plans to marry. The thought of their marriage made Irene feel giddy all over again, and she turned her gaze back down to her plate to hide her smile.

When all the praise and rehashing of the dance the evening before died down, Francesca said lightly, "Now all that is left is to decide what we shall do today."

"Oh, yes," Miss Surton agreed with a giggle. "What shall we do? Lawn tennis was terribly amusing, was it not?"

"Particularly your serve, Ro," her brother Percy replied.

"Oh, you!" She made a pouting face at him. "You, I am sure, will want to go riding again."

"That sounds splendid," Miss Hurley was quick to agree.

"Where would we go?" asked Callie. "We have been all around the estate, have we not?"

Both the Hurleys and Mr. Surton looked rather bemused by the suggestion that any enticement other than being on a horse was needed.

"There are caves not far from here, near the river," Gideon offered. "I have not seen them, but I have been told they are quite interesting."

"The caves!" Lady Teresa gasped. "Oh, no, we cannot go there. They are too dangerous."

"What nonsense." Lady Odelia snorted. "I have been there several times. When we were younger, of course, eh, Pansy? There is nothing dangerous about them, providing one doesn't go wandering off and get lost, that is."

"Lord Cecil never allowed anyone to go there," Lady Teresa responded primly.

"No doubt he didn't want everyone poking about in them," Lady Odelia remarked. "One wouldn't. But I never heard of there being anything wrong with them, have you, Pansy?"

"No, dear," her sister responded, adding kindly to Teresa, "I imagine dear Cecil was just being very careful of you and Timmy. And he did want to protect them from strangers, you know. Said people were apt to damage the formations. But the caves are quite worth seeing. Unusual."

"That sounds like just the thing," Piers said, and all the younger members of the party were quick to agree.

"I am sure that Cook will be able to fill up some picnic baskets for us," Francesca added, with a significant glance at Irene.

Irene knew that look meant that she should arrange for the food baskets with the housekeeper and cook, as she had been the one in charge of dealing with the kitchen and household matters for the week of the party. So as soon as breakfast was over, she made her way to the kitchen to broach the matter.

The housekeeper, Mrs. Jeffries, seemed to have taken a strong liking to Irene, who was not sure about the reason for the woman's attitude, though she suspected it lay in the inadequacies of Lady Teresa and Lady Pansy as mistresses of the house. The housekeeper had turned to Irene with increasing frequency in recent days, and even the formidable Horroughs had consulted with her on the rare occasions when he had been uncertain about an issue concerning the guests.

However, it appeared to Irene that today the smile with which Mrs. Jeffries greeted her was especially bright, and that there was an extra touch of deference in the housekeeper's assurances that she would have the baskets made up and brought down to the caves for the group's luncheon by one o'clock. Irene also noticed several surreptitious glances in her direction from the servants, as well as a good bit of whispering and smiling.

Could it be that the servants already knew about her engagement to Gideon? It seemed impossible, as it had happened only the night before. Of course, the servants always knew everything first. No doubt if Gideon had told his grandmother or great-aunt about it, there had been a maid nearby who had overheard the news.

Irene pretended not to notice their behavior, and as soon as her business with the housekeeper was done, she left the kitchen and returned to her room to change.

Glancing at herself in the mirror as she pulled off her morning dress, it occurred to her that perhaps the servants—and even Lady Odelia—had guessed that something was up simply by looking at her. She had not realized it when she went down to breakfast that morning, but there was a glow of happiness on her features that nothing could conceal. Her cheeks were warm with color, her eyes shone, and her mouth was turned up as if she was just about to break out in a smile.

She studied herself, turning her head this way and that, trying to pull her expression into something more dignified—or at least less transparent. But it took only a minute for her give up, laughing. What did it matter, she thought, if everyone could guess that she was head over heels in love? All she cared about right now was the future that awaited her with Gideon. She could scarcely wait, in fact, to get started on the rest of her life.

But there was the rest of the party to get through—and she rather looked forward to exploring the caves with Gideon—so she quickly changed into her riding habit and pinned the insouciant little cap to her head, angling it just right, so that the glossy black feather curled down to caress the side of her face. High black leather boots and black leather gloves completed her ensemble, and she took a last turn in front of the mirror, pleased with the image she presented. Unlike the high-waisted fashion that was currently the mode in frocks, the fitted jacket of the riding habit showed off her figure quite nicely, and the warm brown color went well with her coloring. Of course, she thought as she left the room with a light step, today she would have felt beautiful in rags.

IRENE RODE BETWEEN Francesca and Calandra on the way down to the caves, leaving Gideon and the other men to entertain the rest of the girls. It would not, after all, be well-mannered to be too obvious about Gideon's preference for her company.

They rode through the meadow and came around to the river, which they followed, led by the Park's head groom. They rode in the general direction of the distant hills, away from both the village and the road back to London. Almost imperceptibly, the lane beside the river began to narrow and the land beyond it to rise, until before long they were riding through a small gorge with limestone bluffs rising up beside them on either side. Finally the head groom stopped and spoke to Gideon, pointing ahead toward a line of bushes at the base of the bluff.

Irene shaded her eyes with her hand and saw a shadow behind the shrubs, darker and more substantial than the lacework of the leaves and branches. She dismounted, as did the others, and they made their way up the slight incline to the entrance of the cave.

The entrance was an ink-black gap in the white rock, and

though it was somewhat sheltered by a large boulder on one side, there was ample room for two people to pass through the gap side by side.

The men had come equipped with lanterns, which they lit now, and the group started into the cave. Francesca and Irene brought up the rear, with Rochford dropping back politely to hold a light for them.

However, they had barely made their way through the gap when Miss Hurley, quite surprisingly, became unnerved by the dark and the smallness of their quarters, not to mention the thought of the mountain of rock pressing down above her head, and she balked, refusing to go any farther. Francesca, suppressing a sigh, said that she would stay outside with the girl, and Mr. Surton, after a last, longing glance at the dark cave beyond, gallantly offered to remain to keep the ladies company. The rest of them went on, a somewhat depleted party.

The cave was a tunnel at first, about the same size as the opening, but as they walked forward, it opened up into a larger room, and here the group stopped, gathering into a loose circle. Irene gazed around her in some awe.

The cave extended in all directions past the reach of the lanterns, and everywhere rocks appeared to grow up from the floor or hang down from the ceiling, slick with moisture, so that they gleamed a little in the lights.

The duke's scholarly friend, Mr. Strethwick, had come along on the expedition, intrigued by the prospect of the caves, and now the shy man, who had kept silent the entire trip, began to babble about the stalagmites and stalactites that lay before them, explaining their formation, going on about salts and minerals and limestone. Irene only half listened, too entranced by the eerie beauty of the scene to care overmuch about its origins.

As Mr. Strethwick talked, the groom went back to their horses and brought in several tall torches, which he planted in the ground and set afire so that the main room of the cave was better lit, and they were able to take their lanterns off with them to explore further.

The duke advised them to remain in a group and not go wandering off on their own, and such was the man's air of authority that no one disobeyed him. Irene was well content to stroll along with everyone else, especially after Gideon fell back to walk beside her.

There was much to see, with smaller tunnels and caves opening off from others. There were odd rippling formations of stone and earth that looked like drapes, and others that seemed like waterfalls frozen in motion. The members of the group pointed out various rocks, saying how one looked like a kneeling man and another like a toadstool, and so on.

Hunger, however, finally drove them back outside, where they found the picnic laid out and waiting for them by the river. Irene started to go over to where Francesca sat, but Gideon wrapped his hand around her wrist.

"No, stay," he murmured in a low voice.

She looked at him and smiled, nodding, then sat down on the rock beside him. He had chosen well, she realized, for the broad rock on which they sat was situated so that, though other people sat on either side of them, their rock jutted out in front of the others, leaving them almost alone together without giving the appearance of privacy or impropriety.

They chatted as they ate, talking more about the caves than about themselves, but the important things were said in their smiles, and in the way their eyes met or his mouth softened when he looked at her. Afterward, Irene remembered little about their conversation, but she would always remember the contentment and peace she felt, the warmth and joy. She would never forget the sun upon her face as she looked up at Gideon, the bright green of his eyes when the sunlight touched them or the rustle of the leaves in the trees as a breeze passed through them.

Later, she knew, she might worry about whether she had made a mistake in saying yes. She might wonder if it would be enough to be Gideon's wife, to know that he valued her as a friend and desired her in his bed, even if he never loved her. Fear might come upon her in the night, and she might cry to herself, knowing that she loved him with all her heart and afraid that he had spoken the truth when he said he could not love.

But at this moment, such worries did not cling to her. She basked in the warmth of his gaze; she remembered his lips upon her mouth and traveling down her skin. Right now, whatever it was he felt for her, it was enough.

She caught Francesca looking at them speculatively once or twice during the meal, and she knew that her friend was not the only one. Gideon's uncle, too, cast more than one glance their way.

After the repast, several people were eager to return to the caves—primarily the duke's scientific friend, who had scarcely paid attention to the delicious food, so intent was he on going over the delights of the cave with Rochford.

Both the Salisbridge girls decided to relax by the river for a while instead of returning to the dark and damp of the caves, which meant that Francesca and Mr. Surton were freed from sitting with Miss Hurley and were able to join the cave party. They all strolled back inside, more at ease this time with the eerie dark interior.

Irene and Gideon chatted and walked about, straying

from the tight-knit group. She felt him slip his hand around hers, and she turned toward him, surprised. He inclined his head to the side, then picked up his lantern and led her farther away from the others. She followed him quietly, and, after a last quick glance around, they slipped into one of the other tunnels.

She covered her mouth to suppress a giggle and concentrated on walking quietly, just as eager as he was to escape the crowd. Finally he deemed them to be far enough away, and he turned, pulling her close to him and kissing her.

"I have been wanting to do that all day," he confided, setting down his lantern on the ground so that he could wrap his other arm around her, too.

"Will you think me very bold if I tell you that I wanted it, too?" she asked, looking up at him flirtatiously.

"I will, indeed, and I thank heaven for it," he replied with a smile, and kissed her again, lightly, on the lips.

Then he laid his cheek atop her head, and they stood that way, simply holding each other for a long moment. He nuzzled her hair and murmured in her ear, "Perhaps we could find a secluded little offshoot and..."

Irene giggled, feeling a trifle giddy. "Stop. You will have me sounding like Miss Surton."

"God forbid," Gideon replied in a heartfelt tone. He raised his head and gazed down at her, then took her lips again in a long, deep kiss.

With a sigh, he released her, and, picking up the lantern, they began to stroll through the tunnel, hands clasped, as aware of each other as they were of the cave around them.

"I told my grandmother and Aunt Odelia that you have accepted my proposal," he told her. "They were, needless to say, delighted."

"I am sure that Teresa will be much less so," Irene remarked drily.

He shrugged. "Fortunately she has nothing to say in the matter. Will you mind having her living at the Park? She could move to another house if she makes you uncomfortable."

"Oh, I shall be able to tolerate her," Irene replied easily. "I would not want to uproot Timothy. After all, he is your family, and you are fond of him, I know."

"I am." He smiled at her. "But I am fonder of you."

"That is good to know. I am sure that I shall put that to the test sooner or later," she went on lightly. "I have been told that I am not an easy person to live with."

"You?" He looked at her in mock amazement, eyes dancing. "Who would dare say such a thing?"

She cast him a speaking glance, and he leaned down to kiss her lightly on the mouth, following it with quick kisses to her eyes and cheeks and chin.

"I like you just as you are," he told her. "An easy person to live with would doubtless drive me mad in two weeks."

"Then I shall do my best to keep you sane," she bantered. In a more serious tone, she went on. "Gideon…there is one thing I would ask of you."

He glanced at her, a little surprised by her tone. "What?"

"I would like my mother to live here, too. She is not happy living with my sister-in-law. She does not say it, but I know it is true, and—"

"Of course," he interrupted her, releasing her hand to put his arm around her shoulders and pull her close. "I assumed that she would live with us. You do not even need to ask."

"Thank you." She smiled up at him.

"I would give you much more than that to have you look

at me in that way," he told her, bending down to kiss her again. His hand slid down her back and curved over her buttocks, pressing her against him.

A fiery tongue of desire licked down through her torso, and she trembled, her hands going up to his chest and digging into his shirt. She wondered, with a little thrill of excitement, what it would be like if he did pull her into some secluded part of the cave.

Their kiss deepened, and he set the lantern down with a clank as he linked his arms around her, pulling her up and into his body, lifting her from her feet. His mouth trailed down her neck and nuzzled into the dark crevice between her breasts, and his breath rasped in his throat.

With a groan, he set her down and took a half step back, sucking in a lungful of air. His eyes burned into her, glittering with passion.

"Sweet bloody hell, but you tempt me!" he grated out. "I have only one stipulation for our marriage—that it be very, very soon!"

"I agree." Irene drew a shaky breath and smoothed her hands down her dress. "Perhaps we should return to the others before we create a scandal."

"Yes, I think you are right."

He picked up the light, and they set off again, but after a few twists and turns, he stopped and cast a look around. "I don't think this is the way we came."

She, too, had been growing uneasy for the last few yards, and she cast a look at him. "We *are* lost?"

"Not very," he said. "But I think we must retrace our steps."

They turned back, following the wide tunnel to where it narrowed. Within a few minutes it opened up into a larger cavern—not as large as the expanse where they had first entered the cave, but nevertheless a high-ceilinged room— one in which Irene was certain they had not been before.

"We are lost!" she exclaimed, a little squiggle of panic rising in her.

He took her cold hand and raised it to his lips. "Don't get anxious. We will find our way back out, I assure you."

He raised the lantern and glanced about the cavern. "It's an interesting place. Look at all the caves opening off this one."

She looked at the darker openings at the edge of the circle of yellow light cast by the lantern. "I hope you don't intend to explore any of them."

"No. But I think I'd like to come back someday and spend more time." He finished turning all around, his light falling on the cave wall closest to them. He paused. "That's odd."

"What's odd?"

He took a step closer to the wall, holding the light nearer to it. "This wall. Look. It isn't like the others."

Irene followed the direction his finger pointed, intrigued despite her uneasiness. "It looks like—well, like rocks piled up."

"Exactly." He set the lantern down at the base of the wall and squatted down. "Not like the solid wall everywhere else. Look."

He reached out and ran a finger down a rock, dislodging moist earth. "These are rocks with earth shoved in between and on top, like a crude wall, but the soil has largely melted away. Look at how much has slid down to the bottom."

Irene frowned, leaning over to brush her fingers over the surface. "You're right. Someone built a wall here. Why?"

He shook his head. "I don't know. But it's odd."

He scooped his hand down the side, dislodging more earth and revealing the stones beneath, then ran his hand up the wall. "It goes up only to here. And it's about two feet wide." He added decisively, "I am going to see what's behind it."

Gideon dug into the wall with both hands, working out a fairly flat rock. It came loose with a scraping sound, and after that the work went much more easily. Irene pulled her riding gloves out of her pocket and put them on, then knelt down to join him. There was an odd feeling in the pit of her stomach, and it grew as they cleared out a larger and larger hole. Behind the rocks lay the deep black of nothingness, and a fetid smell crept out on the air.

There was something very strange about anyone constructing a wall inside a cave. Why would it have been necessary to fill in this hole? She supposed it could lead to something dangerous, a steep drop-off perhaps, but why not just post a sign of warning?

The caves were little used. Clearly, from what Teresa had said, Lord Cecil had thought them dangerous. Irene imagined that others did, as well. She could not help but wonder if that reputation of danger came from something other than physical difficulties. Perhaps criminals used these caves to—to what? Well, she wasn't sure, but it occurred to her that the wall might have been erected to hide some sort of contraband.

Smugglers came to mind. But surely they were too far from the sea here. Thieves, then. People stole things, then hauled them here and hid them—but to what purpose?

She tried to imagine what could be so necessary to hide as to make it worthwhile dragging it all the way up the gorge and through the caves to this out-of-the-way spot. It would have to be something one would want hidden for a long time. But surely most things that one stole were only worth something if one sold them. Thieves did not steal silver and then hide it for years—and how much could one steal, anyway, out here in the country?

Gideon was moving faster as they worked, and the opening widened rapidly. Finally it was large enough that he was able to lift up the lantern and shine it into the hole. They leaned in on either side of the lantern.

The light reached only a few feet, enough to reveal a small denlike cave, not tall enough for a man to stand upright in, that stretched back about six or eight feet. The glow of the lantern bathed the area in a dim light, revealing an object lying about four feet from the opening. It was about five feet long and draped over with a thin white cloth. And it was unmistakably a human form.

CHAPTER TWENTY

IRENE STARED, no sound issuing from her throat. She sat back on her heels abruptly and turned to look at Gideon.

He let out a low curse.

"Selene."

"Oh, my God." Irene's hands went to her cheeks. She realized that she was shaking.

Gideon had put into words the exact thought that had formed in her head. He tore at the rest of the rocks, clearing out the entrance. She reached out and laid a hand on his arm.

"We don't know that."

He paused and cast a look back at her. "I know. Who else would it be?"

"We must not disturb the…the body. Someone may be able to—"

"Identify her?" he asked, and nodded, looking a little calmer. "Yes. You're right. I won't touch…the body. But I have to see."

He pushed the lantern inside and crawled in after it. Irene followed him. Again he turned to her.

"You do not need to do this," he told her. "It will not be a sight fit for a lady."

"I must," she replied. "You are going to look, are you not?"

He nodded and said nothing more to dissuade her. They

crept closer, holding the lantern up so that its light fell fully on the body.

The woman's body had been wrapped like a mummy with some dark, now rotting, material. Over her head and shoulders was draped a thin white material, stained with brown and yellowish marks. Irene realized that the white fabric was actually a petticoat.

Beneath the gauzy white cloth were the wizened, nearly fleshless features of a skull, a few strands of dark hair still clinging to it. Irene sucked in her breath, feeling suddenly a little nauseous and faint. She straightened away from the body and closed her eyes.

"Are you all right?" came Gideon's voice close to her, and she opened her eyes to look into his questioning, concerned ones. "You should not see this. Why don't you go back out?"

She shook her head. "No. I am all right." That was a lie, of course; she still felt a bit queasy. She had never seen anything this macabre. But she was not about to leave Gideon here all alone to face what they both felt sure were the decayed remains of his mother.

She drew a breath. "Is it she?"

He shook his head. "I can't be sure. But who else would it be?" He sighed and took her hand, squeezing it gently. "We must go back and get help. Some other men. My uncle is the only one who might be able to identify her."

Irene nodded, then laid a hand on his arm, looking into his eyes, and said, "Yes, we will, but…are you all right?"

A sad smile curved his lips, and he brought her hand up to his mouth and pressed a gentle kiss against her knuckles. "Yes. It is a long time past. And at least now I know that she did not abandon me."

He leaned his head against hers for a moment, then pulled back. "Come. Let us get the others."

They crawled back out of the oppressive room. It was a relief to stand up in the tunnel. Irene cast a look around.

"Will we be able to find our way back?"

"We will, though it may take a little time. We must leave some things along the way to make sure that we can find our way back."

"I have the ribbons in my hair," she offered. "And my gloves."

"My watch and fobs. Cuff links. We'll find enough to make do."

They started to retrace their steps, leaving an article at every major juncture or turn. They had not gone very far, however, when they heard the faint sound of voices. They stopped, listening, then Gideon cupped his hands around his mouth and shouted, his voice echoing around the cavern.

A moment later, a little louder than before, they heard a man's voice calling, "Radbourne?"

Then another, "Gideon?"

"Piers!" Gideon shouted back. "We're here. Keep coming!"

He and the others continued to exchange shouts, the voices at times receding, but then coming closer again, until at last the glimmer of a light appeared, and a moment later three men with lanterns appeared around the curve of the tunnel. Piers and Gideon's uncle were in front, with Rochford bringing up the rear.

Jasper's face was creased with worry, and even Piers looked concerned. Only the duke was as unruffled as ever, slim and straight in his fawn breeches and dark blue jacket, looking for all the world as if he might have been out for a stroll.

"Thank God, man!" Piers burst out, striding forward. "You had us dead worried. Where have you been?"

"We, um, got a trifle lost, and then…we stumbled upon something."

Something of what Gideon felt must have shown on his face, for whatever the other men had been about to say died on their lips. Rochford's gaze flickered over Gideon, then Irene, and she was suddenly aware of how dirty and disheveled they must appear after digging away the rocks and crawling on their hands and knees into the low cave.

"Show us," was all Rochford said.

They started back, picking up their markers as they went, until they were at the tomb once more. Irene watched as the other men squatted down at the entrance and peered inside. Piers drew in his breath with a gasp, and Jasper went pale and still as death. He cast one quick questioning glance at his nephew.

Gideon shook his head. "I do not know. You are the only one who could tell for sure."

Jasper turned to look back into the cave, and there was such pain on his face that Irene had to turn away from it. He nodded and began to crawl forward, Gideon by his side. Piers watched the two men in shocked fascination, and Rochford turned to Irene.

"Selene?" he asked.

"We fear so."

Piers glanced at them curiously, but obviously realized that this was not the time for a lengthy explanation. Gideon and Jasper had reached the wrapped skeleton.

They heard a muffled exclamation from Jasper, then he

said in a quiet voice, "It is a dressing gown. It— *She* is wrapped in a dressing gown. I—I do not know if it was hers. Help me."

He reached out toward the material, and Gideon moved to help him try to peel it away. It shredded beneath their fingers, some of it falling into pieces and some simply crumbling away into dust.

"Oh, God." Jasper's voice broke, and he reached down. "Her ring. Here is her wedding ring. And this—this pin. I gave it to her. Sweet Jesus. It is Selene. *Selene.*"

Rochford stood up. "Lady Irene, allow me to escort you back to the other ladies. Mr. Aldenham, if you will remain here with the others, I will send the groom back to the Park immediately to bring a cart. Francesca and Irene will take the others back to the house, and I shall return to help you as soon as I have seen everyone off."

Piers nodded. "I'll wait."

"Are you all right?" the duke asked Irene as he led her away from the burial cave.

She nodded. "Yes. I— It was a gruesome sight, to be sure, but…" She shrugged and gave him a half smile. "Anyone will tell you that I am not a very delicate female."

"Thank God for that," Rochford replied easily. "It would be a bit daunting to have to carry an unconscious woman back through all these tunnels. Or one engaged in hysterics."

He smiled at her, and she was surprised at the way his smile lit up his handsome face, lending him a warmth that was usually missing.

"Yes, I imagine that would be somewhat difficult," she agreed, then sighed. "I fear that Gideon will take it hard. He was trying to adjust to the news that his mother had run away, and now to find out that she was murdered…" Irene paused, then continued. "I don't suppose that it could be anything other than murder?"

"I cannot see how," Rochford replied. "Aunt Odelia has told me about Aunt Pansy's story—that Lady Selene ran away with a man. I suppose Lady Selene could have written a note pretending to run away, then come here to kill herself, though I cannot understand her reason for making everyone believe she had left. However, I do not believe that she could have killed herself and afterward draped gauze over her face."

"No. I— It looked as though one side of her head had been…smashed in."

"Devil of a business. At least Cecil's dead. There won't be the agony of a trial."

"You think it was Gideon's father who killed her?"

"He is the one who read the note. The only one, if I understand my great-aunts correctly. I think it must have been he—or his valet. I suppose he could have had his man do it. Owenby was devoted to him."

"But why was Gideon taken?" Irene asked.

"That surpasses my understanding," Rochford admitted. "Ah, there is the main cave up ahead."

"Are you familiar with these caves?" Irene asked.

He glanced at her, surprised. "No. I have never been here before."

"How did you know the way back so well?"

He quirked a brow. "Once we began to suspect that you and Gideon had gone astray—at least longer than one would have expected for a newly engaged couple—" he allowed a small smile "—I marked the way we took to make certain we did not all become lost."

"Of course." Irene smiled to herself. She understood much better now Francesca's remarks about the duke.

"My lady!" The groom was waiting in the main cave, along with Mr. Surton, and he sprang up as he spoke. "Your Grace."

"Lady Irene is quite all right," Rochford assured the men. "I am afraid that she and Lord Radbourne had become rather disoriented, but we found them. I will need your help, Barnes, if you will wait just a moment. Mr. Surton, may I rely on you to see that the young ladies get back to the house safely? I think that Lady Irene should return right away. She is, as you see, somewhat overset by her ordeal."

The duke turned to Irene, murmuring, "You might try to look overset."

Irene raised a hand weakly to her chest. "Mr. Surton, I cannot thank you enough. I fear I feel a trifle faint."

Surton hastened to assure her of his help, and gave her his arm to take her out. The duke turned to the groom and spoke to him in a low voice. The groom looked amazed, but nodded his head without protest and hurried to do as the duke bade.

As soon as Irene and Surton stepped outside, Francesca came forward. "Irene! Are you all right? Is something amiss? Where are the others?"

"I fear I must cut your outing short," the duke said, striding out of the cave after them. "Lady Irene is fine, though a trifle tired. Lady Haughston, if I may speak with you?"

Irene watched as the duke took her friend aside, bending over to talk to her earnestly. Irene saw Francesca raise her hand to her throat in distress, and Rochford reached out as though to touch her arm, then hastily drew his hand back.

He bowed to Francesca instead, and turned, going back into the cave.

Francesca hurried over to Irene. "Oh, my, such a…well, I do not even know what to call it. Are you all right, my dear?"

Irene nodded. "Yes, but we need to get everyone back to the house and then find a way to occupy all the others, so that you and I can explain what has transpired to Gideon's family."

"I shall think of something, never fear."

Francesca swept everyone along, flattering Mr. Surton's helpfulness and fluttering over Irene's wretchedly disordered nerves. They would, she promised, find some other treat for the guests for the rest of the afternoon—perhaps croquet on the wide front lawn?

This idea seemed to please everyone well enough, and they set a good pace back to the house. There was not really much of the afternoon left to arrange for croquet, much less play it, but Francesca set everyone to it anyway, further playing on Mr. Surton's pride by putting him in charge of the whole affair. Then, with a quick word to the butler, Francesca and Irene went into the library to await the women of the family. Lady Odelia and her sister came in a few moments later, looking puzzled, followed by Lady Teresa, who seemed merely disgruntled.

"Francesca?" Lady Odelia began. "What is the meaning of this? Why did you send Horroughs to fetch us?" Her expression changed. "Did something happen to Gideon?"

"No, Lord Radbourne is fine," Francesca hastened to assure the others, and cast a glance at Irene.

Irene nodded. "The thing is, we found something in the caves today. It is— Forgive me, Lady Radbourne," she said to Pansy. "I can think of no easy way to put this. Your son, Lord Jasper, identified it as the body of Lady Selene."

Even Lady Odelia had no words to offer after that statement. After a stunned moment, the women began to ask questions, but Irene was unable to answer them. So they waited, an anxious, quiet little group, for the men to return with the body.

Irene jumped up when at last there was the clatter of riding boots in the hallway outside. A moment later the door opened, and Jasper, Rochford and Gideon strode inside. Irene looked to Gideon. His face was set, his eyes shadowed, and he carried something wrapped in cloth in his hand.

"Jasper?" Pansy rose, looking every bit her age. Her hands trembled, and she clasped them together to stop the shaking. "Is it—is it really Selene?"

Her son nodded grimly. "Yes. I am certain. There was a pin that she often wore, and her wedding ring."

"What happened?" Pansy wailed, looking lost. "How can this be?"

"Did she wander off?" Lady Odelia asked, grasping at straws. "Did she fall or—"

Gideon cut her off harshly. "She was murdered." He looked at his grandmother. "My father killed her."

Lady Pansy sat down as if her legs had given out from under her. "No! That cannot be! Someone must have—have taken her. Stolen her from her room and dragged her there."

"She was killed here," Gideon replied flatly. "We found this tucked into a corner of the cave."

He held out the object in his hand, peeling back the cloth. Jasper turned away as if he could not bear the sight. Irene stared at what lay in Gideon's hand: an ormolu clock with a white marble base. It was smallish for a clock, only four inches wide and twice as tall. And it was mottled with a brown stain, a stain that was also smeared over the cloth that had been wrapped around it.

Gideon's grandmother let out a little shriek at the sight of the clock, and she flung her hands up to her face. "No! No! It can't be."

"It is her clock, is it not?" Gideon asked. "The one that her maid told us had belonged to her mother? The one that Lady Selene kept on her dresser? It was used to smash in her head."

Pansy cried out again and began to sob into her hands.

"Stop," Jasper said, turning back to Gideon, still avoiding the object in his nephew's hand. "It is Selene's clock. I already told you. Leave Mother alone. She knows nothing about what happened."

"Of course not!" Lady Odelia exclaimed, looking shaken. "None of us do. Some—some madman obviously must have broken in here and—"

"Enough!" Gideon grated out. "There has been enough lying, enough deception. My father killed her. And I am going to find out exactly what happened!"

Then he turned and strode rapidly out of the room.

THE OTHERS STARED AFTER HIM, the silence broken only by Lady Radbourne's sobs.

"Now, where the devil is he going?" Rochford asked of no one in particular.

"To Owenby's," Jasper replied. "I will go after him." He started to follow.

"No, stay here with your mother," the duke commanded, taking Jasper's arm and pulling him to a stop. He nodded toward where the two elderly women were huddled together for comfort. "I will go after him."

"You don't know where to go," Jasper protested.

"I do," Irene said, already striding toward the door. "I will show you."

At Rochford's command, the grooms sprang into action, saddling a pair of horses in remarkable time, and Rochford and Irene set out. Gideon had a good head start on them, for he had taken the horse he had just ridden in on, which had not yet been unsaddled. However, Gideon, as his great-aunt had once said, was not at ease on horse, whereas Irene had ridden all her life, and the duke rode as if he might have been born on horseback. Moreover, their horses were fresh, and they took the more difficult but much faster course across fields and meadows, jumping fences and hedges, and coming out just east of the town.

They came galloping up the lane just in time to see Gideon dismount from his horse and storm into the valet's cottage. Rochford and Irene flung themselves off their own horses and, after tying them hastily to the fence, hurried toward the house.

Just as they were about to step inside, the maid came running out, shrieking. When she saw Rochford, she grabbed at his sleeve jacket, jabbering, "Stop him! Stop him, please! He's going to kill him!"

Rochford shook off the girl's hand and continued through the door, as unruffled as ever. Even the crash they heard deep inside the house did not rattle him; he merely strode forward, heading straight toward the noise.

They found Gideon in the kitchen, where apparently he had chased down his father's former valet. Owenby must have fled for the back door, but Gideon had cut him off.

Owenby huddled against the far wall, looking terrified and trapped. Gideon, a fireplace poker in his hand, stood in the center of the kitchen, easily able to move to block the other man's path whether he ran for the back door or the rest of the house.

"Don't deny it!" Gideon roared as Rochford and Irene entered the kitchen, and he brought the poker down on the table with a crash, gouging out a chunk of wood, and causing Owenby to jump and look wildly around, as if he were considering climbing straight up the wall.

"I know he killed her. You or him! Which was it?"

"I— I—" Owenby's hands fluttered nervously from his waist to his throat to the wall behind him.

"Tell me!" Gideon smashed the weapon down again.

"Gideon! Stop," Irene said crisply. "He can't answer, because you are scaring the wits out of him."

Gideon whirled around in surprise. "Irene! Rochford! What the devil are you doing here?"

"Did you think I was going to allow you to kill your father's valet in a fit of anger?" Irene retorted. "I have no intention of spending our wedding night visiting you in gaol."

"Don't be daft. I am not going to kill him."

"Of course not," Rochford agreed, going forward and wrapping his hand around the poker, easing it from Gideon's hand.

Gideon cast him a disgusted look and turned back to the cowering man. "I can still choke you to death," he told Owenby. "And, trust me, I will not hesitate to do so unless you start talking. And quickly. I was not raised as a gentleman."

"I am sure that—Owenby, is it?—will be quite happy to tell us what happened to your mother," Rochford said mildly. "Won't you, Owenby?"

"I didn't do nothing," Owenby wailed, his speech slipping a bit in his distress. "I didn't kill Lady Radbourne. I swear it!"

"I did not think you did," Gideon told him grimly. "My father killed her, I am sure. What I want is for you to tell me why. Tell me what happened."

"I don't know," Owenby told him, looking sullen. When Gideon clenched his fists and took a step forward, the valet cried out, "I don't! It's the God's truth! I wasn't there when it happened. He just—Lord Cecil told me—well, I heard the crash. I was waiting in his room to help him get dressed for bed. And I heard them arguing."

"About what?" Irene asked.

"I don't know. It's the truth. I could hear the voices, but I couldn't tell what they were saying. Except once, he shouted something about having her letters. And when I went in later, there were papers on the fire, burning. I think his lordship threw the letters in there. I think maybe she had tried to take the letters out of the fire, because the poker was lying there, and there was some ash and a coal on the hearth."

"What happened? Did you go in when you heard the crash?" Gideon asked.

"No, my lord. Not right away. It wasn't my place, was it? It was 'tween a husband and wife. It would have been more than my life was worth to have crossed him when he was in one of his moods."

"So you did...nothing?" Gideon's lips curled in a sneer.

"That's right," Owenby retorted defiantly. "I just waited. It wasn't my place."

"When did you enter the room?" Rochford asked before Gideon could lash out at the man.

"Well, after she screamed," he said. "There was some

more yelling, and I heard him tell her he'd never let her go. And then she let out this cry. Something like, 'No!' or 'Go!' or maybe it was just his name. I don't remember. Then she screamed and—and then there was this thud, and some… more thuds. I didn't know what had happened, so I went to the door and, well, then he jerked open the door and saw me. And he pulled me into the room."

The small man hesitated, his gaze flickering from one man to the other anxiously. Finally he went on. "I saw her lying there on the floor. There was a chair turned over—I think that was the first thud I heard. And Lady Selene—she was lyin' on the floor, on her side, and—and I could see she was all limp. Her head—there was blood all over one side of her head. She'd fallen onto the hearth—her head, at least. The rest of her was on the carpet. But I could see that she was dead." He shivered a little at the memory. "She was staring straight at me, like."

"He had hit her with her clock?"

Owenby nodded. "Yeah, it wasn't very big. He must have picked it up and knocked her in the head with it. And then, I think when she fell, he—he hit her another time or two."

The valet crossed his arms in front of him and glared at Gideon. "It wasn't his fault!"

"Not his fault?" Gideon exploded. "He beat her to death!"

"She drove him to it," Owenby fired back. "She made him mad with jealousy. He knew she was sleeping with his brother—oh, yes, I knew it, too. It was clear the way they was always looking at each other."

"But Lord Jasper wasn't even there," Irene pointed out. "He had left for the army some months prior to that."

"I think it was his letters what set his lordship off. He must have been writing her, and Lord Cecil found them."

"So he killed her?" Rochford asked in disbelief.

"He didn't *mean* to," Owenby said staunchly. "He lost his head. He said to me, 'Owenby, I think I've killed her. I don't know what happened. I just picked this up and—'" He paused and repeated, "He didn't mean to do it."

"Well, clearly he meant all the rest of it," Gideon growled. "He was thinking well enough to come up with an elaborate plan."

"I thought of most of it, sir," Owenby corrected him, not without a hint of pride. "I told him he should just pretend that she ran away. But he said that would be too big a scandal, he couldn't do that. And—and then he said we could pretend she was abducted. So that's what we did. I wrapped her up in her dressing gown that was lying out on the bed, and I wrapped one or two of her petticoats around her head. And I cleaned up the blood on the hearth with some more petticoats. Then I wrapped up that clock in her nightgown, and we took her downstairs."

"You took her down to the caves?" Rochford asked incredulously. "All that way? At night?"

"Not then, sir," he replied. "There wasn't time. I carried her through the garden and out to the ruins. I stashed her body there, put a few rocks in front of it. And then I came back and took the boy. I took him—I took him to this man I knew."

"In London?" Gideon asked. "*You* took me to London?"

"No! Not all the way to London. Just to Chipping Camden. There was a chap there that took children you didn't want. And anybody else, either. He wasn't above knocking a fella on the head and taking him to an impress gang. So I took the boy there."

He did not look at Gideon as he said these last few words,

as if refusing to look could somehow help him to separate the boy he had given to a child-thief from the man standing in front of him.

Owenby shrugged. "Then I came back, and we did what we'd planned. Lord Cecil acted like they had been kidnapped. And he pretended to give me that necklace and sent me off to deal with the abductors. But I—I went to the ruins instead, and got her and took her to the caves. And I walled her up, so nobody could stumble on her accidentally. And Lord Cecil, he forbade people going there whenever he could, said it was dangerous."

The three of them looked at Owenby. Irene felt numbed by the man's matter-of-fact recital of Lady Selene's murder. She glanced at Gideon, who also seemed drained. His fury, she thought, had worn itself out, crashing into a kind of cold despair in the face of the valet's story.

"But it still does not make sense," Irene protested. "Why did he have you take Gideon away?" Irene asked. "Why would Lord Cecil get rid of his only son? His heir?"

"The boy saw him. He woke up, I guess at the sound of the voices. The nursery's just above her ladyship's room. And he walked in on them. He saw Lord Cecil hit his mother. And he started screaming, too. That's…that's really when I decided to see what was happening. Lord Cecil knocked him away, trying to shut him up. He was afraid he would waken the household. It knocked him out. And when I came back, well, the boy was still asleep. I think—I think maybe Lord Cecil gave him some laudanum. You know, to keep him asleep. And he told me I would have to get rid of the boy, too, on account of he'd seen…what he'd seen. He couldn't stay there, where he might decide any day to tell everybody what had happened."

"But his own son!" Irene exclaimed.

"What did it matter anyway?" the valet snarled. He looked at Gideon with something close to hate. "From the day he married her, she had never been faithful to him. His brother wasn't the first, just the last. She had a string of lovers, that one." He stared at Gideon, his loathing almost palpable. "You think you're something, don't you? Well, you're wrong. You're no one, you hear me? You're not the earl's son."

CHAPTER TWENTY-ONE

"IT MAKES SENSE," Gideon said calmly.

"What?" Irene looked over at him, startled.

His words were the first he had spoken since they had started the ride back to Radbourne Park. Rochford had tactfully ridden on ahead when they left the valet's cottage, giving Gideon and Irene an opportunity to be alone to discuss the revelations the valet had put before them. But for the first few minutes Gideon had said nothing as he rode, lost in a brown study, and Irene had not wanted to disturb him. He would talk to her when he was ready, she reasoned. However, she had not expected him to say what had just come out of his mouth.

"What makes sense?" she pursued. "I found little about his story that was sensible."

Gideon shrugged. "I am not Lord Cecil's son."

"You don't know that," Irene argued. "All you have is the word of Lord Cecil's valet, and he can have no way of knowing the truth. All he could possibly know is what his employer told him, and we have absolutely no proof that it is true. Even Lord Cecil could not have been sure. The picture Lord Jasper painted of Lady Selene is a far cry from the wanton whom Owenby claims she was. Lord Cecil was doubtless trying to justify his own wicked actions by saying that. He probably felt it made it less a sin to murder her."

"But it makes sense," Gideon said stubbornly, turning his head to look at her. "We have been stymied this whole time by the fact that a man got rid of his own child. We discounted the idea that my father murdered my mother, because we knew he would not get rid of his son and heir. But it would not be so hard, would it, if he knew that I was not really his son?"

"He got rid of you to save his own selfish hide," Irene retorted. "It was cowardice, that was all. After all, if he really thought that you were not his son, he could have repudiated you years ago. He could have charged your mother with adultery and obtained a divorce."

"But that would have entailed a messy scandal, something the family wouldn't have wanted. Moreover, he would have been holding himself up to public ridicule if he laid such charges at my mother's feet, so he went along with the pretense that I was his son. But then, when the opportunity arose for him to get rid of me, as well as wife, he seized it. Had I really been his son, I doubt he would have done so. I was only four. He could have kept me from telling my story, and eventually I would have forgotten it, just as I forgot my childhood. But he saw the chance to get rid of me, and he took it."

"But what about the way you look? And the mark on your back? Lady Odelia said you have the look of the Lilles."

He curved his lip. "Do I? My hair is dark, yes, but my eyes are green. I don't think anyone would mistake Rochford and me for brothers. He is taller, more slender."

"Well, you are not his brother," Irene retorted in some exasperation. "You are cousins, and only second cousins at that."

"Do you not recall how my mother's maid said that I looked

like my mother. That I had her eyes? That everyone went on about how I looked like a Bankes. But she thought I resembled my mother more. Lady Selene's hair was black, as well. And as for that mark, it is a birthmark. Not something I inherited. All it did was prove that I was the boy they had thought was abducted. It does not prove that I am a Bankes."

"Well, there is nothing to prove you are *not!*" Irene snapped.

"Don't you see?" Gideon asked, sounding weary to the bone. "It explains why I feel so strongly that I do not belong here. I don't. I am not a nobleman. My blood is probably that of—of one of the footmen. Or the solicitor in the village— or God only knows who. I am not the Earl of Radbourne. And I cannot pretend to be."

"What are you saying?" Irene asked. "Are you going to— to give up your title?"

"Timothy should be the earl," Gideon said, setting his jaw. "I cannot deprive him of what is by rights his. Do you think I am that sort of person?"

"No. I think you are the sort of person who dislikes aristocrats so much that he wants to deny being one."

"I am not one," he insisted.

"You do not know that."

"I know," he said softly. "I have known, deep down, from the moment Rochford first contacted me."

"How? You could not possibly know?"

"I *know* because I feel it inside."

"That is not enough!" Irene cried. "That isn't knowledge."

Gideon looked over at Irene and pulled his horse to a stop. They were almost to the house; they could see it, rising above the gardens, its windows glinting in the setting sunlight.

He dismounted and reached up to help her down from her horse, then walked over to the low stone wall and stood looking at the house for a long moment before turning back to her.

"I know it," he repeated. "In my blood, in my bones. I am not an earl. Rochford is that kind of man, the sort who can trace his bloodlines back centuries."

Irene came up to stand beside him. "So was my father."

"What do you mean by that?"

"Simply that not all noblemen are the same as Rochford. Like all men, they come in all shapes, sizes and characters. Lord Cecil was the legitimate Earl of Radbourne, and he did not hesitate to kill his wife."

"I know they are not all good. God knows I hope I am a better man than my fath—than Lord Cecil. But I am not a member of…that group. I am not a man who lacks confidence—I have been successful at whatever I set my hand to. But I do not have the quality that every peer I have ever known had, your father included. That certainty, that air of knowing that they were born to high position."

"I think the quality you are talking about is arrogance," Irene told him drily. "And I do not think that one is born to it. I think it is something one is raised to be. You grew up in an entirely different way. That does not change your blood. You are the same man, no matter who your father was."

He nodded. "I know. But it is scarcely fair to Timothy. *He* is my father's son. He should be the Earl of Radbourne, not I. He would have been, if Rochford had not found me. I have to tell them. I have to give up the title."

"You are a very good man," Irene told him, slipping her hand into his.

"I have rarely been accused of that," he answered, with a

faint smile, but when he looked at her, she saw that his eyes were troubled, and he let go of her hand and took a step back from her. "I will no longer be the earl. And I will never know who my father really is. I—" he paused, then continued in a rush, his face set "—I cannot hold you to your promise to marry me. Fortunately, we have not told anyone other than my family, so you will not have to worry about a scandal attaching to your name."

Cold settled onto Irene's heart. She looked at him for a long moment, struggling to speak without bursting into tears. "I beg your pardon? You no longer wish to marry me?"

Gideon's mouth twisted. "No! Of course I still wish to marry you. But I would be a cad to hold you to your promise if I can no longer offer you the life I had offered you. You would not be the Countess of Radbourne but merely the wife of a businessman, and I know how little the wealth I have matters compared to name and family."

"Oh!" Irene stiffened, fury sweeping over her. She stepped forward and slapped him sharply.

Gideon's eyes widened. "What the devil?" He brought his hand up wonderingly to his stinging cheek.

"How dare you even suggest that I—after all I have said to you—after last night!" Irene raged, her eyes glittering. "Do you think that I put a price on my love? That I gave myself to you because of your title? I don't give a fig for your title! Or your wealth! I wouldn't have cared if you were an earl or a rag picker! I came to you because I *loved* you!"

She whirled and ran back to her horse, then mounted and tore away, leaving Gideon staring after her, openmouthed.

SHE RODE BACK to the house on a wave of fury, paying no attention to Gideon shouting her name. She heard the sounds of his horse pounding after her, but she was the better rider, with the better horse, and she outran him to the stables. Hopping off without waiting for assistance, she tossed the reins to the groom and ran for the house. Her chest was tight with fury and pain. She could not wait for Gideon and talk to him now; she only hoped that she could make the sanctuary of her bedchamber before she burst into tears.

She raced up the stairs but did not make it to her room. Jasper, hearing her steps, popped out of the small sitting room beside his mother's bedchamber, a worried frown creasing his forehead.

"Lady Irene!" He looked past her. "Where is Gideon? Is he—"

"He's fine," Irene replied shortly. "I am sorry. If you will excuse me…"

She tried to turn away toward her room, but there was the sound of running footsteps on the stairs and Gideon burst into the hall.

"Irene!"

"Gideon!" his uncle exclaimed, and his frown eased. "Thank God. You are all right."

Gideon stopped and looked at Lord Jasper, then at Irene, his face a study in frustration. Finally he said, "Yes, I am fine. I am sorry to have worried you."

"Rochford told us what Owenby said," Jasper went on. "Your grandmother and Lady Odelia are in the sitting room. Please, come in and talk with us for a moment."

"I will leave you to talk about this in private," Irene said quickly, once again starting toward her room.

"No!" Gideon grasped her firmly by the arm. "You will come with us."

Jasper blinked in surprise at Gideon's words and fierce expression.

"I beg your pardon—" Irene began, her eyes lighting with an even brighter fire.

"Pray, do not spew your venom on me just yet," Gideon told her quickly. "I promise you, you will have ample opportunity to do so in a few minutes. But first, I must settle this. And I do not intend to have you locking yourself away in your room so you don't have to face me."

Irene's brows shot up, and she replied caustically, "Face you? You think I am afraid to face you?"

A grin touched Gideon's face and left just as quickly. "Nay. I do not. 'Tis why I said it. Please, just come with me while I tell them. And then we will have this out."

Irene gave in with little grace and walked with the two men into the sitting room, where Lady Odelia and Lady Pansy sat, waiting for them. Gideon's grandmother occupied the corner of the sofa, looking wilted. Her cheeks were streaked with the tracks of tears, and she clutched a balled-up handkerchief in her hand, using it from time to time to dab at her eyes.

"Oh, Gideon," she wailed when she saw him. "It can't be true." She began to cry again. "That dreadful little man. He is lying, I know it."

Gideon sighed and raked a hand back through his hair. "Lord Jasper said Rochford told you about Owenby." He hesitated, then went on. "Did he relate what Owenby said about…my parentage?"

Lady Odelia's eyebrows lifted almost comically, but her sister only looked confused.

"Your parentage?" Pansy repeated. "I don't understand."

Lord Jasper took a step forward, frowning. "What are you

talking about? The duke said only that Owenby confessed to hiding Selene's body after Cecil killed her. What else did he tell you?"

"That Lord Cecil was not my father," Gideon replied. "I am sorry. I do not mean to cause any of you further distress. But that is what he said. And…I think it is probably true."

Lady Pansy let out a soft little mewl of distress. "No! No! It is not true. Those rumors are false. Yes, it was some time before Selene got with child. But it is clear that you are Cecil's son. Anyone with eyes in his head can see that."

"Yes, you have the look of the Lilles," Lady Odelia added authoritatively, some of her old starch back in her voice. "Just look at Rochford. Look at your uncle."

Irene turned automatically to look at Jasper, as the old woman demanded. She stiffened, her eyes narrowing. Jasper was gazing at Gideon with an expression of pain and regret so sharp that it jolted her. She pivoted slowly to stare at Gideon beside her, an idea forming in her head.

"Of course!" she exclaimed without thinking. She wondered how she could not have realized it before.

Everyone in the room turned to look at her, and Irene blushed.

"I— I'm sorry. But Gideon…"

"What?" He looked at her in some concern. "Is something the matter?"

"Well, um, I think—may we speak privately?"

"Of course. But first I must finish what I came here to say."

"But—wait—" Irene stopped, glancing over at Lord Jasper.

"I think what your future wife wishes to say is this," Gideon's uncle told him. "I believe she just realized why you have the look of the Lilles and of the Bankes, as well. Look at me and you will know what you will look like in twenty-some years."

Gideon stared at him speechlessly.

"Owenby did speak the truth when he said that Cecil was not your father," Jasper went on. "I am."

"You—" Gideon replied blankly.

Jasper nodded. "Yes. I—I have wanted to tell you many times since you returned. But I knew how you felt about us all. I feared that such news would cause you to despise us even more. Especially me. I went away and left you with him. Left both of you with him. I was a fool and a coward. I swear that I would not have done so had I had the slightest inkling what he was capable of doing. I never dreamed— He was not fond of you. He knew, I think, that you were not his. I am sure he suspected that I was your father. Any fool could have seen that I was head over heels in love with Selene from the moment I met her."

"Jasper!" Pansy looked at him in horror. "What are you saying? How could you! You betrayed Cecil?"

"Cecil?" Jasper repeated in amazement. "You are upset because I dared to love Cecil's wife? Cecil was a brute. He murdered Selene. He was a bad-tempered bully, and he never had the sense to appreciate what a jewel his wife was. He betrayed her a hundred times over, yet he railed at her if she so much as smiled at another man. She loved him when she married him. She would not have taken a lover if he had not ground her love for him into dust. Cecil kept a mistress in London for his visits there, yet he never allowed Selene to even go to London for fear some other man would catch her eye. There were the tavern wenches in the village, the barques of frailty in London or Bath, for a little variety when he tired of his mistress and his wife. But he ranted at Selene if she gave a dance to the squire at the assembly or nodded to the doctor in greeting on the street."

Jasper swung away, struggling to gain control of himself, then turned back to Gideon, his voice cold as he continued. "Your mother was a good woman, Gideon. Do not think her loose or wicked, I beg you. She was faithful to my brother for six long years. I was the one who pursued her. And she did not turn to me until my brother had finally broken her heart one too many times. Even then, she hated the deception, the sin of it, and after a few months, she sent me away. I traveled, I studied—I occupied myself in every way I could think of—and I did not come home until you were three years old. Mother had written me about your birth, but I did not realize that you were my son, not Cecil's, until…until Selene told me when I returned. That was when I begged her to leave him, to take you and come away with me. But she would not. She said she could not take you from Cecil, that he believed you were his. She could not take your future inheritance from you. We…for a time, we had what happiness we could, until I could not bear any longer to watch her being his wife. That is when I deserted her the second time." Jasper's face was grim. "You know the rest of the story."

"My God." Gideon stared at him for a long moment. "I scarcely know what to say."

"Say that you forgive me."

"I forgive you," Gideon answered promptly. "I— The truth of it is, I am glad to know it." He smiled a little crookedly. "It is nice to know who my father is. To know that he is not a murderer."

Jasper smiled in relief. "Thank heavens. I feared I might have lost you forever."

"Well, then that is all settled," Lady Odelia said with a

sigh of relief. "It is scandalous, of course, but no one need know about it. I have been thinking, and I believe that the best course is to stay with Cecil's original story and say that Lady Radbourne was abducted. It was obviously the ruffians who took her who killed her and hid her in the caves. And what poetic justice, everyone will say, that her son, returned to his family, is the one who found her and will be able to put her to rest at last."

"But it is not settled, Aunt Odelia," Gideon corrected her firmly. "There is still the matter of Timothy. I am Lord Jasper's son, not the earl's, and not even a legitimate one at that."

"No one need know that," his great-aunt pointed out. "After all, none of us can prove it, now, can we? Cecil accepted you as his son. You were born to his wife in wedlock. I do not see how the succession could fall any other way."

"I cannot deprive Timothy of what should rightfully be his," Gideon argued. "He is the only true son. He should inherit the estate and title, not I."

Lady Odelia groaned. "Well, there can be no question but that you are a Lilles. You are as willful as your great-grandfather."

Beside her Pansy nodded. "Yes, he is very much like Father, but, Odelia, that is not the point, is it?"

"What is the point—that we should let that odious Teresa rule the house again? Timothy is all very well, I suppose. Perhaps he will grow up well enough—though I cannot imagine how, with her for a mother. But there is nothing of the Lilles about him. Or even the Bankes."

"That," Jasper put in firmly, "is because there is no Lilles in him, or Bankes, either."

Once again he had everyone's attention. He shrugged. "You have only to look at him. Lady Odelia is right. I have no idea who Timothy's father is, but I am sure it was not my brother. Cecil could not have children."

"Jasper, no! That was a cruel rumor," his mother objected. "How can you repeat it?"

"It was not just a rumor, Mother, and you know it. It was the truth. Selene was married to the man for six years without conceiving. The only child she gave Cecil was mine. Cecil knew it—he was simply too proud to admit it. Why do you think he accepted Gideon as his son? He knew that he could not produce an heir, so my child, his nephew, was as close as he could come. Why do you think he waited so long to marry again? It was not love for Selene, and obviously it was not hope that she was still alive. It was because he knew that he could not produce an heir anyway, and he had no wish to prove it all over again. With all his mistresses, I never heard of one who had a child by him. You know his reputation hereabouts—we all do. Yet did ever a tavern wench or a maid turn up on our doorstep, claiming to hold his babe in her arms? No. I have no idea how Teresa managed to get him to marry her, but it was two years before she conceived. I am sure she was less naive than Selene. No doubt she did not believe Cecil's accusations, as Selene did, that it was her fault she could not get with child. So she went out and found some other man who could give her the child she needed."

Pansy looked at him with reproach. "How can you say all this? Have you no respect for the dead? For the family?"

"I have no respect for a murderer," Jasper retorted bluntly. "And I am tired of all our secrets. The truth, and you know it, is that Cecil and I caught the mumps when we were children. I was fine. I was only six. But he was twelve years old, and though he recovered, he was sterile."

His mother began to cry again, and her sister snapped, "Oh, hush, Pansy, do. I know he was your son, but really, dear, we all knew he was a rotter even before this news that he killed his wife and turned Gideon over to thieves. If I were you, I would dry my tears and do some good hard thinking over the wrongs you did your grandson and Jasper by keeping silent all these years."

Her sister's eyes widened in dismay. "But I didn't know!"

"Of course you didn't. You are always careful not to know," Odelia retorted. Her sister's eyes welled with tears, and Odelia said, "Oh, don't start up again, please."

Lady Odelia surged to her feet, her last exchange with her sister seeming to have restored her old spirits. "Well, Gideon, there you are. It may not be much, but this is your family. The best you can do for that little boy is to give his mother a house in the city and let Timothy stay here. I'll warrant she'll be more than happy to let him grow up in the country while she enjoys life in town. And you, no doubt, will make sure he has all the advantages. With luck, he will turn out better than either his mother or…well, whoever his father was. You, I fear, will simply have to learn to live with being an earl."

"I promise you, I shall endeavor to do so," Gideon replied.

Jasper stepped forward to speak to him, and Irene seized the opportunity to slip away. She had not made it to the door, however, before Gideon called her name, but she did not look back, only continued out of the room.

"Excuse me," Gideon told his newly found father. "I would like to talk with you. But first I have some very pressing business to attend to."

He hurried out into the hall, half expecting to find Irene

disappearing into her bedchamber, but instead she stood waiting for him in the corridor. Her face was no longer angry, merely weary, and he felt a sharper pang than anything her bright-eyed fury had cost him.

"Irene, please…" He took a step forward, his hand going out to her. "Let me talk to you. Let me explain."

"All right. But let us at least go out into the garden. I do not care to make my personal life the subject of gossip for everyone here."

He nodded, and followed her down the stairs and out onto the terrace. They wound their way through the garden until they came at last to a secluded bench.

Irene turned to face him, straightening her shoulders, and said, "I am sorry for striking you. I hope you will forgive me."

He gave her a faint smile. "Of course I forgive you…if you will forgive me for being a clumsy fool."

She quirked a brow at him. "I suppose you cannot help it."

A short laugh escaped him. "I can always count on you, can't I? You never allow one the easy way."

She shrugged. "Then you are well out of it, are you not?"

"I don't want to be well out of it," Gideon replied. "What I want is to marry you."

She grimaced. "Then I fear you are doomed to disappointment."

"Did you mean what you said?" he asked. "That you love me?"

She lifted her chin. "I am not in the habit of lying. Yes, I love you, but that doesn't mean I have any intention of marrying you."

A smile tugged at one corner of Gideon's mouth. "Not even if I become a rag picker?"

The familiar temper lit her eyes. "Do not mock me! I offered you my love, and you offer me—money and… titles…and…"

"My love," Gideon said simply, going to her and taking her by the arms. He looked down into her face. "I offer you my love. First, last and always. Everything I have is yours. Without you, I fear that none of it would be worth anything to me anyway. But most of all, you own my heart. You have from the moment I first saw you, pointing that gun at my chest, those golden eyes blazing down at me."

"But I—" Irene felt herself begin to tremble with the aftermath of all the tumultuous emotions that had swept through her this afternoon. "You said—" Tears welled in her eyes, and she stumbled to a halt, feeling at once foolish and wonderful.

"I offered to release you because I could not in fairness hold you to your promise. That does not mean I wanted you to *accept* that release. What I hoped was for you to do as you did…." He paused and with a rueful grin, rubbed his cheek. "Although perhaps somewhat less forcefully. I had to give you the chance to choose, knowing everything."

She let out a little sound, half sob, half laugh, and moved into his arms. "Please, do not offer me such chances again."

"I will not," he assured her, wrapping his arms around her tightly and laying his cheek upon her hair. "Believe me. I intend to give you no other chance to get away from me. Fair or foul, you are mine, and I will never let you go."

Irene circled his waist with her arms, pressing her cheek against his chest and drinking in the feel of him, the warmth, the strength, the scent. After a moment, though, she leaned back and looked up at him. "But you said—you told me last night you could not love me. You said you—"

"No doubt I said a number of foolish things," he interrupted her. "I thought— I told myself that I did not love you, that what I felt for you was hunger, desire, friendship, admiration—and it *was* all those things. But this afternoon, when I watched my uncle—my father—as he bent over my mother's body, dead so many years, and I saw the tears well in his eyes…I knew. I knew that was how I would feel if you were taken from me. Twenty, thirty years later—the rest of my life later—I would still ache for you. And I knew that I was only pretending that what I felt was anything but love. I love you."

"Gideon!" Irene flung her arms around his neck and went up on tiptoe to kiss him. "I love you, too."

After a long moment he released her, looked down into her face and smiled. "I think," he said quietly, "that we should leave Aunt Odelia to spread her story about without our help."

"I think that sounds like a very good idea," she replied, smiling back at him.

"I also think that I should tell the servants to send our supper up to us in the tower. I am not, I fear, feeling well enough to join our guests this evening."

Irene's smile broadened. "You know, I believe that I am not feeling well, either."

"Then we agree? I believe this may very well be the second time."

"And the last," Irene put in.

"Then I think we should celebrate the occasion."

He kissed her until she melted against him. Then he slipped his arm around her shoulders, and they strolled off toward the ruins.

EPILOGUE

IT WAS GENERALLY agreed that the marriage of the Earl of Radbourne to Lady Irene Wyngate was the wedding of the year. It was not perhaps the grandest, for it was put on with unseemly haste. But no expense was spared, and there had not been a wedding in years that was so rife with drama and rumors.

It was enough to keep the city buzzing for the whole two months between the announcement of their engagement and the actual wedding in November. There was the matter of the vanished heir returned to his family years later, the abduction that it was whispered was not an abduction at all, not to mention the shiveringly horrifying discovery of the body of the earl's long-dead mother—during a house party, if one could imagine that. And other, much darker things, which none dared mention above a whisper, with a knowing look.

It was rumored to be a love match. And while very few could claim that they actually knew the groom, which gave him a titillating air of mystery, there were many who were well-enough acquainted with the bride to be astounded at the notion that either she or the groom had tumbled headfirst into love.

But none who attended the wedding could deny the glow

of love that shone on the face of both the earl and his new wife as they said their vows. And when they took to the floor for the first dance of their married lives, not even the most hardened heart among the guests could deny a twinge of tearful joy.

Lady Francesca Haughston, standing at the edge of the dance floor, watching them, glowed with a pleasure that owed only a small measure to the lovely silver epergne that Lady Odelia had given to her in gratitude for bringing off the engagement—and which would keep Lady Haughston's household operating through the winter. The truth was that Francesca had come to like both Irene Wyngate and her new husband very much during the time she had spent with them, and she was filled with the happy certainty that their marriage would be a loving one.

The dance ended, and the couple left the floor. Smiling, Irene came toward Francesca, holding out both hands in greeting. "Francesca! I am so pleased to see you!"

Irene was a trifle flushed, and her eyes glittered with pleasure. She was, Francesca thought, the very picture of a beautiful bride. Clearly Gideon, beside her, thought the same thing, for he gazed down upon his new wife in a way that in a softer man would be termed besotted.

"Lady Haughston." He took his eyes from Irene long enough to bow politely to Francesca.

"I wish you both very happy," Francesca said. "Though it is clear that you have no need for my good wishes. Your joy is quite apparent to all."

"It could not keep from being so," Gideon replied, raising his wife's hand to lips and planting a kiss on her knuckles. "I am the luckiest of men." He turned to look at Francesca. "I know that I have you to thank for it."

She smiled. "No, I merely gave you an opportunity. It was you who won her over."

"Despite great resistance," Gideon added, grinning.

"Nonsense. I was merely being logical," Irene told him, her smile as bright as his.

"Logic? Oh, was that it?"

"Yes, indeed. It was quite logical, you see, not to want to enter the married state, given the examples of marriage I had seen. But then, of course, I saw that it was even more logical to say yes to your proposal." She cast a flirtatious look up into his face.

"Indeed?" Gideon responded indulgently. "And how is that, pray tell?"

"Well, as anyone can tell you, it never makes sense to fight love."

"My very intelligent wife," Gideon said and pulled her into his arms for a kiss.

"Gideon!" Irene exclaimed, laughing and blushing, as she emerged from his embrace. "We are in public!"

Gideon bent closer, murmuring in her ear, "Then I can only suggest that we remove ourselves from the public at once."

With a last smile and nod at Francesca, Irene took the arm he offered, and they strolled away through the crowd. Francesca watched them with fondness as they made their way across the floor, stopped frequently by well-wishers.

"Such a lovely couple," said a voice at her elbow, and she turned to see Lady Bainbridge standing beside her.

Francesca smiled a little vaguely at the woman and at Lady Bainbridge's sister, Mrs. Fennelton, who was, as usual, at Lady Bainbridge's side.

"Yes, you must be so proud, Lady Haughston," Mrs. Fennelton added. "Everyone says that you are responsible for the match."

"Thank you," Francesca said politely. "However, I fear that I had little to do with it. I merely introduced them."

"Come, come," said a male voice behind her, and the women turned to see that the Duke of Rochford had strolled over to join them.

The two sisters bridled and simpered at finding themselves being addressed by so great a personage.

The duke favored them with a general smile as he went on. "Lady Haughston is merely being modest. This is, after all, her second triumph this year. She introduced her brother, Viscount Leighton, to *his* bride, as well."

"Oh, yes, of course," Lady Bainbridge agreed. "They were married at the end of the Season. And haven't I heard— isn't there an interesting event expected?"

Francesca's smile was pleasant but dampening of pretensions. "Yes, the family has made an announcement."

"So wonderful," Mrs. Fennelton added, unabashed by the slight reserve in Francesca's tone. "Well, I can see that you do work magic, Lady Haughston. Lady Fornbridge said so to me just recently, but I had no idea you had such a touch."

"La, Your Grace," her sister said with an arch smile at the duke. "Perhaps you should seek Lady Haughston's help. You have been a bachelor far too long, one might say."

Lady Haughston stiffened and cast a quick glance at Rochford.

"Might one?" The duke's smile was somewhat chilly. He turned to look at Francesca and said blandly, "Lady Haughston, I fear, would not wish to take me on. She is too well aware of how ill-suited I am to marriage. Are you not, my lady?"

Francesca's eyes met his for one long moment before she turned toward the other women with a light laugh. "Of course. Everyone knows that the Duke of Rochford is a confirmed bachelor. Now, if you will excuse me…?" She gave them a stiff smile, and turned and walked away.

The duke watched her leave, and for a brief moment, something that might have been regret shadowed his eyes.

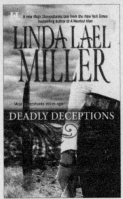

REQUEST YOUR FREE BOOKS!

2 FREE NOVELS
FROM THE ROMANCE/SUSPENSE
COLLECTION PLUS 2 FREE GIFTS!

YES! Please send me 2 FREE novels from the Romance/Suspense Collection and my 2 FREE gifts (gifts are worth about $10). After receiving them, if I don't wish to receive any more books, I can return the shipping statement marked "cancel." If I don't cancel, I will receive 4 brand-new novels every month and be billed just $5.49 per book in the U.S. or $5.99 per book in Canada, plus 25¢ shipping and handling per book plus applicable taxes, if any*. That's a savings of at least 20% off the cover price! I understand that accepting the 2 free books and gifts places me under no obligation to buy anything. I can always return a shipment and cancel at any time. Even if I never buy another book from the Reader Service, the two free books and gifts are mine to keep forever.

185 MDN EF5Y 385 MDN EF6C

Name _____ (PLEASE PRINT)

Address _____ Apt. #

City _____ State/Prov. _____ Zip/Postal Code

Signature (if under 18, a parent or guardian must sign)

Mail to **The Reader Service**:
IN U.S.A.: P.O. Box 1867, Buffalo, NY 14240-1867
IN CANADA: P.O. Box 609, Fort Erie, Ontario L2A 5X3

Not valid to current subscribers to the Romance Collection,
the Suspense Collection or the Romance/Suspense Collection.

Want to try two free books from another line?
Call 1-800-873-8635 or visit www.morefreebooks.com.

* Terms and prices subject to change without notice. N.Y. residents add applicable sales tax. Canadian residents will be charged applicable provinãal taxes and GST. This offer is limited to one order per household. All orders subject to approval. Credit or debit balances in a customer's account(s) may be offset by any other outstanding balance owed by or to the customer. Please allow 4 to 6 weeks for delivery. Offer available while quantities last.

Your Privacy: Harlequin is committed to protecting your privacy. Our Privacy Policy is available online at www.eHarlequin.com or upon request from the Reader Service. From time to time we make our lists of customers available to reputable third parties who may have a product or service of interest to you. If you would prefer we not share your name and address, please check here. ☐

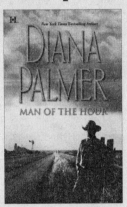

CANDACE CAMP

77243 THE MARRIAGE WAGER   ___$6.99 U.S. ___$8.50 CAN.
77136 A DANGEROUS MAN   ___$6.99 U.S. ___$8.50 CAN.
77135 AN UNEXPECTED PLEASURE ___$6.99 U.S. ___$8.50 CAN.

(limited quantities available)

TOTAL AMOUNT $ _____
POSTAGE & HANDLING $ _____
($1.00 FOR 1 BOOK, 50¢ for each additional)
APPLICABLE TAXES* $ _____
TOTAL PAYABLE $ _____

(check or money order—please do not send cash)

To order, complete this form and send it, along with a check or money order for the total above, payable to HQN Books, to: **In the U.S.:** 3010 Walden Avenue, P.O. Box 9077, Buffalo, NY 14269-9077; **In Canada:** P.O. Box 636, Fort Erie, Ontario, L2A 5X3.

Name: _____
Address: _____ City: _____
State/Prov.: _____ Zip/Postal Code: _____
Account Number (if applicable): _____

075 CSAS

*New York residents remit applicable sales taxes.
*Canadian residents remit applicable GST and provincial taxes.

HQN™

We *are* romance™

www.HQNBooks.com   PHCC0308BL

FLORIDA

RULES OF COURT

VOLUME I – STATE

2015
REVISED EDITION

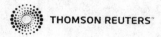
THOMSON REUTERS

Mat #41608291

ISBN: 978–0–314–67324–4